DARKNESS
VISIBLE

DARKNESS VISIBLE

WILLIAM GOLDING

A Harvest/HBJ Book
Harcourt Brace Jovanovich, Publishers
San Diego   New York   London

Requests for permission to make copies of any part of the
work should be mailed to: Permissions Department,
Harcourt Brace Jovanovich, Publishers,
Orlando, Florida 32887.

LIBRARY OF CONGRESS CATALOGING IN PUBLICATION DATA

Golding, William, 1911-
Darkness visible.

Reprint. Originally published:
New York: Farrar Straus Giroux, 1979.
"A Harvest/HBJ book."
I. Title.
[PR6013.035D36   1985]   823'.914   84-22397
ISBN 0-15-623931-0 (pbk.)

Printed in the United States of America

First Harvest/HBJ edition 1985
B C D E F G H I J

CONTENTS

SIT MIHI FAS AUDITA LOQUI

Part One

MATTY

CHAPTER ONE

There was an area east of the Isle of Dogs in London which was an unusual mixture even for those surroundings. Among the walled-off rectangles of water, the warehouses, railway lines and travelling cranes, were two streets of mean houses with two pubs and two shops among them. The bulks of tramp steamers hung over the houses where there had been as many languages spoken as families that lived there. But just now not much was being said, for the whole area had been evacuated officially and even a ship that was hit and set on fire had few spectators near it. There was a kind of tent in the sky over London, which was composed of the faint white beams of searchlights, with barrage balloons dotted here and there. The barrage balloons were all that the searchlights discovered in the sky, and the bombs came down, it seemed, mysteriously out of emptiness. They fell in or round the great fire.

The men at the edge of the fire could only watch it burn, out of control. The water mains were broken and the only hindrance in the way of the fire was the occurrence of firebreaks here and there where fires had consumed everything on other nights.

Somewhere on the northern edge of the great fire a group of men stood by their wrecked machine and stared into what, even to men of their experience, was a new sight. Under the tent of searchlights a structure had built itself up in the air. It was less sharply defined than the beams of light but it was far brighter. It was a glare, a burning bush through or beyond which the thin beams were sketched more faintly. The limits of this bush were clouds of tenuous smoke that were lit from below until they too seemed made of fire. The heart of the bush, where the little streets had been, was of a more lambent colour. It shivered constantly but with an occasional diminution or augmentation of its brightness as walls collapsed or roofs caved in. Through it all—the roar of the

9

fire, the drone of the departing bombers, the crash of collapse—there was now and then the punctuating explosion of a delayed-action bomb going off among the rubble, sometimes casting a kind of blink over the mess and sometimes so muffled by debris as to make nothing but noise.

The men who stood by their wrecked machine at the root of one northern road that ran south into the blaze had about them the anonymity of uniform silence and motionlessness. Some twenty yards behind them and to their left was the crater of the bomb that had cut the local water supply and smashed their machine into the bargain. A fountain still played in the crater but diminishingly and the long fragment of bomb-casing that had divided a rear wheel lay by their machine, nearly cool enough to touch. But the men ignored it as they were ignoring many small occurrences—the casing, the fountain, some fantasies of wreckage—that would have gathered a crowd in peace time. They were staring straight down the road into the bush, the furnace. They had positioned themselves clear of walls and where nothing but a bomb could fall on them. That, oddly enough, was the least of the dangers of their job and one almost to be discounted among the falling buildings, trapping cellars, the secondary explosions of gas and fuel, the poisonous stinks from a dozen sources. Though this was early in the war they were experienced. One of them knew what it was like to be trapped by one bomb and freed by another. He viewed them now with a kind of neutrality as if they were forces of nature, meteors it might be, that happened to strike thickly hereabouts at certain seasons. Some of the crew were wartime amateurs. One was a musician and now his ear was finely educated in the perception and interpretation of bomb noises. The one that had burst the mains and wrecked the machine had found him narrowly but sufficiently sheltered and he had not even ducked. Like the rest of the crew he had been more interested in the next one of the stick, which had struck further down the road, between them and the fire, and lay there now at the bottom of its hole, either a dud or a delayed action. He stood on the undamaged side of the machine, staring like the others down the road. He was muttering.

"I'm not happy. No. Honestly chaps, I'm not happy."

Indeed, none of the chaps was happy, not even their leader whose lips were set so firmly together. For by some kind of transference of effort from them, or by a localized muscular effort, the front of his chin trembled. His crew were not unsympathetic The other amateur, a bookseller who stood at the musician's side and who could never put on his wartime uniform without a feeling of incredulity, could assess the mathematical chances of his present survival. He had watched a wall six storeys high fall on him all in one piece and had stood, unable to move and wondering why he was still alive. He found the brick surround of a window on the fourth storey had fitted round him neatly. Like the others, he had got beyond saying how scared he was. They were all in a state of settled dread, in which tomorrow's weather, tonight's Enemy's Intention, the next hour's qualified safety or hideous danger were what ruled life. Their leader carried out within limits the orders that were sent him but was relieved even to tears and shudderings when the telephoned weather forecast indicated that a raid was impossible.

So there they were, listening to the drone of the departing bombers, estimable men who were beginning to feel that though everything was indescribably awful they would live for another day. They stared together down the shuddering street and the bookseller, who suffered from a romantic view of the classical world, was thinking that the dock area would look like Pompeii; but whereas Pompeii had been blinded by dust here there was if anything too much clarity, too much shameful, inhuman light where the street ended. Tomorrow all might be dark, dreary, dirty, broken walls, blind windows; but just now there was so much light that the very stones seemed semi-precious, a version of the infernal city. Beyond the semi-precious stones, there, where the heart of the fire was shivering rather than beating, all material objects, walls, cranes, masts, even the road itself merged into the devastating light as if in that direction the very substance of the world with all the least combustible of its materials was melting and burning. The bookseller found himself thinking that after the war if there ever was an after the war they would have to reduce the admission fee to the ruins of Pompeii since so many countries would have their own brand-new exhibitions of the broken business of living.

There was an episode of roaring, audible through the other noises. A red curtain of flame fluttered near the white heart of the fire and was consumed by it. Somewhere a tank of something had

11

exploded or a coal cellar had just distilled out its own coal gas, invaded a closed room, mixed with air, reached flashpoint—That was it, thought the bookseller knowledgeably, and now safe enough to be proud of his knowledge. How strange that is, he thought, after the war I shall have time—

He looked round quickly for wood; and there it was, a bit of lath from a roof and lying close by his foot so he bent, picked it up and threw it away. As he straightened up he saw how intently the musician was attending to the fire with eyes now rather than ears and beginning to mutter again.

"I'm not happy. No, I'm not happy—"

"What is it old chap?"

The rest of the crew were also staring more earnestly into the fire. All eyes were aimed, mouths drawn in. The bookseller swung round to look where the others were looking.

The white fire, becoming pale pink, then blood-coloured then pink again where it caught smoke or clouds seemed the same as if it were the permanent nature of this place. The men continued to stare.

At the end of the street or where now, humanly speaking, the street was no longer part of the habitable world—at that point where the world had become an open stove—at a point where odd bits of brightness condensed to form a lamp-post still standing, a pillar box, some eccentrically shaped rubble—right there, where the flinty street was turned into light, something moved. The bookseller looked away, rubbed his eyes, then looked again. He knew most of the counterfeits, the objects that seem endowed with life in a fire: the boxes or papers stirred into movement by localized gusts of wind, the heat-induced contractions and expansions of material that can mimic muscular movement, the sack moved by rats or cats or dogs or half-burnt birds. At once and violently, he hoped for rats but would have settled for a dog. He turned round again to get his back between himself and what he was sure he had not seen.

It was a remarkable circumstance that their captain was the last to look. He had turned from the fire and was contemplating his wrecked machine with the kind of feeling that kept his chin still. The other men drew his eyes to them by not meaning to. They turned away from the fire far too casually. Where there had been a whole set of eyes, a battery of them staring into the melted end

12

of the world, that battery now contemplated the uninteresting ruins from a previous fire in the other direction and the failing jet of water in the crater. It was a sheer piece of heightened awareness, a sense sharpened by dread that made the captain look at once not where they were looking but where they were not.

Two-thirds of the way down the street, part of a wall collapsed and spilt rubbish across the pavement so that some pieces went bowling across the road. One piece struck, of all things, a dustbin left standing on the other side and a metallic clang came from it

"Good God!"

Then the others turned back with him.

The drone of the bombers was dying away. The five-mile-high tent of chalky lights had disappeared, been struck all at once, but the light of the great fire was bright as ever, brighter perhaps. Now the pink aura of it had spread. Saffron and ochre turned to blood-colour. The shivering of the white heart of the fire had quickened beyond the capacity of the eye to analyse it into an outrageous glare. High above the glare and visible now for the first time between two pillars of lighted smoke was the steely and un-touched round of the full moon—the lover's, hunter's, poet's moon; and now—an ancient and severe goddess credited with a new function and a new title—the bomber's moon. She was Artemis of the bombers, more pitiless than ever before.

The bookseller contributed rashly.

"There's the moon—"

The captain rebuked him savagely.

"Where did you think it would be? Up north? Haven't any of you got eyes? Do I have to notice everything for everybody? Look there!"

What had seemed impossible and therefore unreal was now a fact and clear to them all. A figure had condensed out of the shuddering backdrop of the glare. It moved in the geometrical centre of the road which now appeared longer and wider than before. Because if it was the same size as before, then the figure was impossibly small—impossibly tiny, since children had been the first to be evacuated from that whole area; and in the mean and smashed streets there had been so much fire there was nowhere for a family to live. Nor do small children walk out of a fire that is melting lead and distorting iron.

"Well! What are you waiting for?"

13

No one said anything.

"You two! Get him!"

The bookseller and the musician started forward. Half-way down the street the delayed-action bomb went off under a warehouse on the right-hand side. Its savage punctuation heaved the pavement across the road and the wall above it jerked, then collapsed into a new crater. Its instantaneity was dreadful and the two men came staggering back. Behind them the whole length of the street was hidden by dust and smoke.

The captain snarled.

"Oh—Christ!"

He ran forward himself, the others at his shoulder, and did not stop until he was where the air cleared and the heat from the fire became a sudden violent attack on the skin.

The figure was a child, drawing nearer. As they picked their way past the new crater they saw him plain. He was naked and the miles of light lit him variously. A child's stride is quick; but this child walked down the very middle of the street with a kind of ritual gait that in an adult would have been called solemn. The captain could see—and now, with a positive explosion of human feeling—why this particular child walked as it did. The brightness on his left side was not an effect of light. The burn was even more visible on the left side of his head. All his hair was gone on that side, and on the other, shrivelled to peppercorn dots. His face was so swollen he could only glimpse where he was going through the merest of slits. It was perhaps something animal that was directing him away from the place where the world was being consumed. Perhaps it was luck, good or bad, that kept him pacing in the one direction where he might survive.

Now they were so near that the child was not an impossibility but a scrap of their own human flesh, they became desperate to save and serve him. Their captain, indifferent now to the slight dangers that might ambush them in the street, was the first to reach the child and handle him with trained and devoted care. One of the men raced in the other direction without being told, to the phone a hundred yards away. The other men formed a tight and unprofessional knot round the child as he was carried, as if to be close was to give him something. The captain was a bit breathless but full of compassion and happiness. He busied himself with the kind of first aid for burns which is reversed by the

14

medical profession every year or so. In a very few minutes an ambulance came, the team was told all the nothing that was known about the child and he was driven away, the ambulance bell ringing, perhaps unnecessarily.

It was the dimmest of the firemen who expressed the general feeling.

"Poor little bugger."

All at once they were talking to each other enthusiastically about how incredible it was, a kid walking out of the fire like that, stark naked, burnt but going on, steadily making his way towards a glimpse of safety—

"Plucky little bugger! Didn't lose his head."

"They do wonders now. Look at them pilots. Getting faces as good as new they say."

"He might be a bit shrivelled like, down the left side."

"Thank Christ my kids are out of it. And the missus."

The bookseller was saying nothing and seemed to be staring at nothing. There was a memory flickering on the edge of his mind and he could not get it further in where it could be examined; and he was also remembering the moment when the child had appeared, seeming to his weak sight to be perhaps not entirely there—to be in a state of, as it were, indecision as to whether he was a human shape or merely a bit of flickering brightness. Was it the Apocalypse? Nothing could be more apocalyptic than a world so ferociously consumed. But he could not quite remember. Then he was deflected by the sounds of the musician being sick.

The captain had turned back to the fire. He looked down a street that in the event had proved neither as hot as they supposed nor as dangerous. He jerked his attention away from it and back to the machine.

"Well. What are we waiting for? They'll want to tow us if we can be towed. Mason, try the steering and see if you can free it. Wells, come out of that trance! Start tracing the brake lines—quickly now and cheerfully !"

Under the machine, Wells swore horribly and profoundly.

"Now then Wells, you're paid to get your hands dirty."

"The oil went straight into me fucking mouth!"

A burst of sniggering—

"Teach you to keep your mouth shut!"

"What's it taste like, Wellsy?"

15

"Can't be worse'n the canteen!"

"All right lads, turn it up. We don't want the breakdowns to do our work for us do we?"

The captain turned back to the fire. He looked at the new crater half-way down the road. He saw quite clearly in a kind of interior geometry of this and this and that and that how things had been and how they might have been and where he would have been running if he had set off at the very first moment he had realized the child was there and needed help. He would have run straight into the space where now there was nothing but a hole. He would have run into the explosion and he would have disappeared.

There was the clatter of a part falling under the machine and another burst of cursing from Wells. The captain hardly heard it. The skin had seemed to freeze on his body. He shut his eyes and for some sort of time saw that he was dead or felt that he was dead; and then that he was alive, only the screen that conceals the workings of things had shuddered and moved. Then his eyes were open again and the night was as normal as that kind of night could ever be, and he knew what the frost was on his skin and he thought to himself with the cunning immediacy that was part of his nature that it just didn't do to examine such things too closely and anyway the little chap would have suffered just as much and anyway—

He turned back to his own smashed machine and saw that the tow was coming. He came, silent and filled in an extraordinary way with grief, not for the maimed child but for himself, a maimed creature whose mind had touched for once on the nature of things. His chin was quivering again.

The child was called number seven. After the kind of holding operations that had to be performed while he recovered from shock, number seven was the first present he got from the world outside him. There was some small doubt as to whether his silence was organic or not. He could hear, even with the ghastly fragment of ear on his left side, and the swelling round his eyes soon subsided so that he could see well enough. He was contrived a position in which he did not have to be doped very much and spent days and weeks and months in it. But, though the burnt area reckoned as a percentage of the whole made it improbable, he

16

did in fact survive, to begin a long progress through hospitals of one sort of expertise or another. By the time he had come to speak his occasional word of English it was impossible to discover whether it was his native tongue or whether he had picked up the word in hospital. He had no background but the fire. He was known in successive wards as baby, darling, pet, poppet, sweetie and boo-boo. He was at last given a name because a matron put her foot down, a thing of power. She spoke roundly.

"We can't go on calling the child number seven behind his back. It's most improper and injurious."

She was an old-fashioned matron who used that kind of word. She was effective.

The appropriate office was working through the alphabet in rotation, since the boy was only one among the wreckage of that childhood. The office had just presented a baby girl with the name "Venables". The young wit who was given the job of using "w" suggested "Windup", her chief having displayed less than perfect courage in an air raid. She had found she could get married and still keep her job and she was feeling secure and superior. Her chief winced at the name and drew his pen through it, foreseeing a coven of children all shouting "Windup! Windup!" He made his own substitution, though when he looked at what he had written it seemed not quite right and he altered it. There was no obvious reason for doing so. The name had first jumped into his mind with the curious effect of having come out of empty air and of being temporary, a thing to be noticed because you were lucky to be in the place where it had landed. It was as if you had sat silently in the bushes and—My!—there settled in front of you the rarest of butterflies or birds which had stayed long enough to be seen and had then gone off with an air of going for ever, sideways, it might be.

The boy's current hospital accepted "Septimus" as a middle name but made no use of it. Perhaps it had overtones of "Septic". His first name, Matthew, became "Matty"; and as "Seven" was still written on all the relevant papers, no one used his surname. But then, for years of his childhood, all visitors had to peer among sheets and bandages and mechanisms to see any part of him but the right side of his face.

As the various aids to recovery were removed from him and he began to speak more, it was observed that his relationship to

17

language was unusual. He mouthed. Not only did he clench his fists with the effort of speaking, he squinted. It seemed that a word was an object, a material object, round and smooth sometimes, a golf ball of a thing that he could just about manage to get through his mouth, though it deformed his face in the passage. Some words were jagged and these became awful passages of pain and struggle that made the other children laugh. After his turban came off in the period between the primary work and what cosmetic work was possible, the ruin of his half-raw skull and blasted ear was most unappealing. Patience and silence seemed the greater part of his nature. Bit by bit he learnt to control the anguish of speaking until the golf balls and jagged stones, the toads and jewels passed through his mouth with not much more than the normal effort.

In the illimitable spaces of childhood, time was his only dimension. Adults who tried to establish contact with him were never successful with words. He accepted words and seemed to think long about them and sometimes he answered them. But it was a dissociated traffic out there. He was, at this time, to be approached by a method beyond conceptual artifice. Thus the nurse who squeezed him with her arms, knowing just where his body could bear the contact, found the relatively good, relatively undamaged side of his head burrowing against her breast in wordless communication. Being, it seemed, touched being. It was natural that this girl should discount what further thing she had noticed, since it was too delicate, even too private a perception to be called awareness of a symptom. She knew herself not to be particularly intelligent or clever. So she allowed the awareness to float in the back of her mind and paid no particular attention to it, only accepting that she, more than the other nurses, now knew the Matty-ness of Matty. She found herself saying things to herself that would mean one thing to others but something quite different inside her.

"There's Matty thinking I can be in two places at once!"

Then she would find what she had noticed was blown away or rendered massively inaccurate by the words her mind had accidently wrapped round it. But it happened too often and it settled into a pattern of belief that she accepted as a kind of definition of his nature.

Matty believes I'm two people.

Then later and even more privately—*Matty believes I bring someone with me.*

There was a delicacy in her mind that knew this belief to be unique to Matty and not to be discussed. Perhaps she felt a certain delicacy about the nature of her own mind in its surely unusual working. But she felt nearer this child than the others and she showed it in a way that the other children resented because she was pretty. She called him, "My Matty". When she did that it was the first time since his emergence from the furnace that he was observed to employ the complex musculature of his face in a communicative way. The rearrangement was slow and painful as if the little mechanism was in need of oil, but there was no doubt about the end-product. Matty was smiling. But his mouth remained lopsided and closed all the time, which made the smile unchildlike and seemed to concede that though smiling was possible, it was not a common practice and a wicked one if indulged in often.

Matty moved on. He suffered this in animal patience, seeing this was what was going to happen and there was no escaping it. The pretty nurse hardened her heart and told him how happy he would be. She was accustomed to partings. She was young enough to consider him lucky to be alive. Besides, she fell in love and that deflected her attention. Matty went one way and she went the other. Presently the delicate perceptions ceased, for she did not or could not use them on her own children. She was happy and forgot Matty for years until middle age overwhelmed her.

Matty was now fixed in a different position so that skin could be transferred from one part of his body to the other. It was a condition of some absurdity and the other children in the burns hospital, none of whom had much to laugh at, enjoyed his plight. Grown-ups came to entertain and console him but no woman held his undamaged side to her breast. She would have had to contort herself to do so. His smile went unused. There was rather more of him visible now to the casual visitor; and these, hurrying to their own unfortunates, were repelled by the sordid misery in which Matty passed his days, and they flashed sideways at him an uneasy smile which he interpreted with absolute precision. When at last he was cut loose, and having been as much as possible repaired was set on his feet, his smile seemed to have gone for

19

good. The blasting of his left side had given him some contraction of the sinews that growth had not yet redressed, so he limped. He had hair on the right side of his skull but the left side was a ghastly white, which seemed so unchildlike it was an invitation by its appearance of baldness to discount his childishness and treat him as an adult who was being stubborn or just silly. Organizations ground on round him for his benefit but there was little more that could be done with him. His background was probed and probed without result. For all that the most painstaking inquiries could find, he might have been born from the sheer agony of a burning city.

CHAPTER TWO

Matty limped from hospital into his first school; and from that into a school maintained by two of the biggest trade unions in Britain. Here, in the Foundlings School at Greenfield, he met Mr Pedigree. They could be said to have converged on each other, though Matty was going up and Mr Pedigree was going down.

Mr Pedigree had declined from teaching at an ancient choir school through two less historical foundations and a considerable period which he accounted for by foreign travel. He was a slight and springy man with hair of faded gold and a face that was thin and lined and anxious when it was not vexed or arch. He joined the staff at Foundlings two years before Matty got there. The Second World War had, so to speak, disinfected Mr Pedigree's past. He lived therefore, unwisely, in a top room at the school. He was no longer "Sebastian", even to himself. "Mr Pedigree", a figure of the unimportant schoolmaster, was what he had become, and grey was beginning to appear streakily in his faded hair. He was a snob about boys and found the orphans generally repellent with some notable exceptions. There was no use found here for his Classics. He taught elementary geography mixed with elementary history and elementary English Grammar thrown in. For two years he had found it easy to resist his *"times"* and he lived in a fantasy. He pretended to himself that he was always the owner of two boys: one, an example of pure beauty, the other, an earthy little man! His personal charge was a large class into which boys who had given some evidence of having reached their educational ceiling were thrust, there to mark time until they could leave. The headmaster considered that with this lot he could do little harm. This was probably true except in the case of the boy with whom Mr Pedigree had his "spiritual relationship". For there appeared, as Mr Pedigree grew older, an extraordinary kink in the relationship beyond what a heterosexual person might think extraordinary. Mr Pedigree would lift the child on to a pedestal and he would make himself all in all to him, oh yes, all in all; and the little boy would find life wonderful and all things would be made easy for him. Then, as suddenly, Mr Pedigree would turn cold and indifferent. If he spoke to the child it would be sharply; and since it was a spiritual relationship, with not even the touch of a finger on a vellum cheek, what had the child, or anyone else, to complain of?

All this was subject to rhythm. Mr Pedigree had begun to understand that rhythm. It was when the beauty of the child began to consume him, obsess him, madden him—bit by bit, madden him! During that period, if he were not very careful he would find himself taking risks beyond what was common sense. He would find himself driven—the words bubbling over his lips before some other person, a master perhaps—driven to say what an extraordinarily attractive child young Jameson was, one really had to consider him a beauty!

Matty did not immediately go into Mr Pedigree's group. He was given a chance to exhibit his intellectual potential. But hospitals had taken too much of his time as the fire had taken any gloss there might have been about him. His limp, his two-toned face and ghastly ear hardly concealed by black hair swept over the baldness of his skull made him a natural butt. This may have contributed to his development of a faculty—to give it a name—which was to increase throughout his life. He could disappear. He could become unnoticeable like an animal. He had other qualities too. He drew badly but with passion. Leaning over the page, encircling it with an arm as his black hair swung free, he would sink into what he drew as if about to dive into a sea. His outlines were always without a break and he filled each space with colour of absolute evenness and neatness. It was a deed. Also he would listen devotedly to anything told him. He knew large portions of the Old Testament and small portions of the New Testament by heart. His hands and feet were too big for his thin arms and legs. His sexuality—and this was brilliantly perceived by his fellows—was in direct proportion to his unattractiveness. He was high-minded; and his fellows considered this to be his darkest sin.

The Convent School of Saint Cecilia was a hundred yards down the road and the grounds of the two establishments were separated by a narrow lane. On the girls' side was a high wall with spikes on top. Mr Pedigree could see the wall and the spikes from his top room and it brought back memories from which he flinched. The boys could see it too. From the landing and the great window three storeys up outside Mr Pedigree's room you could look over the wall and see the blue dresses and white, summery socks of the girls. There was a place where the girls could get up and peer through the spikes if they were naughty enough or sexy enough, which of course was the same thing. There was a tree on the boys' side that could be climbed and the young creatures could see each other face to face with only the lane between them.

Two of the boys who had taken particularly against Matty's high-mindedness, mostly because they were of exceptional low-mindedness, set out with the directness and simplicity of genius to play on all his weaknesses at once.

"We been talking to the girls, see?"

And later—"They've been talking about you."

And later—"Angy's sweet on you, Matty, she keeps asking about you."

Then—"Angy said she wouldn't mind a walk in the woods with you!"

Matty limped away from them.

Next day they gave him a note, which in a confusion of ideas from the adult world they had printed then signed. Matty inspected the note, torn from a rough workbook like the one he had in his own hand. The golf balls emerged from his mouth.

"Why didn't she write it? I don't believe it. You're having me on!"

"But look, it's got her name there, 'Angy'. I expect she thought you wouldn't believe her unless she signed it."

Shrieks of laughter.

If Matty had known anything at all about girls of school age he would have seen that they would never send a note on such paper. It was an early example of sexual differentiation. A boy, unless deflected, would apply for a job on the back of an old envelope. But if girls got hold of stationery the results were liable to be frightful, purple, scented and strewn with flowers. Nevertheless, Matty believed in the note torn from the corner of a rough workbook.

"She's there now Matty! She wants you to show her something—"

Matty stared from one to the other under lowered eyebrows.

23

The undamaged side of his face flushed red. He said nothing.

"Honestly Matty!"

They crowded in on him. He was taller than they were but stooped by his condition. He laboured at words and got them out.

"What does she want?"

The three heads came as close now as they could get. Almost at once, the redness sank away in his face so that the spots of his adolescence seemed even more definite against their white background. He breathed his answer.

"She didn't!"

"Honestly!"

He looked at each face in turn, his mouth left open. It was a strange look. So a man swimming in the deep ocean might lift his head and stare before him in search of land. There was a trace of light in the look, hope struggling with a natural pessimism.

"Honestly?"

"Honestly!"

"Cross your heart?"

Once more shrieks of laughter.

"Cross my heart!"

Again that aimed, imploring look, movement of a hand that tried to brush aside banter.

"Here—"

He thrust his books into their hands and limped quickly away. They held on to each other, laughing like apes. They broke apart, clamorously collected their fellows. The whole troupe clattered up the stone stairs, up, up, one, two, three storeys to the landing by the great window. They pushed and shoved against the great bar that ran from one end to the other at boy-height, and held the verticals that were less than a boy's width apart. Fifty yards away and fifty feet down a boy limped quickly towards the forbidden tree. Two little patches of blue did indeed show above the wall opposite it on the girls' side. The boys along the window were so entranced they never heard the door open behind them.

"What on earth is all this? What are you men doing up here?"

Mr Pedigree stood in the doorway, nervously holding the doorknob and looking from one end of the row of laughing boys to the other. But none of them minded old Pedders.

"I said what's all this? Are there any of my men here? You, the lad with the lovely locks, Shenstone!"

24

"It's Windy, sir. He's climbing the tree!"

"Windy? Who's Windy?"

"There he is, sir, you can see him, he's just getting up!"

"Oh you are a feeble, nasty, inky lot. I'm surprised at you, Shenstone, a fine upstanding lad like you—"

Scandalized, gleeful laughter—

"Sir, sir, he's doing it now—"

There was a kind of confusion among the leaves of a lower bough. The blue, sexy patches disappeared from the wall as if they had been knocked off by shot. Mr Pedigree clapped his hands and shouted but none of the boys paid any attention. They went cascading down the stairs, and left him there, flushed and more agitated by what was behind him than in front. He looked after them down the well of the stairs. He spoke sideways into the room and held the door open.

"Very well my dear. You can run along now."

The boy came out, smiling confidently up at Mr Pedigree. He went away down the stairs, assured of his own worth.

When he had gone Mr Pedigree stared irritatedly at the distant boy who was coming unhandily down the tree. Mr Pedigree had no intention of interfering—none whatever.

The headmaster heard from the Mother Superior. He sent for the boy who came limping and spotty and anxious. The headmaster was sorry for him and tried to make things easy. The episode had been described by the Mother Superior in such words as hid it behind a veil which the headmaster knew he must lift; and yet he viewed the lifting of a veil with some apprehension. He knew that lifting any veil was liable to uncover more than the investigator bargained for.

"Sit down there, will you? Now. You see we've had this complaint about you. About what you did when you climbed that tree. Young men—boys—will climb trees, that's not what I'm asking you about—but there may be considerable consequences coming from your action, you know. Now. What did you do?"

The unmended side of the boy's face became one deep, red flush. He looked down past his knees.

"You see, my dear boy, there's nothing to be—frightened of. People sometimes can't help themselves. If they are sick then we help them or find people who can help them. Only we must know!"

The boy neither spoke nor moved.

"Show me, then, if that's easier for you."

Matty glanced up under his eyebrows then down again. He was breathing quickly as if he had been running. He took his right hand across and took hold of the long lock dangling by his left ear. With a gesture of absolute abandon he ripped the hair across and exposed the white obscenity of his scalp.

It was perhaps fortunate that Matty did not see how the headmaster shut his eyes involuntarily, then forced them open and kept them open without any change of expression in his face. They both said nothing for a while until the headmaster nodded understandingly and Matty, relaxing, brought the hair back across his head.

"I see," said the headmaster. "Yes. I see."

Then for a while he said nothing but thought of phrases that might go in his letter to the Mother Superior.

"Well," he said at last, "don't do it again. Go along now. And please remember you are only allowed to climb the big beech and even then, up to the second bough. Right?"

"Sir."

After that, the headmaster sent round the various masters concerned to find out more about Matty and it was obvious that someone had been too kind—or perhaps unkind—and he was in a stream that was too much for him. The boy would never pass an examination and it was silly to make him try.

It was for this reason, therefore, that one morning when Mr Pedigree was dozing in front of his class as they drew a map, that Matty came clumping in, books under his arm, and stopped in front of the master's desk.

"Good God boy. Where have you come from?"

It seemed the question was too quick or too profound for Matty. He said nothing.

"What d'you want, boy? Say quickly!"

"I was told, sir. C.3, sir. The room at the end of the corridor."

Mr Pedigree gave a determined grin and wrenched his gaze away from the boy's ear.

"Ah. Our simian friend swinging from branch to branch. Don't laugh, you men. Well. Are you house-trained? Reliable? Brilliant intellect?"

Quivering with distaste, Mr Pedigree looked round the room. If

26

was his custom and entertainment to arrange the boys in order of beauty so that the most beautiful occupied the front row. There was no doubt at all in his mind as to where the new boy should go. At the back of the room on his right, a tall cupboard left enough space for a desk that would be partly concealed by it. The cupboard could not be shifted flush against the wall without blocking a window.

"Brown, you exquisite creature, I shall want you out of there. You can sit in Barlow's place. Yes, I know he'll be back; and then we shall have to do some more arranging, shan't we? Anyway Brown, you're an imp, aren't you? I know what you get up to at the back there when you think I can't see you. Stop laughing, you men. I won't have you laughing. Now then, what's your name, Wandgrave. Can you keep order, mm? Go and sit in that corner and just keep quiet and tell me if they don't behave, mm? Go along!"

He waited, grinning with determined cheerfulness until the boy was seated and partly out of sight. Mr Pedigree found that he could divide the boy by the line of the cupboard so that only the more-or-less undamaged side of his face was visible. He sighed with relief. Such things were important.

"All right everybody. Just get on. Show him what we're doing, Jones."

He relaxed, dallying now with his agreeable game, for Matty's unexpected arrival gave him an excuse for another round of it.

"Pascoe."

"Sir?"

There was no denying that Pascoe was losing what had never been a very high degree of attractiveness. Mr Pedigree wondered in passing what he had ever seen in the boy. It was fortunate the affair had gone very little way.

"Pascoe, dear friend, I wonder if you would mind changing places now with Jameson so that when Barlow comes back—you don't mind being just a *little* further from the seat of judgement? Now, what about you, Henderson. Eh?"

Henderson was in the middle of the front row. He was a child of bland and lyric beauty.

"You don't mind being close to the seat of judgement, do you, Henderson?"

Henderson looked up, smiling, proudly and adoringly. His star

27

was in Mr Pedigree's ascendant. Moved inexpressibly, Mr Pedigree came out of his desk and stood by Henderson, his fingers in the boy's hair.

"Ghastly, dear friend, when did you last wash all this yellow stuff, eh?"

Henderson looked up, still smiling and secure, understanding that the question was not a question, but communication, brightness, glory. Mr Pedigree dropped his hand and squeezed the boy's shoulder, then went back to his desk. To his surprise the boy behind the cupboard had his hand up.

"What is it? What is it?"

"Sir. That boy there. He passed a note to him, sir. That's not allowed is it sir?"

For a while Mr Pedigree was too astonished to answer. Even the rest of the class were silent until the enormity of what they had heard penetrated to them. Then a faint, increasing booing sound began to rise.

"Stop it you men. Now I said stop it. You, what's your name. You must have come straight out of a howling wilderness. We have found a cop!"

"Sir you said—"

"Never mind what I said, you *literal* creature! My goodness what a treasure we've come across!"

Matty's mouth had opened and stayed open.

·It was odd indeed after that, that Matty should adopt Mr Pedigree. It was a sign of the poverty of his acquaintance that he should begin to dog the man and irritate him, since attention from Matty was the last thing he wanted. In fact, Mr Pedigree was on the slope of his rising curve and had begun to recognize where he was in a way that had not been apparent to him in the long distant days of the choir school. He knew now that points on the curve signalled themselves precisely. As long as he admired beauty in the classroom, no matter how overt his gestures of affection, everything was safe and in order. But there came a point where he began—*had* to begin—to help boys with their prep in his own room, forbidden as it was, dangerous and delirious; and there again the gestures would be innocent for a time—

Just now, in the last month of this term, Henderson had been elevated by nature herself to that pre-eminent beauty. Mr Pedigree himself found it strange that there was such a constant

28

supply of that beauty available, and coming up year after year. The month was strange both for Mr Pedigree and Matty, who dogged him with absolute simplicity. His world was so small and the man was so large. He could not conceive of a whole relationship being based on a joke. He was Mr Pedigree's treasure. Mr Pedigree had said so. Just as some boys spent years in hospital and some did not, so he saw that some boys did their bounden duty and reported on their fellows and some did not, even though the result was desperate unpopularity.

Matty's fellows might have forgiven or forgotten his appearance. But his literal-mindedness, high-mindedness and ignorance of the code ensured that he became an outcast. But baldy Windup yearned for friendship, for he did not only dog Mr Pedigree. He dogged the boy Henderson too. The boy would jeer and Mr Pedigree would—

"Not now, Wheelwright, not now!"

Quite suddenly Henderson's visits to Mr Pedigree's room became more frequent and unconcealed and the language in which Mr Pedigree addressed the class became more extravagant. It was the top of the curve. He spent most of one lesson in a digression, a lecture on bad habits. There were very, very many of them and they were difficult to avoid. In fact—and they would find this out as they grew older—some of them were impossible to avoid. It was important however to distinguish between those habits which were thought to be bad and those which were actually bad. Why, in ancient Greece women were thought to be inferior creatures, now don't laugh you men, I know what you're thinking, you nasty lot, and love reached its highest expression between men and between men and boys. Sometimes a man would find himself thinking more and more about some handsome little fellow. Suppose for example, the man was a great athlete, as it might be nowadays, a cricketer, a test player—

The handsome little fellows waited to find out what the moral of this discourse was and how it related to bad habits but they never did. Mr Pedigree's voice trailed off and the whole thing did not so much end as die, with Mr Pedigree looking lost and puzzled.

People find it remarkable when they discover how little one man knows about another. Equally, at the very moment when people are most certain that their actions and thoughts are most hidden in darkness, they often find out to their astonishment and grief how

29

they have been performing in the bright light of day and before an audience. Sometimes the discovery is a blinding and destroying shock. Sometimes it is gentle.

The headmaster asked to see the report books of some boys in Mr Pedigree's class. They sat at a table in the headmaster's study with the green filing-cabinets at their back. Mr Pedigree talked volubly about Blake and Barlow, Crosby and Green and Halliday. The headmaster nodded and turned the reports over.

"I see you haven't brought Henderson's along."

Mr Pedigree lapsed into frozen silence.

"You know, Pedigree, it's most unwise."

"What's unwise? What's unwise?"

"Some of us have peculiar difficulties."

"Difficulties?"

"So don't give these private lessons in your room. If you want to have boys in your room—"

"Oh but the boy's welfare!"

"There's a rule against it, you know. There have been—rumours."

"Other boys—"

"I don't know how you intend me to take that. But try not to be so—exclusive."

Pedigree went quickly, with heat round his ears. He could see clearly how deep the plot was; for as the graph of his cyclic life rose towards its peak he would suspect all men of all things. The headmaster, thought Pedigree—and was half-aware of his own folly—is after Henderson himself! So he set about devising a scheme by which he could circumvent any attempt on the part of the headmaster to get rid of him. He saw clearly that the best thing was a cover story or camouflage. As he wondered and wondered what to do, he first rejected a step as impossible, then as improbable, then as quite dreadful—and at last saw it was a step he would have to take, though the graph was not falling.

He braced himself. When his class was settled he went round them boy by boy; but this time, beginning with awful distaste at the back. Deliberately he went to the corner where Matty was half-hidden by the cupboard. Matty smiled up at him lopsidedly; and with a positive writhe of anguish, Pedigree gave a grin into the space above the boy's head.

"Oh my goodness me! That's not a map of the Roman Empire

30

my young friend! That's a picture of a black cat in a coal cellar in the dark. Here, Jameson, let me have your map. Now do you see Matty Windrap? Oh God. Look I can't spend time loitering here. I'm not taking prep this evening, so instead of going there you just bring your book and your atlas and the rest of it to my room. You know where that is don't you? Don't laugh you men! And if you do particularly well there might be a sticky bun or a slice of cake— oh God—"

Matty's good side shone upwards like the sun. Pedigree glanced down into his face. He clenched his fist and struck the boy lightly on the shoulder. Then he hurried to the front of the classroom as if he were looking for fresh air.

"Henderson, fair one. I shan't be able to take you for a lesson this evening. But it's not necessary is it?"

"Sir?"

"Come here and show me your book."

"Sir."

"Now there! You see?"

"Sir—aren't there going to be any more lessons upstairs, sir?"

Anxiously Mr Pedigree looked into the boy's face, where now the underlip stuck out.

"Oh God. Look, Ghastly. Listen—"

He put his fingers in the boy's hair and drew his head nearer.

"Ghastly, my dear. The best of friends must part."

"But you said—"

"Not *now!*"

"You said!"

"I tell you what, Ghastly. I shall be taking prep on Thursday in the hall. You come up to the desk with your book."

'Just because I did a good map—it's not fair!"

"Ghastly!"

The boy was looking down at his feet. Slowly he turned away and went back to his desk. He sat down, bowed his head over his book. His ears were so red they even had a touch of Matty's purple about them. Mr Pedigree sat at his own desk, his two hands trembling on it. Henderson shot him a glance up under his lowered brows and Mr Pedigree looked away.

He tried to still his hands, and he muttered,

"I'll make it up to him—"

Of the three of them only Matty was able to show an open face

31

to the world. The sun shone from one side of his face. When the time came for him to climb to Mr Pedigree's room, he even took extra care in the arrangement of his black hair so that it hid the livid skull and purplish ear. Mr Pedigree opened the door to him with a shudder that had something feverish about it. He sat Matty down in a chair but himself went walking to and fro as if the movement were an anodyne for pain. He began to talk to Matty or to someone, as if there were an adult understanding in the room; and he had hardly begun when the door opened and Henderson stood on the threshold.

Mr Pedigree shouted,

"Get away, Ghastly! Get away! I *won't* see you! Oh God—"

Then Henderson burst into tears and fled away, clattering down the stairs and Mr Pedigree stood by the door, gazing down them until he could no longer hear the boy's sobs or the noise of his feet. Even then, he stayed where he was, staring down. He groped in his pocket and brought out a large white handkerchief and he passed it over his forehead and across his mouth and Matty watched his back and understood nothing.

At last Mr Pedigree shut the door but did not look at Matty. Instead, he began to move restlessly round the room, muttering half to himself and half to the boy. He said the most terrible thing in the world was thirst and that men had all kinds of thirst in all kinds of desert. All men were dypsomaniacs. Christ himself had cried out on the cross, "Διψῶ!" The thirsts of men were not to be controlled so men were not to blame for them. To blame men for them would not be fair, that was where Ghastly was wrong, the foolish and beautiful young thing, but then he was too young to understand.

At this point Mr Pedigree sank into the chair by his table and put his face in his hands.

"Διψάω."

"Sir?"

Mr Pedigree did not reply. Presently he took Matty's book and told him as briefly as he could what was wrong with the map. Matty began to mend it. Mr Pedigree went to the window and stood, looking across the leads to the top of the fire-escape and beyond it to the horizon where the suburbs of London were now visible like some sort of growth.

Henderson did not go back to his prep in the hall nor to the lavatories that had been his excuse for leaving it. He went towards the front of the building and stood outside the headmaster's door for whole minutes. This was a clear sign of his misery; for it was no mean thing in his world to bypass the other members of the hierarchy. At last he tapped at the door, first timidly, then more loudly.

"Well boy, what do you want?"

"See you, sir."

"Who sent you?"

"No one, sir."

That made the headmaster look up. He saw the boy had been crying very recently.

"What form are you in?"

"Mr Pedigree's, sir."

"Name?"

"Henderson, sir."

The headmaster opened his mouth to say *ah!* then closed it again. He pursed his lips instead. A worry began to form itself at the back of his mind.

"Well?"

"It's, it's about Mr Pedigree, sir."

The worry burst into full flower, the interviews, the assessment of blame, all the vexations, the report to the governors and at the end of everything the judge. For of course the man would plead guilty; or if it had not gone as far as that—

He took a long, calculated look at the boy.

"Well?"

"Sir, Mr Pedigree, sir—he gives me lessons in his room—"

"I know."

Now it was Henderson's turn to be astonished. He stared at the headmaster, who was nodding judiciously. The headmaster was very near retirement, and from tiredness as much as anything switched his determination to the job of fending the boy off before anything irremediable had been said. Of course Pedigree would have to leave, but that could be arranged without much difficulty.

"It's kind of him," said the headmaster fluently, "but I expect you find it a bit of a bore don't you extra work like that on top of the rest, well, I understand, you'd like me to speak to Mr Pedigree wouldn't you, I won't say *you* said so, only say that we don't think you're strong enough for extra work so you needn't worry any more. Mr Pedigree simply won't ask you to go there any more. Right?"

Henderson went red. He dug at the rug with one toe and looked down at it.

"So we won't say anything about this visit to anyone else will we? I'm glad you came to see me, Henderson, very glad. You know, these little things can always be put right if you only talk to a, a grown-up about them. Good. Now cheer up and go back to your prep."

Henderson stood still. His face went even redder, seemed to swell; and from his screwed-up eyes the tears jetted as if his head was full of them.

"Now come along, lad. It's not as bad as that!"

But it was worse. For neither of them knew where the root of the sorrow was. Helplessly the boy cried and helplessly the man watched, thinking, as it were, furtively of what he could not imagine with any precision; and wondering after all whether fending off was either wise or possible. Only when the tears had nearly ceased did he speak again.

"Better? Eh? Look my dear boy, you'd better sit in that chair for a bit. I have to go—I'll be back in a few minutes. You go off, when you feel like it. Right?"

Nodding and smiling in a matey kind of way the headmaster went out, pulling the door to behind him. Henderson did not sit down in the offered chair. He stood where he was, the redness draining slowly from his face. He sniffed for a bit, wiping his nose with the back of his hand. Then he went away back to his desk in the hall.

When the headmaster returned to his study and found that the boy had left he was relieved for a bit since nothing irremediable had been said; but then he remembered Pedigree with much irritation. He debated speaking to him at once but decided at last that he would leave the whole unpleasant business until the first hours of morning school, when his vital forces would have been restored by sleep. Tomorrow would be soon enough, though the whole business could not be left longer than that; and remembering his earlier interview with Pedigree the headmaster flushed with genuine anger. The *silly* man!

However, next morning when the headmaster braced himself for an interview he found himself receiving shocks instead of

34

delivering them. Mr Pedigree was in his classroom but Henderson was not; and before the end of the first period, the new master, Edwin Bell—already "Dinger" to the whole school—had discovered Henderson and suffered an attack of hysterics. Mr Bell was led away but Henderson was left by the wall where the hollyhocks hid him. It was evident that he had fallen fifty feet from the leads or the fire-escape that was connected with them and he was dead as dead. "Dead," said Merriman, the odd-job man, with emphasis and apparent enjoyment, "Dead cold and stiff," which was what had touched off that Mr Bell. However, by the time Mr Bell had been quietened, Henderson's body had been lifted and a gymshoe found beneath—with Matty's name in it.

That morning the headmaster sat looking at the place where Henderson had appeared before him and faced a few merciless facts. He knew himself to be, as he expressed it colloquially, to be for the high jump. He foresaw a hideously complicated transaction in which he would have to reveal that the boy had come to him, and that—

Pedigree? The headmaster saw that he would never have carried on teaching this morning if he had known what happened during the night. It might be what a hardened criminal would do, or what someone capable of minute and detached calculation would do—but not Pedigree. So that who—?

He still did not know what to do when the police came. When the inspector asked about the gymshoe, the headmaster could only say that boys frequently wore each other's gear, the inspector knew what boys were; but the inspector did not. He asked to see Matty just as if this were something on the films or television. It was at this point that the headmaster brought in the solicitor who acted for the school. So the inspector went away for a while and the two men interviewed Matty. He was understood to say that the shoe had been cast, to which the headmaster said in an irritated way that it had been thrown, not cast, it wasn't a horseshoe. The solicitor explained about confidentiality and truth and how they were protecting him.

"When it happened, you were there? You were on the fire-escape?"

Matty shook his head.

"Where were you then?"

They would have known, if they had seen more of the boy, why the sun shone once more, positively ennobling the good side of his face.

"Mr Pedigree."

"*He* was there?"

"No, sir!"

"Look boy—"

"Sir, he was in his room with me, sir!"

"In the middle of the night?"

"Sir, he'd asked me to do a map—"

"Don't be silly. He wouldn't ask you to bring a map to him in the middle of the night!"

The nobility in Matty's face diminished.

"You might as well tell us the truth," said the solicitor. "It'll come out in the end you know. You've nothing to fear. Now. What about this shoe?"

Still looking down, and plain rather than noble, Matty muttered back.

The solicitor pressed him.

"I couldn't hear that. Eden? What's Eden got to do with a gymshoe?"

Matty muttered again.

"This is getting us nowhere," said the headmaster. "Look, er, Wildwort. What was poor young Henderson doing up that fire-escape?"

Matty stared passionately up under his brows and the one word burst from his lips.

"Evil!"

So they put Matty by and sent for Mr Pedigree. He came, feeble, grey-faced and fainting. The headmaster viewed him with disgusted pity and offered him a chair into which he collapsed. The solicitor explained the probable course of events and how a heavier charge might be abandoned in favour of a lesser if the defendant pleaded guilty to render unnecessary the cross-examination of minors. Mr Pedigree sat huddled and shivering. They were kind to him but he only showed one spark of animation during the whole interview. When the headmaster explained kindly that he had a friend, for little Matty Windwood had tried to give him an alibi, Mr Pedigree's face went white then red then white again.

"That horrible, ugly boy! I wouldn't touch him if he were the last one left on earth!"

36

His arrest was arranged as privately as possible in view of his agreement to plead guilty. Nevertheless, he did come down the stairs from his room with policemen in attendance; and nevertheless, his shadow, that dog of his steps was there to see him go in his shame and terror. So Mr Pedigree screamed at him in the great hall.

"You horrible, horrible boy! It's all your fault!"

Curiously enough the rest of the school seemed to agree with Mr Pedigree. Poor old Pedders was now even more popular among the boys than he had been in the sunny days when he gave them slices of cake and was quite amiably ready to be their butt so long as they liked him. No one, not the headmaster nor the solicitor, nor the judge ever knew the real story of that night; how Henderson had begged to be let in and been denied and gone reeling on the leads to slip and fall, for now Henderson was dead and could no longer reveal to anyone his furious passion. But the upshot was that Matty was sent to Coventry and fell into deep grief. It was plain to the staff that he was one of those cases for early relief from school and a simple, not too brainy job was the only palliative if not remedy. So the headmaster, who had an account at Frankley's the Ironmongers at the other end of the High Street down by the Old Bridge, contrived to get him a job there; and like 109732 Pedigree the school knew him no more.

Nor did it know the headmaster much longer. The fact that Henderson had come to see him and been turned away could not be condoned. He left at the end of term for reasons of health; and because the tragedy had been what pushed him out, in his retirement in a bungalow above the white cliffs, he went over the dim fringes of it again and again without understanding it more deeply. Only once did he come across what might be a clue, but even so could not be certain. He found a quotation from the Old Testament, "Over Edom have I cast out my shoe." When he remembered Matty after that he felt a little chill on his skin. The quotation was, of course, a primitive curse, the physical expression of which had been concealed in the translation, like "Smiting hip and thigh," and a dozen other savageries. So he sat and thought and wondered whether he had the key to something even darker than the tragedy of young Henderson.

He would nod, and mutter to himself—

"Oh yes, to *say* is one thing: but to *do* is quite another matter."

37

CHAPTER THREE

Frankley's was an ironmonger's of character. When the canal was cut and the Old Bridge built, it diminished the value of all the properties at that end of Greenfield. Frankley's, in the early days of the nineteenth century, moved into rickety buildings that backed on the towpath and were going dirt cheap. The buildings were indeterminate in date, some walls of brick, some tile-hung, some lath and plaster and some of a curious wooden construction. It is not impossible that parts of these wooden areas were in fact medieval windows filled as was the custom with wooden slats and now thought to be no more than chinky walls. Certainly there was not a beam in the place that did not have here and there notches cut, grooves and an occasional hole that indicated building and rebuilding, division, reclamation and substitution, carried on throughout a quite preposterous length of time. The buildings that at last were subsumed under Frankley's management were random and seemingly as confused as coral growths. The front that faced up the High Street was only done up and unified as late as 1850 and stayed so until it was done up all over again for the visit of His Majesty King Edward the Seventh, in 1909.

By that time, if not earlier, all the lofts and attics, galleries, corridors, nooks, crannies had been used as warehouses and were filled with stock. This was over-stocking. Frankley's held from each age, each generation, each lot of goods, a sediment or remainder. Poking about in far corners the visitor might come across such items as carriage lamps or a sawyer's frame, destined not for a museum but for the passing stagecoach or sawyer who had refused to turn over to steam. True, during the early days of the twentieth century, Frankley's made a determined effort to get as much of the contemporary stock downstairs as possible. This, by a kind of evolution with no visible agent, organized itself into sections or departments devoted to various interests as it might be tools, gardening, croquet or miscellaneous. After the convulsion of the First World War the place grew a spider's web of wires along which money trundled in small, wooden jars. For people of all ages, from babies to pensioners, this was entrancing. Some assistant would fire the jar—clang!—from his counter and when the flying jar reached the till it would ring a bell—Dong! So the cashier would reach up, unscrew the jar, take out the money and inspect the bill, put in the change and fire the jar back—Clang! . . .Clang! All this took a great deal of time but was full of interest and enjoyment, like playing with model trains. On market days the noise of the bell was frequent and loud enough to be heard above the lowing of the cattle that were being driven over the Old Bridge. But on other days the bell would be silent for periods that grew longer as the years revolved. Then, a visitor wandering in the darker and farther parts of Frankley's might find another property of the wooden jars. Tricks of construction might muffle the sound of the bells themselves, and a jar would hiss over the customer's head like a bird of prey, turn a corner and vanish in some quite unexpected direction.

Age was the genius of Frankley's. This complex machinery had been designed as a method of preventing each shop assistant from having his own till. The unforeseen result was that the spider's web isolated the assistants. As a young Mr Frankley took over from the late Mr Frankley and became old Mr Frankley and died, his assistants, kept healthy, it may be, by the frugality and the godliness of their existence, did not die but remained static behind their counters. The new young Mr Frankley, even more pious than his forebears, felt that the overhead railway for money was a slur on these elderly gentlemen and removed it. He was, of course, the famous Mr Arthur Frankley who built the chapel and whose name was shortened to "Mr Arthur" by those gentlemen in their corners whose speech remained uncontaminated by times that were seeing the spread of the horseless carriage. Mr Arthur gave each counter back its wooden till and restored dignity to separate parts.

But the use of the overhead railway had done two things. First, it had accustomed the staff to moderate stillness and tranquillity; and second, it had so habituated them to the overhead method of money sending and getting that when one of these ancient gentlemen was offered a banknote he immediately gestured upwards

39

with it as if to examine the watermark. But this, in the evolution or perhaps devolution of the place, would be followed by continuing silence and a lost look while the assistant tried to remember what came next. Yet to call them "assistants" does their memory scant justice. On bright days, when even the dim electricity was switched off and the shop relied on plate-glass windows or wide, grimy skylights, some of which were interior and never saw the sky, there were restful areas remaining of gloom—corners, or forgotten passageways. On such days the loitering customer might detect a ghostly winged collar gleaming in an unvisited corner; and as he accustomed his eyes to the gloom he might make out a pale face hung above the winged collar, and lower down a pair of hands perhaps, spread out at the level where the invisible counter must be. The man would be still as his packets of bolts and nails and screws and tags and tacks. He would be absent, in some unguessable mode of the mind, where the body was to be left thus to pass life erect and waiting for the last customer. Even young Mr Arthur with all his goodwill and genuine benevolence believed that a vertical assistant was the only proper one and that there was something immoral in the idea of an assistant sitting down.

Since young Mr Arthur was devout, by one of the spiritual mysteries of the human condition it is undeniable that during his reign the assistants became more and more holy. The combination of age, frugality and devotion made them at once the most useless and dignified shop assistants in the world. They were notorious. Young Mr Arthur was exhausted by his Napoleonic decision about the spider's web. He was one of nature's bachelors, less by distaste or inversion than by a diminution of sex drive; and he proposed to leave his money to his chapel. During the Second World War the establishment ceased to pay its way; but minimally. Mr Arthur saw no reason why it should not continue to do so, for the rest of his life. The holy old men were to be supported because they could do nothing but what they were doing and had nowhere else to go. Taxed on this unbusinesslike attitude by the progressive grandson of his father's accountant, Mr Arthur muttered vaguely, "Thou shalt not muzzle the ox that treadeth out the corn."

It is not possible now to discover whether the reintroduction of separate tills had any effect on the speed of the shop's decline. All that is certain is that as the decline became more perilous, by an apparent spontaneity the place made convulsive efforts to save itself. It did not shake off its honourable commitment to the elderly gentlemen who had stood so long and sold so little. But in a first convulsion, it bundled an unimaginable load of oddments away from one loft to another and opened a showroom upstairs! Here was to be seen cutlery and glass; and as all the elderly gentlemen were busy behind their counters, new blood had to be imported. At the time there was none of the right age or cheapness available, so with an air of coming clean and bursting out into the twentieth century, the shop hired—the word "employ" had a masculine dignity—hired a woman. In this long upstairs showroom the electric light—and what is more, with more powerful bulbs than anywhere else in the building—was not turned off, no matter how bright the day, until the front doors had been shut at six. The very way up to this glittering room betokened a basic frivolity that was suited to the goods on display and the sex of their guardian. It was a drumheaded, plaster-moulded survival from the late seventeenth century and there was no way of discovering how anything like that had found itself indoors rather than out. After a short while, to the cutlery and tumblers were added decanters, wine glasses, china, table mats, napkin rings, candlesticks, salt cellars and ashtrays in onyx. It was a shop within as well as above a shop. Yet it seemed a flighty thing, that lighted, drumheaded entrance with the carpeted stairs, the rugs and polished floor, the flash of glass or silver under the wastefully bright lights. Below it the broomsticks remained, the galvanized iron buckets, the rows of wooden-hafted tools. It did not accord well with the pigeon-holes of stained and broken wood, that were filled with nails or pins or tacks or iron or brass screws and bolts.

The old men ignored it. They must have known that it would fail, since the shop, as they were, was in the rip of something uncontrollable, an inevitable decline. Even so, after the upstairs showroom, plastics burst in and would not be denied. Plastics committed enormities in the way of silent buckets and washing-up bowls, sink-baskets, watering cans and trays all of blinding colour. Plastics went even further after that and blossomed as a range of artificial flowers. These all grouped themselves as a kind of bower in the centre of the downstairs showrooms. The bower flung out an annexe of plastic screens and trellises that demanded whimsical garden furniture. Once more, it was a feminine place.

41

Once more, a female was its guardian; and not just a female, but a girl at that. She had a till like everyone else. She experimented with coloured lights and hid herself inside a fantasy grove.

It was into this complex disorder of ancient and modern, this image in little of the society at large, that Matty was projected by the headmaster. His status was ambiguous. Mr Arthur explained that the boy had better come until they found out what use they could make of him.

"I think," said Mr Arthur, "we might make use of him in Deliveries."

"What about the future?" asked the headmaster" —his future, I mean."

"If he does well enough he can go into Despatch," said Mr Arthur, with, as it were, a far-off glance at Napoleon."Then if his head for figures is good enough, he might even move up to Accounts."

"I don't conceal from you that the boy seems to have little ability. But he mustn't stay at school."

"He can start in Deliveries."

Frankley's delivered for ten miles round and gave credit. They had a boy with a bicycle for parcels in Greenfield and two vans for longer or heavier journeys. The second of these vans had a driver and a porter, as he was called. The driver was so crippled with arthritis that he had to be inserted in his seat and left there as long as he could stand it and sometimes longer. This was another of Mr Arthur's unimaginative kindnesses. It kept a man in a job that was a constant trial and terror to him and ensured that two people did one man's work. Though the phrase was not yet widely used, Frankley's was Labour Intensive. It was what was sometimes called "a fine old establishment".

Tucked away at the bottom of the yard that ran along by the small garden of GOODCHILD'S RARE BOOKS, and kept in what was still called the coachhouse, was a forge, complete with anvil, tools, fire, and of course ageing blacksmith, who spent his time making trifles for his grandchildren. This area took Matty and absorbed him. He received pocket money, he slept in a long attic under the rosy, fifteenth-century tiles. He ate well, for this was one of the things Mr Arthur could measure. He wore a thick, dark-grey suit and grey overall. He carried things. He became the Boy. He carried garden tools from one part of the place to another and got

42

customers to sign for them. He was visible part of the time among stacks of packing-cases outside the smithy—packing-cases which he prised open with an instrument like a jemmy. He became adept at opening things. He learnt the measure of sheet metal and metal rod, of angle iron, girders and wire. He could be heard, sometimes, in the silence of business hours tramping unevenly overhead through the lofts and attics among the stock. He would deliver to it strange objects the name of which he did not know, but which would be sold at the rate of perhaps one out of every half a dozen ordered, while the other five rusted. Up there, the occasional visitor might find a set of jacks for an open fireplace or even a deformed packet of the first, snuffless candles. Matty swept here sometimes—swept those acres of uneven planking where all the brush did was to raise the dust so that it hung about invisibly in the dark corners but sneezily palpable. He began to reverence the winged collars in their places. The only boy of his own age or slightly older, there, was the boy who did the local deliveries either on foot or on the bicycle which he regarded as his own. It was already older than he was. But this boy, thick-set and blond with oiled hair that gleamed as seductively as his boots, had perfected a way of remaining away from the establishment that made his visits seem more like those of a customer than a member of the staff. Where the winged collars had achieved, it seemed, a perfect stillness, the other Boy had discovered perpetual motion. Matty, of course, remained too naive to bend circumstances in his direction as the blond Boy had done. He was perpetually employed and never knew that people gave him jobs to get him out of their sight. Ordered by the blacksmith to pick up the cigarette ends in a corner of the yard where he would be hidden, Matty did not grasp that no one would mind if he loafed there all day. He picked up the few cigarette ends and reported back when he had done it.

It was not many months after his arrival at Frankley's that a pattern from his days at Foundlings repeated itself. Already he had passed the bower of artificials and smelt it with a kind of shock. Perhaps it was the intolerable and scentless extravagence of the flowers that made the girl inside so determined to smell sweet. Then, one morning he was told to bring a bundle of new flowers to Miss Aylen. He arrived at the bower, his arms full of the plastic roses on which it had not been thought necessary to imitate the

43

thorns. He looked forward through a gap between his own roses, a leaf meanwhile interfering with his nose. He found that she had made a gap in the wall of the bower by shifting the rose already there from a shelf in front of him. For this reason he was not only able to see through his own roses but into the bower.

He was aware first of a shining thing like a curtain. The curtain was ogival at the top—for she had her back to him—spread very slightly all the way down until it passed out of sight. The scent she wore, obeying its own laws, came and went. She heard him and turned her head. He saw that this creature had a nose that curved out a very short way as if conferring the absolute right of impertinence on its owner, even though at that moment the curtain of hair was caught under it by the turn of her head. He saw also that the line of her forehead was delimited by a line of brow beyond mathematical computation and that under it again was a large, grey eye that fitted between long, black lashes. This eye noted the plastic roses; but she was engaged with a customer in the other direction and had time for no more than a monosyllable.

"Ta."

The empty shelf was under his elbow. He lowered the roses and they cocked up, hiding her from his view. His feet turned him and he went away. "Ta" spread, was more than a monosyllable, was at once soft and loud, explosive and of infinite duration. He came partly to himself near the smithy. Brilliantly he asked if there were more flowers to deliver but was not heard for he did not know how faint his voice had become.

Now he had a second preoccupation. The first, so unlike the second, was Mr Pedigree. When the Boy was sweeping clouds of dust in the loft and when his face had more anguish in its right, expressive side than the occasion would warrant, Mr Pedigree would be there in his mind. When his face contorted with sudden pain it was not the dust nor the splinters. It was the memory of the words screamed at him in the hall—"It's all your fault!" In one very private experience, he had seized a spike and stuck it clumsily into the back of the hand that held the broom. He had watched, a little paler perhaps, the blood turn into a long streak with a drop at the end—and all this because the soundless voice had screamed at him again. Now it seemed to him that this glimpse of part of a face, this fragrance, this hair, filled with a similar compulsion all the parts of his mind that the memory of Mr

44

Pedigree did not inhabit as of right. The two compulsions seemed to twist him inside, to lift him up against his own wishes and leave him with no defences and no remedy but simply to endure.

That morning he drifted away from the yard and climbed the stairs into the lofts. Familiarly he picked his way among packing-cases bursting with shavings, past piled paint, through a room where there was nothing but a set of rusting saws and a heap of hip baths stacked one inside the other, down through rows of identical paraffin lamps and into the long room for cutlery and glass. Here in the centre there was a great skylight of ridged glass that was supposed to let daylight down into the main show-room from a second skylight above it. Looking down, he could see the irradiated glow of coloured lights, could see them move among the ridges as he moved. He could see also, his heart quickening, a vague mass of colour down there that was the flower counter. He knew at once that he would never come this way again without a sideways and downward look at that blurred mixture. He went forward and into yet another loft, empty this one, then a step or two down some stairs. These led down the wall at the farthest point from where the yard was. He put a hand on the guard rail, bent down and peered along under the ceiling.

He could see the mass of artificial flowers but the opening where the customers were dealt with was to one side of him. He could see flowers on this side, and the roses he had stacked all too quickly on the other. All that was visible in the middle was the very top of a light brown head with a white, centre-parting down it. He saw that the only way to do better was to walk along the shop and glance sideways as he passed the bower. He did think for a moment to himself that if one were sufficiently knowing—like for example the blond Boy—one might stop and chat. His heart jumped at the thought and the impossibility of it. He went quickly therefore, but his feet seemed to get in his way as if he had too many of them. He passed a yard from the counter that was not stacked with flowers and looked sideways without moving his head as he passed. But Miss Aylen had bent down and the bower might have been empty for all he could see.

"Boy!"

He broke into a shambling trot.

"Where've you been, Boy?"

But they did not really want to know where he had been,

45

though they would have been amused and liked him better for it if they had known.

"The van's been waiting for about half an hour. Load her up!"

So he hauled the bundles into the van, bundles of metal flung shatteringly into the corner, put down half a dozen folding chairs and finally swung his clumsy body into the seat by the driver.

"What a lot of flowers we've got!"

Mr Parrish, the arthritic driver, groaned. Matty went on.

"They're just like real aren't they?"

"I never seen 'em. If you had my knees—"

"They're good, those flowers are."

Mr Parrish ignored him and set himself to the craft of van-driving. Matty's voice, practically of its own accord, went on speaking.

"They're pretty. Artificials I mean. And that girl, that young lady—"

The noises that Mr Parrish made dated from the days of his youth when he had driven one of Frankley's three horse-vans. He had been transferred to a motor van not many years after such an innovation became available and he took two things with him—his horse-van vocabulary and a belief that he had been promoted. There was no sign at first, therefore, that Mr Parrish had heard the Boy. He had heard everything the Boy said, however— was waiting for the right moment to wrap up his silence, roll it into a weapon and hit Matty over the head with it. He did so now.

"When you address me, my lad, you call me 'Mr Parrish'."

This may well have been the last time Matty ever tried to confide in anyone.

Later that day he was able to go once more through the lofts over the main shop. Once more he glanced sideways at the coloured blur in the ribbed skylight and once more he peered along under the ceiling. He saw nothing. When the shop closed he hurried to the empty pavement in front of it but saw no one. Next day at the same time he got there early, and was rewarded with an exhibition of light-brown hair with honey lights, the apparently naked crooks of knees and the gleam of two long, shining stockings as they disappeared from the platform of a bus to the interior. The next day was Saturday—a half-day—and he was kept busy all morning so that she had gone before he was free.

On Sunday he went automatically to morning service, ate the

large, plain dinner that was served in what Mr Arthur called the Refectory, then wandered out for the walk he was ordered to take for his health. The winged collars snoozed meanwhile on their beds. Matty went along, past GOODCHILD'S RARE BOOKS, past Sprawson's and turned right up the High Street. He was in a curious state. It was as if there was a high, singing note in the air from which he could not detach himself and which was the direct result of some interior strain, some anxiety that could—if you remembered this thing or that thing—sharpen into anguish. This feeling became so strong that he turned back to Frankley's as if sight of the place where one of his problems lay would help to solve it. But though he stood and looked it over, and the bookshop next to it and Sprawson's next to that, he was given no help. He went round the corner of Sprawson's to the Old Bridge over the canal and the iron loo at the root of the bridge flushed automatically as he passed. He stood, and looked down at the water of the canal in that age-old and unconscious belief that there is help and healing in the sight. He had a moment's idea of walking along the towpath, but it was muddy. He turned back, round the corner of Sprawson's, and there was the bookshop and Frankley's again. He stopped walking and looked in the window of the bookshop. The titles did not help him. The books were full of words, physical reduplication of that endless cackle of men.

Now some of the problem was coming into focus. It might be possible to go down into silence, sink down through all noises and all words, down through the words, the knives and swords such as *it's all your fault* and *ta* with a piercing sweetness, down, down into silence—

On the left in the window, below the rows of books (*With Rod and Gun*), was a small counter with a few items on it which were not in the strict canon of bookishness at all. Such was the alphabet and the Lord's Prayer in a hornbook. Such was the carefully mounted scrap of ancient music on parchment—music with square notes. Such was the glass ball that lay on a small stand of black wood just to the left of the old music. Matty looked at the glass ball with a touch of approval since it did not try to say anything and was not, like the huge books, a whole store of frozen speech. It contained nothing but the sun which shone in it, far away. He approved of the sun which said nothing but lay there, brighter and brighter and purer and purer. It began to blaze as when

47

clouds move aside. It moved as he moved but soon he did not move, could not move. It dominated without effort, a torch shone straight into his eyes, and he felt queer, not necessarily unpleasantly so but queer all the same—unusual. He was aware too of a sense of rightness and truth and silence. But this was what he later described to himself as a feeling of waters rising; and still later was described to him and for him by Edwin Bell as entering *a still dimension of otherness* in which things appeared or were shown to him.

He was shown the seamy side where the connections are. The whole cloth of what had seemed separate now appeared as the warp and woof from which events and people get their being. He saw Pedigree, his face contorted with accusation. He saw a fall of hair and a profile and he saw the balance in which they lay, the one the other. The face he had never fully seen of the girl among the artificials was there in front of him. He knew it familiarly but knew there was something wrong with the knowledge. Pedigree balanced it. There was everything right with this plain knowledge of Pedigree and his searing words.

Then all that was unspeakably hidden from him. Another dimension from low on his right to higher on his left became visible with huge letters written in gold. He saw that this was the bottom of the window of the bookshop and that it had GOODCHILD'S RARE BOOKS written in gold. He found that he himself was leaning to one side and, after all, the golden words were horizontal. The glass ball on its stand of black wood had retreated behind the condensation of his breath on the window. The sun no longer blazed in it. Confusedly he remembered that all that day there had been no sun but solid cloud from which rain pricked every now and then. He tried to remember what had happened, then found that as he remembered he changed what had happened. It was as if he laid colours and shapes over pictures and events; and this was not like crayoning in the spaces of a crayoning book where the lines are all set out but like wishing things and then seeing them happen; or even *having* to wish something and then seeing it happen.

After a while he turned away and began to walk aimlessly up the High Street. The rain prickled down and he hesitated then looked round him. His eye fell on the old church, half-way up the left-hand side of the street. He walked more quickly towards it, first thinking of shelter, then suddenly understanding that it was what he had to do. He opened the door, went in and sat right at the back under the west window. He pulled up his trouser-legs carefully and knelt down without really thinking what he was doing. There he was, almost without his volition, in the right attitude and place. It was Greenfield Parish Church, a huge place with side aisles and transept and full of the long, undistinguished history of the town. There was hardly a slab in the floor without an epitaph on it and not much more unlettered space on the walls. The church was quite empty and not merely of people. It seemed to him empty of the qualities that lay in the glass ball and had found some kind of response inside him. He could not make any connection and there was a lump in his throat too big to swallow. He began to say the Lord's Prayer then stopped, for the words seemed to mean nothing. He stayed there, kneeling, bewildered and sorrowful; and while he knelt the painful and extraordinary necessities of the artificials and the brown fall with the honey lights came flooding back.

The daughters of men.

He cried out silently to nowhere. Silence reverberated in silence.

Then a voice spoke, quite clearly.

"Who are you? What do you want?"

Now this was the voice of the curate who was clearing up certain things in the vestry. He had been submitting himself to an austerity of which his vicar knew nothing. He was surprised in this by the sound of a choir boy scrabbling at the vestry door and trying to get in to retrieve a comic he thought he had left. But the voice sounded right inside Matty's head. He answered it in the same place. Before the balance with its two scales, the one with a man's face, the other with a fire of anticipation and enticement, he had a time that was made of pure, whitehot anguish. It was the first exercise of his untried will. He knew, and it never occurred to him to doubt the knowledge, or worse, accept it and be proud of it, that he had chosen, not as a donkey between carrots of unequal size but rather as the awareness that suffered. The whitehot anguish continued to burn. In it was consumed a whole rising future that centred on the artificials and the hair, it had sunk away from the still-possible to the might-have-been. Because he had become aware he saw too how his unattractive appearance would have made an approach to the girl into a farce and humiliation; and thought, as he saw, that it would be so with any woman. He began to weep adult tears, wounded right in the centre of his nature, wept for a vanished prospect as he might have wept for a dead friend. He wept until he could weep no more and never knew what things had drained away from him with the tears. When he had done he found he was in a strange position. He was kneeling but his backside was touching the edge of a bench. His hands were grasping the top of a pew in front of him and his forehead lay on the little shelf where the prayer and hymn books were. As he opened his eyes and focused them he found he was staring down into the wetness of his own tears where they had fallen on stone and lay in the grooves of an ancient epitaph. He was back, in dull, grey daylight with the faint whisper of rain above him on the west window. He saw the impossibility of healing Pedigree. As for the hair—he knew that he must go away.

CHAPTER FOUR

It was typical of Matty's jagged and passionate character that once he had decided to go away he should go as far as humanly possible. It was part of the strange way in which circumstances were apt to adjust themselves round him as he went—as if for all his jaggedness he was fitted for the journey with streamlined farings—that his way to Australia should be made easy. He met what seemed like compassionate officialdom where there might have been indifference; or perhaps it was that those who winced at the sight of his shrivelled ear speeded him out of their sight. It was no more than months before he found himself with a job, a church, a bed in the Y.M.C.A. in Melbourne. All three were waiting for him downtown in Fore Street by the London Hotel. The ironmonger's was not as large as Frankley's but there were storerooms overhead, packing-cases in the yard at the side and a machine shop to stand in for a forge. He might have stayed there for years—for a lifetime—if it had lived up to his innocent belief that by going far and fast he had outdistanced his troubles. But of course, Mr Pedigree's curse came with him. Moreover, either time or Australia or the two together quickly sharpened his vague feelings of bewilderment into downright astonishment; and this at last found words somewhere in his head.

"Who am I?"

To this, the only answer from inside him was something like: you came out of nowhere and that is where you are going. You have injured your only friend; and you must offer up marriage, sex, love, because, because, *because*! On a cooler view of the situation, no one would have you, anyway. That is who you are.

He was also someone who lacked more skin than he knew. When he had come at last to realize just how great an effort even the kindest people had to make not to be visibly affected by his

51

appearance he ducked away from any intercourse he could. It was not just the unattainable creatures (and pausing for forty minutes at Singapore, that doll-like figure in its glittering clothes and standing submissively by the passenger lounge) but a minister and his kindly wife, and others. His Bible, on India paper and in squashy leather, gave him no help. Neither—though in his innocence he had thought it might—did his English voice and emergence from the Old Country. When they were assured that he did not think himself special and did not look down on Australia and did not expect preferential treatment, his workmates were unkinder than they might have been through sheer annoyance at being wrong and missing a treat. Also there was a quite gratuitous confusion.

"I don't care what you're bleeding called. When I say 'Matey' I mean 'Matey'. My bleeding oath!"

—And turning to the Australian equivalent of Mr Parrish—

"Telling me how to speak the King's bleeding English!"

But Matty left the ironmonger's for a very simple reason. The first time he had to take some boxes of china to the Wedding Gifts Department he found it presided over and rendered unspeakably dangerous by a girl both pretty and painted. He saw at once that travel had not solved all his problems and he would have gone back to England there and then except that it was impossible. He did the best he could, which was to change jobs as soon as there was one to be had. He got work in a bookshop. Mr Sweet who ran it was too short-sighted and vague to grasp what a handicap Matty's face would be. When Mrs Sweet, who was not short-sighted or vague, saw Matty she knew why nobody browsed in the shop as they used. The Sweets, who were much richer than English booksellers would be, lived in a country house outside the city and soon Matty was established there, in a minute cottage that leaned against the main building. He was odd-job man; and when Mr Sweet had had him taught to drive, chauffeur between the house and the shop. Mrs Sweet, her face averted, pointed out that his hair would keep in place better if he wore a hat. Some deep awareness of self rather than awareness of identity made him choose a black one with a broad brim. It suited both the mournful, good side of his face, and the lighter, but contracted and more formidable left side where the mouth and eye were both pulled down. It lay so close to the purple knob of his ear that people seldom noticed his ear was anything out of the ordinary. Piece by piece—jacket, trousers, shoes, socks, roll-neck sweater, pullover—he became the man in black, silent, distant, with the unsolved question waiting on him.

"Who am I?"

One day after he had taken Mrs Sweet to the shop and was waiting to bring her back, he stood by the tray of battered books that were displayed outside the shop and all at fifty cents or less. One seemed curious. It had wooden covers on either side and the back was so worn the title was illegible. Idly he picked it out and found it was an old Bible, heavier in wood than squashy leather, though the paper was much the same. He leafed through the familiar pages, stopped suddenly, turned back, then forwards, then back again. He bent his face nearer the page and began to mutter under his breath, a mutter that died away.

One of Matty's characteristics was a capacity for absolute inattention. Speech would wash over him without leaving a trace in his mind. It is likely that in the Australian churches he attended less and less—and in the English churches, and far back in class, at Foundlings—there was talk of the difficulty of moving from one language to another; but explanations must have failed before the present fact of black print on a white page. In the very middle of the twentieth century there was a kind of primitive grating between Matty and the easy world of his fellows that sorted out, it seemed, filtered out, ninety-nine per cent of what a man is supposed to absorb and gave the remaining one per cent the shiny hardness of stone. Now, therefore, he stood, the book in his hands, lifted his head from it and stared aghast through the bookshop.

It's different!

That night he sat at his table with both books before him and began to compare them, word by word. It was after one o'clock in the morning when he stood up and went out. He walked the straight and endless road up and down until the morning when it was time to drive Mr Sweet into the city. When he got back and put the car away it seemed to him that he had never heard before how the quality of bird-noise in the countryside was a kind of mad laughter. It disturbed him so much that he cut a lawn quite unnecessarily, to hide in the noise of the machine. When they heard the first whirr! the flock of sulphur-crested cockatoos that

53

haunted the tall trees round the low house took off, crying and circling, then fled away across the sunburnt grass where the horses grazed—fled to and filled a solitary tree a mile off with their whiteness and movement and clamour.

That evening after high tea in the kitchen he took out his two books and opened them both at the title-page. He read each title-page several times. At last he sat back and shut his book of squashy leather. He took it, went out, across the nearer lawn and along through the vegetable garden. He came to the fence that lay between the garden and the way down to the pool where the yabbies swam. He looked at the miles of moonlit grass that swept away to where there were dim hills on the horizon.

He took out his Bible and began to tear the pages out, one by one. As he tore each, he let the breeze take it, fluttering from his hand to blow away turning over and over into the distance where it was hidden at last among the long grass. Then he went back to his cottage, read in the other Bible between wooden covers for a time, said his mechanical prayers, went to bed and to sleep.

That was the beginning of what was mostly a happy year for Matty. He had a time of conflict with himself when the new girl who served in the village store proved to be pretty; but she was so pretty that she quickly moved on to be replaced by one to whom he could be peacefully indifferent. Happily he moved round the grounds or through the house, his lips moving, the good side of his face as cheerful as one side of a face can be. He never took his hat off where other people could see him and this led to rumours in the village that he slept in it, which was not true. It was not the kind of hat he could sleep in, being broad-brimmed, as everyone knew very well; but the story suited him, matched his withdrawal. The early sun, and always the moon, would find him in his bed, the long smear of black hair lying all ways to one over the pillow, the white skin of his skull and left face disappearing and reappearing as he moved in his sleep. Then the first birds would jeer and he would jerk upright, to sink back for a few moments before he got out of bed. After the bog and the basin he would sit and read, in the book with the wooden covers, his mouth following the words, his good side frowning.

During the day his lips would continue to move, whether he was driving the rotavator through the dust of the vegetable patch, or laying out the hoses, or waiting at traffic lights, the engine idling, or carrying parcels or sweeping, dusting, polishing—

Sometimes Mrs Sweet was near enough to hear.

"—one silver charger of the weight of an hundred and thirty shekels, one silver bowl of seventy shekels, after the shekel of the sanctuary; both of them full of fine flour mingled with oil for a meat offering: 56 One golden spoon of ten shekels full of incense: 57 One young bullock, one ram, one lamb of the first year for a burnt offering: 58 One kid of the goats—"

Sometimes she would hear him in the house as his voice got louder and louder, stuck like a scratched gramophone record.

"21 And he said unto them—said unto them—said unto them—said unto them—"

Then she would hear a few quick steps and know that he had gone into his own place to look at the book lying open on the table. He would come back after a few moments; and through the rub and squeak of the window being polished she would hear him once more.

"said unto them Is a candle bought to be put under a bushel or under a bed? And not to be set on a candlestick?
22 For there is nothing hid, which shall not be manifested; neither was anything kept secret, but that it should come abroad.
23 If any man—"

A happy year, all things considered! Only there were things—as he said to himself once in a moment of quite brilliant and articulate explanation—there were things moving about under the surface. If things moved about *on* the surface there was something to be done. For example, there were explicit instructions as to conduct if a man should defile himself. But how if the thing that moves beneath the surface is not to be defined but stays there, a *must* without any instructions? *Must* drove him to things he could not explain but only accept as a bit of easing when to do nothing was intolerable. Such was the placing of stones in a pattern, the making of gestures over them. Such was the slow trickling of dust from the hand and the pouring of good water into a hole.

It was during this year that Matty ceased to go to a church which had made only perfunctory efforts to retain him. Ceasing to go to church was as much a *must* as the other gestures, and positive. Yet the change from that year to the next, which might have slipped

55

by in the usual well-oiled manner leaving no trace anywhere but on the calendar, came to creak for Matty like a rusty hinge. Mrs Sweet's widowed sister came from Perth to spend the Christmas break and the New Year and brought her daughter. Sight of the girl with her fair hair and a skin to match sent Matty walking the road again until the small hours and it turned his eyes to the sky as if he might find some help there. Then lo! high in the sky he saw a familiar constellation. It was Orion the hunter, glittering, but with his dagger bursting fiery up. Matty's cry stirred the birds awake like a false dawn; and in the silence after they had settled again he understood the roundness of the earth and the terror of things hung in emptiness, the sun moving the witchway, the moon on its head; and when he added in the ease with which people lived in the midst of majesty and terror then the rusty hinge creaked round and the question which went with him always, changed and came clearer.

Not—who am I?

"What am I."

There on the open road in the small hours at New Year a few miles from the city of Melbourne he asked it aloud and stayed for an answer. It was silly, of course, like so much that he did. There was no one awake and up for miles; and when at last he turned away from the spot where he had cried out and then asked his question, though the sun was already lightening the hills on the horizon he still had no answer.

So the winter and the summer and the spring and the autumn were the second year only there wasn't any winter, not really, and not much spring. It was the time when the question seemed to get warmer and warmer under the surface of his mind and his feelings, and then hotter and hotter until he dreamed it night after night. Three nights running he dreamed that Mr Pedigree repeated his awful words and then asked for help. Only Matty was dumb three nights running, struggling under the bedsheet and in his mouth trying to explain—*How can I help until I know what I am?*

After that, when he woke up he found that saying his portion aloud was not the thing to do. It was bad enough having to talk or listen to talk when you had the question there all the time; and because he could not answer the question or know what it meant or how to ask it, certain consequences began to come clear in much the way that the question itself had creaked into a new form. He saw that he must move; and he even had a time of wondering if this might not be the real reason why people moved, or wandered the way Abraham did. Certainly there was desert enough to hand if you drove a few miles, but whether consciously or not, no sooner did Matty understand that he must move, than he saw the necessity of moving *north* to where the fiery jet of Orion's dagger might lie at least more level. A man who moves because he cannot stand still needs a very small impulse to settle his direction. All the same he spent so much time hung up in the sheer impossibility of understanding anything that he had broken into his fourth Australian year before he did what he thought of as shaking the dust of Melbourne from his feet. Because he could not tell, really, why he went, nor what he hoped to find, he spent much time making small arrangements for simplifying life. With some of the wages he so seldom spent he bought a very small, very cheap and hence very old car. He had his Bible between its wooden covers, spare pants, spare shirt, shaving gear for the right-hand side of his face, a sleeping-bag and a spare sock. This was his most brilliant rationalization and he proposed to change one sock a day. Mr Sweet gave him some extra money and what used to be called a "character" which said he was hard-working, scrupulously honest and absolutely truthful. It is some indication of how unattractive these characteristics are when unsupported by anything else, that after Mrs Sweet had said goodbye to him she went into the kitchen and danced a few steps in sheer relief.

As for Matty, he drove off with what he felt was really sinful pleasure. The road led away over the known routes by which he had sometimes taken Mr and Mrs Sweet for Sunday drives but he knew there would come a moment when his wheels would take him away from the prints the Daimler might have left, into a new world. When it came, it was a moment, not so much of pleasure as of sheer delight—all the more sinful of course, since that was his nature.

Matty worked for more than a year after that for a fencing company near Sydney. It got him some more money and kept him away from people for most of the time. He would have left the company earlier only his small car broke down so badly it took him

57

six months' extra work to pay for repairs and get on the road again. The question continued to burn and so did the weather as he moved on towards Queensland. Near Brisbane he needed another job and got it. But he kept it a shorter time than any other he had ever had, including the ironmonger's in Melbourne.

He started as a porter in a sweet factory which was small enough not to be mechanized; and what with the heat, for it was summer, and his appearance, the women swarmed all over the manager demanding his dismissal on the ground that he kept looking at them. In fact they kept looking at him and whispering "No wonder that lot of cream went sour," and so on. Matty, who must have thought himself invisible like an ostrich if he did not look at anybody, was called before the manager and in the process of being given his cards when the door opened and the owner of the factory rolled in. Mr Hanrahan was about half Matty's height and four times his width. His face was fat, with little, darting black eyes always on the watch for something in the corner or behind the door and when he heard why Matty was being dismissed, he looked sideways up into Matty's face, then round at his ear and after that all the way down to his feet and up again.

"And isn't he just the man we've been looking for?"

Matty felt his questions were about to be answered. But as it was, Mr Hanrahan led the way outside and told Matty to follow him up the hill. Matty got into his ancient car, Mr Hanrahan got into his new one and started it, then leapt out again, dashed back to the door, flung it open and stared into the office. He backed away slowly, closing it carefully but watching always, even through the last crack.

The road wound away from the factory through woods and fields and up, a zig-zag up the side of the hill. Mr Hanrahan's house hung on the hillside among strange trees that dripped with orchids and moss. Matty parked behind the new car and followed his new employer up an outside staircase to an enormous living-room that seemed to be walled completely with glass. On one side you could look right down the hill—and there was the factory, looking like an architect's model of itself. Directly he entered, Mr Hanrahan seized a pair of binoculars from the big table and levelled them at the model. He blew out his breath fiercely. He grabbed a phone and shouted into it.

"Molloy! Molloy! There's two girls skulking out at the back!"

But by the time he had said that, Matty was rapt, gazing at the glass on the three other walls. It was all mirror, even the backs of the doors, and it was not just plain mirrors, it distorted so that Matty saw himself half a dozen times, pulled out sideways and squashed down from above; and Mr Hanrahan was the shape of a sofa.

"Ha," said Mr Hanrahan. "You're admiring my bits of glass I see. Isn't that a good idea for a daily mortification of sinful pride? Mrs Hanrahan! Where are you?"

Mrs Hanrahan appeared as if materialized, for what with the window and the mirrors a door opening here or there was little more than a watery conflux of light. She was thinner than Matty, shorter than Mr Hanrahan and had an air of having been used up.

"What is it, Mr Hanrahan?"

"Here he is, I've found him!"

"Oh the poor man with his mended face!"

"I'll teach them, the awesome frivolity of it, wanting a man about the place! Girls! Come here, the lot of you!"

Then there was a watery conflux in various parts of the wall, some darkness and here and there a dazzle of light.

"My seven girls," cried Mr Hanrahan, counting them busily. "You wanted a man about the place did you? Too many females were there? Not a young man for a mile! I'll teach you! Here's the new man about the place! Take a good look at him!"

The girls had formed into a semicircle. There were the twins Francesca and Teresa, hardly out of the cradle, but pretty. Matty instinctively held his hand so that they should not be frightened by his left side which they could see. There was Bridget, rather taller and pretty and peering short-sightedly, and there was Bernadette who was taller and prettier and wholly nubile, and there was Cecilia who was shorter and just as pretty and nubiler if anything, and there was Gabriel Jane, turner-of-heads-in-the-street, and there was the firstborn, dressed for a barbecue, Mary Michael: and whoever looked on Mary Michael was lost.

Cecilia clasped her cheeks with her hands and uttered a faint shriek as her eyes adjusted to the light. Mary Michael turned her swan's neck to Mr Hanrahan and spoke enchanting words.

"Oh Dad!"

Then Matty gave a wild cry. He got the door open and he tumbled down the outside stairs. He leapt into his car and

59

wrenched it round the curves down the hill. He began to recite in a high voice.

"The Revelation of St John the Divine. Chapter One. I. John writeth his revelation to the seven churches of Asia, signified by the seven golden candlesticks. 7 The coming of Christ. 14 His glorious power and majesty. The Revelation of Jesus Christ, which God gave unto him, to show unto his servants—"

So Matty went on, his voice high; and it lowered bit by bit and it was normal as ever it was by the time he had got to—"19 And if any man shall take away from the words of the book of this prophecy, God shall take away his part out of the book of life, and out of the holy city, and *from* the things which are written in this book."

With the "Amen" at the end he found he needed petrol which he got; and while waiting, a kind of after-image of Mary Michael came floating through his mind so he started off again at random, both on the road and in the book—

"22 And Kinah, and Dimonah, and Adadah.

23 And Kedesh and Hazor and Ithnan,

24 Ziph, and Telem, and Bealoth.

25 And Hazor, Hadattah, and Kerioth, *and* Hezron, which *is* Hazor.

26 Amam and Shema—"

And Matty came in the evening unto the city of Gladstone which is a great city. And he sojourned there for many months at peace, finding work as a grave-digger.

But the pattern repeated itself, the question returning and the restlessness and the need to move on to some place where all things would be made plain. So Matty began to think; or perhaps it would be better to say that something began to think itself in Matty and presented the result to him. Thus without his conscious volition he came across the thought: *Are all men like this?* Then there was added to that thought: *No. For the two sides of their face are equal.*

Then: *Am I only different from them in face?*

No.

"What am I?"

After that he prayed mechanically. It was strange about Matty. He could no more pray than he could fly. But now he added a bit in after the petitions for all the people he knew, to the effect that if it was permissible he would be glad if his own particular difficulty could be made easier for him and directly following on that another thought performed itself in his mind, a quotation and a horrible one—*Some have made themselves eunuchs for the sake of the kingdom of God*. He had that thought in a grave, which was the best place for it. It got him out of the grave in a kind of instant resurrection and he was miles up the coast in a land of violent and wicked men before he could put the quotation out of his mind. The wicked men did it for him. He was stopped by police who searched him, and the car, and warned him that murder had been done on the road and would be done again, but he went on because he did not dare go back and there was nowhere else to go. He had looked at a map in a petrol station but his years in the land had not taught him the difference between a country and a continent. He went ignorantly expecting the journey to Darwin to be a few miles and with convenient petrol stations and stores for food and wells for water. He had no interest in acquiring knowledge and the Bible, though it was full of wildernesses and deserts, did not mention the incidence of wells and petrol stations in the outback. So he turned off what was already no major highway and he got thoroughly lost.

Matty was not frightened. It was not that he was brave. It was that he could not realize danger. He was not *able* to be frightened. So he lurched and bumped on, juddered and slid and thought he would like a drink but knew he had none, watched the needle of the fuel indicator drop lower and lower until at last it bounced on the pin, and still there was nothing but the merest track and then the car stopped. It did not do so dramatically or in a position of apparent drama. It stopped where scrubby thorns fledged a soil that looked rather like sand and where the only break in the prickly horizon was the low hump of three trees, not all together, but spaced all along on the north hand and seeming distant. Matty sat in the car for a long time. He saw the sun go down ahead of him and the sky was so cloudless that even down at the edge of it the sun mixed and clotted for a while among the thorns before it managed to lug itself down out of sight. He sat and listened to the noises of the night but by now they were familiar enough and even the thumping passage of a large animal among the thorns was not at all frightening. Matty composed himself in the driver's seat as if it were the proper place and went to sleep. He did not

61

wake up until the dawn; and what woke him was not light, but thirst.

He could not be frightened; but he could be thirsty. He got out of the car into the chilly dawn and walked round as if he might come across a pool or a snack bar or a village store; and then, without any preparation or much thought he began to walk forward along the track. He did not look round until a strange warmness on his back made him turn and stare at the rising sun. There was no car under it, only scrub. He started to walk again. As the sun rose, so did his thirst.

The literature of survival had passed Matty by. He did not know about the plants that hold water in their tissues, nor about digging holes in the sand or watching the behaviour of birds; nor did he feel the excitement of adventure. He just felt thirsty with a burning back and the wooden covers of the Bible bouncing against his right hip-bone. It may not even have occurred to him that a man could walk and walk until he dropped and still not find water. So he went on in the same stubborn way that he had done everything all his life, even back at the beginning of it.

By midday strange things were happening to the bushes. They were floating about sometimes as if Mr Hanrahan had got them into his strange living-room. This interfered with Matty's view of the track or what he thought was the track and he stopped for a bit, looking down and blinking. There were large, black ants running round at his feet, ants that apparently found the heat encouraging and an incentive to work for they were carrying huge burdens as if about to achieve something. Matty considered them for a while but they had nothing to say to his condition. When he looked up again he could not see which way the track went. His own footprints were no help for they curved out of sight and the scrub lay all around. He examined the close horizon as carefully as he could and decided that in one direction there was a thickening of its texture or additional denseness and additional height. It might be trees, he thought; and with trees there would be shade so he decided to go in that direction if it lay anywhere in the sector to the west. But at midday, that near the equator, even with a sextant it is very difficult to take your bearing from the sun and all that happened was that Matty, looking up, took a step to the rear and fell flat on his back. The fall made him breathless and for a moment among the wheeling rays and flashes from the meridian there seemed to be a darkness, man-shaped and huge. He got to his feet and of course there was nothing, just the sun falling vertically so that when he got his hat on again the shadow of the brim lay on his feet. He found the direction of the thickening and tried to think whether it was the sensible direction or not but all that came into his mind was a stream of Biblical injunctions about the size of seas of brass. They set him seeing water in flashes and this got mixed into the mirrors in Mr Hanrahan's room and his own lips out there felt like two ridges of rock in a waste land. So then he was pushing through scrub that came up to his shoulders and beyond it was a tall tree full of angels. When they saw him they jeered and flew and circled and then streamed away through heaven so that he saw clearly that they meant him to follow and jeered because he could not fly. But he could still move his feet and he pushed on until he stood under the tree that held its leaves sideways to the sun and gave no shade and all there was round the tree was a little space of bare and sandy soil. He got his back against the trunk and winced at the pain for he was burnt through his jacket. Then there was a man standing at the edge of the bare sand and he was an Abo. He was the man, Matty saw, who had been there, up in the air and between him and the sun when he fell. Matty now had the chance to examine him all over and carefully. The man was not so tall, after all, really rather short. But he was thin and this seemed to make him taller. The long, wooden stick with the burnt black point which the Abo held upright in one hand was taller than either of them. The Abo, Matty saw, had a cloud in his face, which was reasonable enough, seeing how he had materialized in the air under the sun. He was bollock naked too.

Matty took a step away from the tree and spoke.

"Water."

The Abo came forward and peered into his face. He jerked his chin up and spoke in his language. He gestured hugely with the spear, tracing out a great arc in the sky, which included the sun.

"Water!"

Now Matty pointed into the cloud that hid the Abo's mouth, then into his own mouth. The Abo gestured with his spear towards the densest of the scrub. Then he took out of the air a small, polished stone. He squatted, put it down on the sandy soil and muttered to it.

63

Matty was appalled. He scrabbled his Bible out of his pocket and held it over the stone but the Abo went on muttering. Matty cried out again.

"No, nc!"

The Abo looked impenetrably at the book. Matty thrust it back into his pocket.

"Look!"

He scuffed a line in the sand and then another that crossed the first. The Abo stared at it but said nothing.

"Look!"

Matty flung himself down. He lay, his legs stretched down the first line, his arms held wide on either side along the second. The Abo at once leapt to his feet. The cloud in his face was split by a wide flash of white.

"Fucking big sky-fella him b'long Jesus Christ!"

He leapt into the air and landed with a foot on either outstretched arm, a foot in the crook of either elbow. He stabbed down on this side and that with his fire-hardened spear into the open palm. He jumped back high, and he landed with both feet in Matty's groin and the sky went black and the Abo disappeared into it. Matty rolled up like a leaf, like a cut worm, screwed his body up and the waves of sickness increased like the pain until they carried his consciousness away.

When he came to he knew he was badly swelled up so he tried to move on hands and knees but the sickness swamped him again. So it being his nature, he got upright with the world reeling and he kept his legs apart and his belly dragged so that he held himself in with both hands so as not to lose anything down there. He went towards the place where he seemed to remember there had been some thickness beyond the scrub. But when he was through the thickness he came into an open space with trees a little further off. In the open space and stretching all along from as far that way to out of sight on this was an electrified fence. He turned, mechanically, to go along it but a car hooted behind him. He stood still, humbly and dumbly and the car was a Land Rover that came by his left shoulder slowly then stopped. A man got out and came across. He wore an open-necked shirt and jeans and a digger's hat turned up at the side. He peered into Matty's face and Matty waited like an animal not being able now to do anything else.

"My oath. Been done have you? Where's your cobber? Mate? Matey?"

"Water."

The man manoeuvred him gently towards the Land Rover, hissing between his teeth now and then as if Matty were a horse.

"You have been done my old son oh dear oh dear. What *has* been at you? Gone ten rounds with a roo? Drink this. Easy!"

"Crucified—"

"Where's your oppo?"

"Abo."

"You seen an Abo? Crucified? Here. Show us your hands. That's no more than scratches."

"A spear."

"Little thin man? With a little fat woman expecting and two nippers? That'll be Harry Bummer. The bleeding sod. I expect he let on he didn't know English didn't he? Moved his head like this, didn't he?"

"Just one Abo."

"They'll have been grub-hunting likely, the others I mean. He's never been the same since they made that film about him. Tries it on all the tourists. Now let's have a gander at your doolies mate. You're in luck. I'm the vet, see? What about your chum?"

"Alone."

"Oh my word. You been in there by yourself? You could go round and round in there you know, just round and round. Now careful, easy does it, can you lift up? Let me get my arm under and then pull your pants down. Oh my word as we say in Aussieland. If you was a bullcalf I'd say someone hadn't done a neat job. Oh dear. We'll put 'em in a sling. Of course in my line of business I'm generally moving in the other direction if you follow me."

"Car. Hat."

"All in good time. Let's hope Harry Bummer doesn't find it first, the ungrateful sod. After all the education he's had. Keep 'em wide apart. I expect after all they'll find he hasn't spoilt your chances, ruined the family jewels, clumsy it was. I've often looked at a bullock and wondered what he'd say to me if he could. What's this in your pocket? Oh, a preacher are you? No wonder old Harry—Now you lie still. Try to brace yourself with your hands. It'll jolt a bit but we can't help that and the hospital isn't far, not really. Didn't you know? You were nearly in the suburbs. You didn't think you were really in the outback did you?"

He started the engine and moved the Land Rover. Very soon Matty lost consciousness again. The vet, looking back at him and seeing that he had passed out, put his foot down and bumped and slewed through the sandy soil and on to the side road. As he went he talked to himself.

"Got to tell the police I suppose. More bleeding trouble. Not that they'll catch old Harry. He'll have an alibi with a dozen of them. This poor Pom could never tell them apart."

CHAPTER FIVE

Matty came to in hospital. His legs were strung up and he had no pain. There was pain later on but nothing his stubborn soul could not cope with. Harry Bummer—if it had been he—never found the car, which was brought in for Matty with his spare shirt, pants and third sock. His wooden Bible lay on the night table by the bed and he went on learning his portions from it. He had a period of fever when he mouthed inarticulately, but when his temperature was normal he fell silent again. He was calm, too. The nurses who attended to him so intimately found his calmness unnatural. He lay, they said, like a log and no matter how sordid the necessity he submitted to it with a still face and said nothing. The ward sister at one point gave him an aerosol to keep his privates cool, explaining delicately why it was touch and go with some vessels, but he never used it. At last his legs were cut down and he was allowed to sit out, be wheeled out, to limp out with sticks and finally to walk. His face had acquired an immobility in hospital on which the disfigurements seemed painted. From long stillness his movements had become more deliberate. He no longer had a limp, but he did walk with his legs kept slightly apart as if he were a freed prisoner whose body had not yet rid itself of the memory of chains. He was shown photographs of various Abos, but after a dozen, he spoke the great Caucasian sentence.

"They all look the same to me."

It was the longest sentence he had spoken for years.

His adventure was publicized and a collection taken up so that he had some money. People thought he was a preacher. Yet those who got in touch with him were baffled by a man of so few words, so awful and grave a face yet who did not seem to have opinions or a purpose. Yet still inside him the question pressed, altering now and becoming more urgent. It had been *who I*, then become *what am I*; and now through the force of his crucifarce or crucifiction by the black man leaping on him out of the sky it changed again and was a burning question.

What am I for?

So he moved round the curious tropical city. Where he walked now, clad in black and with a face that might have been cut out of particoloured wood, the old men sitting on the iron seats under the orange trees fell silent until he had passed towards the other end of the park.

Convalescing, Matty wandered round and round. He sampled the few chapels and those who moved towards him to ask him to take off his hat, came close, saw what they saw and went away again. When he could walk as far as he liked he would go and watch the Abos in their lean-tos and shacks round the edge of the city. Most of the time their actions were only too easily to be understood; but now and then they would do something, no more than a gesture, it may be, that seemed to interest Matty profoundly, though he could not tell why. Once or twice it was a whole mime that absorbed him—a game perhaps with a few sticks, or the throwing of pebbles with marks on them, then the absorbed contemplation of the result—the breathing, the blowing, the constant blowing—

The second time he saw an Abo throw the pebbles, Matty hurried back to the room he had been found in the Temperance Hotel. He went straight through into the yard and picked up three pebbles and held them—

Then stopped.

Matty stood for half-an-hour, without moving.

Then he laid the pebbles down again. He went to his room, took out his Bible and consulted it. Then he went to the State House but could not get in. Next morning he tried again. He got no further than the polished wooden information desk where he was received courteously but got no understanding. So he went away, bought matchboxes and then was to be seen, day after day, arranging them before the door of the State House, higher and higher. Sometimes he would get them more than a foot high, but they always fell down again. He gathered groups for the first time in his life, children and layabouts and sometimes officials who stopped on their way in or out. Then the police moved him away from the door out on to the lawns and flowerbeds; and there, perhaps because he had moved away from officialdom, people and children laughed at him louder. He would kneel and build his tower out of matchboxes; and sometimes, now, he would blow at them like an Abo blowing on the pebbles and they would all fall down. This made people laugh and that made children laugh; and now and then a child would dart forward while the tower was abuilding and blow it down and everyone would laugh and sometimes a naughty boy would dart forward and kick it over and people would laugh but also cry out and object in a friendly manner since they were on Matty's side and hoped one day he would manage to get all the matchboxes balanced one on the other since that seemed to be what he wanted. So if a naughty, energetic boy—but they were all naughty, energetic boys and quite capable of saying "Go up Baldhead!" except that they did not know what was under the hat and there are no bears in the Northern Territory—kicked, struck, spat, jumped and knocked the match-boxes over, all the grown-ups would cry out, laughing, shocked, nice women out to do the shopping, and pensioners, cry out—"Oh no! The little bastard!"

Then the man in black would move back on his knees and sit on his upturned heels and he would look round slowly, round under the brim of his black hat sweeping round at the laughing people; and because his face like particoloured wood was inscrutable and solemn, they would fall silent, one by one on the, by now, watered grass.

After seven days Matty added to his game. He bought a clay pot and gathered twigs; and this time when everyone started laughing at his matchboxes, Matty put the twigs together with the pot on top and tried to light them with the matches but could not. Crouched down in black by his twigs and pot and matchboxes he looked silly and a naughty boy kicked his pot over and all the grown-ups cried out "Oh no! You little sod! That's *reely* naughty! You might have broke it!"

Then, as Matty gathered his matchboxes and twigs and pot together, everyone drifted away. Matty went away too, watched absently by a park-keeper.

The next day, Matty had moved out to where the twigs would not be damp from the water that the automatic jets sprinkled on the grass lawns by the State House. He found a kerb near the central parking lots, a kind of nonplace with rank grass and seeding flowers, rank under the vertical sun. Here it took him a little longer to gather a group. In fact he was an hour at his building and might have got his matchboxes all vertically arranged the way any game of patience will come out at last given enough time but there was a little wind and he could never get more than eight or nine on top of the other before they fell over. However, at last the children came and stopped and then the adults and he got his attention and his laughter and a naughty boy and "Oh no, the wicked little sod!" So then he was able to lay his twigs and put the pot on top and strike a match and light the twigs and he got more laughter and then applause as if he was a clown who had suddenly done something clever; and through the laughter and the applause you could hear the crackling of the twigs under the pot and the twigs blazed and grass blazed and the flower seeds went bang, bang, bang and a great flame licked across the wasteland and there were shrieks and screams and people beating each other out and the children and people scattering and the screech of brakes as they ran into the road and the crash as cars shunted each other and cries and curses.

"You know," said the secretary, "you mustn't do it."

The secretary had a thatch of silver hair that was as carefully arranged, as carefully wrought as a silver vessel. He had the same accent, Matty could hear, as old Mr Pedigree had had all those years ago. He spoke mildly.

"Will you promise me not to do it again?"

Matty said nothing. The secretary leafed through some papers.

"Mrs Robora, Mrs Bowery, Mrs Cruden, Miss Borrowdale, Mr Levinsky, Mr Wyman, Mr Mendoza, Mr Buonarotti—an artist do you think?—You see when you singe as many people as that—and they are very, very angry—oh no! You really must not do it again!"

He put the paper down, laid a silver pencil on it and looked across at Matty.

"You're wrong, you know. I believe your sort of person always has been. No, I don't mean in the, the content of the message. We know the state of things, the dangers, the folly of taking a meteorological gamble; but we are elected you see. No. You are wrong in supposing that people can't read your message, translate your language. Of course we can. The irony is—the irony always

70

was—that predictions of calamity have always been understood by the informed, the educated. They have not been understood by the very people who suffer most from them—the humble and meek—in fact, the ignorant who are helpless. Do you see? All Pharaoh's army—and earlier than that the firstborn of all those ignorant fellahin—"

He got up and went to the window. He stood looking out of it, his hands clasped behind his back.

"The whirlwind won't fall on government. Trust me. Neither will the bomb."

Still Matty said nothing.

"What part of England do you come from? The south, surely. London? I think you would be wise to return to your own country. I can understand that you won't stop what you are doing. They never do. Yes. You had better go back. After all—" and he swung round suddenly—"that place needs your language more than this one."

"I want to go back."

The secretary sank easily into his chair.

"I'm *so* pleased! You are not really—You know, we felt what with that most unfortunate episode with the native, the Aborigine—did you know they *insist* on being called Aboriginals as if they were adjectives?—but we did feel that perhaps we owed you something—"

He leaned forward over his clasped hands.

"—And before we part—tell me. Do you have some kind of, of perception, some extra-sensory perception, some second sight—in a word, do you—*see*?"

Matty looked at him, mouth shut like a trap. The secretary blinked.

"I only mean, my dear fellow, this information you feel called on to press on an unheeding world—"

For a moment or two Matty said nothing. Then slowly at first but at the last with a kind of jerk, he got himself upright on the other side of the desk and stared not at the secretary but over him out of the window. He convulsed but made no sound. He clenched his fists up by his chest and the words burst out of his twisted lips, two golfballs.

"I feel!"

Then he turned away, went out through one office after another and into the marbled hall then down the steps and away. He made some strange purchases and one, a map, that was not so strange and he put everything he had into his ancient car, and the city knew him no more. Indeed Australia knew him no more as far as eccentricity is concerned. For the short remainder of his stay he was noticed for nothing but his black clothes, and forbidding face. Yet if human beings had little more to do with him in Australia there were other creatures that had. He drove for many miles with his curious purchases and he seemed to be looking for something big rather than small. He wanted, it seems, to be low down and he wanted to find some water to be low down with and he wanted a hot and fetid place to go with it all. These things are specific and to be found together in known places but it is very difficult most of the time to get close to them by car. For this reason Matty took a winding course in strange places and often enough had to sleep in his car. He found hamlets of three decaying houses with the corrugated iron of their roofs grinding and clanking in a hot wind, and not a tree for miles. He passed by other places of Palladian architecture set among monstrous trees where the red galahs squawked and lilies loaded the tended pools. He passed men riding round and round in little traps drawn by horses with a delicate high step. At last he found what no one else would want, looked at it in the bright sunlight—though even at noon the sun could scarcely pierce through to the water—and he watched, perhaps with a tremor that never reached the outside of his face, the loglike creatures that slipped one after another out of sight. Then he went away again to find high ground and wait. He read in his Bible with the wooden covers and now, for the rest of the day he trembled slightly and looked closely at familiar things as if there was something in them that would bring comfort. Mostly of course he looked at his Bible, seeing it as if he had not looked at it before and noticing for what that was worth how the wood of the cover was boxwood and he wondered why and thought aimlessly it might be for protection which was strange because surely the Word did not need it. He sat there for many hours while the sun took its wonted way over the sky and then sank and the stars came.

The place he had looked at now became additionally strange in the darkness which was thick as the darkness an old-time photographer thrust his head into under the velvet. Yet every other sense would have been well enough supplied with evidence. Human feet would have felt the soft and glutinous texture, half water half mud, that would rise swiftly to the ankles and farther, pressed out on every side with never a stone or splinter. The nose would have taken all the evidence of vegetable and animal decay, while the mouth and skin—for in these circumstances it is as if the skin can taste—would have tasted an air so warm and heavy with water it would have seemed as if there was doubt as to whether the whole body stood or swam or floated. The ears would be filled with the thunder of the frogs and the anguish of nightbirds; and they would feel too, the brushing of wings, antennae, limbs, to go with the whining and buzzing that showed the air too was full of life.

Then, accustomed to the darkness by a long enough stay and willing—it would have to be by sacrifice of life and limb—to trade everything for the sight, the eyes would find what evidence there was for them too. It might be a faint phosphorescence round the fungi on the trunks of trees that had fallen and were not so much rotting as melting away, or the occasional more lambent blueness where the flames of marsh gas wandered among reeds and floating islands of plants that lived as much on insects as on soupy water. Sometimes and suddenly as if they were switched on, the lights would be more spectacular still—a swift flight of sparks flashing between tree trunks, dancing, turning into a cloud of fire that twisted in on itself, broke, became a streamer leading away which incomprehensibly switched itself off to leave the place even darker than before. Then perhaps with a sigh like a sleeper turning over, a big thing would move washily in the unseen water and loiter a little further away. By then, feet that had stayed that long would have sunk deep, the mud moving to this side and that, the warm mud; and the leeches would have attached themselves down there in an even darker darkness, a more secret secrecy and with unconscious ingenuity, without allowing their presence to be felt would have begun to feed through the vulnerable skin.

But there was no man in that place; and it seemed impossible to one who had inspected it from far off and in daylight that there ever had been a man in the place since men began. The sparks of flying life came back as if they were being chased. They fled in a long streamer.

A little while later the reason for this flight in one direction was

73

evident. A light, and then two lights, were moving steadily behind the nearer forest. It showed treetrunks, hanging leaves, moss, broken branches in silhouette, lighting them and bringing them into a brief local visibility so that sometimes they seemed like coals or wood in a fire, black at first, then burning, then consumed as the twin sidelights wound onward through the forest to the marsh, each light bringing with it a dancing cloud of flying things, papery and whitish. The old car—and now its engine—had warned away everything but the flying creatures so that even the frogs had fallen silent and dived—stopped two trees away from the mysterious darkness of the water. The car stopped, the engine died, the two sidelights faded just a little but were still bright enough to light up the flying things and a yard or two of mould on this side of what must have been a track.

The driver sat for a while without moving; but just when the car had been silent and motionless long enough for the noises of the place to begin again, he jerked open the right-hand door and got out. He went to the boot, opened that and brought out a number of objects that clanked. He left the boot open, came back to the driver's seat and stood for a while, staring towards the invisible water. After he had done that, he became suddenly busy and incomprehensible. For he was pulling off his clothes so that his body appeared in reflected light from the sidelights, thin and pale, and to be investigated at once by some of the papery flying things and a great many of those that hummed or whined. Now he brought a curious object from the boot, knelt down in the mould and began, it would seem, to take the object apart. Glass clinked. The man struck a match, brighter than sidelights, and what he was doing—but there was no one to see—became comprehensible. He had on the ground before him a lamp, an antique practically, he had the globe and the chimney off and he was lighting the wick and the papery things whirled and danced and flared and were consumed or crawled away half burnt. The man turned the wick right down, then put on the tall funnel and the glass globe. After that, when he was sure the lamp stood straight and safe in the mould, he turned to the first set of objects. He worked at them and they clanked and everything was inscrutable except inside of the man's head where his purpose was. He stood up, no longer quite naked. There was a chain round his waist and on this chain, heavy steel wheels were slung; one, and that the one of greatest weight, lay over his loins so that he was absurd but decent even when nothing could see him but the natural creatures that did not matter. Now he bent down again but for a moment had to steady himself by clutching at the door of the car because the heavy wheels made kneeling straight down a very difficult business. But at last he was there, kneeling, and slowly he turned up the wick; and now the white globe of the lamp took over from the sidelights and the trees and the undersides of the leaves. The mould and moss and mud came solid like things that would still be there in daylight and the white, papery things went crazy round the white globe and across the gleaming water, so flat, so still, a frog stared at the light through two diamonds. The man's face was close to the white globe and it was not the light that made a difference on this left side where the eye was half closed and the corner of the mouth twisted.

Now he lifted the lamp and got himself up, slowly, by holding onto the door. He got upright, with the clanking wheels round his waist and the lamp, now held high, the foot of it even, above his head. He turned and walked slowly, deliberately, towards the water. Now the mud did feel human feet, the warm mud moving away to this side and that as this foot pressed and sank and then that foot. The man's face was additionally contorted now as if with unutterable pain. His eyes flickered shut and open, his teeth gleamed and gritted, the lamp shook. He walked in, his feet went, his calves, his knees, strange creatures touched him underwater or snaked away over the rippled surface and still he went, down and in. The water rose past his waist and to his chest. The frog broke out of the hypnosis of the light and dived. The water at past this midpoint of the pool was at the man's chin; and then suddenly, higher. The man floundered and the water washed. For a yard it may be, he was out of sight and there was nothing to be seen by whatever was watching but an arm and hand and the old lamp with its bright white globe and the dancing crazy creatures. Then black hair floated wide on the water. Down there underneath he was thrusting strongly into the ooze with his feet and he got his head up and grabbed a breath. After that he rose steadily towards the other side and the water ran from him and from his hair and his wheels; but not from the lamp. Now he stood; and though the air was hot and the water steamed he began to shudder, shudder deeply, convulsively, so that he had to hold the lamp with both

75

hands to keep it upright and from falling in the mud. As if this shuddering was some kind of sign, thirty yards away across the water, a huge lizard turned and loitered off into the darkness.

The man shuddered less and less. When he was no more than trembling he picked his way round the pool and back to the car. It was all solemnity and method. He held the lighted lamp up carefully, heaved it four times at four points of the compass. Then he turned down the wick and blew it out. The world returned to what it had been. The man loaded the lamp and the wheels and the chain into the boot. He dressed. He arranged his curious hair and set his hat firmly on it. He was quiet now, and a drift of fireflies came back and danced over the faint gleam of the water each to its own image. The man got into the driver's seat. He pressed the starter and had to do it three times. It was perhaps the strangest noise of all in that wilderness, the suburban sound of the starter and then the engine catching. He drove slowly away.

Matty set out, not by air, though he could just about have afforded the cheapest one-way fare, but by sea. It may be that the air was too presumptuous and high for him; or it may be that hidden away at the back of his mind was not the sight of the dollgirl in Singapore with her glittering clothes, but just an unease over the whole question of Singapore Airport, a gleaming Wickedness detached from any substance. For certainly he now moved easily among women as among men, looked and was struck no more by the one than the other, and would not have avoided the Wanton with her cup of abominations in fear for his peace of mind or virtue.

He gave his car away but took what other few things he had. He tried to ship as a seaman; but there was no place for a man of his age whatever it was, who was skilled in odd-jobbing, sweet-packing, grave-digging, car-driving in difficult circumstances and, pre-eminently, in Bible-studies. Nor did it matter that he had testimonials from many kinds of people, all of whom wrote of his probity, reliability, honesty, fidelity, assiduity (Mr Sweet), discretion, without mentioning that they had found these qualities really rather repulsive.

So he went at last to the docks with his small suitcase which contained the shaving material for the right side of the face, one spare pair of pants, one spare shirt, one spare black sock, one

76

flannel, one bar of soap. He stood for a while looking up at the side of the ship. At last he looked down at his feet and appeared to be lost in thought. At last he lifted the left foot and shook it three times. He put it down. He lifted his right foot and shook it three times. He put it down. He turned round and looked at the port buildings and the low line of hills that was all a continent could muster from its inside to bid him farewell. He seemed, or would have seemed, to look through those hills at the thousands of miles over which he had travelled and at the hundreds of people that for all his care he had, if not met, at least seen. He stared round the quay. In the lee of a bollard there was a pile of dust. He went to it quickly, bent down, took a handful and strewed it over his shoes.

He climbed the ladder, away from the many years he had spent in Australia, and was shown the place he had to sleep in with eleven others, though none of them had arrived. After he had stowed his one suitcase he went back up again to the deck and stood again, still, silent and staring at the continent he knew he was seeing for the last time. A single drop of water rolled out of his good eye, found a quick way down his cheek and fell on the deck. His mouth was making little movements, but he said nothing.

CHAPTER SIX

While Matty was in Australia Mr Pedigree came out of jail and was cherished by a number of societies. He had a little money coming to him from his mother's will, for that ancient lady had died while he was still inside. It gave him, not so much freedom, as a degree of mobility. He was able therefore to break away from those who were trying hopelessly to help him and made for central London. He very soon went straight back to jail. The next time he came out he had aged many more years than the period of his sentence for his fellows had, as he said to himself, weeping with self-pity, *cottoned on*. He had never had any spare flesh and now a little of what he could not well spare was worn away. He was lined, too, and bent and there was no doubt about the grey that was spreading through the faded straw of his hair. He had sat to begin with on a bench in a London terminus and had it up-ended under him by the police at one o'clock in the morning and it may be that this experience removed any magnetism there was in London, for from that time he worked his way to Greenfield. That was, after all, where Henderson had been; in death Henderson had been subsumed into Mr Pedigree's mind as the desired perfection. He found that there was a hostel in Greenfield that he had never known of before—would not have had to know of before. It was heartlessly clean and the large rooms were divided into separate cubicles, each with a narrow bed, a table and chair. Here he lived and from here he made his expeditions: one to the school where he gazed through the gate and saw the place where Henderson had fallen and the fire-escape above it and the edge of the leaded roof. There was no reason in law why he should not go closer; but he had joined or was in the process of joining the wall-creepers, men of decayed appearance who keep a wall at their side so as to be sure there is at least one direction from which trouble will not come. He was now the sort of man whom a policeman feels in his bones should be moved on; and consequently he began to feel himself that he ought to be moved on and whenever he saw a policeman, moved himself on or sideways round a corner as soon as possible.

Yet he still had his little income and except for his compulsion—which in many countries would not have got him into trouble—he was without vice. He had next to nothing and lived on it without feeling any hardship. He owned what he stood up in. His Victorian paperweights had gone, sold alas before the market blew up, and his few netsukes—though they had fetched more—all gone except one. This was a netsuke he called his lucky charm and kept in his pocket so that it was always there to be fingered, smooth ivory, the whole thing no larger than a button which of course it really was, the two boys merging so excitedly and excitingly. Sometimes the netsuke burned his fingers. It was after one of these burnings that he made what was now becoming one of his regular trips to jail. This time the possibility of an operation was put to him; at which he began to scream on and on, piercingly and mindlessly, so that even the Home Office psychiatrist gave up. When he came out he went back to Greenfield again; and it was as if his brain had now settled into simple patterns, rituals both of action and belief. On the first day of his arrival he came down the High Street, noting as he did so how there were more and more coloured people about. He crept down until he found himself facing the front of Sprawson's with the bookshop and Frankley's on one side of it and the Old Bridge humped up on the other. There was an antique public lavatory on the root of the bridge this side. It was a cast-iron structure, pictorially impressive, not so much stinking as smelly and not so much dirty as with the appearance of dirt (that black creosote) rather than the substance. Here, too, by a technological marvel of the eighteen-sixties the cistern filled and flushed, filled and flushed night and day, sure as the stars or the tides. It was the scene of the moderate triumph that had sent Mr Pedigree back to jail on the last occasion; but he did not return solely with a rational hope or desire. He came back because he had been there before.

He was developing. Over the years he had moved from a generous delight in the sexual aura of youth to an appreciation of all the excitement attendant on breaking taboos if the result was

79

sufficiently squalid. There were public lavatories in the park of course, and more by the central car stack, there were some in the market—oh there were public lavatories dotted round the place, far more of them than anyone without Mr Pedigree's specialized knowledge would guess. With school barred for ever, they were the next step in some direction or other. He was now about to leave the protection of the wall at the end of Sprawson's when he saw a man come out of the house and walk up the street. Mr Pedigree peered after him, then looked back at the urinal, then back at the receding man. He made up his mind and loped, bending and swaying up the High Street. As he went he straightened up. He passed the man and turned.

"Bell, isn't it? Edwin Bell? Aren't you left from my time? Bell?"

Bell faltered to a stop. He gave a kind of high whinny.

"Who? Who?"

The years, all the seventeen of them, had made a great deal less difference to Bell than to Pedigree. Though Bell had also had his troubles, they had not included the awful problem of putting-on weight. He had kept, too, the singular garb of an undergraduate of the late thirties, all except the Bags, and there was about him, the carriage of his snub nose, the tiny evidence of authority exercised and assertion without contradiction.

"Pedigree. Of course you remember me! Sebastian Pedigree. Don't you remember?"

Bell jerked upright. He drove his fists deep into his overcoat pockets, then brought them together in panic in front of his privates. He gave a kind of wail.

"Hu–llo! I—"

And fists driven deep, nose up, mouth open, Bell began to tiptoe, as if by this simple tactic he could lift himself above his embarrassment; and so doing was nevertheless reminded that to pass by on the other side was not the action of a liberal person and therefore he came down again which made him stagger.

"Pedigree, my dear fellow!"

"I've been away you see, rather lost touch. Retired and thought—oh yes, I thought I might as well look up—"

Now they were facing each other, the crowd in its many colours moving round them. Bell stared down into the old man's face, the lined and silly mask that looked up at him so anxiously.

"I might look up the old school," said the lined face sillily and

80

piteously. "I thought you'd be the only one left from my time. Henderson's time it was—"

"Oh I say, Pedigree—you—I'm married you see—"

Insanely he began to ask Pedigree if he was married too and then managed to stop himself. Pedigree never noticed.

"I just thought I'd look up the old school—"

And there, floating in the air between them was the quite clear and specific knowledge that if Sebastian Pedigree put his foot inside the school buildings he would be taken up for loitering with intent; and the equally clear and specific knowledge that if Edwin Bell took him in arm-in-arm the law would stand back for the time being and it wasn't worth it for either of them only Pedigree would think it was; and taking Pedigree in was what a saint would do probably, or Jesus or maybe Gautama and certainly Mahomet, let's not think of Mahomet in this instance as it will get me into deep waters and *Christ* how am I going to get rid of him?

"So if you were going that way—"

Edwin jerked up on his toes again. He struck his buried fists together convulsively.

"Oh bother! I've just remembered! My, my—I must go back at once. Look Pedigree—"

And now he had turned, striking a vivid coloured female with his shoulder.

"—I'm so sorry, so sorry, so clumsy! Look Pedigree, I'll keep in touch."

He turned to tiptoe down the street and knew without looking that Pedigree was coming after him. So then there was a kind of confused charade in which Edwin Bell, his privates still concealed by fists as well as clothes, ducked and wove through the saried marketeers, followed as closely as possible by Pedigree while both of them talked at once as if silence would allow something else to be heard, something deadly. It turned in the end—when they had reached Sprawson's and there was a clear danger of Pedigree coming right upstairs, past the solicitor's office, right up to the flat—into a naked avowal, a terrified prohibition from Edwin Bell, hands out, palms facing outward and his voice high—

"No, no, *no!*"

He broke away as if there was a physical bond between them and fled away up the stairs, leaving Pedigree alone in the hall and still talking about the possibility of coming back to the school and about Henderson as if the boy were still there. Then, when Pedigree stopped he became aware of where he found himself, in a private building with that glass door there leading down to the garden, stairs leading up both sides, and doors, one at least for a firm of solicitors. So Mr Pedigree became once more a wall-creeper, moving out and down two steps to the stone pavement in front of Sprawson's. Then he hurried across the street to the comparative safety of shop fronts and looked back. He glimpsed Edwin's face at an upper window with Edwina's beside it and then the curtain hurriedly pulled back.

It was thus that Mr Pedigree on his return became a problem not merely to the police who knew something about him, if not all, not merely to the park-keeper and the young man in a grey raincoat whose duty it was to head off the likes of Mr Pedigree, but precisely to Edwin Bell, the only man left from the old times in Greenfield. The process by which Mr Pedigree felt himself connected to Bell defied reason. Perhaps he needed a link with what passed for normality, since now his rituals began, bit by bit, to consume him. Thus, after leaving Bell, or rather after Bell left him, Mr Pedigree went towards the seductive urinal on the Old Bridge and would have gone in but a police car shoved its nose over the crest of the bridge and he went nimbly for his age down the steps and sheltered on the towpath under the bridge as if from rain. He even held out a palm in a dramatic gesture, then examined it for possible drops of water before walking away along the towpath. He did not want to walk along the towpath but he was facing in that direction and the police car had made the road behind him painful. So Mr Pedigree went widdershins round a circle that was in fact a rectangle. He went along the towpath, past the old stables behind Sprawson's, past the jumble of roofs that was the back parts of Frankley's the Ironmongers, past the long wall that cut off the almshouses from the perils of water; and coming then by a kissing gate on his left (with Comstock Woods on his right) through the footpath to the side streets and then left again, past the almshouses, Frankley's, Goodchild's and Sprawson's in reverse order; then left once more and in furtive triumph, the police car defeated, to the roots of the Old Bridge and the black urinal again.

What was strange and sad and sane was not his abortive meeting with Bell—a meeting which Bell, having backed away,

82

took very good care not to have repeated—but the fact that there were no meetings at all. Sim Goodchild had been dimly visible beyond the books in his shop window. As Pedigree came past Sprawson's for the second time there had been the sound of a woman's voice raised high, where Muriel Stanhope was embarking on the quarrel that would send her finally to Alfred and New Zealand. High walls, less penetrable than brick, than steel, walls of adamant lay everywhere between everything and everything. Mouths opened and spoke and nothing came back but an echo from the wall. It was a fact so profound and agonizing, the wonder is there was no concert of screaming from the people who lived with the fact and did not know that they endured it. Only Sim Goodchild in his bookshop whimpered occasionally. The others, Muriel Stanhope, Robert Mellion Stanhope, Sebastian Pedigree, thought it was their individual and uniquely unfair treatment by a world that was different for everyone else. But for the Pakistanis, the men in their sharp suits, the women in gaudy colours with a corner snatched across the face, but for the Blacks, the world *was* different.

So Mr Pedigree came out of the urinal and walked back up the High Street, keeping as close as possible to any convenient wall. He glanced back at the upper window in Sprawson's but of course the Bells were no longer visible. He made for the park. He went in, past the notice-board with its list of necessary prohibitions, with what for him was an air of complete security. He was near the bottom of his graph after all. He was able therefore to find a seat and sit on its iron slats and finger the netsuke in his pocket as he spied out the land. He was, as he sometimes said to himself, window-shopping. The children were in groups, some with balls, some with balloons, some trying not very successfully to fly kites in the light wind. The adults were dotted about on the seats—three pensioners, a courting couple with nowhere to go and the young man in a grey raincoat whose presence was not unexpected to Mr Pedigree. In the far corner were the lavatories. Mr Pedigree knew that if he got up and went there the young man would follow and watch.

Regularly, since now there was the possibility of meeting Bell as well as visiting the Old Bridge, Mr Pedigree rotated, day after day, through his own rounds of Greenfield. It was at this time that there was a curious kind of epidemic in the town. People only thought of it as an epidemic when it was past its height and nearly over. Then they thought back, or some of them did and felt they knew where the blame was to be laid, right back, even to the first day, because the first day was so soon after Mr Pedigree met Bell on his latest emergence from retirement. It was a young woman seen, a white woman trotting from Pudding Lane into the High Street. She wore platform shoes and that made her trot even more comical than it might have been, because she was the sort of young woman who can only run with her hands up at either side and with her feet kicking out this way and that—a method of progress which allows of no acceleration. Her mouth was open and she was saying "Help, help, oh help!" in a die-away voice almost as though she was talking to herself. But then she found a pram by a shop with a baby in it and that seemed to quieten her because after she had examined the baby and jogged the pram for a bit she wheeled it away without saying anything, only looking round her nervously or perhaps sheepishly. The same day Sergeant Phillips had a real cause to look sheepish because he found a pram with a baby in it outside Goodchild's Rare Books and neither Sim Goodchild nor his wife Ruth had any idea of how it got there. So Inspector Phillips had to push the pram all the way up the High Street to his car and then radio a description. The mother was soon identified and had left the pram complete with baby outside the Old Supermarket next door to the Old Corn Exchange. There were a few days then and it started all over again. But for a month maybe, prams were moved as if someone was trying to draw attention to himself and using this as a kind of sign language. Mr Pedigree was watched; and though he was never caught at it, the pram-shifting stopped and that month simply became the one people remembered when you couldn't leave a pram unattended. They forgot a rather nasty confrontation between Mr Pedigree (entering the Old Supermarket in search of cereal and carrying the minute pot of Gentleman's Relish he had obtained from George's Superior Emporium) and some ladies who saw him threading his diffident way between the prams that were parked outside like boats moored at a landing stage. As Mrs Allenby remarked to Mrs Appleby over coffee when they discussed the affair in the Taj Mahal Coffee Shop, it was lucky for Mr Pedigree this was England. Of course she did not call him Mr Pedigree but that ghastly old creature.

There was nothing to connect Mr Pedigree with the pram-pushing. But as Sim Goodchild agreed with Edwin Bell, people of Pedigree's sort often had a degree of cunning in the pursuit of their perversions that was the result of not being able to think about anything else. It was true. In this respect, except for the fleeting interests that Mr Pedigree's expensive education sometimes gave him, he was like Matty and dedicated to one end only. But unlike Matty he knew only too well what that end was, what it had to be; and watched it approach or found himself compelled to approach it, with a perpetual kind of gnawing anxiety which aged him far more than the mere flow of time. It is not recorded anywhere if there was a single person living in Greenfield who pitied him. Certainly those ladies at the supermarket who were prevented from scratching his eyes out would have screamed a rebuke at anyone who had suggested it was possible he had never touched a pram at all. And after he had got away from them it could not be a coincidence that Greenfield prams seemed to be safe from interference thereafter.

So Mr Pedigree kept out of the High Street for a while, going no nearer it than Foundlings, round the corner, where he sometimes hoped to see Edwin Bell, who took care not to be visible. The old man, stuck like a broken gramophone record, would stand outside the railings, mourning for the perfected image of little Henderson, and cursing the boy with the mended face, who at the time had landed at Falmouth in Cornwall from a Greek cargo boat and had gone back to ironmongering, locally, the Bible when consulted having told him to make no more than a Sabbath journey. It was the same day that the ladies tried to maim Mr Pedigree that Matty in Cornwall, and for a most extraordinary reason, started to keep the following journal.

CHAPTER SEVEN

17/5/65

I have bought this book to write in and a biro because of what happened and I want to keep the book for evidence to show I am not mad. They were not like the ghost I saw in Gladstone it was a ghost it must have been. These appeared last night. I had read my portions and then repeated them from memory and I was sitting on the edge of my bed taking my shoes off. The time was eleven forty I mean eleven forty when it began. At first I thought it is cold for May and then my room is cold but it got colder and colder. All the warmth went out of me like being drawn out. Every hair on my person, I mean every short hair not the long hair on my head which prickled but every short hair stood up each on a lump. It is what people call being frightened and now I know it is awful. I could not breathe or call out and I thought I should die. Then they appeared, to me. I cannot properly say how. Remembering changes it. I cannot say how. But I am not mad.

18/5/65

They did not come back tonight. No, last night I must say now. I waited until twelve o'clock and when it struck I knew they would not come. What can it all mean I ask myself. The one was in blue and the other in red with a hat on. The one in blue had a hat too but not as expensive. They appeared and stayed I do not know how long from eleven forty just looking at me. It was awful. The ghost was without any colour at all but these were red and blue like I have said. I cannot say how I see them when I see them I just see them but it is different remembering. Is it a warning I ask myself, have I left something undone. I searched back and could not find any except of course my great and terrible sin, which I would undo if I knew how but the Bible sent me here and he is not here so what am I to do. It is all hidden. I gave many signs nearly two years ago in Darwin Northern Territory and nothing has happened. It is to try my faith.

17/5/66

I take up my pen a year after to say they came again. I knew they would as soon as I felt the cold and the warmth drawing out of my person. I waited but they did not speak but still looked at me. I cannot tell when they went away. They came at after eleven and went away before the clock struck just like a year ago. Perhaps they come every year. I think perhaps it is something to do with my feeling that I am at the centre of an important thing and have been always. Most people do not live into their thirties without knowing what it is to be frightened and most people are afraid of ghosts and do not see spirits.

21/5/66

I was reading at the table Revelations when I understood. At once it was like when the spirits appear but they did not. I went cold, shivering and the short hairs on my person stood up. I saw that a FATEFUL DAY is coming by reason of the calendar. At first I did not know what to do. This must be why the spirits appeared before me. They must come again to tell me what to do. My waiting on them is a wave-offering. I must make a heave-offering but have so little it is difficult to see what I have left for a heave-offering.

22/5/66

I thought in the shop what would be a heave-offering but it is so awful I am holding it back.

23/5/66

I bind to lift up more of what I eat and drink then place it on the altar. I bind to lift up all of what I speak except what must be spoken. There is almost no time left. I pray all the time I can.

30/5/66

At first with eating so little I felt great pain and weakness but then I found a way of seeing all that I had not eaten offered up on the altar and this helped me. Also cold water is alright to drink but I have a great and live memory of tea hot tea with milk and sugar like in Melbourne. Sometimes I can even smell the tea and feel how hot it is. I wondered then I might be being ministered to as it is said. Mr Thornbury tells me I should see a doctor but he does not understand. Because I have made a heave-offering of my talking it is not right for me to explain to him.

31/5/66

I have been among the Baptists and Methodists and Quakers and the Plymouth Brethren but there is no dread anywhere and no light. There is no understanding except sometimes when I repeat my portion inside from memory. When I go among these different people they question me sometimes. Then I lay my hands over my mouth and see by the way they smile that they understand a little. Now I have been cold all day, thinking of the calendar. I thought in these exceptional circumstances the spirits might come back but now it is past twelve and though I got colder as the clock struck nothing happened because I tell myself the cup is full but not yet *pressed* down and overflowing. Also I said to myself it would start perhaps when it started first down under and then remembered it is said *in the twinkling of an eye* so it would be in Melbourne, Sydney, Gladstone, Darwin, Singapore, Hawaii, San Francisco, New York and Greenfield also in Cornwall at the same instant.

1/6/66

It is terrible to see the days pass, the cup already full and waiting to be *pressed down*. I eat nothing and only drink a little cold water. Today as I came upstairs to my room I stumbled for weakness but it is no matter with the time so short. It came to me in a flash, a great opening while I was just writing those last words, a hand was laid on me and I understood what I must do on THE DAY. It is my task to give Cornwall ONE LAST CHANCE!!

4/6/66

There are no preparations to make. Tomorrow I will watch all night *lest we be taken sleeping*. It seems to me that on 1/6/66 a voice told me what to do but I cannot be sure. It is all mixed up like when the display counter was turned over by that great dog.

6/6/66

I watched all night having put everything ready the day before. It was much harder to cut myself than I had thought but I made an offering of it. A bird sang at first light and I had the dreadful expectation that it had sung for the last time. I took blood and wrote on the paper in letters each as long as my thumb the awful number 666. I put the paper as instructed in the band of my hat so that the number was to be seen from in front. I repeated my portion as I thought I should not have the opportunity later but be in judgement and was in great dread at the thought. Then I walked out. The streets were so empty that at first I thought judgement had already been done and I left of all the world alone but later I saw it was not so as people were bringing food to market. I believe some were stricken and some even brought to recollection when they saw me bearing the awful number through the streets on my head and written in blood. I went through all the churches and chapels in the town with my hat on except those that were locked. At each of these I knocked three times then shook the dust of the threshold off my feet and walked away. All this time I was very tired and in such terror I could hardly walk. But when it was dark I went back to my room, on hands and knees up the stairs and waited until midnight when I began to write this so that not to make a lie of it the number should be 7/6/66. Many people will know the carnal and earthly pleasures of being alive this day and not brought to judgement. No one but I have felt the dreadful sorrow of not being in heaven with judgement all done.

11/6/66

I have looked for the judgement that was to be done on the sixth but cannot find it. Sara Jenkins died, may she rest in peace, and a son was born to the doctor's wife in the cottage hospital. There was a slight accident at the bottom of Fish Hill. A boy (P. Williamson) fell off his bike and sustained a fracture of the left leg. His will be done.

15/6/66

It is a great relief to me to think that all these people have time now in which to repent. Yet in that relief I feel a great grief and when not a grief I feel a great emptiness and my question comes again. What am I for, I ask myself. If to give signs why does no judgement follow. I will go on because there is nothing else to do but I feel an emptiness.

18/6/66

They came back. I knew they would as soon as I felt the cold and my hairs rise up. I was more ready this time because I had thought while serving in the shop what to do. I asked them in a whisper so as not to be heard through the partition by Mr Thornbury if they were servants of OUR LORD. I expected them either to say nothing or to speak out loud, or perhaps whisper, but it was a mystery instead. For when I had whispered I saw they held a great book between them open with HIS NAME there in shining gold. So it is alright but still dreadful of course. The hair on my person will not lie down all the time they are there.

19/6/66

They will not speak in a common way. They hold out beautiful white papers with words on or whole books faster than newspapers being printed like you see on the television. I asked them why they came to me. Then they showed on a paper: We do not come to you. We bring you before us.

2/7/66

They came again tonight, the red spirit with the expensive hat and the blue spirit with a hat but not so expensive. They are hats of office I cannot say what I mean. Also the red robes and the blue

90

robes. I do not know how I see them but I do. I am still frightened when they come.

11/7/66

Tonight I asked them why they brought me before them out of all the people in the world. They showed: You are near the centre of things. This was what I had always thought but as I felt the pride of it I saw them both much dimmed. So I hurled myself down inside, down as far as I could and I stayed like that. But they went away, or as I should say, put me from them. Now my fear is not just the cold, it is different. It is deeper and it is everywhere. I got cold when they came but not like I did when they first came and my hair just prickles a bit.

13/7/66

The fear is everywhere and mixed in with it is being sorry, grieving, but not me only being sorry but everything. This feeling is there even when they are hidden from me.

15/7/66

There is too much to put down but I must put it down for evidence. Great things are afoot. They have been four times, always after I have repeated my portion. The first time they brought me before them I asked them why they brought me before them. They showed: We work with what we have. I was put in great satisfaction by this reply and asked what I was for, my old question. They showed: That will appear at the appointed time. The next time they were there I asked what I was, the older form of my great question and they showed: That will appear too. The third time they brought me before them was very terrible to me. I asked them what they would have me do. Then the red one showed: Throw away your book. I thought he meant this book and I started up from the edge of the bed—for that is where I seem to be sitting when they bring me to them—and reached out for the book to tear it. But as I did so the red one showed very plainly: Let the record of our meetings alone. We mean you are to throw away your Bible. At this I think I cried out and they thrust me away from

91

them so that they were hidden. I could not sleep all night I was so frightened, and next day in the shop Mr Thornbury asked me what was the matter. I said I had a bad night which is true. I wondered all day if they had thrust me away from them for ever as being unworthy of a place near the centre of things and I thought that if they came back—or rather I must remember it is difficult—if they bring me before them I will have some questions to test them. Satan may appear as an angel of light so much more easily as a red or blue spirit with hats. They did come that night, the fourth time it was in a row. I asked them at once, Are you both true servants of OUR LORD? At once they held up between them the great book with HIS NAME in shining gold. I watched very closely for I knew that THAT NAME would strike Satan down and burn him like an acid. But the beautiful paper was the same as ever and the gold too. Then, for I had determined not to be mistaken, I said though frightened and cold, What do you mean by HIM. Then they showed: We worship HIM THE LORD OF THE EARTH AND THE SUN AND THE PLANETS AND ALL THE CREATURES THAT ARE ON THEM. At that I flung myself down inside myself and whispered, What does HE want of me? I am willing. Then they showed: Obedience and to throw away your Bible. It was a quarter to ten. I put on my charity greatcoat and took my Bible and walked out into the night all the way to the headland. It was very dark with clouds and there was a sound all the time of wind and sea that got louder as I got nearer. I stood right on the edge and saw nothing in the dark but some white patches down below where the water was moving round the rocks. I stood there some time in fear to throw and in fear to fall though I think to fall would have been easier. I waited for a while hoping that the order would be cancelled but there was nothing but the sound of the wind and sea. I threw my Bible as far out into the sea as I could. Then I returned very weak and thirsty and failed at the knees as I climbed the stairs. But I managed at last and came at once into their presence. I whispered, I have done it. Then they held out the great book between them and I saw that it was full of the comfortable words.

17/7/66

They brought me before them and showed: Though every letter of the book is from everlasting to everlasting the great part of it that

92

you have learnt by heart is what your condition needs and was laid down for you from the beginning. I said it was terrible knowing what to do or what not to do in such a matter. It was like being on a tightrope high up over a street. Then they showed: Be obedient and you shall not fall.

25/7/66

Tonight they showed at once when I came before them: Now you are to go on a journey. I said I am willing, where am I to go? Then they showed: That will be revealed to you presently. But we are pleased with your ready acceptance and as a reward we allow you to ask us what you like provided you have not asked it before and been answered. Then I thought for a while and asked them why they did not come or rather bring me before them every night. They showed: Know that we see your spiritual face and it so badly scarred by a sin that we have to summon up great courage to look at you. But all the same you are the best material that can be obtained in the circumstances. I asked at once what had scarred my spiritual face and I wept bitter tears when they showed me what I had already guessed. For however ignorant a man is he always knows his sins until he is lost if there can be any like that. Yes it is the terrible wrong I did my dear friend though perhaps I should not call him that he was so high above me, Mr Pedigree. Indeed, not a day passes but at some time of it I hear what he said to me as they took him away. No wonder my spiritual face dims the light the spirits bring with them, and that lies around them.

27/8/66

They have not brought me before them for a long time. When they do that I am cold and frightened but when they do not I am lonely even with people about. I have a great wish to obey them in this journey they talk about. Is my wish to go away from Cornwall a being led by them, I ask myself. Sometimes when the spirits do not appear and I remember my Bible floating away in its wooden covers or sinking down my hair prickles a bit still and I go cold but it is not the same cold. But then I remember I am at the centre of things and must be content to wait no matter how long.

93

22/9/66

I take up my pen to write that they have not brought me before them for more than a period of three weeks. I know I must wait but worry sometimes in case they do not bring me before them because I have done something that is wrong. Sometimes when I am far down I wish dearly that I had a kind wife and some little children. Sometimes I have a great wish to return to what I may call my home, that is, Greenfield, the town where Foundlings was.

25/9/66

They came again. I said I did not know whether the saying to me that I was to go on a journey was all or that it was right to wait for more instructions. They showed: You are right to wait. You are now to eat and drink more to get up your strength for the journey. You are to go to Curnow's Store and choose among the second-hand bikes you saw there for one to ride. You are to learn to ride it.

3/10/66

They showed: We are pleased with your progress in strength and in riding the bike. In a little while we shall send you on your journey. We are pleased with you and allow you to ask us any questions you like. Then I was bold to ask something that had been on my mind for several months. When I was at a stand for progress I offered up speaking as a heave-offering. Now I said they allowed me to eat and drink more. Could I perhaps speak more too for in my young days I was a great talker and not ever content with yea and nay but spoke many unsanctified words. When I had said this to them I saw their light dimmed and there was a silence in heaven for a space of half an hour. So I offered myself up on the altar. At last they showed: You are so often in our thoughts familiarly that we do not always remember how naturally wicked you earthly creatures are. Then the spirit dressed in red (I think he is some kind of president) showed: Your tongue was bound so that in the time of the promise which is to come you shall speak words like a sword going out of your mouth. I thanked

94

them both very much but mostly the spirit in red as he is a higher spirit than the other. Then they showed: Seeing you are a friend of ours in the spiritual kingdom for all your terrible face and earthly wickedness we will allow some relief to your wish to talk. You may if the pain of not talking is past putting up with (and as it is a spiritual pain we know it is three times worse than an earthly pain) you may, in a dark place preach a sermon to the dead. But let no living person hear. I was much comforted by this and thanked them again.

7/10/66

It is easier to drive a car than to learn to ride a bike when you are a grown man but today my knees and elbows seem better and the bruising has gone down. I am much stronger and do not fail on the stair as I did or when carrying boxes in from the yard.

11/10/66

They came and showed: You are to ask Mr Thornbury for a rise and when he refuses it you are to shake the dust of Cornwall off your feet and go to Greenfield to the employment exchange there. You are to take no thought for what kind of work there is but accept what is offered.

12/10/66

Mr Thornbury refused the rise. He said I was worth it but with business as it is he could not afford it. He gave me a testimonial to whom it may concern saying I had worked for him for two years was sober, hard-working and scrupulously honest. I feel bad that he is not a Godly man. What will become of him I ask myself.

19/10/66

Exeter is not a good place to stop. It is better to choose B and B in the country but a woman by herself would not let me in because of my face. My bike stands up to it. If the spirits had not told me to buy the bike I should have gone by train and it would have been cheaper. I am spending money like a rich man. The weather continues fine.

The country is very open between Salisbury and Basingstoke with a great deal of long straight road. All day I saw rainstorms on every side but they did not come nigh me. I take it as a sign that my journey is a hallowed one and the spirit of Abraham encloses it.

28/10/66

Greenfield is much changed. I had a thought to go to Foundlings but of course my dear friend Mr Pedigree would not be there since he was despised and rejected. No one would know what had become of him. I may do so later. There is much new building and crowds of people. There are many more black and brown men and women, the women wear all kinds of costumes but the men not. There is a heathen temple built right next door to the Seventh Day Adventists!! When I saw this and also the mosque I was torn by the spirit. I had a great desire to prophesy Thou Jerusalem that slayest the prophets and sitting on the saddle with one foot on the pavement I had to clap both hands over my mouth to keep it in. But the church is still there. I went in and stayed for a time in the same seat where it happened how many years ago I ask myself. Also looking in Goodchild's Rare Books but the glass ball is gone and that part is filled with books for children, two of them stories from the Bible. The employment exchange was shut for the day so I found a bed and cycled round a bit. Then I came back here to repeat my portion.

29/10/66

In the employment exchange the man took all my testimonials and read them and thought well of them. He said he thought he had a place for me in a school. I felt very strange at once, thinking of Foundlings and Mr Pedigree and all that sad story, but no. He said it is Wandicott House School which is some way out in the country wait while I ring them. He telephoned the school and read out my references to the man at the other end and they laughed with each other which surprised me for there is nothing in my references to laugh at even by carnal men. But then the man said the bursar wanted me to come straight away for an interview and bring my references. I rode down the High Street and over the Old Bridge over the canal where there are a lot more boats than there used to be. I rode along through Chipwick then up a bridle path in a deep groove under trees. (I did not ride up, that would be a lie, I pushed my bike up.) Then I went down the other side of the downs into Wandicott village where the school is, and where I am now. It is six miles from Greenfield with the downs in between. Captain O. D. S. Thomson D.S.C. R.N. Rtd. interviewed me. He asked me how much money I wanted. I said enough to keep soul and body together. He mentioned a sum and I said it was too much and would cause me trouble. He was silent for a while and then explained about inflation and that I could leave the spare money with him and think no more of it unless needed. I am to be at every man's beck and call. When he said that I understood with joy that it was exactly what the spirits wanted and that my task is to be obedient unless asked to do what is wrong.

30/10/66

I have a room with the head gardener but he is gruff and sullen and does not want me to use his toilet as there is one by the harness room about fifty yards away. I do not use a toilet often since I have given up so much of my earthly living.

7/11/66

The spirits have not brought me before them since the night of 11/10/66. They have put it all on me. As they showed it is my responsibility to always remember how I am near the centre of things and all things will be revealed. This evening I spent sewing a patch on my rough trousers (the spare pair of army surplus) where the saddle had worn it.

12/11/66

This school is not at all like Foundlings. I did not know there were schools like this. The boys are rich and noble and have more people looking after them than there are children. You can walk for a mile and still be inside the grounds although some of them

97

are fields with cattle. You would think that the drive from the gates to the school was an ordinary road it is so long with trees over it. I have nothing to do with the children of course but only with the lowest people. Mr Pierce the head gardener has a down on me. He takes a delight I think in giving me hard things to do and humble things too but it is the only way I may learn what I am for. I have a half-day off every week. Mr Braithwaite says I can have evenings off by arrangement but I would sooner work.

20/11/66

I help the gardeners weeding and picking things. Mr Pierce is still gruff and sullen and gives me jobs to dirty me it is his nature. I have helped Mr Squires in the garages. We have our own pumps.

22/11/66

I have nothing to do with the boys but the masters speak to me sometimes and the headmaster's wife, Mrs Appleby. She does not seem to mind my face but inside she does and I daresay speaks about it when I am not there.

24/11/66

I fetched a rugby ball for the boys from some bushes and they did not mind me at all but looked and thought me strange I believe but did not mind.

26/11/66

At last I got up my courage even though the spirits had not told me and cycled to Foundlings. I stared through and could see the place where all the hollyhocks used to be and S Henderson fell. All is as it was. While I looked someone opened Mr Pedigree's window (I mean the one at the top that opens on to the leads and where I saw S Henderson come away after I had followed him and waited). It was a woman I saw by the shape of her arm. Perhaps she was cleaning the room. Of course I could not see my poor friend. But what I did see was the young master who discovered Henderson's body after he fell. It was Mr Bell and he is much much older. I was sitting on my bike by the pavement when Mr Bell dressed the same way as he used to be, with his big scarf came out of the front door just by the headmaster's study then came out of the gate and walked away down the High Street. I was moved to follow him and he went into Sprawson's by the Old Bridge. It was a great grief to me that he passed me where I sat on my bike without recognizing me that is the truth. It seems I have no part left in Greenfield which was what I came to think of as my home, not supposing my one friend was still there but in my mind seeming to connect him with it.

31/12/66

Tonight while I was waiting for the clock in the Wandicott church to strike twelve (and then some of the masters who have stayed on for the holiday will ring a peal for the New Year it is done not for godliness but in fun) I read through this book from the beginning. I began it as evidence of the spirits visiting me in case I should be thought mad and taken up and put away in a mental hospital as happened to R. S. Jones in Gladstone but I see I have recorded much else as well. Also I find in myself that I have written down words instead of speaking them and it is a little comfort. The spiritual life is a time of trial and without the comfortable words and the spirits telling me I am at the centre of things and all shall be made plain I should be tempted to do as R. S. Jones and do a mischief to myself. For the question that I now ask, what am I and what am I to do is still unanswered and I must *endure* like a man holding up a heavy weight. The peal is ringing and I wish I could weep but it does not seem possible.

5/2/67

A wonderful thing has happened. The weather has been so cold the playing fields are frozen and the boys not playing. They go for walks in the estate instead. I was cleaning out a corner by the harness room (for Mr Pierce will find work for me even when the air is freezing and the earth not to be turned even by a pick) when three boys came by and stopped. It is rare for them to be near me but they stood and watched. Then the biggest who was white asked me why I wore a black hat! I had to think very quickly because though I do not speak more than is necessary these were children which He said must be suffered etc. I decided that it was a part of obedience to do as they asked and they asked me to reply to them. So I said to keep my hair tidy. This made them laugh and one said I was to take off my hat. I did and they laughed so loud I had to smile and I saw they did not mind my mended face at all but thought someone had had a joke with me. I was a clown for them. So I lifted the hair away from the bald side showing them my bad ear and they were very interested and not a bit frightened or horrified. After they went away I felt more happy than at any other time. I put my hat back on and continued to clean the corner but I thought that if only I could put all right with my friend Mr Pedigree I would then prefer to live among children and in this very school than anywhere else. Can it be that what I am for is something to do with children I ask myself.

13/4/67

I helped the groundsmen taking down the rugby posts. They did not work as hard as they should. One was telling the others how Mr Pierce makes money by selling garden produce on the side when it ought to be used for the school. They also told me about some of the parents of some of the boys but soon stopped talking to me when they found out how little I answered. They said two of the men about the place were detectives and one of the gardeners I wonder which it cannot be Mr Pierce surely. But it is not my business I remind myself. I am much troubled as to whether I should tell Captain Thomson D.S.C. R.N. Rtd. about Mr Pierce and the garden produce.

20/4/67

I have a bad cold and a temperature making all things move about and shake. But when I was repeating my portion the spirits came again they were just the same as ever, the red one and the blue one. They showed: We are pleased with your obedience to Mr Pierce though he is a bad lot. He will be paid out for it. However to comfort you we allow you to ask what you like and if it is lawful we will answer. I asked what had troubled me off and on for a long time, which is why so little effect was visible in Cornwall when I carried the awful number written in blood through the streets. They showed: Judgement is not the simple thing you think. The number did much good not only in the town but as far afield as Camborne and Launceston. Ask on. Then I thought and asked if my spiritual face was healed or still ugly for them. They then showed: No it is still dreadful to us but we bear it cheerfully for your sake. Ask on. Then I said, hardly knowing what I did, Who am I? What am I? What am I for? Is it to do with children? Then they showed: It is a child. And when you bore the awful number through the streets a spirit that is black with a touch of purple like the pansies Mr Pierce planted under the rowan was cast down and defeated and the child was born sound in wind and limb and with an I.Q. of a hundred and twenty. Ask on. At this I cried out What am I? Am I human? and heard Mr Pierce turn over in bed with a great honk of a snore and the spirits removed me from them but gently. It seems to me that perhaps this night I do not need sleep.

22/4/67

It must have been nearly three o'clock in the morning I think that quite suddenly I sweated streams and streams and felt a great need of sleep after all. So I slept and next day was hard put to it to do the work that Mr Pierce laid on me. But I am happy to think that what I am for is to do with these little boys though Mr Pierce tries to keep me away from them. 120 was the I.Q. of Jesus of Nazareth.

2/5/67

Today I went into Greenfield on my half-day. Mrs Appleby the headmaster's wife who often speaks to me asked me to get her some things and it was so strange when she said, You can get them at Frankley's! So I went in. Then I looked at GOODCHILD'S RARE BOOKS and was a little sorry that the glass ball was not there any longer, sold I suppose or I might have bought it. Only also when I was looking in the window two little girls came from Sprawson's where I took the fireirons all that time ago and looked in the window at the children's books. They were so beautiful like angels and I was careful to turn my bad side away. They went back into Sprawson's and the door of the shop was open so I heard a woman inside say that Stanhope's little girls were everything to each other. I got on my bike and rode away but I could not help wishing that they were who I am for. I do not mean I looked at them in the way I looked at Miss Lucinda or the daughters of Mr Hanrahan all that is done with I think, gone out of my mind as if it had never been. It is very strange all the events of 20/4/67 are cloudy so that I cannot remember clearly if the word in the book was child or children. Perhaps I am to do not with the children of this school but the little girls, Stanhope they are called or one of them but I would like it to be both. While waiting to find out what I am for I shall keep an eye on them on my half-days. The next time the spirits call me before them I shall ask about the little girls. One of them is dark and one fair. I add them to my list for praying for.

9/5/67

The spirits have not brought me before them. Today on my half-day, I went in to Greenfield again to see if I could see the little girls but they did not appear. I may not see them very often but that will be as God wills of course. I looked at their house. It is a big one but a firm of solicitors lives in one part and there is a flat.

13/5/67

The spirits came again. I asked at once about the little girls and they showed: That will be as it will be. I then had a sudden fear that I was in danger of committing a sin by preferring these little girls to anything else. They did not wait for me to whisper this to them but showed at once: You are right. Do not go into Greenfield unless you are sent. They seemed a bit severe with me I thought. They thrust me away from them quickly. So I am once again in the position of doing a hard thing. I must be content with my lot and talking now and then to the little boys and trust that there are good spirits (angels) looking after the little girls which of course there are. And as they are everything to each other they do not need me.

Part Two

SOPHY

CHAPTER EIGHT

What Mrs Goodchild had said to Mr Goodchild was quite true. The twins, Sophy and Toni Stanhope, were everything to each other and they hated it. If they had been identical it might have been better but they were as different as day and night, night and day you are the one, night and day. Even when Matty saw them, within a week of their tenth birthday, Sophy had a sharp idea of how different they were. She knew that Toni had thinner arms and legs and a less smooth, pink curve from her throat right down to between her legs. Toni's ankles and knees and elbows were a bit knobbly and her face was thinner like her arms and legs. She had big, brown eyes and ridiculous hair. It was long and thin. It was not much thicker than—well if it had been any thinner it wouldn't have *been* at all: and as if preparing for disappearance it had entirely got rid of its colour. Sophy on the other hand knew that she herself lived at the top end of a smoother and rounder and stronger body, inside a head with dark curls all over it. She looked out through eyes that were a bit smaller than Toni's with masses of long, dark eyelashes round them. Sophy was pink and white, but Toni's skin, like her hair, had no colour in it. You could see through it in a way; and Sophy, without bothering to know how she knew, knew pretty well the Toni-ness of the being who lived more or less inside it. "More-or-less" was as near as you could get because Toni did not live entirely inside the head at the top, but loosely, in association with her thin body. She had a habit of kneeling and looking up and saying nothing that had a curious effect on any grown-up present. They would go all soppy. What made this so maddening was that at these times, Sophy knew Toni wasn't doing anything at all. She wasn't thinking and she wasn't feeling and she wasn't being. She had simply drifted away from herself like smoke. Those huge, brown eyes, looking up from the falls of lintwhite hair! It was magic and it worked. When it happened, Sophy would disappear inside herself if she could, or remember the precious times when there had not been any Toni. There was one with a whole roomful of children and music. Sophy could do the step and would have liked to do it for ever, one, two, three, hop, one, two, three, hop; calm pleasure in the way that threeness always brought the other leg for you to do a hop with, and for some reason, no Toni. Pleasure too because some of the children could not do this simple, lovely thing.

There was also the long square. Later she thought of it as the rectangle, of course, but what was remarkable was that she had Daddy to herself, and Daddy had actually proposed a walk, thus causing her such a confusion of delight that only later had she understood why he did it. She might have been a trouble to him if she had missed Toni! But for whatever reason, he actually took her by the hand, she reaching up and looking—bah!—with a simple trust in that handsome face and they had descended the two steps, passed between the small patches of grass and were on the pavement. He had wooed her, there was no other word for it. He had turned them right and shown her the bookshop next door. Then they had stopped and looked in the huge window of Frankley's the Ironmongers and he had told her about the lawn-mowers and tools and said that the flowers were plastic and then had taken her on past to the row of cottages with the words on a shield over them. He had told her they were almshouses for women whose husbands had died. Then he had turned her right down a narrow lane, a path it was and then through a kissing gate and they were on the towpath by the canal. Then he had explained about barges and how there used to be horses. He turned right again and stopped by a green door in the wall. Suddenly she understood. It was like taking a new step, learning a new thing, the whole place came into one. She saw that the green door was at the bottom of their garden path and that he was already getting bored in a princely way, standing there on the towpath before the blistered paint. So she ran on, getting too close to the water and he caught her as she intended but angrily, just at the steps up to the Old Bridge. He positively lugged her up them. She tried to get him to stop by the public convenience at the top but he would not. She tried to take him straight on after he had turned right again, tried to make him go with her up the High

Street but he would not and they did turn right and there was the front of the house. They had come round and back to it and she knew he was angry and bored and that he wished there was someone else about to take charge of her.

It was in the hall that the little conversation had taken place.

"Daddy, will Mummy come back?"

"Of course."

"And Toni?"

"Look child, there's no need to worry. Of course they'll be back!"

With her mouth open she had looked after him as he disappeared into his column room. She was too young to say the thing in her mind that would be like killing Toni. *But I don't want her back*!

However, on the day when Matty saw them they were indeed being more or less everything to each other. Toni had suggested they ought to go to the bookshop next door and see if there were any of the new books there that would be worth having. With a birthday next week it might be worth dropping hints to the current auntie, who needed prodding. But when they got back from the shop Gran was in the hall and the auntie was gone. Gran packed for them and took them away in her little car all the way down to Rosevear, her bungalow near the sea. This was such an excitement it put books and aunties and Daddy clean out of Sophy's mind, so that their tenth birthday flew by without her noticing. Besides, at that time she discovered what fun a brook was. It was much better than a canal and moved with a chatter and pinkle. She walked by it in the sun among tall grasses and buttercups, the buttery petals with their yellow powder so real at head height making distance itself, space so real. There was so much green and sunlight coming from everywhere at once; then when she parted the greenness which was what the grasses were, she saw water between here and there, that farther bank, outland, water moving between, Nile, Mississippi, trickle, dabble, ebble, babble, prick and twinkle! And then the birds that stalked through the jungle down to the edge of outland! Oh that bird all black with a white keyhole on the front of its head, and the tweeting, squeaking, chirping brood of fluffies climbing and scrambling and tumbling among the grasses at its back! They came out into the water, mother and chicks all ten on a string. They moved on with the brook and Sophy went right out

107

into her eyes, she was nothing but seeing, seeing, seeing! It was like reaching out and laying hold with your eyes. It was like having the top part of your head drawn forward. It was a kind of absorbing, a kind of drinking, a kind of.

The next day after that, Sophy went looking through the long, buttery flowers and grasses of the meadow to the brook. As if they had been waiting for her all night, there they were the same as ever. The mother was swimming away down the brook with the string of chicks behind her. Every now and then she said, "Kuk!" She was not frightened or anything—just a bit wary.

This was the first time Sophy noticed the "Of course" way things sometimes behaved. She could throw a bit but not much. Now—and this was where the "Of course" thing came in—now there was a large pebble lying to hand among the grasses and drying mud, where no pebble had any business to be unless "Of course" was operating. It seemed to her she did not have to look for the pebble. She just moved her throwing arm and the palm of her hand fitted nicely over the smooth, oval shape. How could a smooth, oval stone be lying there, not under the mud or even under the grass but on top where your throwing arm can find it without looking? There the stone was, fitted to the hand as she peered past the creamy handfuls of meadowsweet and saw the mother and chicks paddling busily down the brook.

When you are a small girl, throwing is a difficult thing and, generally speaking, not something you practise for fun, hour after hour, like a boy. But even later on, before she learnt to be simple, Sophy could never quite understand the way in which she saw what would happen. There it was, a fact like any other, she *saw* the curve which the stone would follow, saw the point to which the particular last chick would advance while the stone would be in its arc. "Would be", or "Was"? For also, and this was subtle—when she thought back later it did seem that as soon as the future was comprehended it was inescapable. But inescapable or not she could never understand—at least, not until a time when understanding itself was an irrelevance—how she was able, left arm held sideways, upper arm rotating back from the elbow past her left ear in a little girl's throw—was able not merely to jerk her upper arm forward but also to let go the stone at the precise moment, angle, speed, was able to let it go unimpeded by the joint of a finger, a nail, pad of the palm, to follow—and really only half

108

meant—to follow in this split and resplit second as if it were a possibility chosen out of two, both presented, both foreordained from the beginning, the chicks, Sophy, the stone to hand, as if the whole of everything had worked down to this point—to follow that curve in the air, the chick swimming busily forward to that point, last in line but having to be there, a sort of silent *do as I tell you*: then the complete satisfaction of the event, the qualified splash, the mother shattering away over the water, half flying over it with a cry like pavements breaking, the chicks mysteriously disappearing, all except the last one, now a scrap of fluff among spreading rings, one foot held up at the side and quivering a little, the rest of it motionless except for the rocking of the water. Then there was the longer pleasure, the achieved contemplation of the scrap of fluff turning gently as the stream bore it out of sight.

She went to find Toni and stood tall among the meadowsweet with the tall buttercups brushing her thighs.

Sophy never threw at the dabchicks again and understood why not, perfectly well. It was a clear perception, though a delicate one. Only once could you allow that stone to fit itself into the preordained hand, preordained arc, and only once do so when a chick co-operates and moves inevitably to share its fate with you. Sophy felt she understood all this and more; yet knew that words were useless things when it came to conveying that "More", sharing it, explaining it. There, the "More" was. It was, for example, like knowing that never, never would Daddy walk again with you round the long square, the rectangle, past the other side of the outer stable door. It was like knowing, as you did, certainly, that the wooing Daddy would not be with you because he wasn't anywhere, something had killed him or he had killed himself and left the hawk's profile stuck at the top of the calm or irritated stranger who spent his time with an auntie or in the column room.

Which was perhaps why Gran's and the brook and the meadow were such a relief, because despite the fact that the meadow was where you learnt about "More", you could use it for sheer pleasure. So as the holiday lengthened, in the cheerful, buttercup-plastered enjoyments of the water-meadow and butterflies and dragonflies, and birds on boughs and daisy chains, she thought *rowdily* of that other thing, that arc, that stone, that fluff as no more than a slice of luck, luck, that was what it was, luck explained everything! Or hid everything. Making a daisy chain with little Phil or being Indians in a wigwam with Toni, the two of them in a rare state of oneness, she knew it was luck. In those times, dancing times, singing times, times of going to a newness and meeting new people who should not be allowed to go away (but did)—the tall woman with red hair, the boy only a bit younger than herself who let her put on his blue denims with the red animals sewn on them, the big hat, party times—oh, it was luck and who cared if it wasn't? It was also, that summer, the last time they went to Gran's and the last time Sophy inspected dabchicks. She left Toni looking for small insects in the grass by the lane and waded away through the longer grass, meadowsweet and docks of the meadow and when she saw the mother with her chicks she chased them along the brook. The mother uttered her warning cry, harsh, staccatissimo and swimming faster, the chicks too, faster and faster. Sophy ran beside them until at last the mother took off with her shattering noise and foam and the chicks disappeared. They disappeared instantly, as it were into thin air. At one moment there was the fluffy string of them straining to go faster, necks out, feet whipping under the water; then the next instant there was a *phut!* sound and no fluffies. It was so astonishing and baffling that she stopped running and stood watching for a while. Only after she had seen the mother come part-way back and swim busily in the brook, brandishing her cry like a hammer, did Sophy find that her own mouth was open, and close it. After, it may be, half an hour, the mother and chicks came back together and Sophy chased them again. She found that the chicks did not vanish into thin air but thin water. There was a point in their fear where it turned into hysteria and they dived. No matter how small they were—and these were about as small as chicks could be—if you chased them, at last they would dive and get clean away from you no matter how fast you ran and how big you were. She brought this astonishing news back across the field to Toni, half in admiration of the chicks and half in irritation at them.

"Silly," said Toni. "They wouldn't be called dabchicks if they didn't."

That reduced Sophy to putting out her tongue and waggling her fingers beside her head, thumbs in ears. It was unfair the way Toni behaved, sometimes, of being miles away, certainly nowhere near her thin body with its empty face; and then proving carelessly, to be present. She would come down out of the air and be inside her

110

head. Then with what you could only call a wrench, she would bring things together that no one else would have thought of, and there you were with something decided, or even more irritating, something seen to be obvious. But Sophy had learnt to qualify her early dismissal of the Toni-ness of Toni. She knew that when the essential Toni was seated, perhaps a yard above her head and off-set to the right, it was not always doing nothing or sliding into sleep or coma or sheer nothingness. It might be flitting agilely among the boughs of invisible trees in the invisible forest of which Toni was the ranger. The Toni up there might be without thought; but then, it might equally be altering the shape of the world into the nature it required. It might, for example, be taking shapes from the page of a book and turning them into solid shapes. It might be examining with a kind of remote curiosity the nature of a ball made from a circle, a box from a square or that other thing from a triangle. Sophy had discovered all this about Toni without really trying. After all, they were twins, kind of.

After Toni had pointed out the connection between the behaviour of the dabchicks and their name, Sophy felt cheated and annoyed. The magic disappeared. She stood over Toni wondering whether she should go back and chase the dabchicks again. She saw in her mind that the thing to do was not to chase the dabchicks down the brook but up it. In that way the movement of the water would help you and hinder them. After that, you could keep up with them and watch them carefully under water and see where they came up. After all, she thought to herself, they must come up somewhere! But really, her heart wasn't in it. The secret was no longer a secret and of no use to anyone but the silly birds themselves.

She pulled her hair out of her ears.

"Let's go back to Gran."

They laboured through the bursting fertility of the meadow towards the hedge and as they went, Sophy wondered whether it would be any use asking Gran how explanations took the fun out of things; but two things put the whole matter out of her head. In the first place, they met little Phil from the farm—little Phil from the farmhouse with his curls, just like little Phil in *The Cuckoo Clock*, and they went off to play with him in one of his father's fields. There, little Phil let them examine his thing and they showed him their things and Sophy suggested they should all get

111

married. But little Phil said he had to go back to the farm and watch telly with his mum. After he left, they found a red pillar-box at the crossroads and had fun posting stones in it. Then, in the second place, when they got back to the bungalow Gran told them they were going back to Greenfield next day because she was going into hospital.

Toni pulled some unexpected knowledge out of whatever place she kept it in.

"Are you having a baby then, Gran?"

Gran smiled in a kind of tight way.

"No I'm not. Nothing you'd understand. I'll probably come out feet first."

Toni turned to Sophy with her usual air of speaking from a height.

"She means she's going to die."

After that Gran did a bit of packing for them which seemed mostly to be flinging things about. She seemed very angry, which Sophy thought unfair. Later when they were in bed and Toni in that sleep where she seemed not to breathe at all, Sophy lay thinking, until it was so late it was quite, quite dark. The hospital and Gran and dying made the darkness shivery. She examined, despite herself, the whole process of dying as far as she knew about it. Oh indeed, it was shivery—but exciting! She flung herself round in bed and spoke out loud.

"I shan't die!"

The words sounded loud, as if someone else had said them. They sent her down under the bedclothes again. It was down there that she found herself, as it were, forced to think of the place, the bungalow, as if it were now all part of this new thing, Gran's dying—Gran's bedroom where the bed seemed almost too big for the floor, the huge furniture crammed into the little rooms as if a great house had been contracted; the huge, dark, sideboard with carved squiggles and the cupboards you were not to open as in Bluebeard, the present darkness, that was like some creature sitting in each room; and Gran herself, made mysterious, no, dreadful, by coming out of hospital, monstrously feet first. It was at that very point that Sophy made her discovery. The mystery of things and Gran coming out feet first drove Sophy in on every side into herself. She understood something about the world. It extended out of her head in every direction but one; and that one was secure because it was her own, it was the direction through the back of her head, *there*, which was dark like this night, but her own dark. She knew that she stood or lay at the extreme end of this dark direction as if she were sitting at the mouth of a tunnel and looking out into the world whether it was dusk or dark or daylight. When she understood that the tunnel was there at the back of her head she felt a strange kind of shiver that shot through her body and made her want to escape from it into daylight and be like everybody else; but there was no daylight. She invented the daylight, there and then, and filled it with people who had no tunnel at the back of their heads, gay, cheerful, ignorant people; and presently she must have fallen asleep because Gran was calling them to wake up. At breakfast in the kitchen Gran was very cheerful and said they mustn't pay too much attention to what she said, everything would be all right probably and nowadays they could do wonders. Sophy heard all this and the long chat that followed without listening to it, she was so interested to see Gran, couldn't take her eyes off her because of this enormity, Gran was going to die. What made everything odder was that Gran didn't understand. She was trying to cheer them up as if *they* were going to die which was silly and to be dismissed in view of the plainly visible outline that now surrounded Gran, cutting her off from the rest of the world in her movement towards coming out of the hospital feet first. However, there was more of interest to be extracted and Sophy waited impatiently for all the things Gran was saying to cheer them up and as soon as there was a pause in the long explanation of however much they loved her they were young and would find other people which was what she had been meaning to tell them—in the subsequent drawing of Gran's breath, Sophy managed to get out her question.

"Gran, where are you going to be buried?"

Gran dropped a plate and burst into some quite extraordinary laughter which turned into other noises and then she positively rushed out and slammed the door of her bedroom. The twins were left at the kitchen table not knowing what to do, so they went on eating, but in respectful silence. Later Gran came out of her bedroom, kind and sunny. She hoped they wouldn't be too sorry for their poor old Gran and would remember the good times and what fun they had had all three together. Sophy considered that they had had no fun at all, all three of them and that Gran could snap if you got your shoes too dirty but she was beginning to learn what not to say. So she watched Gran who still had that curious outline round her, watched with solemn eyes over her mug while Gran talked sunnily. They were going to be very happy when they went back to Daddy because a new lady would be looking after them. Gran called her an au pair.

Toni asked the next question.

"Is she nice?"

"Oh yes," said Gran, in the voice that meant the opposite of what she was saying, "she's very nice. Your Daddy would see to that, wouldn't he?"

Sophy was not concerned to think about the new auntie because of the outline round Gran. Toni went on asking questions and Sophy was left to her own thoughts and observations. There was nothing particular about Gran (except the outline) to show that she was going to die so Sophy altered things round a bit to consider what the result would be. It was with disappointment and a little indignation that she saw how Gran's dying might very well cut her off from the buttery meadow and the dabchicks and little Phil and the pillar-box. She very nearly put this point to Gran, but thought better of it. And there—Toni must have said something! Gran was off again, the bedroom door slamming. The twins said nothing but sat; and then, simultaneously they caught each other's eyes and burst into a fit of the giggles. It was one of those rare moments when they really were everything to each other and enjoyed it.

Gran came out later, not so sunny, put their luggage together and drove them to the station in complete silence. This move towards home deflected Sophy into a consideration of the future. She asked a question which carefully avoided any point of contact with Gran and Gran's future.

"Shall we like her?"

Gran understood that one.

"I'm sure you will."

Then after a while and two traffic lights she spoke again in that voice which always meant the opposite of what it said.

"And I'm sure she'll be devoted to the two of you."

When they got back to Greenfield they found that the "au pair" was their third auntie. She appeared to have come out of the room across the landing like the other two, as if that bedroom produced

114

aunties like butterflies in warm weather. This third one was certainly more like a butterfly than the other ones had been. She had yellow hair, she smelt like a ladies' hairdressers' and she spent a long time each day putting things on her face. She had a way of speaking that was unlike anything the twins could hear, either in the house, or down in Dorset, or in the street from white, yellow, brown or black faces. She informed the twins that she came from Sydney. Sophy thought at first that Sydney was a person and that caused some confusion. However, the au pair, Auntie Winnie as she was called, was cheerful and quick once she was satisfied with her face. She whistled and sang a lot and smoked a lot and though she made so much noise she did not irritate Daddy in the slightest. When she wasn't making a noise herself, her transistor radio did it for her. Everywhere that Winnie went the transistor was sure to go. By listening to the transistor you could tell where Winnie was. When Sophy understood that Sydney was a big city on the other side of the world, she was encouraged to question Winnie.

"Isn't New Zealand on the other side of the world too?"

"'Spose so, dearie. Never thought of it like that."

"An auntie a long time ago. Our first auntie she was. Well she said Mummy was gone to God. Then Daddy said she'd gone to live with a man in New Zealand."

Winnie screamed with laughter.

"Well, it's the same kind of thing me old sweetheart, innit?"

Winnie changed things a lot. The stables down at the end of the garden path were now officially the twin's own house. Winnie persuaded them that they were proud and lucky to have a house of their own; and they were young enough to believe her for a time. Then later, of course, when they got used to it, there was no need to change anything. Daddy was particularly pleased and pointed out to them that they would no longer be annoyed by the sound of his typewriter. Sophy, who had sometimes been lulled to sleep by the secure sound of the typewriter, saw this as just another indication of what Daddy (Daddy out there, through there, along there, Daddy at a distance) of what Daddy really was. But she said nothing.

Winnie took them to the sea. This was going to be a great thing but it went all wrong. They were on sand among a huge crowd of people, most of them in deck-chairs with children scattered

115

between. The sun wasn't shining and it sprinkled rain now and then. But what went wrong was the sea itself, and it went wrong even for the grown-ups. The twins were inspecting a rippled inch or two at the very edge of the water when there were shouts and people started to run away up the beach. The sea had a line of foam·on it which came near and turned into a green hollow of water and this fell on them and there was a time of screaming and choking and Winnie wading with them both under her arms, then leaning forward and straining while the water tore at them and tried to take them away. So they all three went home at once. Winnie was so angry and they were all shivering and the transistor had stopped working and Winnie seemed quite different without it. The first thing she did when they were home again and dry was to take the transistor to be mended. But the wave—and no one could explain it, not even grown-ups, though they talked on the telly about it—the wave had a nasty habit of returning when you were asleep. Toni seemed unaffected by it but Sophy suffered. She woke several times to hear herself screaming. It was odd about Toni, though. Just once, when the two of them were squatting in front of the telly and watching a fun thing about all the various adventures you could get up to, as for example, hang gliding, there were included some shots of people surf-riding in the Pacific. At one moment the screen was full of a wave approaching, and the camera zoomed right up, right in, so you were right inside the immense green hollow. Sophy felt a terrible pang in her stomach and a fear of everything and she shut her eyes to keep out the sight though she could still hear the wave, or some wave or other, roaring and roaring. When the telly said now how about a change from water to air and she knew it would show pictures of parachutes she opened her eyes again to find that her untwinlike twin, Toni of the bleached hair and indifference to everything, had fainted clean away.

After that, for a long time, weeks and weeks, Toni was more often than not up in the air in her private forest or whatever it was. Once, when Sophy mentioned the wave (it being absent) to give herself an agreeable shiver there was a long silence before Toni answered.

"What wave?"

Winnie's transistor came back from the shop and went everywhere with her again. Once more you might hear a tiny orchestra

116

playing in the kitchen or a man's voice coming down the garden path at knee height. When the twins were taken up the High Street past the new mosque to the school and introduced to the milling children, the small man's voice went with them and left them there holding each other's hands as if they liked each other. Winnie fetched them after school which made some of the children laugh. Some of them were men, almost, at least, some of the black ones were.

Winnie lasted much longer than the other aunties, seeing how different she was from Daddy. She moved into his bedroom, transistor and all. Sophy disliked this but could not really tell why. Winnie arranged that the twins could use the old green door from the stables onto the towpath. She said to Daddy that they had to get used to the water.

This meant that for a time that summer and autumn the twins explored the towpath, from the Old Bridge with its tablet saying that someone had built it—though not perhaps with the stinky-poo urinal on the top—all the way, oh a mile or two perhaps by a path narrowed between brambles and loosestrife and stands of reed, all the way to the other bridge right out in the country. There was a wide pool by that bridge with a decaying barge in it, a boat much older than the line of motor boats and rowing boats and converted (but decaying) thises and thats across the canal from the green door. Once they even went so far they climbed up a track on the other side of the canal, up and up along a deep groove with trees hanging over on either side, up and up till they came out on the very ridge of the downs and could see the canal and Greenfield on one side and a valley full of trees on the other. They were late home that time but nobody noticed. Nobody ever noticed and sometimes Sophy wished they would. But then Sophy knew in a direct sort of way that Winnie had pushed them down the garden path into the stables—and very comfortable they were, what lucky children!—simply in order to get them out of the way and as far as possible from Daddy. They could do what they liked in the stables, dressing up from among the ancient trunks that seemed to hold the spillage of all history, the Stanhope family from way back, curling irons and hoops, dresses, shifts, materials, unbelievably a wig, faintly scented and with a trace of white powder lingering in it, shoes, and they lugged all this around and tried most of it on. Only they were not allowed to have other children in without permission. By the time the business of the wave had settled down a bit and sunk away into the place where occasional nightmares came from, Sophy began to think that she and Toni were being forced to be everything to each other again. She thought this so clearly one day that she tried pulling Toni's hair to prove that they weren't. But by now Toni had evolved her own way of fighting, flailing wildly with thin arms and legs and all the time looking nowhere with her big brown eyes, that it seemed she had escaped and left her thin and lengthening body behind her to inflict whatever it could of random injury and pain. Sophy began to find fighting unsatisfactory. Of course, at the school there were such tough children, men almost, it was best to keep out of that sort of trouble and leave the centre of the playground to them. So they played in the stables, parallel, so to speak, or walked primly in the High Street, conscious of difference among the black and yellow and brown, or went for quite wild walks along the towpath between the canal and the woods. They found a way of getting on the old barge, which was very long inside and had cupboards. It had an old sort of lavatory in a cupboard right up at the front end, so old it was no longer stinky-poo, or at least no more than the rest of the barge was.

So that year wore away unnoticed, what with school and living in the stables and having Mr and Mrs Bell to the stables for tea in a very grown-up way; and then they were out of thick trousers and sweaters and into jeans and light shirts and their eleventh birthday showed up on the horizon. Toni announced that it would be a good thing to go looking for books that they might like for their birthday. Sophy understood completely. Daddy would give them money, it was easier than thinking about them. Books chosen by Winnie would be ridiculous. They would have to make her mind up for her without her knowing since there was all this pretence of secrecy about birthday presents and she had to think it was her own idea. They went, therefore, from the stables at the bottom of the garden up the path under the buddleias, up the steps to the glass door into the hall, past Winnie who was playing her transistor in the kitchen, past Daddy who was playing the electric typewriter in his column room, then down the two steps to the front of the house where it looked up the High Street. They turned right to GOODCHILD'S RARE BOOKS and there they were, between the two

118

boxes outside Goodchild's window, the sixpenny box and the shilling box, all full of books no one would ever think of buying.

Mr Goodchild was not in the shop but Mrs Goodchild was at the back doing some writing at the desk by a door that led somewhere. The twins paid no attention to her, even after they had got the door open and been ever so slightly startled by the ting! of the shop bell. They looked round the books for children but had most of them in the stables anyway because books were the kind of thing that seemed to come from every direction, and though often interesting were not particularly precious. Sophy soon saw these books were too simple and she was about to go when she saw that Toni was examining the old books on the shelves with her particular silent attention so Sophy waited, turning over *Ali Baba* and wondering why anyone would want it when there were the four thick volumes in Daddy's column room to be taken away if you felt like it. Then the old man who was so helpful to little boys in the park came in. Toni ignored him because by then she was right inside a grown-up book but Sophy greeted him politely because though she did not like him she was curious about him; and the one thing all the aunts and cleaning women and cousins were keen on was being polite to everybody. Certainly he came under the interdict of not-talking-to-strange-men-in-the-street, but Mr Goodchild's bookshop wasn't a street. The old man poked about among the books for children, then he went up the shop to where Mrs Goodchild was sitting. At the same time old Mr Goodchild came in ting! from the High Street and immediately talked in a joky kind of way to the twins. But before this had got properly under way he saw the old man and stopped. In that silence they all heard the old man who was holding out a book to Mrs Goodchild say, "For my nephew, you know." Then Toni, who had had her nose in a grown-up book but had seen him out of the back of her head, said helpfully that he had forgotten the one he had put in the right-hand pocket of his raincoat. After that things were fast and mixed. The old man's voice went shrill as a woman's, Mrs Goodchild stood up and talked angrily about police and old Mr Goodchild walked up to the old man and demanded the book now and no nonsense or else. The old man came in a sort of dance, a twisting of the body, inward movement of the knees with arms almost flailing but not quite, and his high woman's voice complaining, down the shop by the shelves and under the cases and Sophy opened the door for him, ting! and shut it after him, because that too had a bit of the *meant* about it that sometimes happened. Mr Goodchild's face stopped being red quite quickly and he turned towards the twins but Mrs Goodchild talked to him first in the voice and words they were not supposed to understand.

"I can't think why they've let that man out of you-know-where again. He'll simply do it all over again, and there'll be some other poor little mite—"

Mr Goodchild broke in.

"Well at least now we know who's been taking the children's books."

After he had said that he became silly again, bowing to the twins.

"And how are the Misses Stanhope? Well, I trust?"

They answered him in beautiful unison.

"Yes thank you, Mr Goodchild."

"And Mr Stanhope? He is well?"

"Yes thank you, Mr Goodchild."

There was no question of being well as Sophy realized already. It was a thing people said, just as wearing a tie was something they did.

"I think, Mrs Goodchild," said Mr Goodchild in a more than usually silly way, "that we can offer the Misses Stanhope some liquid refreshment?"

So they went with comfortable Mrs Goodchild who was never silly, but calm and matter-of-fact, into the shabby sitting-room through the door at the back of the shop, where she sat them side by side on a sofa in front of a television set that was switched off and went away to get the fizzy drinks. Mr Goodchild stood in front of them, smiling and rocking on his toes and said how nice it was to see them and how he and they saw each other most days, didn't they. He had a little girl of his own, well she was a big girl now, a married lady with two little children but a long way away in Canada. It was half-way through his next sentence, which was about how much pleasanter a house was with children in it—and of course he had to add something silly like, "or not children precisely, let us say a pair of delightful young ladies like you," whereas when they left home if they went a long way away—half-way or somewhere in this twisting sentence Sophy had a naked realization of her own power should she care to exercise it, to do

120

anything she liked with Mr Goodchild, that large, old, fat man with his shopful of books and his silly ways, she could do absolutely anything she liked with him only it would not be worth the trouble. So they sat, toes only just reaching the old carpet and gazed at things over their fizzy drinks. There was a large notice on one wall that said in big letters how BERTRAND RUSSELL would address GREENFIELD PHILOSOPHICAL SOCIETY in the Assembly Rooms on HUMAN FREEDOM AND RESPONSIBILITY at such and such a date. It was an old notice and getting dim and seemed odd since it was stuck or hung where most people would put a picture; but then in the rather gloomy light Sophy saw under the big BERTRAND RUSSELL, in small print, Chairman, S. Goodchild, and understood, more or less. Mr Goodchild went on talking.

Sophy asked what interested her.

"Mrs Goodchild. Please, why was the old man taking books?"

After that there was quite a long pause before anyone spoke. Mrs Goodchild took a long drink of her instant before she said anything.

"Well dear, it's stealing, you see."

"But he's old," said Sophy, looking up over the rim. "He's old as old."

After she said that, Mr and Mrs Goodchild looked at each other over their instant for quite a time.

"You see," said Mr Goodchild at last, "he wants to give them to children as presents. He's—he's sick."

"Some people would say he's sick," said Mrs Goodchild, meaning she wasn't one of some people, "and needs a doctor. But others—"and it sounded as if Mrs Goodchild might be one of the others—"just think he's a nasty, wicked old man and that he ought to be—"

"Ruth!"

"Yes. Well."

Sophy could feel and almost see those shutters coming down that grown-ups had in constant supply when you wanted to know something really interesting. But Mrs Goodchild went off round a corner.

"What with W. H. Smith taking over and ruining the assembly rooms and the supermarket giving away paperbacks it's hard enough keeping the place together without nasty old Pedigree helping us on the road to ruin."

121

"At least we know now who's been doing the shoplifting. I'll have a word with Sergeant Phillips."

Then Sophy saw him change the subject behind his face. He became fatter, rosier, beaming with his head a bit sideways. He spread out, his cup in one hand and the saucer in the other.

"But with the Misses Stanhope to entertain—"

Toni spoke in the pause, using her faint, clear voice in which every syllable was as precise as a line in a good drawing.

"Mrs Goodchild. What is Tran-scend-en-tal Phil-os-oph-y?"

Mrs Goodchild's cup rattled in her saucer.

"God bless the child! Does your daddy teach you words like that?"

"No. Daddy doesn't teach us."

Sophy saw her fly away again and explained the thing to Mrs Goodchild.

"It's the name on a book in your shop, Mrs Goodchild."

"Transcendental Philosophy, my dear," said Mr Goodchild in a jokey voice that had nothing to be jokey about, "might on the one hand be called a book full of hot air. On the other hand it might be considered the ultimate wisdom. You pays your money as they used to say and you takes your choice. Beautiful young ladies are not generally considered to stand in need of an understanding of Transcendental Philosophy on the grounds that they exemplify in themselves all the pure, the beautiful and the good."

"Sim."

It was evident that nothing was to be learnt from Mr and Mrs Goodchild. For a little while longer Sophy and Toni did their "remarkable children" thing, then said together—it was one of the few benefits of twinship—that they must go now, got down, did their "thank yous" demurely, to hear as they retreated down the shop old Mr Goodchild going on about "enchanting children" and Mrs Goodchild breaking in—

"You'd better have a word with Phillips this afternoon. I think old Pedigree is having one of his beastly times again. They ought to put him away for good."

"He wouldn't touch Stanhope's little girls."

"What difference does it make whose child it is?"

That night in bed, Sophy did a long brood that was almost a Toni, a drifting away up into the boughs. "Stanhope's little girls?" It seemed to her that they weren't anyone's little girls. She sent

122

her mind round the circle of people who impinged: Gran, who had disappeared together with Rosevear and all that, Daddy, the cleaning women, aunts, a teacher or two, some children. She saw clearly that they belonged to each other and to no one else. As she didn't like belonging to Toni and contrariwise, it was clear she wouldn't like belonging to anyone else either.. And then—that personal, that wholly isolated direction at the back of your head, the black place from which you looked out on things so that all of those people, even Toni, *out there*—how could the creature called Sophy who sat there at the mouth of the tunnel behind her belong to anyone but herself? It was all silly. And if belonging was like being twin with a lot of people out there the way Daddy had lived with aunts and the Bells with each other and the Goodchilds with each other and all the others—but Daddy had his column room to disappear into and when he had disappeared into his column room—she saw suddenly, knees up to her chin—he could go further, do a Toni and disappear into his chess.

When she thought that, she opened her eyes and the room came into view with a glimmer from her dormer so she shut them again, wishing to stay inside. She knew she was not thinking the way grown-ups thought and there were so many of them and they were so big—

All the same.

Sophy became very still and held her breath. There was the old man and the books. She saw something. She had been told it often enough but now she *saw* it. You could choose to belong to people the way the Goodchilds and Bells and Mrs Hugeson did by being good, by doing what they said was right. Or you could choose what was real and what you knew was real—your own self sitting inside with its own wishes and rules at the mouth of the tunnel.

Perhaps the only advantage of being everything with a twin and knowing the exact Toni-ness of Toni was that in the morning Sophy had no hesitation in discussing the next step with her. She suggested they should steal sweets and Toni not only listened but contributed ideas. She said they would use a Paki shop because the Pakis couldn't keep their eyes off her hair and she would hold the man's attention while Sophy did the actual stealing. Sophy saw the reasonableness of this. If Toni let her hair fall over her face, then tried in a deliberately baby-way to get it clear and looked up through the tresses it was like doing a bit of magic. So

123

they went to the shop kept by the Krishna brothers and it was simply too easy. The younger Krishna was standing in the doorway and talking in a liquid voice to a blackie—"Now you go off you black fellow. We are not wanting your custom." The twins sidled past him and inside the shop the older Krishna came forward from between sacks of brown sugar that were open for the scoops and said the shop was theirs. Then he positively forced curious sweets on them and added some curious sticks which he said were incense and refused to be paid for anything. It was humiliating and they abandoned the project, seeing that if they tried it on Mr Goodchild's books it would be much the same;.and the books were silly anyway. There was another thing that now presented itself to Sophy. They had more toys than they wanted and more pocket money than they wanted. All Daddy's cleaning women and cousins ensured that. Worst of all, they found there was a group of kids at their school who were doing the same thing only on a larger scale, *really* stealing and sometimes breaking in and then selling the loot to those children who could afford to buy it. Sophy saw that stealing was wrong or right according to the way you thought, but both ways it was boring. Being bored was the real reason for not stealing, the reason that counted. Once or twice she thought about this matter so piercingly it was as if right and wrong and boring were numbers you could add and subtract. She saw, too, in this particularly piercing way that there was another number, an x to be added or to be subtracted, for which she could find no value. The combination of the piercingness and the fourth number made her panicky and would have settled into a chilly fear, if she had not had the mouth of the dark tunnel to sit at and know herself to be not Sophy but *This. This* lived and watched without any feelings at all and brandished or manipulated the Sophy-creature like a complicated doll, a child with all the arts and wiles and deliberate delightfulness of a quite unselfconscious, oh a quite innocent, naive, trusting little girl—brandished her among all the other children, white, yellow, brown, black, the other children who surely were as incapable of inspecting this kind of sum as they were of doing the others in their heads and had to write them down laboriously on paper. Then, suddenly, sometimes, it would be easy—flip!—to go out there and to join them.

This discovery of what-is-what might have seemed very

important except that their eleventh birthday was the start of a really dreadful month for Sophy and perhaps for Toni, though Toni did not seem to be as affected. It was on the birthday itself. They had a cake, bought from Timothy's and with ten candles round the top with one in the middle. Daddy actually came all the way down from the column room to share in the tea and he was jokey in the way that did not suit him or his hawk's face that always made Sophy think of princes and pirates. He told them after only the slightest many happy returns and before they'd even blown out the candles. He told them he and Winnie were getting married so they'd have what he called a proper mother. Sophy knew a lot of things in the burning moment after he stopped speaking. She knew the difference between Winnie keeping her clothes in the aunties' room and paying Daddy visits; and Winnie going straight in there to undress and get in bed and be called Missis Stanhope and perhaps (because it happened in stories) having babies that Daddy would want the way he didn't want the twins, his twins and nobody else's. It was a moment of deadly anguish—Winnie with her painted face, her yellow hair, her strange way of speaking, and her smelling like a ladies' hairdressers'. Sophy knew it couldn't happen, couldn't be allowed to happen. All the same, that was no comfort and she couldn't get her mouth together to blow but it went wider and she began to cry. Even the crying was all wrong because it began in sheer woe but then because she was exhibiting it before Winnie, and worse, before Daddy, thus informing him how important he was, it got mixed up with rage. Also she knew that even when she had done with crying, the fact would still be there, massive and unbearable. She heard Winnie speak.

"Over to you, cobber."

Cobber was Daddy. He came and said things over her shoulder, touched her so that she twisted herself away and there was silence after a time. Then Daddy roared in a terrible voice.

"Christ! Children!"

She heard him thumping down the wooden stairs into the coachhouse and then hurrying up the garden path. The door into the hall slammed so hard it was a wonder the glass didn't break. Winnie went after him.

After she had got rid of all her tears without improving the situation she sat up on her divan bed and looked across at Toni on

125

hers. Toni was the same as usual except that she was a bit pink in the cheek—no tears. She simply said in an offhand voice:

"Cry-baby."

Sophy was too miserable to answer. She wanted nothing so much as to get right away and abandon Daddy, forget him and his treachery. She rubbed her face and said they should go along the towpath because Winnie told them not to. They did this at once though it seemed weak and nowhere near a reply to the awful news. Only by the time they had got to the old boat by the broken lock Winnie and Daddy did seem a bit smaller and farther away. They mooned about on the boat for a bit and they discovered a clutch of duck's eggs that had been left there a long time. When she saw the eggs, everything came quite clear in Sophy's head. She saw how she would torment Winnie and Daddy, go on and on tormenting them till she had driven them both mad and away, both taken away like Mr Goodchild's son in the mental hospital.

After that things happened the way they were intended to happen. They fell together in a kind of "Of course" way, as if the whole world was co-operating. It was meant that when they got back to the birthday cake and ate some of the icing—there was no sense in leaving it—they should decide to open the old leather trunk they had been told not to and find the bunch of rusty keys there. The keys opened everything usually kept shut. That night, sitting up in bed, her knees against her new breasts, Sophy saw clearly that one of the old eggs was meant for Winnie. She found herself overcome with a passionate desire in the darkness to be Weird—there was no other name for it, Weird and powerful. She frightened herself and curled down in the bed but the dark tunnel was still there; and in that remote security she saw what to do.

Next day she found how easy it was. You just looked for the areas of inattention with which grown-ups were so liberally supplied and walked through them. You could do it quite briskly and no one could see or hear you. Therefore, briskly she unlocked the drawer in the little table by Daddy's bed, broke the egg in it and walked away briskly. She put the key back with the others on the heavy ring that quite obviously had not been used for years and felt it was the nearest she could get to being Weird but not really satisfactory. That day she was so preoccupied in school that even Mrs Hugeson noticed and asked what was the matter. Nothing of course.

That night in her bed under the dormer in the stables she brooded about being weird. She tried to join things together about weirdness but could not. It was not arithmetic. Everything floated, the private tunnel, the things that were meant and oh, above all, the deep, fierce, hurting need, desire, to hurt Winnie and Daddy up there in the bedroom. She brooded and wished and tried to think and then brooded again; and presently her feelings made her want so desperately to be weird for this occasion that she saw in a kind of supposing that burnt how it should have been. Now she saw herself glide up the garden path, through the glass door, up the stairs, gliding through the bedroom door to the big bed where Daddy lay and Winnie curled, her back to him. So she went to the little table which now had three books on it by the bedside lamp and she thrust her hand with the egg through the locked wood and she broke the egg beside the other one, so eek, so stinky-poo, so oof and pah and she left the two messes there. Then she turned and looked down and she aimed the dark part of her head at sleeping Winnie and gave her a nightmare so that she jerked in bed and shrieked aloud; at which the shriek kind of woke Sophy—though it could not wake her as she had never been asleep—and she was in her own bed with her own shriek and she was deadly frightened by the weirdness and she cried out after her own shriek, "Toni! Toni!" But Toni was asleep and off away wherever it was so Sophy had to lie for a long time, curled up, frightened and shaking. Indeed she began to feel that going on being weird would be too much and that grown-ups would win after all, because too much weirdness made you sick. But then Uncle Jim appeared from fucking Sydney.

At first everyone had fun with Uncle Jim, even Daddy, who said he was a natural comedian. But not more than a week after the birthday party that had gone wrong Sophy noticed how much time he was beginning to spend with Winnie; and she wondered about it all and was a bit scared that she might have produced him by being weird. After all, he did kind of dilute the situation, she said to herself, proud of having found a word that was even better than just the right word, he diluted everybody's feelings and made them—well, dilute.

On the seventh of June, that being approximately a fortnight after the birthday, when Sophy was already accustomed to thinking of herself as eleven, she was behind the old rose bush and

127

squatting down, and watching the ants being busy about nothing when Toni came flying down the garden path and up the wooden stairs to their own room. This was so astonishing that Sophy went to see. Toni wasted no time in explanations.

"Come."

She grabbed Sophy's wrist, but she resisted.

"What—?"

"I need you!"

Sophy was so astonished she allowed herself to be led. Toni went quickly up the garden path and into the hall. She stood outside the door of the column room and put her hair straight. She held on to Sophy's wrist and opened the door. Daddy was there, looking at a chess set. The Anglepoise light was switched on and lowered over it, though the sun was shining outside.

"What do you two want?"

Sophy saw that Toni had gone bright red for the first time in memory. She gave a little gasp, then spoke in her faint, colourless voice.

"Uncle Jim is having sexual relationships with Winnie in the aunties' bedroom."

Daddy stood up very slowly.

"I—you—"

There was a pause of a kind of woollen silence, prickly, hot, uncomfortable. Daddy went quickly to the door, then across the hall. They heard him on the other stairs.

"Winnie? Where are you?"

The twins ran, Toni white now, ran to the glass door down into the garden, Sophy leading. Sophy ran all the way down to the stables again, she hardly knew why or why she was excited and frightened and scared and triumphant. She was up in the room before she saw that Toni had not come with her. It was perhaps ten minutes before she came, slowly and still even whiter than usual.

"What happened? Is he angry? Were they doing that? Like in the lectures? Toni! Why did you say 'I need you?' Did you hear them? Did you hear him? Daddy? What did he say?"

Toni was lying on her tummy, her forehead on the backs of her hands.

"Nothing. He shut the door and came down again."

After that, there was a pause of about three days; and then

128

when the twins came back from school in the afternoon they walked through a furious grown-up row. It was high above their heads and Sophy walked away from it down the garden path, half hoping that weirdness was working but wondering in a gloomy sort of way if all that really worked was what Toni had done, in letting Daddy know a secret. But whichever it was, that was the day it was all done with. Winnie and Uncle Jim went away that very evening. Toni—who did not, it appeared, concern herself with the idea of being weird at a distance—had stayed as close to the grown-ups as she could and reported helpfully to Sophy what she had heard without trying to explain it. She said Winnie had gone with Uncle Jim because he was a digger and she was sick of fucking Poms it had all been a mistake anyway Daddy was too fucking old and the kids were a consideration and she hoped there were no hard feelings. Sophy was half-sorry and half-glad to know that she had not got rid of Winnie by being weird. But Uncle Jim was a real loss. Toni dropped one piece of information which did show Sophy how carefully her twin had planned and gone about the whole scheme.

"She had a passport. She was a foreigner. Her real name wasn't 'Winnie'. It was 'Winsome'."

This struck the twins as so funny they were happy with each other for quite a while.

There were no more aunties after Winnie, and Daddy spent regular times in London at a club and doing his chess broadcasts. There was a long series of cleaning ladies who did the bit of the house that wasn't occupied by the solicitors and the Bells. There was also a sort of cousin of Daddy's who stayed every now and then, overhauled their clothes, told them about periods and God. But she was a colourless character not worth being friends with or tormenting.

In fact, after the disposal of Winnie time stopped. It was as if after climbing a slope they had both come to a plateau, the edges of which were out of sight. Perhaps this was partly because their twelfth birthday went unnoticed by Daddy, there being no Winnie or other auntie to remind him. Both twins were made aware in the course of that year that they had phenomenal intelligence, but this was no news, really, except that it did explain why all other children seemed so dim. To Sophy the phrase "phenomenal intelligence" was a useless bit of junk lying in her mind and not

129

really connected to anything that would be worth having or doing. Toni seemed the same, unless you knew her the way that Sophy did. It showed, perhaps, in the way that they quickly found themselves in different classes for certain subjects, though not all. It showed itself more subtly in the way that Toni would sometimes say things offhand that settled a question for good. You could tell then that long thought had preceded the words; but there was no other evidence for it.

Periods, when they happened, hurt Sophy and enraged her. Toni seemed indifferent to them, as if she could leave her body to get on with its job and be away somewhere herself, out of the whole business of feeling. Sophy knew that she herself had these long, still times; but she knew they weren't thinking, they were brooding. It was when she had a period and it hurt that she began to brood again—for the first time since Winnie—on the whole business of being weird and what there was in it. She found herself doing some strange things too. Once, near Christmas, she went into the deserted aunties' room and then had to think—why did I come here? She brooded some more—standing by the head of the stripped single bed on which the ancient electric blanket, creased and stained with iron mould, seemed ugly as a surgical appliance—brooded on the *why* and decided that she had had some vague wish to find out what an auntie was and what they had in common; and then, with a shiver of a kind of dirty excitement and also disgust she knew that she wanted to find out what there was about them that made Daddy summon them to his bed. While she was thinking that, she heard him come out of the column room and run up the stairs two at a time if not more, slam the bathroom door—and then there was running water and all that. She thought of the duck's egg by his bed and wondered why no one had ever said anything about it; but with him in the bathroom there was no chance of going in his bedroom to see. She stood there by the single bed and waited for him to go down.

Any reasonable auntie would have been glad to get out of that room. There was an old rug by the bed, a chair, a dressing-table and large wardrobe and nothing else. She tiptoed to the window and looked down the garden path to the dormers of the stabling. She opened the top drawer of the dressing-table and there was Winnie's little transistor lying in the corner. Sophy took it out and

130

examined it with a comfortable feeling of security from Winnie. She felt a bit of triumph as she switched on the set. The battery was still live so that a miniature pop group began to perform miniature music. The door opened behind her.

It was Daddy, standing in the door. She looked at him and saw why Toni had such a white skin. There was a long silence between them. She was the first to speak.

"Can I keep it?"

He looked down at the little leather-sheathed case in her hands. He nodded, swallowed, then went away as swiftly as he had come, down the stairs. Triumph triumph, triumph! It was like capturing Winnie and keeping her caged and never letting her out—Sophy sniffed the case carefully and decided that none of Winnie's scent had clung to it. She took it away, back to the stables. She lay on her divan bed and thought of a tiny Winnie shut there in the box. It was silly of course, to think that—but as she said that to herself she had a thought to go with it; having a period is silly! Silly! Silly! It deserves to have a duck's egg, a stink, some dirt.

After that Sophy became addicted to the transistor with Winnie inside it. She thought it likely that all transistors had their owners inside them and so it was lucky this one was already tenanted. She listened often, sometimes with her ear against the fairing of the speaker, sometimes pulling the earplug out of its niche and being private to herself. It was that way she heard two talks which spoke not to the little girl with her smiling face (little friend of all the world) but directly to the Sophy-thing that sat inside at the mouth of its private tunnel. One was about the universe running down and she understood that she had always known that, it explained so much it was obvious, it was why fools were fools and why there were so many of them. The other talk was about some people being able to guess the colour of a greater percentage of cards than they should be able to, statistically speaking. Sophy listened enthralled to the man who spoke about this nonsense, as he called it. He said there was no magic and how if people could guess these so-called cards more than they ought, statistically speaking, then fiercely, oh so very fiercely, the man's eyes must be popping out, *statistics must be re-examined*. This made even the Sophy-creature giggle because she could swim in numbers when she wanted. She remembered the duck's egg and the little

131

Sophy-child walking through those areas of inattention; and she saw that what they missed out of their experiments in magic which gave them no or little result, was just the stinky-poo bit, the breaking of rules, the using of people, the well-deep wish, the piercingness, the—the what? The other end of the tunnel, where surely it joined on.

In the evening when these things came together, she jumped clean out of bed and the desire to be weird was like a taste in the mouth, a hunger and thirst after weirdness. It seemed to her then that unless she did what had never been done, saw something that she never ought to see, she would be lost for ever and turn into a young girl. Something pushed her, shoved her, craved. She tried to get the rusty dormer open and did so, just a crack; then more than a crack as if the door of a vault were grinding on its hinge. But all she could see in the evening light was the canal shining. But then there were footsteps on the towpath. She did a violence to her head, thrusting it sideways in the crack and yes, she could see now what was never before oh not by living people seen from this angle, not just the towpath and the canal but along the towpath to the Old Bridge, yes, more of the Old Bridge and yes, the filthy old stinky-poo urinal, whiff whiff; and there was the old man who stole books from Mr Goodchild going in and she kept him there she did! She willed him to stay in the dirty place, like Winnie in the transistor, would not let him come out, she bent her mind, frowning, teeth gritted, she brought everything down to one point where he was in the dirty place and kept him there; and a man in a black hat went cycling primly out over the Old Bridge into the country and a bus heaved this way over it and she kept him there! But she could not hold on. The man in the black hat went cycling out into the country, the bus went on into Greenfield High Street. Her mind inside her let go so that she could not tell whether she was keeping the old man in the dirty place or not. All the same, she thought as she turned away from the dormer, he stayed in there and if I can't be sure I kept him in, I can't be sure I didn't. Then all at once because she had let go of her mind and become the Sophy-child again in her pyjamas out in the centre of the moony room, fear descended over her like a magician's tall hat and froze her flesh so that she cried out in panic.

"Toni! Toni!"

But Toni was fast asleep and stayed that way even when shaken.

In their fifteenth year at a specific hour or even instant, Sophy felt herself come out into daylight. She was sitting in class and Toni was the only other girl of her age in the room. The rest were seniors with lumpy breasts and big bums and they were groaning as if the algebra was glue they were stuck in. Sophy was sitting back because she had finished. Toni was sitting back because she had not only finished but evaporated and left her body there with its face tilted up. That was when it happened. Sophy *saw* as well as knew, that there was a dimension they were moving through; and as she saw that she saw something else too. It was not that Toni was Toni the wet, though she *was* a wet hen and always would be, but yes, she was beautiful, a beautiful young girl—no, not beautiful with her smoke-grey hair afloat, her thin, no slim body, her face that could be seen through—she was not just beautiful. She was *stunning*. It was a pang clean through Sophy to see that so clearly; and after the pang, a kind of rage, that wet hen Toni of all people—

She asked to be excused, went and examined herself urgently in the grubby mirror. Yes. It was not like Toni's beauty but it was alright. It was dark of course, and not to be seen through, not transparent, but regular, pretty, oh God, *healthy,* outdoor, winning, inviting, could be strong and yes that would be the best side for a photograph; in fact very satisfactory indeed if you didn't have always at your side the wet hen for which or whom there was now no easy word—So Sophy stared into the grubby mirror at her reflection, seeing all things in the daylight that had brightened and cleared so suddenly. That evening after the French verbs and American history she lay on her divan and Toni on hers. Sophy wrenched up the volume of her new transistor so that it blared for a moment, a challenge perhaps, an insult even, or at least a rude jab at her silent twin.

"Do you mind, Sophy!"

"Doesn't make any difference to you does it?"

Toni half knelt, changing her position. With her new, daylight eyes, Sophy saw the impossible curve alter and flow, from the line of the forehead under the smoky hair, down, round the curve of the long neck, the shoulder, include the suggestion of a breast, sweep round and end back there where a toe moved and pushed off a sandal.

"It does as a matter of fact."

"Well you'll have to go on minding then, my deah, deah Toni."

"I'm not Toni any more. I'm Antonia."

Sophy burst out laughing.

"And I'm Sophia."

"If you like."

And the strange creature drifted away again, leaving her body to lie there, as it were, untenanted. Sophy had a mind to blow the roof off with the radio but it seemed an action out of that childhood which they had so suddenly left behind. She lay back instead, looking at the ceiling with the big spot of damp. With another jolt of awareness she saw that this new daylight made the dark direction at the back of her head all the more incredible yet all the more evident; because there it was!

"I've got eyes in the back of my head!"

She sat up with a jerk, conscious of the words spoken aloud, then the turn of the other girl's head and the long look.

"Oh?"

Neither of them said anything after that and presently Toni turned away. It was impossible that Toni should know. Yet Toni did.

There are eyes in the back of my head. The angle is still there, wider, the thing called Sophy can sit looking out through the eyes, the thing which really is nameless. It can choose either to go out into the daylight or to lie in this private segment of infinite depth, distance, this ambushed separateness from which comes all strength—

She shut her eyes with sudden excitement. She made a connection that seemed exact between this new feeling and an old one, the one of the rotten egg, the passionate desire to be weird, to be on the other side, desire for the impossibilities of the darkness and the bringing of them into being to disrupt the placid normalities of the daylight world. With her front eyes shut it was as if those other eyes opened in the back of her head and stared into a darkness that stretched away infinitely, a cone of black light.

She came up out of this contemplation and opened her daylight eyes. There the other figure was, curled on the other divan, child and woman—and surely expression too, not of the futile pinpricks

134

of light with its bursting and efflorescence, but of the darkness and running down?

It was from that moment that Sophy ceased to make many of the gestures that the world required of her. She found a measuring rod in her hand. Look at "ought" and "must" and "want" and "need". If they were not appropriate at the moment to the sweet-faced girl with the optional eyes at the back of her head, then she touched them with her wand and they vanished. Hey presto.

When they were fifteen-and-a-bit, the staff said Toni should go to a college but Toni wasn't certain and said she might prefer to model. Sophy didn't know what she would do but saw no point in going to college or loading your body with someone else's clothes day after day. It was while she was still in the position of not really believing that it would come to the point of living in the outside world that Toni went off to London and was away quite a time, which infuriated the school and Daddy. The thing was that after a few days, girls being supposed to be a fragile commodity, Toni became a genuine missing person and listed by Interpol, as on the telly. The next anybody knew was that she turned up in Afghanistan of all places, and in deep trouble because the people she had accepted a lift from were running drugs. It seemed for a while that Toni might have to stay in jail for years. Sophy was astonished by Toni's daring and a bit jealous, and decided to get on with her own further education. The first thing she did, being certain that by now Toni must have got rid of her virginity, was to examine her own by means of a strategically placed mirror. She was not impressed. She tried a couple of boys who proved incompetent and their mechanisms ridiculous. But they did teach her the astonishing power her prettiness could wield over men. She examined the traffic situation in Greenfield and saw the best place, by the pillar-box a hundred yards beyond the Old Bridge. She waited there, refused a truck and a man on a motorbike and chose the third one.

He drove a small van, not a car, he was dark and attractive and he said he was going to Wales. Sophy allowed him to pick her up by the post-box because she thought he was very likely telling the truth and never seeing him again would be that much easier if it was what she wanted. Ten miles out of Greenfield he drove down a side road, parked in the skirts of a wood and enveloped her,

135

breathing heavily. It was she who suggested they should go into the wood and there she found there was no doubt about his competence at all. He hurt her more than she had thought possible. When he had ended his part of the affair he pulled out, wiped himself, zipped himself and looked down at her with a mixture of triumph and caution.

"Now don't you go telling anyone. See?"

Sophy was faintly surprised.

"Why should I?"

He looked at her with less caution and more triumph.

"You were a virgin. Well. You aren't, now. I've had you, see?"

Sophy took out the tissues she had brought with her for the purpose and wiped a trickle of blood from her thigh. The man said, in high humour and to no one in particular:

"Had a virgin!"

Sophy pulled on her pants. She was wearing a dress rather than jeans, which was most unusual but another bit of foresight. She looked curiously at the man who was now evidently delighted with life.

"Is that all?"

"What d'you mean?"

"Sex. Fucking."

"Christ. What did you expect?"

She said nothing, since it was not necessary. She then had a lesson in the extraordinary nature of men, if this specimen was anything to go by. This instrument of her initiation told her what a risk she had run, she might have been picked up by anyone and lying there at this very moment strangled, she must never, never do such a thing again. If she were his daughter he would take the strap to her, letting herself get picked up and she only seventeen, why she might, she might—

By this time Sophy lost patience.

"I'm not sixteen yet."

"Christ! But you said—"

"Not till October."

"Christ—"

It was a mistake. She saw that at once. It was another lesson. Always stick to the simplest lie like the simplest truth. He was angry and frightened. But then as he blustered about deadly secrets and how he'd find her and cut her throat she saw how

136

slight and silly he was, all this about never letting on, forgetting him, if she said a word—if she mentioned *anyone* had picked her up. Bored, she broke it to him.

"I picked you up, silly."

He made for her and she went on quickly before his hands touched her.

"That card I posted when you stopped by me. It had the number of your van on it. It's to my Dad. If I don't pick it up—"

"Christ."

He took an uncertain step among the leaves.

"I don't believe you!"

She recited the number of his van to him. She told him he was to take her back to where he had found her and when he swore, mentioned the card again. Finally, of course, he drove her back, because, as she told herself, her will was stronger than his. She liked that idea so much that she broke her recent resolve and told him in so many words. It made him very angry all over again but pleased her. Then what was. the most extraordinary part of the whole thing, he got positively wet, telling her she was a lovely kid really and she shouldn't waste herself on this sort of thing. If she waited for him at the same place and time next week, they'd go together regular. She'd like that. He had a bit of money—

To all this Sophy listened silently, nodding occasionally, since that was what kept him planning. But she would not tell him her name or give him her address.

"Don't you want to know my name then, kiddy?"

"As a matter of fact, not."

"'As a mattah of fact not.' Christ stone the fucking crows. You'll be murdered one of these days. Straight, you will."

"Just put me down by the post-box."

He shouted after her that he would be at the same place, same time, next week and she gave him a smile to get rid of him and then walked a long way home by all the sidestreets and alleys she could think of so that the van could not follow. She was still in the grip of her astonishment at it meaning so little. It was so trivial an act when you subtracted the necessary and not-to-be-repeated pain of the first time. It meant nothing at all. There was little more sensation to it than feeling the inside of your cheek with your tongue—well, there *was* a little more but not much.

137

They said too, whoever it was said, that the girl cried afterwards.

"I didn't cry."

At that, her body gave a long shudder, all on its own, and she waited for a bit, but nothing more happened. Of course, the sex lectures always added in the bit about pair-bonding and about achieving orgasm which might not happen to a girl for quite a long time—but really so trivial an act and significant only in the possible, though quite unbelievable outcome. It seemed to her, walking home by way, at last, of the towpath, vaguely right that this thing they made so much fuss about—wrestling with each other on the box or grunting at it on the wide screens, all the poetry and music and painting and everybody agreeing it was a many-splendoured thing, the simplest thing, well it *was* very nearly the simplest thing and so much the worse, yes, vaguely right in view of how the whole thing is running down—well, it was silly.

She agreed mildly with Daddy's cleaning lady that she was home early from school, listened for the electric typewriter then remembered it was the afternoon of his school broadcast, and went to the bathroom where she washed herself out as in the films and was faintly repelled by the mess of blood and spunk, and—reaching far in, her lower lip hurting between clenched teeth—she felt the pear-shaped thing stuck inside the front of her stomach where it ought to be, inert, a time bomb, though that was hard to believe of yourself or your body. The thought of the possible explosion of the time bomb started her even more elaborately probing and washing, pain or not; and she came on the other shape, lying opposite the womb but at the back, a shape lying behind the smooth wall but easily to be felt through it, the rounded shape of her own turd working down the coiled gut and she convulsed, feeling without saying but feeling every syllable—*I hate! I hate! I hate!* There was no direct object to the verb, as she said to herself when she was a little more normal. The feeling was pure.

But washed and cleaned out, menstruated and restored, this active hate sank down like a liquid to the bottom of things and she was a young girl again, felt she was; a young girl conscious of listening to the sound of space, confused over the possibilities of weirdness since the word was used in several ways, conscious of

138

resisting the proposal of teachers that you should make one last effort to use your unquestioned intelligence; or—and suddenly—a giggly girl about clothes and boys and who was going with whom and yes isn't he gorgeous and catch phrases and catch music and catch pop stars and catch and catch as catch can be simple.

All the same, with Toni not yet retrieved and staring into her own bland face, she was worried over it meaning nothing, even though that in itself was about as simple as you could get. She thought round the whole circle of people she knew, even dead Gran and forgotten mother and she saw they were shapes and it worried her. It was almost better being forced to be everything with someone you didn't really like than this living with yourself and to yourself. With a confused and fundamentally ignorant expectation that wealth and sophistication would make a difference—and besides, now she was sixteen!—she picked up an expensive car, only to find that the man inside was much older than he looked. This time the exercises that took place in the wood were not painful but more prolonged and she did not understand them. The man offered her more money than she had ever seen before to perform various actions for him, which she did, finding them a bit sick-making but not more so than the inside of her own body. It was only when she got home—Yes, Mrs Emlin, school *is* out early—she thought: *Now I am a whore!* After the bathroom she lay on her divan, thinking about being a whore, but even if she said it out loud it didn't seem to change her, didn't seem to touch her, just was not. Only the roll of blue five-pound notes was real. She thought to herself that being a whore didn't mean anything either. It was like stealing sweets, a thing you could do if you wanted, but boring. Not even rousing the Sophy-creature to say—*I hate!*

After that she put sex on one side as a discovered, examined and discarded bit of triviality. It became nothing more than playing with yourself lazily in bed to the accompaniment of quite unusual or what seemed like quite unusual imaginings, very private indeed.

Antonia was flown home and had terrific cold rows with Daddy in the column room. There was a little, a very little, communication in the stables but Toni was not inclined to give a blow by blow account of her life. Sophy never knew why or how Toni and

139

Daddy worked it, but before long Toni was living in a hostel in London which was official and would keep her safe from everything. She said she was an actress and tried for it, but the odd fact was that despite her intelligence and her transparency she wasn't any good. There seemed little for her but the university but she swore she wouldn't go and began to talk wildly about imperialism. Also freedom and justice. She seemed to have even less use for boys or men than Sophy had, though they swarmed after her remote beauty. No one was really surprised when she disappeared again. She sent them a defiant postcard from Cuba.

Sophy got a job that demanded nothing. It was in a travel agent's and after a few weeks she told Daddy she was moving up to London, but would keep her bit of the stables.

He looked at her with evident dislike.

"For God's sake go and marry somebody."

"You're no advertisement for marriage, are you?"

"Neither are you."

Later when she thought that one over and understood it, she had half a mind to go back and spit in his face. But as a remark the farewell at least served to confirm her in her understanding of how deeply she hated him; and even more than that—how much they hated each other.

CHAPTER NINE

Runways Travel was boring but undemanding. Despite what she had told Daddy she travelled up to it every day for a bit, and then the manager's wife found her a room which was good but expensive. The manager's wife produced plays for a small amateur group and persuaded Sophy to act but she wasn't any better than Toni. She went out with boys a few times and fended them off from the boring sex stuff. Really what she liked was to lie in front of the television and watch programmes indifferently, advertisements or even the Open University, and let it all go by her. She went to the flicks sometimes, usually with a boy and once with Mabel, the lanky blonde who worked next to her, but without much enjoyment. Sometimes she wondered why nothing mattered and why she felt she could let her life trickle out of her hand if she wanted to, but most often she did not even wonder. The thing at the mouth of her tunnel brandished a pretty girl who smiled and flirted and even sounded earnest now and then—"Yes I *do* see what you mean! We're destroying the world!" But the thing at the mouth of the tunnel said without sound—*as if I cared*.

Someone—Daddy? a cleaning woman?—sent on a postcard from Toni. This time the print round the picture was Arab writing. All Toni said was, "I (and then she had crossed out the I) We need you!!" Nothing else. Sophy put it up on the mantelpiece of her bedsitter and forgot all about it. She was seventeen and not to be fooled by the pretence that they were everything to each other.

A ponderously respectable person began to visit her desk and ask questions about voyages and flights she suspected he had no intention of taking. At his third visit he asked her to come out with him and she did in an exhausted kind of way since it was what was expected of a girl who is seventeen and pretty. He was Roland Garrett, and after the first two times she went out with him—once to the flicks and once to a disco where they didn't dance because he couldn't—he said she should take a room in his mother's house. It would be cheaper. It was. She got it almost for nothing. When she asked Roland why it was so cheap he said his mother was like that. He was protecting a girl, that was all. It seemed to Sophy that the protecting came from Mrs Garrett but she did not say so. Mrs Garrett was a haggard widow with dyed brown hair and little substance to her body other than its skeleton. She stood in the open doorway of Sophy's room, leaning against the doorpost with her skinny arms folded and a dead fag-end hanging from one corner of her mouth.

"I expect you have trouble being so sexy dear, don't you?"

Sophy was folding underwear in a drawer.

"What trouble?"

There was a long pause then, which Sophy did not feel inclined to break. Mrs Garrett broke it instead.

"Roland's very steady you know. Very steady indeed."

Mrs Garrett had large eye-hollows that looked as if they had been charred. Her eyes, deeply set in them, seemed extra bright, extra liquid by contrast. She put up a finger and touched one hollow delicately. She elaborated.

"In the civil service dear. He has very good prospects."

Sophy understood why she had got the room for next to nothing. Mrs Garrett did her best to thrust them together and quite soon Sophy had shared his narrow bed with that freedom which stemmed from the pill; and he performed correctly as if it were a bit of civil service work or bank business or duty. But he seemed to enjoy himself, though as usual there wasn't much in it for Sophy. Mrs Garrett began to keep on at Sophy to consider herself engaged. It was fantastic. She saw that Roland couldn't get himself a girl and his mum had to do it for him. Being tied to Roland with his prospects was a thought that made her shudder and giggle. Of course there was a bit of warm pleasure in it, and on her side a faintly pleasurable contempt for them both, as she said to herself, putting words to what wouldn't really go into them. Roland had a car and they looked at places and pubs and she said why not this new thing, hang gliding, you know. He said I'd never let you do a thing like that it's dangerous. She said of course not I mean you. However, he taught her to drive, more or less, complete with L-plates; and he wanted to meet her father.

142

Amused, she took him to Sprawson's and of course it was Daddy's day in London. So they went through to the stables. Roland displayed a kind of automatic interest in the layout as if he were an architect or archaeologist.

"It'll have been for the coachman and the grooms and ostlers. You see? They must have built it before the canal because now you couldn't get a coach out. That's why the house went downhill."

"Downhill? Our house?"

"There'll have been other stables along there—"

"They're just warehouses for storing things. When I was little there used to be a big ironmonger's. Frankley's, I think."

"What's beyond that door?"

"Towpath and canal. And the Old Bridge just along with the dirtiest loo in town."

Roland looked at her sternly.

"You shouldn't say things like that."

"Sorry, dad. But I live—lived here you know. Me and my sister. Come and see." She led the way up the narrow stairs.

"Your father could do this place up and let it as a cottage."

"It's our place. Mine and Toni's."

"Tony?"

"Antonia. My sister."

He peered about.

"And this place was yours."

"Belongs to both of us—belonged to both of us."

"Belonged?"

"She hasn't been home for ages. Don't even know where she is."

"All these places where pictures were stuck up!"

"She had a religious thing. Jesus and all that. It was *so* funny. Christ!"

"And you?"

"We aren't alike."

"Twins, though."

"How did you know?"

"You told me."

"Did I?"

Roland was picking over the pile on the table.

"What are these? Girlish treasures?"

"Don't men have treasures?"

"Not this sort."

"That's not a doll. It's a glove puppet. Fingers in here. I used to do this a lot. Sometimes I felt—"

"Felt what?"

"It doesn't matter. I made this thing in pottery. It rocks all the time because I didn't get the bottom quite flat. All the same, they fired it. To encourage me, Miss Simpson said. I never made any more. Too boring. It does for tidying things into."

Roland picked out a tiny pearl-handled knife with a blade of soft silver folded into it. She took it from him and when she opened the blade to show him, the whole thing was still no more than four inches long.

"This is for protecting my honour. It's the right size."

"And you don't know where."

"Where what?"

"Toni. Your sister."

"Politics. She got politics the way she got Jesus."

"What's in that cupboard?"

"Skeletons. Family skeletons."

All the same, he opened the cupboard door just as if she had told him he could; and that pointless freedom annoyed her so that somewhere in her mind a question was asking itself—why is he here? Why do I put up with him? But by that time he was pawing all her old dresses, even the ballet one, and all still faintly perfumed. He took hold of a handful of frills, then suddenly turned to her.

"Sophy—"

"Oh not now—"

All the same, he put his arms round her and began making swooning noises. She sighed inwardly but laid her arms round his neck since she had found that in this business it was less bother to comply than to exercise will. She wondered resignedly what the order of service would be this time and of course it proved to be Roland's usual routine, what you might call his ritual. He tried to put her on the divan and at the same time remove both their essential clothing without interrupting the kind of swooning eagerness he thought most seductive. She was obedient, since he was relatively young and strong, passably good to look at, with wide, flat shoulders and a flat stomach. Yet even so as she complied, somewhere or other the question was asking itself—as

144

if *this* was murmuring from where it lay ambushed, even in daylight, at the mouth of the tunnel—a question concerning life which they said was so important, you must live your life, you only have one life to live, et cetera—life so trivial if it must be organized round such pointless activities as Antonia's Jesus or politics or ponies or this grunting and heaving. So she lay, clamped down by flesh and gristle and bone. The thing was faceless, no more than a mop of hair shaking by her left shoulder. Now and then the mop paused, turned into a puzzled face for a moment or two and went back to the shaking mop again.

"I do what you want, don't I?"

"There's more to it than that—"

And he set to again, if anything, with a more determined energy. So lying there with his weight on her she tried to find out what more there was to it. The weight was—pleasant. The movement was natural and—pleasant. Just so, even the varying degrees of obedience she had experienced with the old man in the big car had been pleasant in some way, like the money; a kind of entry into an area not of secrecy but—outrage. And this prolonged and rhythmic activity about which there was so much talk and round which such a—social dance—was organized? This—ludicrous—intimacy which must be sort of intended since the parts fitted so well? and Roland, irritating Roland, and suddenly exasperating Roland was moving faster and faster as if this were some sort of athletic activity, a private dance after the public one. There *was* sensation, no doubt of that; and she made some words in her head to describe that sensation which surely would be of more interest, more intensity, with a different head to shake by her shoulder.

The words pleased her so much that she said them aloud.

"A faint, ring-shaped pleasure."

"What?"

He collapsed on her, gasping, and angry.

"You meant to put me off—and when I was—and for you, too!"

"But I—"

"For Godssake, girl—"

Some deep rage boiled out of her. Her right hand found it still held the familiar shape of the little knife. She jabbed it fiercely into Roland's shoulder. Distinctly she felt the skin resist, then puncture and give way as a separate substance from the flesh

145

into which the blade slid, a meaty moment—Roland gave a howl, then jerked away and went bending and doubling up round the room cursing and groaning with one hand clapped to his shoulder. She lay still, spread on the divan and felt inside her the breaking of the skin and the smooth slide of the blade. She held the tiny thing up before her eyes. There was a thin, red smear on it.

Not mine. His.

Something strange was happening. The feeling from the blade was expanding inside her was filling her, filling the whole room. The feeling became a shudder then an unstoppable arching of her body. She cried out through her clenched teeth. Unsuspected nerves and muscles took charge and swept her forward in contraction after contraction towards some pit of destroying consummation into which she plunged.

Then for a timeless time there was no Sophy. No *this*. Nothing but release, existing, impossibly by itself.

"I'm still bleeding!"

Sophy came back, sighing gustily, drowsily. She got her eyes open. He was kneeling by the bed now, hand still clapped to his shoulder. He whispered:

"I feel faint."

She giggled then found herself in a yawn.

"So do I—"

He took his hand from his shoulder and peered into the palm.

"Oh. Oh."

She could see his shoulder now. The wound was so small and faint and blue. The blood had come out mostly from the pressure of his palm. By contrast with the tiny puncture there was so much of him, such muscle, such a silly, square, male face. She felt almost affectionate in her contempt.

"Have the bed for a bit. No. Not Toni's. Mine."

She got off it and he lay there, hand once more covering his shoulder. She dressed and sat for a while in the old armchair that they had talked of re-covering but of course had never re-covered. Stuffing was still coming out of one arm. Roland began to whiffle and snore but faintly as if he had swooned in his sleep. Sophy returned to contemplating the upheaval in her own body that had changed so much, lighted up so much, calmed so much down. Orgasm. That was what the sex lectures called it, what they had all talked about, written about, sung about. Only

146

no one had said what a help a knife would be—kinky?

All at once a world fell into place. It was all part of—a corollary? Extension?—of that axiom discovered when sitting in a desk ages and ages ago. It was all part of being simple. With *their* films and books and things; with *their* great newspaper stories of hideous happenings that kept the whole country entranced for weeks at a time—oh yes, of course, all outraged and indignant like Roland, and perhaps all frightened like Roland—but all unable to stop reading, looking, going with the feel of the blade sliding in, the rope, the gun, the pain—unable to stop reading, listening, looking—

The pebble or the knife to the hand. To act simply. Or to extend simplicity into the absolute of being weird whether being weird meant anything or not—as it must when magic efforts *fester* with dirt—

To be on the other side from all the silly pretence. To be.

Roland made a honking noise, then sat up.

"My shoulder!"

"It's nothing."

"I must get one, quick."

"Get what?"

"Anti-tet."

"Anti-what?"

"Tetanus. Lockjaw. Oh Christ. Injection. And—"

"Of all the—!"

But it was what he did. She only just managed to get a seat in his car, he was so preoccupied and violent.

"What happened when you were a boy if you fell down?"

But he was too busy driving. He took his large and violated body to the hospital not caring whether she came or not. He came back from the room where it had been punctured—more expertly perhaps—and slid in a dead faint to the floor. When he had recovered a bit, he drove her back in silence to his mother's house and went into his room without a word.

Sophy mutinied. She went out by herself, back to the disco called The Dirty Disco, which was supposed to be a joke, but it was actually filthy. Even her jeans and the sweatshirt she had pulled on with BUY ME stencilled on it seemed sweet by comparison. The noise was solid but she had not been there for more than a few seconds when a young man pushed through the dancers

147

and pulled her to her feet. He proved to be everything, marvellous, inventive, and oh so strong without thinking about it; and he lifted them to a level where Sophy discovered she was marvellous, too. Soon there was a space round them so that in their twoness they were wilder and wilder, going from one extravagance to the next endlessly. All the place began to applaud so that there was as much clapping and cheering as music, except the beat of course, the beat in the floor. When the beat stopped they stood looking at each other, panting. Then he muttered *see you* and went back to his table where there was another man, and a nignog grabbed her and dragged her into the dance. When he let her go she went looking for the young man and they met half-way like old friends and he shouted to her (his first words!): "Two minds without a single thought." It seemed the sun rose or something. This time, by an agreement that neither of them needed mention, they put virtuosity on one side and shouted their whispered inquiries at each other. She glimpsed the other man sitting at the table but she knew this one, Gerry, oh yes, this one was no more queer than she was and everything had happened at once.

He shouted.

"How's your father?"

"My father?"

As she said that, the beat stopped—stopped more suddenly than Gerry was able to—so that his reply was shouted into the silence.

"The bloke you were with the other night—the elderly gentleman in the lounge suit!"

When he heard himself he clapped both hands over his ears but took them away at once.

"Oh my God! But what's a girl like you, etc.? There—they're off as the monkey said. We fit like the hand and the glove."

"Mm?"

"Consummate."

"Well of course."

"Promise?"

"Necessary?"

"Still. Bird in the hand, you know. No? Not tonight Josephine?"

"It's not that. Only—"

Some sort of necessary preparation. Wash Roland off me. Wash them all off me.

"Only?"

"Not tonight. But I promise. Faithfully. Cross my heart. There."

So they sat and he gave her his address and they sat and at last Gerry said he was falling asleep and they parted for the time; and only when they had parted did she remember they had no special date for meeting. A black man followed her back to the house so she rang the bell since the door was not only locked but bolted. After the briefest of pauses Mrs Garrett unlocked and unbolted and let her in; and glanced across at the black man loitering on the other pavement. After that she followed Sophy up to her room and stood in the doorway, not leaning against the doorpost but upright this time.

"You're learning, aren't you?"

Sophy said nothing but looked back good-humouredly at the eyes gleaming so liquidly in their charred cups. Mrs Garrett licked her thin lips.

"It's one thing with Roland. Boys will be boys. Men, I mean. And then, he'll settle down. I know things are different nowadays—"

"I'm tired. Goodnight."

"You could do worse, you know. Much worse. Settle down. I wouldn't say anything about him."

"Him?"

"The nig."

Sophy burst out laughing.

"Him! But after all—why not?"

"Why not indeed! I've never heard—"

"And then—I *do* like to be able to see what I'm doing."

"You like to *see!*"

"Just a joke. Look. I'm tired. Really."

"Have you and Roland had a tiff?"

"He went to the hospital."

"He never! Why? On a Sunday? Was he—"

Sophy scrabbled in her shoulder bag. She found the little knife and took it out. She began to laugh but thought better of it.

"He got cut. With my fruit-knife. Look. So he went to get a what d'you call it. Anti-tet."

"Cut?"

"He thought it might be dirty."

"He always was—but what was he doing with a thing like that?"

149

The words *peeling fruit of course* formed in Sophy's mind and rose to her lips. But looking at those liquidly glistening eyes she understood suddenly how easy it was to deny them anything—any entry. They could not look in. All this Sophy in here was secure. Those eyes in Ma Garrett's face were no more than reflectors. All they saw was what light gave them. You could stand, allowing your own eyes to receive and bounce back the light; and the two people behind, each floating invisibly behind her reflectors need not meet, need give nothing. Need say nothing. All simple.

But then, still looking, she saw more. In immediate contradiction, whether it was from knowledge of the world up to that moment, whether it was to be read in the subtlest changes in the woman's stance or in her breathing or in the arrangement of her face, Sophy saw more than those twin reflectors intended. She saw the words approach Ma Garrett's lips, *You'd better leave*, and hang there, inhibited by other thoughts, other words, *What would Roland say, she might just do, and if he's hooked on her*—

Sophy waited, remembering simplicity. Do nothing. Wait.

Ma Garrett did not precisely slam the door, but closed it with such an elaborate absence of noise it was just as good an indication of anger. After a moment or two, listening to quick steps on the stairs, Sophy let her breath out. She went to the window and there was the nig still standing on the other pavement and looking across inscrutably at the house; but as she watched, he glanced to one side then ran away round the corner. A police car cruised down the street. Sophy stood for a while, then undressed slowly and remembered the fullness, the clearing out of want and urgency like the fall of a great arch; and it was easier to give the credit for it not to Roland at all but to nameless masculinity. Or if it must have a name, give it Gerry's name, Gerry's face. There was tomorrow.

CHAPTER TEN

All that day it seemed to Sophy that nothing could be sillier than having to tell people what it would cost them to fly to Bangkok or how to get to Margate from Aberdeen; or how to get from London to Zürich with a stop-off somewhere, or how to take a car to Austria—not only silly as could be but more and more boring as the day dribbled away. When the job was done she hurried back to the house and watched the clock till it was just possible the disco would be open and away she went. Every now and then she ran a few steps, as if afraid she would be too late rather than too early. But Gerry wasn't there. And Gerry wasn't there. And Gerry still wasn't there. At last she danced a bit and fended off mechanically with a smile like on a statue. She saw it was all intolerable, all quite, quite impossible too; and short of being weird—how the old thoughts could come back!—if a man won't be where you want him, there is only one thing to do.

Next morning, instead of going to work she went straight to the address that Gerry had given her. He woke, late and frowsty, to hear her at the door. He fumbled to let her in with eyes half-shut. She edged in sideways with her load of belongings in shopping bags. She had an apology for her own untidiness on the tip of her tongue but abandoned it when she saw the room and smelt it.

"Phew!"

Despite himself he was ashamed.

"Sorry about the mess. I haven't shaved either."

"Don't shave."

"You want me without or with?"

It was a hangover. With a kind of automatic libidinosity he reached out at her but she swung a carrier bag in the way.

"Not now, Gerry. I've come to stay."

151

"Christ. I must go to the loo. And shave. Oh hell. Make some coffee will you?"

She got busy in the dirty corner where the sink was. It could be considered a flat if you shut one eye and—she thought this as she cleared a space for the kettle—if you could shut your nose. They said men were less sensitive to smells anyway.

Gerry himself cleaned up astonishingly well. When he was dressed as well as shaved, she sat on the chair and he sat on the unmade bed and they looked at each other over the mugs of coffee. He was satisfactorily taller than she was but on the slight side and loosely put together, with a head and face that in daylight was—well, pretty was wrong and handsome wouldn't do either, so why bother? Rhythm—and as if he saw the word in her head, having looked in right past the reflectors—he began a sort of toneless whistling, the sketch of a tune and one finger beat on the side of his coffee mug—rhythm was everything to him, which was why—

"Gerry, I'm out of work."

"Sacked?"

"Left. Too boring."

The sketched tune stopped, to be replaced by a whistle of surprise that did achieve some tone. Overhead, a brief argument flared and there were a couple of thumps then comparative silence.

"Desirable neighbourhood. Hang on a moment."

Gerry put down his coffee, pulled out a cassette player and switched it on. The air swingled. Relieved, he took up the rhythm, nodding his head, eyes closed for the time being, ripe lips pursed; lips that would—that would avoid the four-letter word which she never used herself so that this could not be pair-bonding as with ducks, was it?

"What bird were you with, then?"

"No bird, dear thing. Chap I know."

His eyes flicked open, large, dark, and he smiled at her round them. What girl could pass up that smile, those eyes, that dark hair with its forward flop—?

"Yeah?"

"Fairly thick night."

"Is that all?"

"Word of an officer and gentleman."

"So *that's*—"

"That's. Care to see my commission? Once you have it, you have it even when you've declined a posting. Second lieutenant. Imagine being shot at in Ulster. Paff!"

"Have you been shot at? Really?"

"Well. I would've been if I'd stayed in."

"I wish I'd seen you in uniform."

He pulled her to the bed and hugged her. She hugged him back and kissed him. His gestures became more intimate.

"Not now, Gerry. It's too early. I wouldn't be fit for anything later."

"There's nothing to do later. Not till they open."

All the same he took his hands off her.

"Look, dear thing. You'll have to sign on for social security. But I was looking to you for the occasional hand-out."

She doted down at him in recognition of what they shared right from those first few seconds; the complete acceptance of what each was; or what each thought the other was.

"We'd better not let on we're living together."

"Oh. So we're living together are we?"

"Sheer gain, mathematically."

"And you could always earn a bit on the side."

"Mm?"

"Red lamp in the window."

"Too much like work. I've—well. What about you?"

"Dodgy market. Know any rich old ladies?"

"No."

"Used to be loads of them. We were talking about it last night. Nowadays they're all poor old ladies. Unfair to junior officers. No, dear thing. It's social security or paff paff."

"Paff?"

"Mercenary. Make you at least a captain if you can produce evidence of being an O and G in herself's forces. Loads of lolly."

"That's all very well for you—"

"Oh is it my God? Not so hot if you get wounded or captured. Time was, you used not to get wounded or captured. Nigs had a decent sense of who was who. Now you get shot like those poor bastards. Then again, I've got prospects, sort of—no. I'm not telling you, sweet thing, chubby prattler."

She took him by the arms and shook him.

153

"No secrets!"

"You trying to get rid of me? You need my social security as much as I need yours."

She collapsed, giggling on his chest. The words popped out.

"Thank God I don't have to pretend any more!"

For a day or two, what with the Employment Exchange and trying to make Gerry's flat habitable for two people, she had some time away from him and spent it thinking about him. No indeed, they did not, must not use that four-letter word, the many-splendoured, but all the same, when you are young and have told yourself what nonsense so much is, you cannot help an occasional glance at the current situation and say to yourself—is this it? You examine the curious fact that this twin, this discovered twin, could outrage and yet not annoy. There were those moments when a funny struck them both and they fell towards each other, hugging and giggling and not needing to say anything—also those moments when a smile round those big eyes, or fall of a lock of hair on his forehead could be a sweetness in the stomach—oh, he was sweet!

And there standing at the pigeon-hole, with the faceless servant of the unemployed public behind it, her soul said aloud, "You are sweet!" only to come plummeting down as the face flashed into an amazed smile then blushed scarlet. Moreover, she thought, as she handed in the completed form, moreover I know he doesn't work because he can't work, it's not in him. How can a child work? Now he has all of me and my body, he is waiting without knowing it for the box of bricks or the train set—

The fourth night, Gerry told her about his friend Bill.

"Quaint character. He was shot at as it happens. They got his C.O. so he opened up and knocked off half a dozen of them."

"He really shot people?"

"So they slung him out! Imagine! What in hell do they think soldiers are for?"

"I don't know what you're talking about."

"He said it was tops. Smasheroo. Stands to reason, doesn't it? All those millions—wouldn't be done if it wasn't natural to do it. For God's sake. Christ. I mean!"

"Oh you—yes, yes!"

"Bloody silly the whole thing."

154

"This friend of yours, Bill—"

"He's a bit thick mind you. But then you don't want privates to go thinking, do you? Perfect other rank, I'd have said. End up in a red coat at Chelsea. And then they go and chuck him out!"

"But *why?*"

"Didn't I tell you? He enjoyed it you see. He likes killing. The natural man. So they told him he didn't ought not to have done it, as he put it. Said he supposed they thought he should have had tears in his fucking eyes. Pardon his French."

"He sounds like Uncle Jim. Was he an Aussie?"

"British to the backbone."

"Fun to meet him."

"Well you will. He's not a handsome chap like me, my sweet, but remember whose doggie you are."

"I bite."

So she did.

They met Bill in a pub. He had some money, only just enough for the three of them and he was vague about the source. He was much older than Gerry but treated him with awful respect and even called him "sir" once or twice, which made Sophy smile. He was physically rather like Gerry, but with less forehead and more jaw.

"Gerry's told me about you."

Bill sat very still. Gerry broke in.

"Nothing you'd mind old sport. That's all over—"

"Of course he doesn't mind, do you Bill?"

"She really all right sir, Gerry?"

"What's it like, Bill?"

"What's what like Miss, Sophy?"

"Killing people."

There was a long silence. Gerry gave a sudden shudder then took a long drink without stopping. Bill surveyed her, stonily.

"They give us ammo."

"Bullets, you'd call them, dear thing. Live rounds."

"I mean—was it sort of led up to? Was everything arranged, so that when you did it, it was like finding a stone ready for throwing—kind of?"

"We was briefed."

Now it was her turn to be silent for a while. What do I want to know? I want to know about pebbles and the hissing in the

155

transistor and the running down, running down, endless running down!

"I'm sick of all the things they say. Pretending life is what it isn't. I want—I want to know!"

"Nothing to know, dear thing. What is. Bed and board."

"That's right sir, Gerry. You got to look at the facts."

"And what happens?"

"Bill. I think she means when you knock one off."

Then there was more silence. Staring at him, Sophy saw a faint smile come in Bill's face. The direction of his gaze altered. Slid over her body, came back till he glanced at her eyes again. Then he looked away. She knew, with a tiny prickle of the flesh, what was happening. She said the words inside her head. *He fancies me!* Oh how much he fancies me!

Bill was looking at Gerry.

"Tarts is all the same."

He looked back at her with the faint smile of his awareness round the mouth.

"You squeeze, see? Pip! He falls down."

"All fall down, dear thing. Nothing to it. Ringa ring."

"Does it hurt? Does it take long? Is there any—is there much—"

The smile widened into one of more accurate comprehension.

"Not if it's a neat shot, see? One wriggled. I give him another. Finee."

"It's a highly technical matter, Sophy dear. Don't trouble your pretty head. Leave it to us splendid male beasts. Yours not to reason why."

Bill was nodding and grinning into her face as if they understood each other. Oh how he fancies me; and no you don't, she said to herself, not with a bargepole as they say, you dumb animal!

She looked away.

It soon became evident that the two men had not met merely to drink. After a certain amount of allusive talk, they stopped, with Bill looking at her again. Gerry patted her shoulder.

"Honeybunch. Wouldn't we care to go and powder the little nose?"

"Powder your own, dear thing!"

"Haw," said Bill with his best imitation of a debby voice. "Powdah your own. Sorry, miss. Sophy, I mean."

156

But she went, for all that, because it didn't much matter and she smelt a secret to be worked out later.

The next day Gerry said he had a date and he was very excited and shivering a bit. That was when she found out that he was on pills, tiny black things that could be hidden under a thumbnail or lost in a crack between two boards. He came back very late at night. He was white and exhausted and she made a joke of it, saying it must have been some bird, *some* bird he'd been with. But she knew what it was all about when he slipped a gun, real or model, back in the drawer. She had sex with him and ended in their single bed with his head on her naked breast. All the same, he was Gerry again next day and produced a wad of notes he said he'd won at the dogs, having forgotten, apparently, that she had seen the gun. So it all came out. He and Bill did a job now and then. They had a high old time for a day or two. Once they met Bill and his current girlfriend. She was a card, Daisy, a punk, six-inch heels, cheap trouser-suit, dead white face, dead black eye make-up, straw hair like a rick, plastered down on one side and sticking straight up on the other. It seemed to Sophy that one meeting was enough, but it turned out she had something to do with Gerry's black pills.

Gerry took her to another party with no Daisy and no Bill, but some very odd types. It was a party in a real flat with several rooms. There was much music and chat and drink and they went just the two of them, as Gerry said Bill's face wouldn't fit. He meant her to be debby and straight because of the man he was contacting, but things went wrong in a very odd way. Somehow as the noise increased into a party roar some of the people began playing a silly game with a piece of paper with a blotch of ink on it. You had to say how many things it was like and some of the answers were wonderfully dirty and witty. But when Sophy had her turn she looked at the black shape in the middle of the paper and nothing happened at all. Then without any kind of intermission she found she was lying on the sofa and staring at the ceiling and there was no party roar and people were standing round and looking down at her. She got up on one elbow and saw the woman who was giving the party standing by the open door of the flat and talking to someone who was outside it.

"Nothing my dear Lois, nothing at all."

"But that dreadful screaming and screaming!"

157

Gerry took her away, explaining that she had fainted from heat, and it was a day or two before she worked the whole thing out and knew why her throat was sore. But that night, after they had left the party, Gerry said they needed some calm. So the next evening they sat, drinking quietly in a pub, and watching the telly that was fastened high up in one corner. Indeed, Sophy, puzzling over the darkness inside her, began to find it a bit too quiet and suggested they should move on. But Gerry said to hang on. He was watching the box intently and smiling.

"Christ!"

"What gives?"

"Fido! My old friend Fido!"

It was indoor athletics. A young man bulging with sinew and muscles was performing on the high rings. To Sophy he seemed like every other young competitor in the hall; but perhaps that was because he wore a face of such stern dedication.

"Fido! He was in with me—"

"Was?"

"Teacher now. PT. Some posh school or other. Wandicott."

"I know Wandicott. Knew of Wandicott. It's out our way, beyond Greenfield."

"Oh good show, Fido! Splendid fellow! Dear God he's sweating like the Sunday roast."

"What do they do it for?"

"Showing off to their girls. Winning prizes. Getting promotion. Health, wealth, fame—show's over."

Sophy persuaded Gerry and Bill to let her help. Daisy didn't come, didn't want to come, it wasn't her scene. They did three shops and came away with just over two hundred pounds. The risk seemed appalling to Sophy and she persuaded them to try Paki shops. It was certainly job-satisfaction for a bit. Pakis dwindled when Gerry pointed his fake gun at them. Sophy improved their technique by making Bill tell them that the organization would bomb the shop if there was any trouble. It was fun to see how the Pakis bundled money into the bag as if it was sweets or incense. They couldn't get rid of it fast enough.

Sophy did some arithmetic with it, putting risk on one side of an equation and the money on the other. She talked to Gerry in bed.

"It's no good, you know."

He yawned in her ear.

"What isn't?"

"Robbing the till."

"Old soul! Have you got religion?"

"Too much chance of being caught."

"One in a hundred."

"And when you've done a hundred shops?"

There was a long pause.

"I mean—who's got the money? The real money, I mean. The stuff to set you up for life, set you free, go where you like, do what you like—"

"Not banks my poppet. They've learnt too much. Advanced technology."

"Arabs."

She felt him shaking with laughter.

"Invasion is just not on. We'd need all three services. Good night, gorgeous."

She put her lips close to his ear and giggled at the sheer outrage of her idea.

"Where do they send their children to school?"

This time the pause was even longer. Gerry broke it at last.

"Christ all bleeding mighty. As Bill would say. Christ!"

"Wandicott School, Gerry. Where your friend is. It's stiff with them. Princes—the lot."

"My God. You—you really are—"

"Your friend—what was it—Fido? Gerry—we could grab a boy and hide him and ask—we could ask a million, a billion and they'd pay it, they'd have to pay—they'd have to pay or we'd—Gerry kiss me right now yes feel me fuck me we'd have a prince in our power to bargain with and if that's good more he'd be hidden and tied up and gagged and if oh if ah nothing nothing nothing on and on and on and on oh oh oh—"

So then there was another time of lying side by side, she with her arm across the chest of a Gerry who seemed wrecked and confused in the darkness. Then when he did breathe evenly she shook him—shook him hard.

"I wasn't joking or pretending. It wasn't just a thinking to come with. I mean it. Not this fiddling with shops! We might as well be stealing milk bottles!"

"It's too much."

159

"It isn't too much for us, Gerry. It's just enough for me. We'll be caught if we go on doing shops because it's small. But this—We need one big thing, a thing so monstrous no one would bother to defend against it—"

"It's too much. And I want to kip."

"I want to talk. I'm not going on with shops. That's flat. If you want me, you'll—We could be rich for life!"

"Never."

"Look Gerry. At least we can go down and see what the school's like. Meet your friend Fido. Get him in, perhaps. We could go and see how things are—"

"Not bloody likely."

"We'll drive down there and see what's possible."

"No we won't."

There was a long silence which she did not choose to break this time. Then when he was breathing evenly again, she spoke to herself, silently.

Oh yes we will, my sweet. You'll see!

CHAPTER ELEVEN

They parked the car where the tree-covered track led up to the crest of the downs. They walked up and found that the old road along the top was deserted and windy. Clouds and bright sun succeeded each other, like takes in a film, across the rounded greennesses and indigo horizon. Nothing moved but the clouds. Even the sheep seemed to prefer motionlessness. A mile ahead of them the downs rose to a blunt top. The track led over the top then on, bump after bump away into the remote centre of the country. Sophy soon stopped.

"Wait a minute."

He turned to her, grinning. He had plenty of colour and the hair was flopped over his forehead. She thought dizzily, as she got her breath back, that he had never been so beautiful.

"Not a natural walker are you, my beloved?"

"Your legs are longer."

"Some people call this fun."

"Not me. I wonder why they think so."

"Beauties of nature. You are a beauty of nature and so—"

She twisted out of his arms.

"We're doing a job! Can't you keep your mind on it?"

They walked on, side by side, a country-visiting pair. Gerry pointed to the concrete stand at the top.

"That's a base for triangulation."

"I know."

He looked at her in surprise. But unfolded the map.

"We spread this out on the plate and look round."

"Why?"

"Sheer pleasure. Everybody does it."

"Why?"

161

"Actually I *am* enjoying it quite a lot, you know. Takes me back to all that 'Forward men!' and so on."

"What do we look round at?"

"We identify six counties."

"Can we?"

"It's always done. Great British tradition identifying counties. Never mind old thing, I won't press it. Notice anything about the air?"

"Should I?"

"But they've written whole books about it!" And standing by the concrete pillar, his hair and the map fluttering, he began to sing, " 'Give to me the life I love, let the lave go by me—' "

From deep inside her she was shaken by a gust of sheer rage.

"For God's sake Gerry! Don't you know who—" She caught herself up and went on quickly. "I'm edgy. Can't you see? You don't know what it's like to be—Sorry."

"OK. Look, Sophy. This isn't going to work, is it?"

"You said. You agreed."

"A recce."

They stared at each other across the pillar. It seemed to her that something, the air perhaps, was reminding him of other places and other people. He was firm and drawing back almost as if he might—escape.

The man in the van. *My will is stronger than his.*

"Gerry dear. We aren't committed to anything. But we've spent three days on the job already. We know he uses the right of way and that we'll meet him there by accident. We'll make contact, that's all. Argue later."

He still stared at her from under his fluttering hair.

"One thing at a time."

She moved round the pillar and squeezed his arm.

"Now then, map-reader. Where is it?"

"The right of way leads down from this place—see the dotted line? Down there is what you saw from the other side of the valley yesterday. He brings the boys up this dotted line towards us then turns to his left and circles back. Healthy country run."

"Just about right. Come on."

The right of way led down at the side of a wire fence that seemed to stretch without a break into clumps of trees in the bottom of the valley. Sophy pointed to a huddle of grey roofs.

162

"That's it."

"Over there on the other side where the trees are is where we were yesterday."

"And there they are!"

"Christ yes. Dead on time. And there he is. Tell him a mile off. Well. He is a mile off or near enough. Notice his high-stepping action? Come on."

The boys were coming up from the hollow with its glimpsed leaden roofs. They were a string of bobbing red objects, small boys in some sort of red sports outfit, and a larger bit of red bounced up and down in pursuit of them. The whole string trotted up the hill and the patch of red behind it became a wiry young man in a scarlet tracksuit who ran with an exaggerated knees-up action and now and then shouted at the boys in front of him. Gerry and Sophy stopped and the boys ran past, looking at them and grinning. The young man stopped too and stared.

"Gerry!"

"Fido—we saw you on the box!"

The young man called Fido gave a bellow that halted the boys. He and Gerry slapped each other's backs, punched ribs and exchanged badinage. Fido was introduced. Fido was, or had been, Lieutenant Masterman but pointed out at once that he answered to the name of Fido or Bow Wow or Doggie but Fido mostly.

"Even the boys," he said triumphantly. "They all call me Fido."

Though Fido was only of average height he was splendidly developed. He had less head than face and his features were weathered by exposure. Sophy knew, from what Gerry had said, that Fido's chest had been expanded by weight-lifting, his legs by assiduity on the trampoline and his balance by hair-raising exploits on any rock face within reach. His hair was dark and curly, his forehead low and his manner imperceptive.

"Fido is a positively national athlete," said Gerry, with what Sophy recognized as malice. "You'd never believe his snatch."

"Snatch?"

"Weight-lifting. D'you know how much?"

"I'm sure it was enormous," cried Sophy, curving at Fido. "It must be marvellous to be able to lift as much as that!"

Fido agreed that yes it was rather marvellous. Sophy emitted

163

some perfume at him and allowed all the lines to stretch in his direction. There was a mutual expansion of pupils. Fido's eyes were rather small and the expansion improved them. He told the boys to stay where they were but jump about a bit. Gerry said they'd seen the name of the school on the map and having seen Fido on the box thought that they might look him up—and now here he was!

"Keep warm, you men," shouted Fido. "We'll be going on in a jiffy."

"You must be an inspiration to them, Mr Masterman."

"Fido, please. I come when you whistle."

He danced, fisted the air a bit then gave an ejaculatory laugh that really was rather like a bark. He went on to say that she could whistle for him when she liked and it would be a pleasure.

Gerry broke in.

"How's the job, then, Fido?"

"Schoolmastering? Well, you can see I manage to keep fit on it. Do a lot of this stuff. Of course, it's not the same as proper road-work. You can't have the little men really going at it. So most days I carry weights. Besides—" He glanced round them cautiously, inspected the downs, bare of all but sheep and boys. "I have to keep a careful eye on them you know."

Sophy trilled.

"Oh Fido! You're stuck away here at the end of nowhere—"

He leaned towards her, reached out a hand to grasp her arm, then thought better of it.

"That's just it. You see the little fellow there? No—don't let him know you're looking. Be subtle about it like me. Out of the corner of your eye."

Sophy looked. The little boys were just little boys, that was all, except that three of them were black and two brown. Most were the usual sort of whiteish.

"The one thumping the nig?"

"Careful! He's *royal*!"

"But Fido, how thrilling!"

"His parents are really nice people, Sophy. Of course they don't get down here much together. But she actually spoke to me, you know. She said, 'Build him up, Mr Masterman.' She has a marvellous memory for names. They both have. He follows weight-lifting with keen interest, you know. He said,'What d'you

164

reckon your limit'll be in the snatch?' I tell you, as long as we have them—"

Gerry tapped him on the shoulder and turned him from his exclusive attention.

"And you have another job as well as running the P.T.?"

"I'm not saying, am I? The little men don't know, you see. But it's such a load—why, good Lord, the lad his little highness was toughing up—and take that little brown fellow for example—he's the son of an oil sheik. Got to call him a prince, though of course it's not the same. More like a laird who's struck it lucky when deer-stalking or something. His old man could buy this country."

"I expect he has," said Gerry with uncharacteristic feeling. "Nobody else would."

"You mean his father's really rich, Fido?"

"Billions. Well. Mustn't let the old gluteus maxima get a chill. Sophy, you two—I'm free for a bit round about four. Tea in the village? Scones? Home-made stuff?"

Before Gerry could answer, Sophy accepted.

"Super, Fido!"

"The Copper Kettle then. About half an hour. See you."

"We'll be there."

Fido gave her a last expanded pupil then bounded off up the track. He chased the little boys about and made noises like a dog tormenting cows. The little boys responded with mooing and shrieks of laughter. Fido was evidently popular. Sophy stared after him.

"They actually spend their time lifting up weights?"

"For God's sake, you saw them on the box!"

"So I did."

"Dear thing, you're not into the modern scene."

She saw that for all his twinship he was irritated by the traffic in pupils and she was pleased and amused.

"Don't be dumb, Gerry. It couldn't have happened better."

"I'd forgotten what a thick oaf he is. Christ."

"He's our way in."

"Yours, you mean."

"You agreed to it."

"I'm only just beginning to find out what we've taken on. You heard what he said. They'll have the works here, the complete works! We're probably on tape already."

"I don't believe it." She moved close to him. "You don't know about being invisible, do you?"

"I'm a soldier. Try and find me when I want to hide."

"Not just hiding. I've known it for these last three days. *We're invisible*. No, not because of some magic or other—though perhaps—but anyway; not because of magic; but just *because*. That he's here and you know him. That I can—manage him—Sometimes there are coincidences; but sometimes the arrangement of things is—deliberate. I know about that."

"Well I don't."

"When I was in the travel agency I did a lot of looking-up tables and things, and dates and numbers. I understand them. I really *do* understand them, you see, the way Daddy understands his chess and all that. I'm just not used to putting that kind of knowing into words. Perhaps it won't go anyway. Listen. Those numbers. The girl who was there when I first got there. Well. She was a dim blonde. She was a smasher too. The manager knew how to pick them. Not all that good for business, but why should he worry? You'd have popped your eyes at her, my dear. But she, she was dim. D'you know? I watched her use tables to work out what ten per cent of a bill came to!"

"Just the way she should be. Keep a lot of chaps very happy."

"The point is this. She had to fill in a date and it went, the seventh day of the seventh month of the seventy-seventh year; so it was seven, stroke, seven, stroke, seven, seven. Well. Alice filled it in, looked at it with her bulging great blue eyes, gave her idiotic laugh—the one the manager said was like a bird-trill—he was wet, he couldn't keep his hands off anything; and she said, 'It's quite a coincidence, isn't it?' "

Gerry turned away and began to walk down by the wire.

"So it was."

"But—"

She ran after him, caught his arm and pulled him round.

"Don't you see, dear, my, my lovely—it wasn't! A coincidence comes out of the, the mess things are, the heap, the darkness and you can't tell how—But these four sevens—you could see them coming and wave goodbye to them! It was the system—but coincidences—more than coincidences—"

"Honest to God, Sophy, I don't know what you're on about."

"Everything's running down. Unwinding. We're just—tangles.

166

Everything is just a tangle and it slides out of itself bit by bit towards something that's simpler and simpler—and we can help it. Be a part."

"You've got religion. Or you're up the wall."

"Being good is just another tangle. Why bother? Go on with the disentangling that will happen in any case and take what you can on the way. What it wants, the dark, let the weight fall, take the brake off—"

A truth appeared in her mind. *The way towards simplicity is through outrage.* But she knew he would not understand.

"It's like the collapse of sex."

"Sex, sex, there's nothing like sex! Sex for ever!"

"Oh yes, yes! But not the way you mean—the way everything means, the long, long convulsions, the unknotting, the throbbing and disentangling of space and time on, on, on into nothingness—"

And she was there; without the transistor she was there and could hear herself or someone in the hiss and crackle and roar, the inchoate unorchestra of the lightless spaces.

"On and on, wave after wave arching, spreading, running down, down, down—"

The leaden roofs of the school came back into focus then moved out of it as she stared up into Gerry's worried face.

"Sophy! Sophy! Can you hear me?"

That was why this vast body she inhabited was being moved backwards and forwards; and becoming known now as a girl's body, and man's hands shaking it by the shoulders.

"Sophy!"

She answered him with lips that could hardly move.

"Just a moment can't you? I was speaking to—of—I was someone—"

His hands stilled but held her.

"Take it easy then. Better?"

"Nothing wrong." As the words fell out of her mouth she saw how funny they were and started to giggle. "Nothing wrong at all!"

"We need a drink. My God, it was like—I don't know what it was like!"

"You're so wise, my dear!"

He was peering closely into her face.

167

"I didn't approve one little bit, old soul. It was damned weird, I can tell you."

With that, there was clear daylight, sun, breeze, downs, a known date and place.

"What did you call it?"

"Bloody worrying for a moment."

"You said 'Weird'."

All things flowed together. Power filled her.

"You talked about guards round this place and about tapes. But we're in a special time. They come, you see. It's not that they can't see us. It's that they don't. Why when I was small—It's the tangle untangling, sorting itself, slipping and sliding. You must be simple. That's the real thing."

"I'm beginning to realize you're an oddball. Not sure we ought to go on. There are things I just don't—"

"We'll go on. You'll see."

"Not if I say no. I'm in charge."

"Of course, dear."

"I'll go exactly as far as things are—possible. When we reach the impossible we'll stop. Understand?"

She gave him an especially brilliant smile which he kissed in a protective kind of way. He took her hand and they walked down the wire in silence. Lovers out walking.

The Copper Kettle was empty except for its fake eighteenth-century furniture and fake horse-brasses. Here they sat, viewed indifferently by a cretinous girl, and waited for Fido. He came breathlessly. Gerry played up, acting out sparks of at first amused jealousy; and then, she saw, putting a little more than acting into it. Fido was soon barking. He had brought some photographs with him. One showed him receiving a medal on a rostrum. Sophy saw to her surprise that he had not won the event but come third. Encouraged by her intense interest in his activities he took a sheaf of photographs out of his breast pocket and exposed them to her. Here was Fido, all gleaming muscle and sinew and lifting weights. Here was Fido rock-climbing and suspended, grinning over a hideous gulf. Here was Fido at the trampoline, caught upside-down in mid-air. When Sophy admitted provocatively that she had some small doubt as to the importance of all these activities, Fido simply didn't understand her. Did she mean it was dangerous? A girl might well feel that—

168

Sophy took her cue.

"Oh but it *must* be terribly dangerous!"

Fido meditated.

"Took a tumble rock-climbing."

Gerry spoke nastily from the place where they were ignoring him.

"Wasn't that when you fell on your head?"

Fido responded with a precise catalogue of his injuries. Sophy broke in, hoping to conceal her giggles.

"Oh but it's not fair! Why can't we—?"

Gerry gave a positive guffaw.

"You! Christ!"

But Fido was already pointing out those areas of sport in which he thought female participation was allowable.

"And croquet," said Gerry. "Don't forget croquet."

Fido said he wouldn't; and gave Sophy a conquering look from his expanded pupils. After tea he walked them some way to the bus that would take them to Gerry's car. They received a pressing invitation from him to return; and the fact that it was directed wholly at Gerry was the only false thing about it.

Sophy kissed Fido goodbye so that he barked again and she willed her scent into him. When at last they were alone in the car, Gerry looked at her, half in anger, half in admiration.

"You were half-way up his flies. Christ!"

"He might be useful. He might even come in with us."

"Don't be wet, dear thing. You may be fatal but you can't do miracles."

"Why not?"

"Think you're something out of history, don't you?"

"I don't know any history."

Gerry revved the engine viciously.

"Don't need to. Whore's instinct."

He was silent after that and she considered his point of view. It was, she saw, peculiarly male. Here was Gerry—who would quite calmly suggest she should keep them both by using men and had been serious about it, she was certain—getting worked up by her approach to ridiculous Fido. Brooding on this she found it all rooted in men's need to see. Possible customers were faceless. But Gerry knew Fido.

Two days later they had a letter from Fido repeating his

169

invitation. Gerry was all for ignoring it, they must have been out of their minds. When Sophy said she had to think, she saw Gerry take this as meaning, "I want to do nothing." He patted her, got pilled up and went off with Bill to arrange a job. Sophy rang Fido from a callbox. She said she didn't think she and Gerry should come down. Interrogated insistently by Fido she admitted she had thought they weren't easy together and Gerry had been, well, not difficult but thoughtful. She couldn't bear the idea of breaking up an old friendship that way. No! For her part she would have liked nothing better. In fact—

She refused to be drawn on the fact. But then she heard along the miles of wire how Fido barked as a brilliant idea came to him. He invited her to a meeting in South London where she could watch him lift weights and afterwards they could discuss the situation.

The weight-lifting competition, in which Fido won his section, struck her as so funny that that side of it was almost compensation for the pervading smell. Afterwards Fido, breathing quickly, conveyed to her that he found her exceptionally desirable. She waited for the pass; and it was an invitation to come to the school on parents' day. Sophy, who had expected a straightforward proposition, found this as comic as weight-lifting.

"I'm not a parent."

He explained it was the day when parents saw how agile he had made their little men. She allowed herself to be persuaded and began to suspect that the actual proposition when it came might be a moral one. Married—to a weight-lifter! Fido obviously thought that Gerry once out of sight would be out of mind as well. She listened as he, with a kind of egotistical innocence, displayed his life before her—his grandmother's money, and that line out to the royals on which he placed such weight, intimating that one day he might be able to present her to them, or to one of them, if she agreed to come.

"Mind," he said. "I'm not promising anything. I can only present you if I'm commanded."

So she went to parents' day, conspicuously inconspicuous in a cotton dress and straw hat. No royals were present and this cast a profound gloom over Fido, only lightened by a word or two with Lord Mountstephen, and the Marquis of Fordingbridge. Sophy inspected Fido's bedsitter and found that it resembled an annexe

170

to the gym except for the rows of photographs. She knew now that any idea of getting Fido in with them would be pointless. It was not that he would find it wrong. He would find it dangerous in a way that did not apply to rock-climbing. It would not be his scene. Nor was there any future for his girlfriend or wife. Fido's offer of companionship and sex would be limited to what was unavoidable between the competitions. The sex would be a quick use of the body, healthy when taken in moderation. The only other use he had for a woman was as an audience for his physical perfection. Most masculine of men—how narrow his hips, how tucked in behind him the hard rondures of his bum! How wide his shoulders and glossy his skin!—He had all the narcissism of a woman or a pretty boy. He enjoyed the beauty of his flesh more than Sophy enjoyed the beauty of hers. She knew all this, even while he put his arms round her, and the school drum-and-fife band made noises on the playing fields outside the window and the summery parents drifted round the various exhibitions. Nevertheless, she let him have her on his narrow, bachelor bed, and the exercise was only a little less boring than resisting him. But he had yet another surprise for her, announcing when he had finished that they were engaged. On the way back to London it seemed to her more and more incredible that these valuable children should be so freely available to inspection once you had joined the peculiar club that surrounded them. But she thought to herself—it's simple—I'm inside!

Daisy's bloke came out of jail so Bill had to move on quick. He came to tell them all about it so the three of them held a council of war in Gerry's unkempt, uncleaned room that they called his flat. The last job had been a flop—much danger and little money. The two men were inclined to listen to Sophy if only for the sake of a little harmless fantasy. But when she began to describe the school and suggest routes, Gerry patted her as if she were a child herself.

"Sophy, like I said, they'll have gadgets you just wouldn't believe. For example. You walk along a path. A chopper with a gadget could follow you half an hour after you passed just by the bit of warmth where you'd walked. If you hid in a wood they could spot you by the lovely warmth, yum, yum, of your body. On the screen you'd look like a fire."

"He's right, see? You got to be careful."

171

"Let's plan a smack at a bank, old soul. That's dicing with death, but not *absolument* daft."

"But this is new, don't you see? And who cares about gadgets? Once we'd got him—Fido showed me the layout. I can find out anything we want. *Anything*. That's—power. He introduced me to the headmaster's wife. You see, Daddy's fearsomely well thought of, the last of the Mohicans and all that—last of his family, I mean Bill, never mind. And after all, I mean—chess!"

"None of them would tell you everything, Miss. There's always something. He wouldn't even know."

"Couldn't have put it better myself, old thing. Covering fire. Think you're in the clear, then paff! All fall down. Besides—wrong league."

"Look, Gerry. It's new. That's why it'll work. We—me and 'Toinette, my sister Toni—we did their tests. You think too highly of people's intelligence. They aren't you know. They're mostly the ones who fail or score about a hundred. We did the tests without trying. Well, *I* know what an asset we've got with me inside. We'll need more people, more information—I'll get it. We'll need weapons, explosives perhaps, we'll need safe places to hide ourselves or him. This place? Maybe—and the stables and the old barge. There's a cupboard, an old loo—"

"We'd need a safe way of getting out ourselves—Christ!"

"Fuck me, sorry Miss."

She reached for the transistor. It was no longer Winnie's ancient machine. This one fitted easily into the palm of her hand. She switched it on and voices from some other life filled the room.

Yes. It's a black one. Moving your way. Over.

Gerry laughed.

"You don't suppose they'd use a channel you could get at with that thing?"

It's not ridiculous, she thought. Why am I so certain I am not being ridiculous? Under her arm the flat voices were talking at intervals. *Yes, if you say so. No, I said it's a black one.* Perhaps they were not police. Perhaps—what? Inside a radio and out there in infinite space that included the world there was audible mystery and confusion, infinite confusion. She moved the control, destroying the voices, passed through music, a talk, a quiz, a burst of laughter, some foreign languages, loud, then faint. And she moved the control back and found the point between all stations;

172

and immediately in the uncleaned room which seemed always to smell of drains and food, and to be organized, or disorganized round an unmade bed—the very light from the window seeming dusty and dim as if the whole world were no more than an annexe to the room—immediately there came the voice of the darkness between the stars, between the galaxies, the toneless voice of the great skein unravelling and lying slack; and she knew why the whole thing would be simple, a tiny part of the last slackness.

Running-down. Dark.

A voice came back faintly on the verge of the hissing. *I couldn't get the number. I said it's a black one.*

A wave of happiness and delight went over and through her.

"It's going to be simple."

"Who says so?"

"Think."

It was a triumph of the will. As if a hand was on them the two men began to discuss the operation they so plainly did not believe in. They began to isolate problems and put them aside unsolved. Sophy thought of the school as she knew it and the people there. She became indifferent to the ineffectual and random kind of suggestions that they tossed from one to the other. She heard nothing of what they said but the tone, understanding by it how they felt themselves to be pawing at a steel wall that surrounded such a centre of the privileged and valuable. In the end they came to a full stop. Bill went off at last. Gerry got the whisky out of the drawer in which he had hidden it. They drank bit by bit as they undressed and then had sex, Sophy absently.

"Your mind's not on your work."

"Have you noticed, Gerry, how through this thing we understand each other more?"

"No I haven't."

"Well. We're closer."

Then there was a time in which he convulsed and gasped and grabbed and groaned and she waited for it to be over. She patted his back and ruffled his hair in a companionable sort of way.

He grunted into her shoulder.

"Can't be closer than two-in-a-bed."

"I said 'understand'."

"Do we?"

"Well. I understand you."

173

He purred.

"Tell me about myself, doctor."

"Why should I?"

"It's this recurrent nightmare I have, doctor—may I call you Sigmund?—about a disgusting wench—"

"I wonder. I'm sure you don't dream, Gerry. You daydream about money, you lovely man. Masses of money."

"My oh my. I ought to beat you up to satisfy the neighbours. But remember, by the way, that I'm in command."

"You?"

"Well fo' lan's sake honey chile! Sleep time."

"No."

"Insatiable."

"Not that, it's the school. It's those questions—"

"Dead end."

She said nothing for a while, thinking how easily he gave up and how he must be pushed.

"I shall go back."

He rolled over on his back, stretched, yawned.

"Sophy, pet. Are you getting a thing about him?"

"Fido? My God, he's such a bore! Only after the three of us talked about it, I can see how much I'll have to find out. That's all."

"Remember whose doggie you are."

"Wuff wuff O my God. Still—if he ever got me into bed it would be out of sheer boredom. Premarital sex."

He smiled at her sideways, boyishly, winningly.

"If it's absolutely necessary. But please, please dear thing, don't enjoy it."

She felt a certain pique.

"My fiancé is not like that. He's in training. All the same, Gerry, I think you might at least pretend to be jealous!"

"We all have to make sacrifices. Tell him if he'll sell us a boy he can have me too if he wants, the splendid male thing that he is. Has he improved his snatch?"

"You don't know what I put up with. The headmaster's wife thinks that as soon as we're married we should start a family straight away. She's all for families straight away. I'll need more money."

"We're short. You know that."

174

"I have to dress the part. Phyllis isn't too keen on slacks."

"Phyllis?"

"Phyllis Appleby. Headmaster's wife. Cow."

"It's all a lot of nonsense. Nighty night."

"Fido? Bless you my love, divine to hear you! Oh super! I was afraid you might be out with the little men. Yes I know it was going to be Saturday but oh my sweet good, good news! There's been a rearrangement at the agency and do you know it gives me three extra days—yes *with* pay! I'm coming down to you right away!"

"Oh that's jolly good, Sophy, jolly good! Bow wow!"

"Wuff wuff!"

"It'll be great! Of course, by the way, you know I'll be working and I'm in training."

"I know dear. I think you're marvellous. You're doing what? Sorry, I can't hear you, it's this line—you're doing what? You're developing what? You're developing your deltoids? Oh super darling, where are they? Can I help?"

Inside the receiver a tiny voice began to talk about deltoids. She held it away from her and looked at it with distaste. The tiny voice continued to talk. She waited, idly watching a man walk past with a horrid, two-tone face. The tiny voice called her—

"Sophy! Sophy? Are you there?"

"Sorry darling. I was looking for more change. You'll be glad to see me?"

"Rather! Mrs Appleby was asking after you. Listen. I'll try and get you a room in the school."

"Oh super. Then we could—"

"Training! Training, dear!"

"Can you fix it? Ask matron. I'm sure she fancies you."

"Oh go on, Sophy, you're pulling my leg!"

"Well I'm jealous darling. That's why I'm coming down early now I have the chance to keep an eye on you."

"You don't need to. I'm not like Gerry."

"No. True."

"You haven't seen him?"

"Good heavens no! If a girl's got you—"

"And if I've got a girl—bow! wow!"

175

"Wuff! Wuff!"

(Christ.)

"The usual bus?"

"The usual bus."

"Sophy darling, I must go—"

"Until this afternoon then. I'm sending you a great big kiss along the wire."

"And one back for you."

"*Darling!*"

She put down the receiver and stood for a moment looking at it and the tiny figure of Fido beyond it, physically so attractive if you fancied a kind of a statue. She spoke in her outside girl's voice.

"Eek!"

So she got the bus and it humped over the Old Bridge and along to Chipwick and then round the downs into the next valley and Wandicott village where Fido managed to meet it. She put outrage, whether successful or not, out of her mind. Yet she had to act and could not entirely live her part. For though the five days were too full to be unpleasant actively, yet there was a constant kind of glee in her (a song in my heart) that she had a list of things to find out about the school and could tick them off in her mind one after the other, though some had to be approached carefully as a bird sitting on a nest. If Fido had had an ounce more wit or been slightly less preoccupied with the splendours of his own anatomy he might have questioned her insistence on knowing who looked after what. The little boys pleased her too and they were desirable, edible, even. They did not call her 'Miss' or 'Sophy'. Solemnly, from the biggest down to the smallest, they called her 'Miss Stanhope'. They opened doors for her, picked up anything she dropped. When she asked a boy a question he did not say 'How should I know?' but 'I'll find out for you, Miss Stanhope,' and ran off to do so. It was most peculiar. While Fido was working she quite enjoyed watching these edible little boys, so bland and pretty. Watching one of these infinitely precious objects she found herself saying inside herself. *Lovely my pet! I could eat you!*

As for Fido, it was a relief that he was in training. But they did have sex once. He came to her where she sat under the dying elms and watched the little boys play cricket.

"Come along Sophy to my room after lights-out. I'll leave the door ajar."

176

"But you're in training darling!"

"It's good for the system once in a while. Besides—"

"Besides what?"

"Well. We're engaged and all that."

"Darling!"

"Darling! Oh well played Bellingham!"

"What did he do?"

"But wait till lights-out as I said."

"What about the duty master?"

"Old Rutherford?"

"I don't want to run into him going his rounds and be taken for a wicked woman."

Fido looked cunning.

"You'd be going to the loo, he'd think."

"Well then, Fido, why don't you come to my room?"

"You'll get me the sack."

"What! In this day and age? For God's sake Fido, they think—I mean, look at this ring! We're engaged! We're in the nineteen-seventies!"

Fido displayed an unusual perceptivity.

"No we aren't, Sophy. Oh dear no. Not here."

"Well. You could be going to the loo as convincingly as I could."

"You know as well as I do it's not in your direction."

So annoyed, but resigned and thinking it a reasonable price for the precious information that was stored unforgettably in her pretty head, she agreed that she should go to his room; and that night did so. She had never felt so indifferent, so divorced from sensuality or emotion. She lay like a log; and this, it seemed, was just as agreeable to Fido as a fuller co-operation would have been. After he had pleased himself, and, as she thought, relieved himself, she could hardly make the smallest token gesture of affection. She spoke to him in the whisper that the place demanded.

"Finished?"

It was a real pleasure to be back and alone in the room that the headmaster's wife had found for her. The next day, as if sex were something that drove them apart rather than united them, they parted with the merest of pecks.

"Goodbye, Sophy."

"Goodbye Fido. Have some good deltoids."

This time, she went straight to the flat. Gerry was there, turned in after a session at the pub that had taken him far into the dreary reaches of the afternoon. He lifted his head off the pillow and looked at her blearily as she flung her four plastic shopping bags on the bed.

"For Christ's sake!"

"God, Gerry, you do look a mess!"

"Got to go to the loo. Make some—"

"Coffee will you?"

It was instant coffee and ready by the time he came out of the loo. He pushed both hands through his hair and stared into the shaving mirror that was propped on the shelf over where the open fireplace had been.

"God."

"Why don't we leave this filthy place? Get a better pad. We don't have to live in Jamaica."

He slumped on the edge of the bed, took the coffee and engrossed himself in it. Presently, one hand supporting his bowed head, he held the empty mug out to her with the other.

"More. And the pills. Twist of paper, top left-hand."

"Are they—"

"You're making my head ache. Keep quiet, will you, playmate?"

This time she brought some coffee for herself as well and sat on the bed by his side.

"I think it's Phyllis."

"Mm? Phyllis?"

"Mrs Appleby. Headmaster's wife."

"What's she got to do with it?"

Sophy smiled to herself.

"She's training me. I've passed the first inspection good as gold. Schoolmaster's wife. Now she's on to—you just wouldn't believe. Women, particularly with small boys about, have to be so careful of their person."

"Rape?"

"No, you grotty thing!"

"I know that word. You've been talking to small boys."

"Listening. But personal hygiene, dear. That's what she's on about."

"She thinks you stink. B.O. they used to call it."

178

"Perfume. That's what she's on about. 'I wear the merest trace, Sophy, dear.' "

She lay back on the bed and laughed at the ceiling. He grinned and straightened up as if the coffee or the pills or both, were working for him.

"All the same I know what she meant."

"Do I reek?"

He reached out absently and began to mould her nearer breast.

"Lay off Gerry. It's the wrong time of the day."

"Exhausted by Fido's enormous sex drive. How many times did he have you?"

"He didn't have me at all."

Gerry put his mug on the floor, took hers from her, set it down, then turned over so that he was lying partly on her. He smiled into her eyes as he spoke.

"What a liar you are, old soul."

"If it comes to that, dear thing, how many times have you had it off while your little girl has been unavoidably absent?"

"Nary a once, honest to God, marm."

Then they were both laughing at each other, twins. He bowed down and laid his head by hers, face down. He nuzzled his face into her hair and murmured so that his breath tickled her ear.

"I've got such a hard-on I could get right up between your tits and make your teeth rattle."

But he didn't. He lay there, breathing lightly, lighter than Fido. She freed a curl that was pulling and murmured back.

"I've got all the answers to those questions."

"Goldfinger would be pleased with you. You do keep on, don't you?"

"Will Bill have a hangover too?"

"He never gets a hangover. God is too good to him. Why?"

"Well Christ! Another council of war!"

He looked at her, shaking his head wonderingly.

"Sometimes I think you're—you never give up, do you?"

So once more the three of them met in the gloomy room and the two men went about it and about. She made no suggestions herself, only answered questions they asked her about the set-up. But it became clearer and clearer to her that they were drifting away from the real world into fantasy. For a while she went with them, and then, bored, she began to invent fantasies for herself, pictures inside her mind, impossible daydreams that she knew for what they were. They would have a helicopter which lowered a hook and snatched one of the black, brown or white highnesses literally. They dug a secret tunnel. They got themselves invulnerable bodies and irresistible strength so that they strode in with bullets bouncing from their skin and the hands of men sliding from their more-than-human flesh. Or she became all-powerful and could alter things as she pleased so that the boy was snatched out of his bed and through the silent air to the place—what place? With a shiver of waking she saw what the place was, and where it was; and as if that place thought rather than her mind, the idea came with it.

The two men were silent, looking at her. She could not remember speaking but smiled sleepily from the one to the other. She could see how relieved they were to have proved the whole thing impossible. When she spoke, her words were as gentle as her smile.

"Yes. But what would they do in the night, if there was a big bang and a fire?"

The silence went on and on. At last Gerry spoke, in a voice that was carefully controlled.

"We don't know about that. We don't know what would burn. We don't know where the kids would go. We don't know anything. Not about that. For all you've told us."

"He's right, miss. Sophy."

"Well. I'll go back. I'll go back as often as necessary. We've started this thing and we won't—"

Bill stood up abruptly.

"Well then. Till you've been back. Cor."

The other two waited until he had gone.

"Cheer up, Gerry! Do a daydream about money!"

"Oh my oh my. Is Bill chicken? Honey chile, just be very, very careful!"

"Trouble is I haven't a good excuse for going back."

"Passion."

"I'm suppose to be working at Runways, clot."

"Say they sacked you."

"Spoil my image."

"You sacked them. Better yourself."

"But I can't go rushing back to Fido—"

"Go down in a panic and say he's knocked you up."

180

"Knocked me up?"

"Enceinte. Preggers."

Pause.

"Like I told you, field-marshal, I didn't have it off with him."

"Tell him I've made him a father."

Then they were rolling over and over each other with explosions of sniggers and giggles that turned suddenly into sex, pre-occupied, wounded, experimental, libidinous, long, slow and greedy. When their unsynchronized orgasms had let them down, back into the crumpled bed and into the grey light from the grimy window, Sophy could not even be bothered to repair her lips but lay there in a kind of trance of consent.

"One day, Gerry, you'll be the filthiest old man."

"Filthy old woman yourself."

The grey light washed through Sophy like a tide.

"No. Not me."

"Why not you?"

"Don't ask me. You wouldn't understand anyway."

He sat up abruptly.

"Psychic are we? Snap out of it. What do I keep you for?"

"In all this luxury?"

"I'll say one thing for you, angel. You aren't a libber."

That made her laugh.

"I like you, twin. I really do! I think you're the only person for whom—"

"Yes yes?"

"Never mind. Like I said, I'll go. I could have left my ring down there. So precious my dear and besides it's not just the money it's the sentimental value—oh Fido darling I've done a terrible thing can you ever forgive me? No it's not Gerry—but dearest I've lost our ring! Well of course I've been crying! Oh darling it must have cost at least two pounds fifty—where shall we ever find that sort of money again? You know, Gerry, he's—what's the meanest thing there is?"

"You're pretty mean with hand-outs."

"One of these days I shall swipe you."

"Yum yum."

"Will you keep this bloody ring for me? No—come to think of it, I'd better find it somewhere in the school, hadn't I? More convincing."

"Don't forget to look under Fido's pillow."

"You are *the*—"

And then out of the complications too vast for understanding, out of the lies not admitted but nevertheless known to be lies, out of the surmises and the complexities and the seamy side they collapsed in each other's arms, shaking with mutual laughter.

So she took her ring back to Wandicott House and got a shock. For one thing, when Fido heard the ring was lost he was very angry indeed and told her what it had cost. It was considerably more than two pounds fifty and some of it was still outstanding. For another thing, the news that pretty Miss Stanhope had lost her engagement ring flashed through the school and brought it to a full stop. The whole place reorganized itself. Masters whose names she did not know revealed themselves as leaders of men. As for the boys—! But of course the operation, though it was ideal for her purpose, was not without a certain degree of embarrassment. Dr Appleby, the headmaster, impressed on everyone the first thing to do was to establish with precision Miss Stanhope's exact movements during every moment of her previous stay; and though Phyllis Appleby with practised ease turned his remarks in the direction where they would sound as little silly and suggestive as possible, he had nevertheless sown a seed. The news, therefore, that Miss Stanhope had visited her fiancé's room to inspect his photographs was greeted with a solemnity that creaked. Sophy managed to weep and this was a huge success. Fido was told gently by Phyllis what a lucky man he was, that a ring was only a ring and that what a girl really *needed* was to be assured by her fiancé that she was ten thousand times more precious than any mere object. The headmaster came near to ticking Fido off.

"You know, Masterman, what it says in the Bible. 'The price of a good woman is above rubies.' "

"It was an opal."

"Ah well. We're not superstitious, are we?"

It was a great relief when Sophy or the odd-job man—this bit was not quite clear—found her ring under one of the dying elms. It must have been the odd-job man because she was heard thanking him effusively and smiling at him sweetly for all his awful face. But when she told Fido he ought to reward the man, Fido appeared never to have seen or heard of him. The only real draw-

182

back after that was that Phyllis insisted they should take her car and go for a drive together. Oh never mind the reading lesson! She would take it herself, so long as the little men didn't have to be told how to spell "accommodation". Now you two young people go off and be alone for a bit. Fido don't sulk! And don't be a brute! Girls aren't like your soldiers you know! They need—Sophy, take him off and pull his ears for him. Go over to have a look at the abbey, the west front is simply marvellous!

So they drove off. Fido doing it moodily and unhandily but gradually thawing and simmering down, then heating up a bit so that he became amorous. Sophy happy in the knowledge that this was the last time she would have to put up with him, explained that it wasn't any good today. He did know that about girls, didn't he? Apparently he did; but not much else; and the information made him moody again.

All at once Sophy's boredom with him flowed over. It even spilled out to Gerry and Bill and Roland and the whole world of men. She thought to herself, I won't go back to the flat tonight. I'll ring the pub and ask them to give Gerry a message and I'll sleep in the stables and to hell with it. I need something bigger, I—need something I—

Respect? Admire? Fear? Need?

She made him drop her in Greenfield High Street and because she was in such a temper with him, the outside girl was even more flashing as she walked briskly down the street to Sprawson's. Jauntily she swung her plastic bags past the laundromat, the Chinese takeaway, Timothy Krishna, Portwell Funeral Directors, Subadar Singh's Gent's Best Suiting. Gaily she greeted Mrs Goodchild as she crossed to the front door, still so splendid in its eighteenth-century manner. She nudged sideways through the door into the hall and a solicitor's clerk proceeding in the other direction hoped she was a client but feared not; and Edwin Bell, climbing the stairs to his flat over the solicitor's office thought—I know that positively breezy way of coming in—Sophy, dear Sophy is back!

Sophy listened outside the column room but heard nothing, so walked straight in to use the telephone.

"Daddy!"

He accepted a peck but cried out as her arm brushed the table.

"Mind what you're doing! Damn it must you girls be so

183

confoundedly clumsy? You're supposed to be—where's the other one—Antonia?"

"How should I know? Nobody knows."

"Oh of course. Well. Neither of you need think I'm going to pay for more flips by air. If it's a question of money you might as well know straight away—"

"It isn't a question of money, Daddy. I just came to see you. After all, I'm your daughter. Forgotten?"

"You want to use the phone."

Pause.

"Later perhaps. What's this thing?"

He looked down at the scattered pieces and began to arrange them again on the little machine.

"They call it a computer but it isn't really. More what I'd call an adding machine. It works through a few variables and then—"

"Can it think?"

"Did they teach you nothing at school? There! Look at that for a move. The thing's moronic. I've worked out a way of mating it with white to move, in eight moves. And you're supposed to pay hundreds of pounds for it!"

"Why bother?"

"I'm supposed to review the thing. There's a certain mild interest in working out from what it does how they've made it. Takes me back to my code-breaking days."

She picked up her bags to leave and was amused to see how he sat back and with a conscious effort set himself to show a little interest, like a father in a book.

"Well. How are things, er, Sophy?"

"The agency was too, too boring."

"Agency? Oh yes!"

"I'm thinking of looking for something else."

He had set his fingertips together, legs stretched under the desk, was looking sideways at her. He smiled and his face lit up, was conspiratorial—was—and she saw at once with what ease he must have persuaded the aunties to come one after the other out of the bedroom across the landing.

"Have you got a boyfriend?"

"Well. What do *you* think?"

"I mean, are you—going steady?"

"You mean am I having it off with a bloke?"

184

He laughed soundlessly up at the ceiling.

"You won't shock me, you know. We used to have it off too. Only we didn't call it that and we didn't talk about it so much."

"All those aunties after Mummy—went. When Toni pushed off with the Butlers she was looking for Mummy, wasn't she?"

"That crossed my mind."

The awareness at the mouth of the tunnel spoke but used the voice of the outside girl.

Lightly.

"I hope it didn't come between you and your toys."

"Toys? What are toys? How would you define toys?"

"Mummy didn't like chess either, I suppose."

He became restless. It was not so much movement as a kind of deliberate stillness out of which his voice came a tone higher and with a hint of strain in it.

"Use the phone if you like. I'll go. Private I suppose. Only I don't ever want to talk about her. Understand that."

"But I *do* understand that!"

He blared out at her.

"Like hell you do! What do you know, any of you? This, this romantic stuff, this, this—"

"Go on. Use the word."

"It's like stinking treacle. It swallows, drowns, binds, enslaves—*that*—" and he gestured sweepingly over the desk with its litter of papers and games—"that's life. A meanwhile, a what the man said, a surcease, even a cleanness in the stink in the wetness, the milk, nappies, squallings—"

He stopped; then went on in his normal, cold voice.

"I don't want to seem unwelcoming. But—"

"But you're busy with your toys."

"Precisely."

"We're not very wholesome are we?"

"That's a good word."

"You, Mummy, Toni, me—we're not the way people used to be. It's part of the whole running down."

"Entropy."

"You don't even care enough about us to hate us, do you?"

He looked at her and moved his body restlessly.

"Push off, er, Sophy. Just go away."

She stood there, half-way to the door, between her plastic

185

shopping-bags full of gear. She looked back at his frown, the old-fashioned hair-do with its side parting, the collar and tie, the grizzled sideburns, the lines on his stripped face, his eagle's face that nevertheless was so wholly male. All at once she understood. It had been so, always so, back beyond the birthday when she had lost him for ever, back to the time of the rectangle and the tiny girl looking up and *woo'd*, yes woo'd for those few minutes, that half hour; was so even now, not in a Gerry way or Fido way or Bill way or, or—but in a wide passion rooted beyond the very stars in which *I fancy you* was trivial as a single bubble on a stream, a nothing, a joke—

Her mouth began to talk in a cover-up, partly arch girl, concerned daughter, partly fugitive from this last piece of outrage.

"But look Daddy, you can't go on living by yourself. You'll get old. You'll need, I mean you can say sex is trivial but what do you do about it, I mean—"

And then, facing him, unable to take her eyes off his face, the severe, masculine mouth, the eagle's beak, the eyes that surely could see as far as she through a brick person—*then*, both hands trapped by her sides by the swinging bags, her splendid, idiotic body took charge, and before him, her unbra'd breasts rose up, their vulnerable, tender, uncontrollable, enslaving points hardened, stood out and lifted the fabric of her shirt in a sign as clear as if it had been shouted. She saw his eyes move their focus from her own, move down, past her flushing face and throat until they stared straight at the overt signal. Her mouth opened, shut, opened.

"What do you do—"

At these words that she could only just hear over the pounding of the blood in her ears she saw his eyes lift to hers. There was a redness in his cheeks too. His hands had shifted back and were clutching the arms of his revolving chair. His nearer shoulder was hunched as if to get between them and he was staring at her round it. Then, as if to demonstrate his freedom, boldness, his power to say anything that might be thought unsayable, he spoke directly into her face. He even swung his chair round a little to show there was no concealment, not even from his shoulder. His words were like blows, driving them apart, destroying them, hurling her away from the toy room, the column room, the room that was so secure from people.

186

"What do I do?" Then with a hissing kind of hatred—"You want to know? You do? I masturbate."

So there they were, he, crouched in his chair, trapped between his hands, she by the door, trapped between her bags. With great deliberateness, as if he himself were a lay figure, a puppet which he was rearranging, he shifted his position, his head moved to look down at the chess machine, body moved round and forward, the hands lifted one after the other from the arms of the chair; picture of a man absorbed in his study, his job, his business, his all, his. What a man is for.

She stood there; and for once the presence at the mouth of the tunnel was not able to make itself felt. There was too much of outside girl. Her face felt swollen and water was building up under and behind her eyes.

She swallowed, looked at the window, then back at his indifferent profile.

"Don't we all?"

He did not reply but stayed where he was, looking down at the chess machine. He picked up a biro in his right hand and held it ready but for nothing. The hand and the biro stayed there, shaking slightly. She felt full of lead, full of pain unexpected and not understood; and this storm of emotion that filled the room was like a physical thing and must surely be confined to a cuboid shape by the walls, not understood, only one thing understood, the great slash he had made between the two of them, through what had not existed, oh no, could never have existed, and where there was severance, goodbye and good riddance, cruel and contemptuous act of will.

"Well—"

Her feet seemed stuck to the floor, stuck in it. She pulled them out of the floor with an effort that made her stagger, turned, and was swung at least partly by the weight in her either hand and went through the idiotic business of getting the door wider open, then pulling it to with one foot behind her. It closed on the silent figure with the quivering hand and she hurried through the hall, got the glass door open somehow, then pulled it to with one foot behind her, like the other door, more or less fell down the steps, hurried along the asphalt under the buddleias, past the riot of rosemary and mint and the straggling roses that were overtaken by their own stock. She climbed the narrow stair to the old room with the dormers and collapsed on the cold comfort of her divan. Then she began to cry, and rage against everything. It was in the middle of this rage that she heard an unspoken sentence from her own inside that the secret of it all was outrage; so she looked among her hot tears, her rage and hatred for the outrage that would go with the unravelling, and there it was right in the front of her mind so that she stared at it. There was a girl (oh not with an addled egg in her hand) going up the garden path with her girl's body, her scent and her breasts, laughing she went, back to the hall, the door, flung it open and there laughing offered what she had to him; and now a real, solid girl's body staggered down the stairs and along the path after the phantom girl, up the steps, got open the glass door; and the electric typewriter was going and going, chattering the apegame in the column room and she could not, *could not*, her body would not, *would not*, and she came away, tears streaming and she got back to the unaired divan and lay there, failed in outrage, and seething with the hatred that was a thing all on its own, bitter in the mouth and the belly, worse than bitter, acid burning.

At last she lay without either thought or feeling, and with a sentience that neither commented nor criticized but was a naked and unemotional "I am" or perhaps "It is". Then the interior, nameless thing was there again, the thing that had sat from everlasting to everlasting, staring out. Now, for an aeon at the mouth of its tunnel it stared out and was aware, too, of that black angle, direction behind that stretched, widening, as far as there was to stretch. The thing examined the failure to outrage, noted it; was aware that there would be some other occasions for outrage; even said (but silently) a word.

Presently.

Sophy became aware of the divan, the place, her body, her ordinariness. She felt how diagonally across her right cheek a wrinkle in the coverlet had pressed it and had done so with more effect than usual because the flesh of that cheek was pulpy with a suffusion of the blood of rage and hatred and shame. She sat up and swung her feet off the divan. She went to the mirror, and there it was, the crease mark on a face that tears had reddened round eyes even redder.

Sewn in with red worsted.

Who had said that? An auntie? Toni? Mummy? Him?

She became very busy talking to herself.

"This will never do, my old soul! We must repair the damage, mustn't we? A girl's first duty is to get herself up as a lollipop a nice bit of crumpet what would our dear fiancé think or our dear boyfriend? Or our dear—"

Someone was coming very softly up the wooden stairs. There was almost no sound from the feet and only the faintest of creaks from the weight. She saw a head appear, a face, shoulders. It was a dark head of hair and curly as her own. The eyes under it were dark in the delicate face. A scarf, a long raincoat open, to show a trouser-suit too sharp for Greenfield, trousers tucked into the tops of long, high-heeled boots. The girl drew clear of the stairs and stood looking across at her expressionlessly. Sophy stared back. Neither of them said anything.

Sophy felt in her shoulder bag, got out her lipstick and mirror, busied herself repairing her face. It took quite a time. When she was satisfied, she put the things back in the bag and dusted off her hands. She spoke conversationally.

"I couldn't get mine under a wig as easily as that. Contact lenses too. Or did you cut it?"

"No."

"Palestine. Cuba. And then—I know where you've come from."

A faint, far-off voice from behind the face on which a new face had been marked out by make-up.

"Obviously."

"England's turn, is it? The superior, blinding bastards!"

"We're considering. Looking round."

As if to demonstrate this, Toni began to move round the room, peering at the places on the wall where the pictures had been. All at once, Sophy felt a kind of glee that awoke in the depth of her body and bubbled up, not to be quelled.

"Have you seen him?"

Toni shook her head. She picked at a scrap of a picture still sticking to the plaster. The glee bubbled up and up.

"You said 'We need you.' Well?"

"Well?"

"You have men. Money. Must have."

Without moving her feet, Toni sank down and sat on the end of the divan, very slowly. She waited. Sophy stared out of the

189

dormer and at the blind windows of the old house.

"I have access. And a project. Know-how. It's saleable."

Now she, in her turn, sank down on to the divan slowly and faced the enigmatic contact lenses.

"My deah, deah Antonia. All over again! We're going to be everything to each other."

Part Three

ONE
IS
ONE

CHAPTER TWELVE

Next door to Sprawson's, in Goodchild's shop, Sim Goodchild sat at the back and tried to think about First Things. There were no people browsing along his shelves so it should have been easy. But as he told himself, what with the jets soughing down every minute to London airport and the monstrous continental trucks doing their best to break down the Old Bridge, any thought was impossible. Moreover he knew that after a moment or two on First Things (getting back, he sometimes called it) he knew he would be likely to find himself brooding on the fact that he was too fat, also as bald as bald and with a cut at the left corner of the chin, acquired in the process that morning of shaving a jowl. He said to himself you could work of course. You could do a bit of rearranging and fool with the job of reticketing so as to limp after inflation. It was really the only sort of thought possible in all the town-racket, what with being bald and old and breathless. You could also brood on what to do in the large sense, as a businessman. The oil shares were all right and would last their lifetime. They provided the bread and butter; but no jam. The shop wasn't providing any jam either. What to do? How bring in the Pakis? How the Blacks? What brilliant and unique stroke of the antiquarian bookseller's craft would prise that crowd of white people away from the telly and bring them to read old books again? How to persuade people of the essential beauty, lovableness, humanity even, of a beautifully bound book? Yes. You could brood on that for all the rumpus, but not on First Things.

This was the point in his daily brooding when he was accustomed to finding himself stood on his feet by a kind of interior pressure. The pressure was the memory of his own shortcomings and he stood up because if he did not the memories would take on time and place, which was intolerable. He stared at

Theology, Occult, Metaphysics, Prints, the *Gentleman's Magazine*—and flash! the very episode which he had stood on his feet to avoid shot bang into awareness.

About a month ago, the auction.

"£250, £250. Any advance? Going for the last time at £250—"

That was when Rupert Hazing from Midland Books had bent to him.

"This is where I step in."

"What? With one year missing?"

Rupert's mouth had stayed open. He had glanced at the auctioneer then back at Sim. It had been enough. While Rupert hesitated the books had been knocked down to Thornton's of Oxford.

That was sheer wantonness, not helping the business but hindering Rupert. For fun. The diabolical *thing* down there disporting itself. And you could not embark on the long voyage of reparation that could make all well, could not give Rupert Hazing all the volumes of the *Gentleman's Magazine* for £250 with, say, ten per cent on top for himself—could not do it because, to change the metaphor, this latest piece of wantonness was only a bit on the top of the pile. The pile was a vast heap of rubbish, of ordure, of filthy rags, was a mountain—it did not matter what one did, the pile was too big. Why pick the last bit of filth off the top?

Sim blinked and shook himself as he always did at this point and came up out of the pile to the modified daylight of the shop. This was the bold, the cynical point in his mornings when he walked down between Novels, Poetry, Literary Criticism on the one hand and Bibles, Prayer Books, Handicrafts and Hobbies on the other. It was the point where he sneered at himself and his ancestors and the good old family business now going so inexorably to the dogs. He was accustomed even to sneer nowadays at the children's books he had arranged, years ago, at one side of the great plate-glass window. Ruth, when she came in from shopping the first time after he had done it, had said nothing. But later when she had brought his tea to him at the desk she had glanced away down the shop.

"I see you are changing our image."

He had denied it but of course it was true. He had seen Stanhope's little girls coming up the street hand-in-hand and quite suddenly he had felt every speck of dust in the shop was made of

194

lead, and that he was made of lead and that life (which he was missing) was bright and innocent like the two children. With a kind of furtive passion he had begun to buy children's books, new ones at that, and arrange them in the left side of the window. Sometimes parents bought a book at Christmas, and rarely, in between, for birthdays, perhaps, but the addition to turnover was imperceptible.

Sim sometimes wondered whether his father's display there had had the same kind of furtive and obscure motivation. His rationalist father had set out a skrying glass, the *I Ching* complete with reeds, and the full set of Tarot cards. Sim understood his own motive only too well. He was using children's books as a bait for the Stanhope twins, who would be some substitute for his own children—Margaret, married but in Canada, and Steven, incurable in that ward where his parents met him week after week for a period of complete non-communication. The brilliant little girls had indeed come in, hardly tall enough to reach the doorknob but with the calm assurance usually connected with privilege. They had examined books with the solemn attention that kittens will give with their noses. They had opened books and turned over page after page, surely faster than not only they but anyone else could read. Yet they seemed to be reading: the fair one—Toni—turning from a child's book to take down an adult one; then the other giggling at a picture while the dark curls shook all over her little head—

Ruth understood though it must have been bitter for her. She had them into the sitting-room for lemonade and cake, but they did not come back. After that, Sim would stand in his doorway when they went to school, first with the au pair and later on their own. He knew exactly when to stand, abstracted, and have his minute gift bestowed on him regally.

"Good morning Mr Goodchild."

"And good morning to the Misses Stanhope!"

So they grew in beauty. It was Wordsworthian.

Ruth emerged from the sitting-room to go shopping.

"I saw Edwin yesterday. I forgot to tell you. He's coming to see you."

Bell lived in part of Sprawson's; they had a flat. Once upon a time, Sim had envied the Bells for living so close to the twins. But

195

that was past. The girls were little girls long ago—ten years ago, not so long after all—and quite beyond children's books.

As if she saw his thought, Ruth nodded at the left-hand side of the shop window.

"You should try something else."

"Any suggestions?"

"Household. BBC Publications. Dressmaking."

"I'll think."

She went away up the High Street among the foreign costumes. Sim nodded and went on nodding, agreeing about the children's books but knowing he wouldn't change them. They would get their dust of lead. They said a stubborn something. Abruptly he turned to the books piled by his desk; the books from Langport Grange to be sorted and priced—work, work, work!

It was work he enjoyed—work that had kept him in his father's business. Bidding was a trial, for he was a coward and not willing to chance his arm. But sorting afterwards—it was almost like panning for gold. You stalked the job lot, your eye having caught the tell-tale glint; and after the dreadful time of bidding—*there* was the first edition of Winstanley's *Introduction to the Study of Painted Glass* in perfect condition!

Well. It happened once.

Sim sat down at his desk but the door flew open, the bell rang and it was Edwin himself, larger than life or would-be larger than life, in his check coat and yellow, dangling scarf—Bell, still dressed as an *undergrad* of the thirties and lacking only the Oxford Bags to be a complete period piece.

"Sim! Sim!"

A gust of wind, a kind of Edward Thomas crossed with George Borrow wind on the heath, great Nature, but all the same, cultivated, cultural and spiritually *sincere*.

"Sim! My good Sim! The man I have met!"

Edwin Bell strode up the shop and sat himself like a lady riding sidesaddle on the corner of the desk. He banged down the text book he was carrying and the copy of the *Bhagavad Gita*. Sim leaned back in his chair, took off his spectacles and blinked at the eager face seen so indistinctly against the light.

"What is it now, Edwin?"

"The man—Ecce homo—if that isn't too disastrously blasphemous and really do you know Sim I don't think it is? The most incredible creature with an effect—I am, do you know, I am—excited!"

"When were you not?"

"At last! I genuinely feel—It's a case of everything comes to him who waits. After all these years—I know what you're going to say—"

"I wasn't going to say anything!"

"You were going to say that my swans were always geese. Well. So they were. I admit it freely."

"Theosophy, Scientism, the Mahatma—"

Edwin subsided a little.

"Edwina implied much the same."

It must have been intended from the beginning of the universe, this marriage between Edwin and Edwina Bell. There was more to the obviousness of the intention than the coincidence of the name. They looked so much like each other that unless a person knew them very well they had a kind of transvestite appearance simply by reference to each other. On top of that, Edwin had a high voice for a man and Edwina a low voice for a woman. Sim still winced at the memory of one of his early telephone conversations with them. A high voice had replied so that he had said "Hullo Edwina!" The voice replied "But Sim, it's Edwin!" Then when next he had been answered by a low voice he had said "Hullo Edwin!" only to hear—"But Sim, it's Edwina." When they walked up the High Street from Sprawson's or from their flat in Sprawson's, they would both have much the same scarf blowing from much the same open overcoat. Edwina's hair was a little shorter than Edwin's and she had rather more bosom. It was a useful distinction.

"Edwina always did have more sense than you, I think."

"Now Sim, you're just saying that because it's what people say about wives when they can't think of anything else. I call it the Little Woman Syndrome."

The phone rang.

"Yes? Yes, we do. Hold on a moment please. It's in good condition. Seven pounds ten, I'm afraid—I mean seven fifty. We have your address? Right. Yes, I will." He put the phone back, made a note in his desk diary, sat back again and looked up at Edwin.

"Well? Out with it!"

Edwin smoothed down the hair at the back of his head with a gesture exactly like Edwina's. Growing together.

"It's this man as I said. The Man in Black."

"I've heard that before. The Man in Black. The Woman in White."

Edwin gave a sudden, triumphant laugh.

"But it's not so, Sim, not so! You couldn't be more wrong if you tried! You see, what you're being is *literary!*"

"Bookseller after all."

"But I haven't told you—"

Edwin was leaning across the desk, sideways, his eyes bright with enthusiasm, mouth open, short nose projecting in search, in passion, in anticipation. Sim shook his head with weary but still good-humoured affection.

"Believe Edwina, Edwin. She has more bosom than you O God why did I say that I mean—"

But once more, as on all the other occasions with all those other people, the thing was irretrievable. There were rumours about the Bells' sex life, everyone knew the rumours and nobody said—surely now Bell was blushing against the light, flushing, rather, the good humour of his excitement changed to anger? Sim jumped up and struck the desk with his fist.

"O curse it curse it curse it! Why do I do it, Edwin? Why in the name of God must I do it?"

Bell was looking away at last.

"You know we once nearly, very nearly, took out a libel writ?"

"Yes. I did. Do. They said so."

"Who's 'They'?"

Sim gestured vaguely.

"People. You know how it is."

"I do indeed, Sim. I do indeed."

Then Sim was silent for a while, not because he had nothing to say but because he had too much. Everything he could think of had a double meaning or was likely to be misunderstood.

At last he looked up.

"Two old men. Got to remember that. Only a few more years. Getting a bit ingrown, silly, perhaps, more than we—more than I am by nature if that's possible. Only it can't, *can't* amount to no more than this, can it? This kind of dull, busy preoccupation with trivialities—I would do this and that but on the other hand there is

198

that and this, have you read the papers, what was on the box, how is Steven, I can let you have it at eighty-five pence with postage and never, never a dive into what must be the deep—I'm sixty-seven. You're—what is it?—Sixty-three. Out there are the Pakis and Blacks, the Chinese, the Whites, the punks and lay-abouts, the—"

He stopped himself, wondering a little why he had gone on so long. Edwin stirred on the corner of the desk, stood up and stared away at Metaphysics.

"I taught the other day for a whole period with my flies open."

Sim kept his lips together but heaved once or twice inside. Edwin appeared not to notice. He was looking clean through the row of books, away and away.

"Edwin. You were telling me about this man."

"Ah yes!"

"A Franciscan friar? A Mahatma? A reincarnation of the first Dalai Lama who wants to build a Potala in Wales?"

"You're jeering."

"Sorry."

"In any case it wasn't the Dalai Lama. Just a Lama."

"Sorry. Sorry."

"The Dalai Lama is still alive so it couldn't have been."

"O God."

"But this—afterwards I found I was—not crying, because the implications of the word are a bit childish, a bit babyish—but weeping. Not for sorrow. For joy."

"One for sorrow."

"Not any more."

"What's his name? I like to have a name to hold on to."

"Then you're out, my dear man, right out. That's the core of it. No names. Rub them off. Ignore them. Think of the mess, the ruckus, the tumultuous, ridiculous, savage complications that language has made for us and we have made for language—oh confound it, now I've started to orate!"

"He wants to get rid of language and has approached two people, you and me via you, who depend on language more than anything else for their existence! Look at these books!"

"I see them."

"Think of your classes."

"Well then!"

"Don't you see? You talked once about being more worried by *faux pas* than sin. Precisely at that point you are invited to make a huge sacrifice that would stand our worlds on their—on its—head—the deliberate turning away from the recorded word, printed, radioed, televized, taped, disced—"

"No, no."

"Good God, Sim, you're older than me! How long have you got? How long can you wait about? I tell you—" And Edwin gestured so widely his greatcoat swung open—"this is it!"

"The odd thing is, you know, that I don't care how long or how short I've got. Oh yes. I don't want to die. But then, I'm not going to, am I? Not today, at any rate, with a bit of luck. There'll come a day and I shan't like it. Probably. But not today. Today is infinity and triviality."

"You won't take a chance?"

Sim sighed.

"I foresee the resurrection of the Philosophical Society."

"It was never dead."

"Resumption then. How wordy we are!"

"Transcendentalism—"

The word acted like a pulled trigger on Sim. He simply ceased to listen. The great wheel, of course, and the Hindu universe, alleged to be identical with the one the physicists were uncovering; skandhas and atavars, recession of the galaxies, appearance and illusion—and all the time, Edwin talking more and more like a character in one of Huxley's less successful novels! Sim at this point began silently to rehearse his own particular statement. It is all reasonable. It is all equally unreasonable. I believe it all as much as I believe anything that is out of sight; as I believe in the expanding universe, which is to say as I believe in the battle of Hastings, as I believe in the life of Jesus, as I believe in—It is a kind of belief which touches nothing in me. It is a kind of second-class believing. My beliefs are me; many and trivial.

Then once more he could hear Edwin and he looked up at him and nodded, a tiny typical dishonesty implying *I see what you mean, yes, I was listening.* The fact that Edwin was still talking sent him spinning away into his customary astonishment at the brute fact of Being and the brute fact that all he believed in as real, as deeply believed in, not as second-class belief, was himself as the man said because he felt himself thinking that he felt himself thinking that he felt awareness without end—

He found himself nodding again. Edwin went on speaking.

"So tell me. How did he know I am a seeker? Where is it written on me? On my forehead like a caste mark? Are there tribal cuts on my cheeks? Put aside all the technicalities, clairvoyance, second sight, extrasensory perception, all the skrying, seeing, the Gift—he simply knew! And as we walked I found myself—now this is the point, I found not that he spoke but—"

Edwin paused and looked as nearly furtive as a man of his open appearance could.

"You're not going to believe this, Sim. He didn't speak. I did."

"But of course!"

"No, no, not for me! For him! Somehow I was finding words for him—I was never at a loss—"

"You never have been. We both have what my mother called tongues hung in the middle that wag both ends—"

"Just so! Just so! He at one end, I at the other. And then—walking along the gravel path towards the elms they haven't cut down yet—as the rain pricked and the wind came and went—"

Edwin stopped. He got up from the desk. He thrust his hands deep into his pockets. The overcoat shut in front of him like drawn curtains.

"—I spoke in more than words."

"You sang, perhaps."

"*Yes*," said Edwin, without a trace of humour. "Exactly so! That is to say I experienced more than words can say; and I experienced it there and then." A small black boy pressed his face to the plate glass, looked into the impenetrable innards of the shop and ran away. Sim looked back at Edwin.

"There's always come a point when I have had to take your say-so. Can't you understand, Edwin, that I'm fettered by a kind of social politeness? I've never been able to say to your face what I actually think about it all."

"I want you to come along. Back to the park."

"Have you arranged a meeting?"

"He'll be there."

Sim passed a hand over his baldness then shook himself in irritation.

"I can't leave the shop whenever I like. You know that. And Ruth is out shopping. I couldn't possibly leave until—"

The shop bell rang and of course it was Ruth. Edwin turned back to Sim triumphantly.

"You see?"

Now Sim was really irritated.

"That's trivial!"

"It all hangs together. Good morning, Ruth."

"Edwin."

"Still going up, dear?"

"Just the penny here and there. Nothing to worry about."

"I was explaining that I can't leave the shop."

"Oh but you can. Cold lunch. I shall be glad to sit."

"And you see again, my dear Sim? Trivial of course!"

Driven, Sim became stubborn.

"I don't want to come!"

"Go with Edwin, dear. Do you good. Fresh air."

"It won't be any good, you know. It never is."

"Up you get."

"I don't see why I—look Ruth, if Graham's comes through tell them we haven't got a full Gibbon after all. One volume of *Miscellaneous* is missing. But we've the full *Decline and Fall* in good condition."

"That's the first edition."

"Price as agreed for the *Decline*. New dicker for the rest."

"I'll remember."

Sim got his overcoat, his scarf, his woollen gloves, his squashy hat. Side by side they walked up the High Street. The bell struck eleven from the tower of the community centre. Edwin nodded at it.

"That's where I met him."

Sim did not answer, and they passed the community centre, from whose graveyard the tombstones had not yet all been moved, in silence. Harold Krishna, Chung and Dethany Clothing, Bartolozzi Dry Cleaning, Mamma Mia Chinese Takeaway. In the door of Sundha Singh's Grocery Store one of the Singh brothers was talking liquidly to a white policeman.

The temple and the new mosque. The Liberal club closed for repairs, graffiti on every available surface. Up the Front. Kill the Bastard Frunt. Fugglestone shoe repairs.

Edwin swerved round a Sikh woman in her brilliant costume only partly hidden by her raincoat. For twelve yards or so Sim

202

followed him among white men and women waiting for a bus. Edwin spoke over his shoulder.

"Different when I came, wasn't it, after the war? London wasn't crawling all over us. The Green was still a village green—"

"If you shut one eye, it was. Ponsonby was vicar. You met this man of yours in there, you said."

"I wanted to see young Steven's wood sculpture. He'll go some distance—not far; but it's already a fallout from using the place as a community centre—there was also an exhibition of what's his name's photographs of insects—you know the man I mean. Fascinating. Oh yes. The Little Theatre Group was rehearsing that thing of Sartre's—you know—*In Camera*—in the, the north annexe—"

"You mean the north transept where they used to reserve the sacrament."

"Now Sim! You old stick-in-the-mud! You weren't even a communicant! Remember we're multi-racial and all religions are one, anyway."

"Try telling them that in the mosque."

"What do I hear? Has the Front been getting to you?"

"Don't be obscene. This man—"

"I met him just where the—no it wasn't. The font was on the other side. But he was standing under the west window, staring down at one of the old inscriptions."

"Epitaphs."

"I teach books, you know. I live by them too. The school does, after all. Yesterday after meeting him, I suddenly thought when I was talking about Shakespeare's own Histories—Good Lord, *that's* why he didn't bother about having his stuff printed! He knew, you see. Well, he would, wouldn't he?"

" 'Venus and Adonis'. 'Rape of Lucrece'. Sonnets, to you."

"A young man. The letter killeth. Who said that?"

"You found it in print."

"Some of the time we were both silent. I mean very silent. During one of these silences I found something out. You see, the silence was seared by the passage of these ghastly jets; and I knew that if, *if* we, or he, could find a place with the quality of absolute silence in it—that was why he was in the community centre, I think. Searching for silence—disappointed of course. So we were talking for only part of the time. Or rather I was. Have you ever

203

noticed that I talk a lot, almost logorrhoea, talking for the sake of it? Well I didn't. Not then."

"You're talking about yourself. Not him."

"But that's the point! Part of the time I—well, I spoke *Ursprache*."

"German?"

"Don't be a—God, how lucky they were, those old philosophers and theologians who spoke Latin! But I forgot. No they weren't. It was a kind of print—one remove from. Sim. I spoke the innocent language of the spirit. The language of paradise."

Edwin was looking sideways defiantly and flushing. Sim felt his own face go hot.

"I see," he muttered. "Well—"

"You don't see. And you're embarrassed. I don't see either and I'm embarrassed—"

Edwin covered his privates again with his two fists thrust into the overcoat pockets. He spoke fiercely. "It's not the thing, is it? Awfully bad form, isn't it? A bit methodist, isn't it? Back street stuff isn't it? Just talking with tongues, that's all. Now the moment is gone I can't re-experience it. I can only remember, and what's a memory? Useless clutter! I should have it down and sewn into the lapel of my jacket, here, somewhere. Now we're both blushing like a couple of naughty schoolgirls who've been caught using a bad word. In for a penny in for a pound. You're for it, Sim. Treat it as science, that'll make it feel better. I'm going to describe that memory as exactly as—I said seven words. I said a small sentence and I saw it as a luminous and holy shape before me. Oh, I forgot, we're being scientific aren't we? Luminous would pass. Holy? Right then—the *affect* was one commonly associated in religious phraseology with the word 'Holy'. Well. The light was not of this world. Now laugh."

"I'm not laughing."

They walked on in silence for a while, Edwin with his head turned sideways, in defence and suspicion. He struck a small Eurasian with his shoulder and exploded into the social Edwin which always seemed more real than any other of his private committee.

"I'm so sorry—inexcusable clumsiness—are you sure—oh really it was too bad of me! You're not hurt? Thank you so much, so very very much! Good day. Yes. Good day!"

Then as suddenly switched off, the defensive Edwin looked back at Sim as they walked.

"No. I don't believe you are. Thank you."

"What were the words?"

Astonished, Sim saw a positive tide of red sweep up Edwin's neck, up his face, his low forehead, and vanish under his tough but grizzled hair. Edwin swallowed once and over the knotted scarf it was possible to see how his prominent Adam's apple bobbed up and down. He gave a self-conscious cough.

"I can't remember."

"You—"

"All I have left is a memory of sevenness and a memory of that shape, imprecise as it was, but now crystallized—colourless, now alas—"

"You've done an Annie Besant."

"But that's exactly it! *That's* exactly the difference! I've done it or rather it's been done—Our geese—have been those whose opinions we thought might be helpful, whose philosophies, whose religions, whose codes might be what we were looking for; and what would eventuate tomorrow or the day after or the year after in some kind of illumination—the difference is that this was it! Was tomorrow, the year after next! I don't have to explain, Sim, I am not looking for anything—I found it, there in the park, sitting beside him. He gave it me."

"I see."

"I was a little downcast you know when you—Dejected. Yes, I was cast down."

"My fault, sorry. Uncivil of me."

"It all falls together as it should. I don't think he would object to a man having and carrying about with him the written word rather than the printed—so, so long as he had copied it out himself—"

"Are you serious?"

"You would write down yourself and keep private to yourself—you know, Sim, I've just remembered. That's coming together. He took my book from me."

"What book?"

"A paperback. Nothing important. He took it and went away into the public lavatory and of course when he came back—well he didn't give it back."

"You've forgotten. Like the seven words."

205

"There was one thing he did, though. He picked up a matchbox and a stone. Then he very carefully balanced the matchbox on the arm of the seat with the stone on top of it."

"What did he say?"

"He's not got a mouth that's intended for speaking. Good Lord, what have I said? That's exactly it! Not intended for speaking!"

"What happened to the matchbox and the stone?"

"I don't know. Perhaps they're still there. Perhaps they fell off. I didn't look."

"We're crazy. Both of us."

"He can speak of course, because he said 'Yes'. I'm nearly sure he said 'Yes'. He must have done. I'm quite sure in my mind that he said some other things. Yes, he said quite a bit concerning 'secrecy'."

"What secrecy for God's sake?"

"Didn't I tell you? That's the other thing. No reproduced words. No permanent names to anything. And no one must know."

Sim stopped on the pavement so that Edwin had to stop as well and turn to him.

"Look Edwin, this is fantastic nonsense already! It's masonic stuff, inner circle stuff, conspiratorial—don't you understand? Doesn't he understand himself? You could get up in the High Street or the Market Place and speak; you could get up and shout, you could use a loudhailer and no one, but no one, would give a damn! The jets would still come over, the traffic pass, the shoppers the coppers the teeny boppers and all, and no one would even notice. They'd think you were advertising fivepence off at the supermarket. We're damned with our own triviality, that's what it is—secrecy? I've never heard anything so silly in my life!"

"Nevertheless—you see, I have brought you to the gates of the park."

"Let's get it over."

They stood together a few yards inside the gates, while Edwin swung on his heel looking round. Groups of children were playing here and there. The attendant stood only a few yards from the public lavatory, watching the children morosely as they ran in and out or took each other there.

Edwin discovered the man behind them with a great start. Sim, turning as well, found himself looking straight into the man's face. There was something a little stagey about his appearance, as if he were got up to play a part. He wore a broad-brimmed black hat and a long black overcoat, into the pockets of which his hands were thrust as Edwin's were thrust into his. He was, Sim saw, exactly the same size as he was so that they met eye to eye. Yet the man's face was strange. The right side was browner than a European's would be, yet not so distinctly brown as to type him as Hindu or Pakistani and certainly he was no Negro, for his features were quite as Caucasian as Edwin's own. But the left side of his face was a puzzle. It seemed—thought Sim for a moment—as if he held a hand mirror which was casting faint light from the grey, misty day which lowered the colour of that side a tone or two. In that side, the eye was smaller than the right one and then Sim knew that this lighter shade was not a reflection but a different skin. The man, many years before, had had a skin graft that covered most of the left side of his face and was perhaps the reason why Edwin had said he had a mouth not for speaking, because the skin held that side of the mouth closed as it held the eye nearly closed, an eye, perhaps, not for seeing. A fringe of jet-black hair projected down under the black hat all round and on the left side there was a mulberry-coloured thing projecting through rather longer black hair. With a sudden lurch of his stomach Sim saw that this thing was an ear, or what was left of it—an ear imperfectly hidden by the hair and suggesting immediately that its appearance dated from the event that had occasioned the skin graft. Of all sights he had not expected to see such deformation. It made him wince to look at it. His mouth that had opened in the first movement of some social advance, stayed opened and he said nothing. It was not necessary because he could hear Edwin talking eagerly at his side and with that particularly loud, braying note that was a parody teacher's and so often taken off behind his back. But Sim paid no attention to what Edwin was saying. His own gaze was held by the man's one-and-a-half eyes and his half-mouth not meant for speaking and the extraordinary grief that seemed to contract it as much as the pull of the skin. Moreover, the man seemed to be outlined—but this must be some quirk of psychology—against his background in a way that made him the point of it.

Eyes held, Sim felt the words rising through him, entering his throat, speaking themselves against his own will, evoked, true.

"My inclination is to think that all this is nonsense."

207

The man's right eye seemed to open wider; and the effect was as if a sudden gleam of light came from it. Anger. Anger and grief. Edwin answered.

"Of course it's not what you expect! The paradox is that if you had thought a bit, Goodchild, you'd have known it couldn't be what you expect!"

A particularly snarling jet soughed louder and louder down over them. At the same moment the High Street seemed to be invaded by a whole string of articulated juggernauts. Sim raised a hand to his ear, more in protest than in hope of keeping the noise out. He glanced sideways. Edwin was still speaking, his short nose lifted, the hectic on his cheeks. It sounded like a comminatory psalm, overthrowing, trampling down.

Sim could only tell what he himself said because he was inside with it.

"What are we getting ourselves into?"

Then the jet had passed, the juggernauts were grinding themselves away, to turn right and go round to the spur of the motorway. He looked back at the man and found with a jolt of surprise that he had gone. A kind of mash of surmises, most of them ridiculous, filled his mind; and then he saw him, ten yards off and striding away, hands in long coat pockets. Edwin was following.

They went like that, the three of them, in single file along the main, gravelled path. Grief and anger. The two so mixed they had become a single, settled quality, a strength. Again, words seemed to find their own way up his body towards his throat like bubbles in a bottle; but with the man's face hidden ahead there he contrived to keep them in.

I'd expected some kind of Holy Joe.

As if they shared a mind, Edwin slackened his pace and drew alongside.

"I know it's not what anyone would expect. How are you doing?"

Unwillingly, again, and cautiously—

"I'm—interested."

They were approaching an area where children were playing. There were swings, a see-saw, a small, metal roundabout, a slide. As they moved towards the centre of the park the road noises—and there, now, was the sudden roaring, rattling passage of a train—tended to be muffled as if the trees round the edge of the green did indeed muffle sound as they hindered sight. Only the jets soughed over, one every two or three minutes.

"There! Did you see!"

Edwin had reached sideways and grasped Sim's wrist. They were stopped and looking forward.

"See what?"

"That ball!"

The man had not slackened his pace and was getting ahead of them. Edwin lugged again at Sim's wrist.

"You must have noticed!"

"Noticed what, for—"

As if he were talking to a particularly dim pupil Edwin began to explain.

"The ball that boy kicked. It shot across the gravel and through his feet."

"Nonsense. It went between his feet."

"I tell you. It went *through* them!"

"Optical illusion. I saw as well, you know. It went between them! Be your age, Edwin. You'll be having him levitate next."

"Look, I *saw* it!"

"So did I. And it didn't."

"Did."

Sim burst out laughing and after a moment or two Edwin allowed himself to smile.

"Sorry. But—look. As clearly—"

"It didn't. Because if it did—you see, Edwin the, the miracle would be trivial. More than trivial. What difference would it make if the ball struck and bounced off? Or did in fact, as I am sure it did, happen to find a passage between his feet in an unusually neat but still possible way?"

"You are asking me to doubt the evidence of my own eyes."

"For God's sake! Haven't you seen a conjurer? He's unusual, he's extraordinary, he embarrasses me and so do you, but I'm not going to have a trick of the light or a minimal coincidence stuffed down my throat as a violation of the natural order, as a miracle if you prefer the word."

"I don't know what word to use. It was another dimension, that's all."

"Scientistic top-dressing."

"His life, as far as I have shared it—and that's a matter of minutes—well, it may be hours—is thick with that sort of—phenomenon."

"Why isn't he in a laboratory where the controls are?"

"Because he has something more important to do!"

"More important than the truth?"

"Yes. Yes, if you like!"

"What then?"

"How should I know?"

But the man had stopped by a seat that was set by the gravelled path. Sim and Edwin stopped too, a few yards short of the seat, and Sim had a moment or two of feeling acutely foolish. For now, plainly, they were following the man not as if he were another man but as if he were some rare beast or bird with whom there was no possibility of human intercourse but whose behaviour or plumage or pelt was of interest. It was silly, since the man was no more than some sort of white man dressed all in black, and with a head on him, the one side of which had received severe damage many years ago and been imperfectly repaired; and who—all this Sim told himself with increasing comfort and increasing amusement—who was very reasonably annoyed at what life had done to him.

Edwin had stopped talking and was looking where the man was looking. There was a scatter of children playing, little boys mostly but also a small girl or two on the edge of the group. There was also a man. He was a slender old fellow, seeming, thought Sim, older than I am, the oldest man in the park, this childish morning, a slender, rather bent old fellow with a mop of white hair and an ancient pepper-and-salt suit, a suit far, far older than the children, a good suit, a too good suit, a suit that gentlemen used to have made for them in the days when there were gentlemen and waist-coats were worn; also brown, elastic-sided boots, but no coat on this childish morning, together with an anxious, rather silly face—the old man was playing ball with the children. It was a big ball, of many colours. The old fellow or perhaps old gentleman or just old man was active, springy, and he threw the ball to one boy and had it back and then to another boy and had it back and all the time he was working his way—him and the boys—towards the lavatories, with an anxious and gleaming smile on his thin face.

What am I seeing?

210

Sim swung round on his heel. The park attendant was nowhere to be seen. There were, after all, many groups of children and one man cannot be everywhere. Edwin was looking outraged.

The old man, with an agility that the years had not impaired very much, kicked the ball hard with his shiny boot and laughed and giggled with his thin mouth. The ball beat the boy, beat all the boys. The ball flew and bounced and came as if the old man had intended it, bounce, bounce, and the man in black held up his hands with the ball in them. The old man, giggling and waving, waited for the ball back and the man in black waited and the children. Then the old man with a loping, a springy catlike run came across to the path, but began to slow and stop smiling and even stop panting and he bent a little, just a very little and examined each of them in turn. No one said anything and the children waited.

The old man lowered his chin and looked up at the man from under white, springy eyebrows. He was a clean old man, unnaturally clean in his suit, however worn. His voice was expensively educated.

"My ball, I think, gentlemen."

Still no one said anything. The old man gave his silly, anxious giggle again.

"Virginibus puerisque!"

The man in black held the ball against his chest and looked at the old man over it. Sim could only see the undamaged side of his face, his undamaged eye and ear. The features had been regular, attractive, even.

The old man spoke again.

"If you gentlemen are connected with the Home Office, then I can only assure you that the ball is my ball and that the little men at my back are undamaged. To put the matter clearly, you have nothing on me. So please, give me my ball and go away."

Sim spoke.

"I know you! All those years ago—in my shop! The children's books—"

The old man stared.

"Oh, so it's a meeting of old acquaintances is it? Your shop? Well allow me to tell you, sir, we pay as we go, these days, no credit allowed or given. I paid! Oh yes I paid all right! Not for that but for life you see. You don't understand, do you? Ask Mr

211

Bell, there. He brought you. But I've paid so don't any of you dun me. Give me that ball! I bought it!"

Something was happening to the man in black. It was a kind of slow convulsion, and it shook the ball at his chest. His mouth opened.

"Mr Pedigree."

The old man started. He stared into the melted face, peered, head on one side as if he could look under the white skin of the left side, searched all over, from the drawn mouth to the ear on that side, still so imperfectly hidden. The stare became a glare.

"And I know you, Matty Woodrave! *You*—all those years ago, the one who didn't come and had the face, the cruelty, the gall to, to—Oh I know you! Give me that ball! I have nothing but—it was all your fault!"

Again the convulsion, but this time with the grief and anger made audible—

"I know."

"You heard him! You're my witnesses, gentlemen, I hold you to it! You see? A life wasted, a life that might have been so, so beautiful—"

"No."

The word was low, and grated as if from somewhere that was not accustomed to making speech. The old man gave a kind of snarl.

"I want my ball, I want my ball!"

But the whole attitude of the man before him who held the ball so firmly against his black-clad chest was a refusal. The old man snarled again. He glanced round and cried out as if he had been stung; for the children had run or drifted away and were mixed among the playing groups spread round the park. The old man loped out into the empty space of grass.

"Tommy! Phil! Andy!"

The man in black turned to Sim and faced him over the ball. With great solemnity he held the ball out in both hands and Sim understood that he must take it with an equal solemnity. He even bowed a little as he took the ball between his two hands. The man in black turned away and walked after the old man. As if he knew they had made the first step of following him, he gestured on one side of him in a gesture of admonition, without looking round. Don't follow me.

212

They watched him right across the grass until he disappeared behind the lavatory. Sim turned to Edwin.

"What was all that about?"

"Some of it is clear at any rate. The old man. Pedigree, his name is."

"I said, didn't I? He used to shoplift. Children's books."

"Did you prosecute?"

"Warned him off. I understood him. He wanted the books as bait, the old, old—"

"There, but for the grace of God."

"Don't be sanctimonious. You've never wanted to go round interfering with children, neither have I."

"He's a long time there."

"Spend a penny just like anyone else."

"Unless he's having trouble with the old man."

"It's such a particularly contemptible business. Let's hope we don't see him again."

"Who?"

"The old fellow—what did you call him—Pettifer?"

"Pedigree."

"Pedigree, then. Disgusting."

"Perhaps I'd better have a look—"

"What at?"

"He might be having—"

Edwin trotted across the grass towards the lavatory. Sim waited, feeling not just foolish but disgusted, as if the ball was a contamination. He wondered what to do with it; and the memory of the clean old man with his disgusting appetite made him wince inside. He turned his mind aside to things that were really clean and sweet, thinking of Stanhope's little girls. How exquisite they had been and how well-behaved! What a delight it had been to watch them grow; though no matter how wonderfully *nubile* they became they could never surpass that really fairy delicacy of childhood, a beauty that could make you weep—and of course they hadn't turned out just as they should but that was as much Stanhope's fault as theirs and Sophy was so pretty and so friendly—good morning Mr Goodchild, how is Mrs Goodchild? Yes it is isn't it? There was no doubt about it, the Stanhope twins shone in Greenfield like a light!

Edwin was coming back.

213

"He's gone. Disappeared."

"You mean he's gone away. Don't exaggerate. There's a gate out to the road among the laurels."

"They've both gone."

"What am I supposed to do with this ball?"

"You'd better keep it, I suppose. We'll see him again."

"Time I was going."

Together they walked back along the gravel path but before they had gone more than fifty yards, Edwin stopped them.

"About here."

"What?"

"Don't you remember? What I saw."

"And I didn't."

But Edwin was not listening. His jaw had dropped.

"Sim! Now I understand. Oh yes, it all hangs together! I'm one step nearer to a complete understanding of—if not what he is—of how he works, what he is doing—That ball that went round or through—He let it go. He knew it was the wrong ball."

CHAPTER THIRTEEN

Ruth was being fanciful. This was most unusual for her since on the whole she was a down-to-earth woman; but now she had a feverish cold and was staying in bed. The Girl minded the shop now and then, though Sim was always nervous when he did not have both her and the shop in sight, but he had quite often to take hot drinks upstairs and persuade Ruth to drink them. Each time he did this he had to stay a bit because of the fancifulness. She lay on her side of the double-bed where the children had been begotten a generation ago. She kept her eyes closed and her face shone with perspiration. Now and then she muttered.

"What did you say, dear?"

Mutter.

"I've brought you some more hot drink. Wouldn't you like to sit up and drink it?"

Ruth spoke with startling clearness.

"He moved. I saw him."

An almost physical anguish contracted Sim's heart.

"Good. I'm glad. Sit up and drink this."

"She used a knife."

"Ruth! Sit up!"

Her eyes flickered open and he saw them focus on his face. Then she looked round the bedroom and up at the ceiling where the sound of a declining jet was so loud it seemed visible. She put her hands down and heaved herself up.

"Better?"

She shuddered in the bed and he draped a shawl round her shoulders. She drank, sip after sip, then handed the glass back without looking at him.

"Now you're what they used to call all-of-a-glow you'll feel better. Shall I take your temperature again?"

215

She shook her head.

"No point. Know what we know. Too much noise. Which way is north?"

"Why?"

"I want to know. I must know."

"You're a bit hazy still, aren't you?"

"I want to know!"

"Well—"

Sim thought of the road outside, the High Street, the Old Bridge. He pictured the enlacement of canal and rail and motorway and the high jet road searing across them all.

"It's a bit difficult. Where would the sun be?"

"It keeps turning, and the noise!"

"I know."

She lay back again and shut her eyes.

"Try and sleep dear."

"No! Not. Not."

Someone was hooting in the road outside. He glanced down through the window. A juggernaut was trying to get on to the Old Bridge and the cars massing behind it were impatient.

"It'll be quiet later."

"Mind the shop."

"Sandra's there."

"If I want anything I'll thump."

"Better not kiss you."

He laid his forefinger on his lips then transferred it to her forehead. She smiled.

"Go."

He crept away downstairs, through the living-room and into the shop. Sandra was sitting at the desk and staring straight at the big shop window without a trace of expression. The only thing that moved was her lower jaw as it masticated what seemed to be a permanent piece of chewing-gum. She had sandy hair and sandy eyebrows imperfectly concealed by eyebrow pencil. She was rather fat, she wore bulging jeans and Sim disliked her. Ruth had chosen her out of the only three applicants for a job that did not pay much, was dull by modern standards and required no intelligence at all. Sim knew why Ruth had chosen the least attractive, or most unattractive of the applicants and agreed with her, ruefully enough.

"Could I have my chair, Sandra, do you think?"

Sarcasm was wasted on her.

"I don't mind."

She got up. He sat down, only to see her wander across to the steps which he used for reaching the high shelves and perch her large bottom on it. Sim watched her savagely.

"Wouldn't it be better, Sandra, if you kept on your feet? It's what people expect you know."

"There isn't any people and there hasn't been. And there won't be not now it's so near lunch. There hasn't been anybody not even the phone."

All that was true. The turnover was becoming ludicrous. If it weren't for the rare books—

Sim experienced a moment of exquisite inferiority. It was no good expecting Sandra to understand the difference between this place and a supermarket or a sweet shop. She had her own idea of that difference and it was all in favour of the supermarket. There was life in the supermarket, fellows, talk, chat, light, noise, even muzak on top of the rest. Here were only the silent books waiting faithfully on their shelves, their words unchanged, century after century from incunabula down to paperbacks. It was a thing so obvious that often Sim found himself astonished at his own capacity for finding it astonishing; and he would move from that point to a generalized state of astonishment that he felt obscurely was, like the man said, the beginning of wisdom. The only trouble was that the astonishment recurred but the wisdom did not follow. Astonished I live; astonished I shall die.

Probably Sandra felt her weight. He looked at her and saw how her broad bottom overflowed the step. Then again, she might be having a period. He stood up.

"OK Sandra. You can have my chair for a bit. Until the phone rings."

She heaved her bottom off the step and wandered down the shop. He saw how her thighs rubbed each other. She sank into the chair, still chewing like a cow.

"Ta."

"Read a book if you like."

She turned her eyes on him, unblinking.

"What for?"

"You can read I suppose?"

" 'Course. Your wife asked me. You ought to know that."

Worse and worse. We must get rid of her. Get a Paki, a lad, he'd work. Have to keep an eye on him though.

Don't think that! Race relations.

All the same they swarm. With the best will in the world I must say they swarm. They are not what I think, they are what I feel. Nobody knows what I feel, thank God.

But they were to have a visitor, perhaps a customer. He was trying the door now—ting! It was Stanhope, of all people. Sim hurried down the shop, hands washing each other in the appropriate manner, his personalized bit of play-acting.

"Good morning Mr Stanhope! A pleasure to see you. How are you? Well, I hope?"

Stanhope brushed it all aside in his usual manner and went straight to the point, a technical one.

"Sim. Reti. *The Game of Chess*. The nineteen thirty-six reprint. How much please?"

Sim shook his head.

"I'm sorry, Mr Stanhope, but we do not have a copy."

"Sold it? When?"

"We never had one, I'm afraid."

"Oh yes you did."

"You are at perfect liberty—"

"It's a wise bookseller that knows his own stock."

Laughing, Sim shook his head.

"You won't catch me out, Mr Stanhope. Remember I've been here since my father's day."

Stanhope hopped briskly up the steps.

"There you are, poor condition."

"Good Lord."

"Knew I'd seen it. Haven't been in for years, either. How much?"

Sim took the book, blew dust off the top, then looked at the flyleaf. He did a rapid calculation.

"That'll be three pounds ten. I mean three fifty of course."

Stanhope reached into his pocket, grumbling. Sim, unable to resist, heard his own voice going on without, apparently, his volition.

"Yesterday I saw Miss Stanhope. She passed the shop—"

"Who—one of mine? That'll be Sophy, idle little bitch."

"But she's so enchanting—they're both so enchanting—"

"Be your age. That generation's not enchanting, any of it. Here."

"Thank you, sir. They've always been such a pleasure to us, innocence, beauty, manners—"

Stanhope gave a cackle of laughter.

"Innocence? They tried to poison me once, or damn nearly. Left some filthy things in a drawer by the bed. Must have found the spare house-keys and then *plotted*—bitches! I wonder where they found those beastly little monsters?"

"A practical joke. But they've always been so kind to us—"

"Perhaps you'll meet them, you and Bell at your meetings."

"Meet them?"

"You *are* looking for a quiet place aren't you?"

"Edwin said something."

"Well then."

Stanhope nodded at him, looked briefly towards Sandra then withdrew, ting! A loud thump came from the ceiling. Sim hurried upstairs and held Ruth while she brought up some phlegm. When she was better she asked who he had been talking to.

"Stanhope. Just a chess book. Fortunately we had it in stock."

Her head turned from side to side.

"Dream. Bad dream."

"Just a dream. Next time it'll be a good one."

She drifted off to sleep again and breathed easily. He tiptoed down into the shop. Sandra was still sitting. But then the shop bell tinged again. It was Edwin. Sim made shushing noises and then breathed the reminder melodramatically.

"Ruth's poorly. She's asleep up there—"

Edwin's declension from noise to near silence was as dramatic.

"What is it, dear Sim?"

"Just a cold and she's getting better. But you know at our kind of age—not that she's as old as me, of course; but all the same—"

"I know. We're in the bracket. Look, I have news."

"A meeting?"

"We are all there is, I'm afraid. Yet I'm not afraid, really. Many are called, et cetera."

"Stanhope's place."

"He told you?"

219

"He was here just now. Dropped in."

Sim was faintly proud of Stanhope having dropped in. Stanhope was, after all, a celebrity, with his column, broadcasts and chess displays. Ever since chess had moved out of the grey periphery of the news and with Bobby Fischer edged into the full limelight, Sim had come to an unwilling respect for Stanhope.

"I'm glad you didn't object."

"Who? I? Object to Stanhope?"

"I've always had the feeling that your attitude to him was faintly, shall we say, illiberal."

Sim cogitated.

"That's true, I suppose. After all, I've spent my life here, like him. We're old Greenfield people. You see, there was a bit of scandal and I suppose I'm prudish. When his wife left him. Women, you know. Ruth has no time for him. On the other hand his twin girls—they've been a delight to us all, just to watch them grow up. How he can ignore, could ignore such, such *charmers*— let them grow up any old how—"

"You will be able to sample the charm again, although at second hand."

"They're not!"

"Oh no. You wouldn't expect it, would you? But he says we can use their place."

"A room?"

"It's the stabling at the end of the garden. Have you been in?"

"No, no."

"They used to live there, more or less. Glad enough to get away from Stanhope, if you ask me. And he from them. They took it over. Didn't you know?"

"I don't see what's so special about it."

"I know the place. After all, I live at the top end of the garden. I should, don't you think? When we came here first, the girls even invited us to tea there. It was a kind of dolls' tea party. They were so solemn! The questions Toni asked!"

"I don't see—"

"You old stick-in-the-mud!"

Sim made himself grumble.

"Such an out-of-the-way place. I don't see why you can't use the community centre. After all, that way we might get more members."

"It's the quality of the place."

"Feminine?"

Edwin looked at him in surprise. Sim felt himself begin to blush, so he hurried on his explanation.

"I remember when my daughter was at college, once I went into the hostel where she was living—girls from top to bottom—good Lord, you'd never believe perfume could be so penetrating! I just thought, if it's where a couple of—Well. You see."

"Nothing like that at all. Nothing whatsoever."

"Sorry."

"Don't apologize."

"This quality."

Edwin took a turn round one of the middle bookcases. He came back, drawing himself up, beaming. He threw his arms wide.

"Mmm-ah!"

"You seem very pleased with yourself."

"Sim. Have you been in the, the community centre?"

"Not since."

"It's all right of course. Just the thing and it's where I met him—"

"I'm not, you know—not as impressed as you are, no not half as impressed. You'd better understand that, Edwin. I don't doubt that to you in particular—"

"Just listen. Now."

"I am. Go on."

"No, no! Not to me. Just listen."

Sim looked round him, listening. The traffic produced a kind of middle range of noise but nothing unusual. Then the clock struck from the community centre and like an extension of the sound he heard the clang of a fire engine's alarm bell ring as the machine nosed over the Old Bridge. A jet whined down, mile after mile. Edwin opened his mouth to speak, then shut it, holding up one finger.

Sim felt it with his feet, more than heard it—the faint vibration, on and on, as a train rocked across the canal and drew its useful length through the fields towards the midlands.

There came a thump on the ceiling.

"Just a minute. I'll be back."

Ruth wanted him to wait outside the door while she went to the loo. Thought she might come over queer. He sat on the attic stairs,

221

waiting for her. Through the shot-window he could see that men were already opening up the jumbled roofs that had held Frankley's ridiculous stock. Presently the breakers would come with their flailing ball and chain, though it was hardly needed. They had only to lean against the old place and it would collapse. More noise.

He came back to the shop to find Edwin perched on the edge of the desk and talking to Sandra. He felt indignant at the sight.

"You can go along now, Sandra. I know it's early. But I'll lock up."

Sandra, still ruminating, took a kind of loose cardigan from the hook behind the desk.

"'Bye."

He watched her out of the shop. Edwin laughed.

"Nothing doing there, Sim. I couldn't interest her."

"You—!"

"Why not? All souls are of equal value."

"Oh yes. I believe."

Indeed I do. We are all equal. I believe that. It is more or less a fourth-class belief.

"You were going to explain a crazy idea to me."

"They used to build churches by holy wells. Over them sometimes. They needed it, water, it was stuff you drew up out of the earth in a bucket, the earth gave it you. Not out of a pipe by courtesy of the water board. It was wild, springing, raw stuff."

"Bugs."

"It was holy because men worshipped it. Don't you think that infinite charity would fix that for us?"

"Infinite charity is choosy."

"Water is holiness. Was holiness."

"Today I have not struck a believing streak."

"And now; as water was then, so something as strange and unexpected and necessary in our mess. Silence. Precious, raw silence."

"Double-glazing. Technology has the answer."

"Just as it put the wild holiness in a pen and conducted it demurely through a pipe. No. What I meant was random silence, lucky silence, or destined."

"You've been there now, in the last few days?"

"As soon as Stanhope offered us the place. Certainly. There's a

222

kind of landing passage at the top of the stairs with the rooms opening out. You look through small dormers, that way to the still, untouched canal, the other way into the green of the garden. Silence lives there, Sim. I know it. Silence is there and waiting for us, waiting for him. He's not aware of it yet. I've found it for him. The holiness of silence waiting for us."

"It can't be."

"I wonder how it comes about? Certainly there's a sense of going down, of all the town being built up there and this being, as it were, at the bottom of steps, shut away, a kind of courtyard, a private place farther down into the earth almost holding the sunlight like a cup and the quiet as if someone was there with two hands holding it all—someone who no longer needed to breathe."

"It was innocence. You said—a kind of dolls' tea party. That's sad."

"What's sad about it?"

"They've grown up, you see. Look, Edwin. There's some trick of the building, some way in which sound is reflected away—"

"Even the jets?"

"Why not! Somehow the surfaces will have done it. There'll be a rational explanation."

"You said it was innocence."

"My aged heart was touched."

"Put that way—"

"Have the girls left any traces behind them?"

"The place is still furnished, more or less, if that is what you mean."

"Interesting. Do you think they would be interested? The girls, I mean."

"They aren't home."

Sim was on the point of explaining that he had seen Sophy walking past the shop but thought better of it. There was a touch of curiosity in Edwin's face whenever he heard an inquiry about them—almost as if the non-events, the strange, sensual, delightful and poignant linkage that did not exist except in the world of a man's supposing, were not private, but out there, to be detected, read like a book, no, like a comic strip, part of the generation-long folly of Sim Goodchild.

Because he was old, felt himself to be old and irritable with

223

himself as much as with the world, he did a violence to his accustomed secrecy and revealed a small corner of the comic strip.

"I used to be in love with them."

There—it was out and blinding.

"I mean—not what you might think. They were adorable and to be, be cherished. I don't know—they still are—well she is, the brunette, Sophy, or was still when I last saw her. Of course the fair one—Toni—she's gone."

"You old romantic."

"Paternal instinct. And Stanhope—he really doesn't care about them you know, I'm certain; and then with those women—well that's all a good while ago. One felt they were neglected. I wouldn't have you for the world think—"

"I don't. Oh no—"

"Not that—"

"Quite."

"If you see what I mean."

"Absolutely."

"Of course my child—our children—were so much older."

"Yes. I see that."

"So it was natural with two such decorative little girls living practically on our doorstep."

"Of course."

There was a long pause. Edwin broke it.

"I thought tomorrow night if that's convenient for you. It's his evening off."

"If Ruth is well enough."

"Will she come?"

"I meant if she's well enough to be left. What about Edwina?"

"Oh no. No. Definitely. You know Edwina. She met him, you see. Just for a minute or two. She's so, so—"

"Sensitive. I know. I can't think how she can bear her job as almoner. The things she must see."

"It is a trial. But she makes a distinction. She said plainly afterwards. If he were a patient it would be different. You see."

"Yes I see."

"In her own free time it's different you see."

"Yes."

"Of course if there were an emergency."

"I understand."

224

"So it'll just be the three of us, I'm afraid. Not many is it, when one remembers the old days."

"Perhaps Edwina would care to come and sit with Ruth."

"You know how she is about germs. She's as brave as a lion really, you see, but she has this thing about germs. Not viruses. Just germs."

"Yes, so I believe. Germs are dirtier than viruses. Germs probably have viruses, would you say?"

"She simply has this thing."

"She's not a committee. Women often aren't. Are you a committee Edwin? I am."

"I don't know what you mean."

"Oh Lord. Different standards of belief. Multiply the number of committee members by the number of standards of belief—"

"I'm still not with you, Sim."

"Partitions. One of me believes in partitions. He thinks, for example, that although Frankley's is on the other side of this wall—or is until they knock the place down—the wall remains real and it's no good pretending otherwise. But another of my members—well, what shall I say?"

"Perhaps he'll pierce a partition."

"Your man? Let him do it really, then, and beyond doubt. I know—"

I know how the mind can rise from its bed, go forth, down the stairs, past doors, down the path to the stables that are bright and rosy by the light of two small girls. But they were asleep and remained asleep even if their images performed the silly dance, the witless Arabian thing.

"Know what?"

"It doesn't matter. A committee member."

All is imagination he doth prove.

"Partitions, my majority vote says, remain partitions."

One is one and all alone and ever more shall be so.

Edwin glanced at his watch.

"I must rush. I'll let you know the time when he gets in touch."

"Late evening is best for me."

"For the whole committee. Which one had a thing about the little girls?"

"A sentimental old thing. I doubt he'll bother to come."

He ushered Edwin out of the shop door into the street and gestured courteously to his hurrying back.

A sentimental old thing?

Sim sighed to himself. Not a sentimental old thing but the unruly member.

At eight o'clock, Ruth being propped up with a good book and his stomach rather distended with fish fillet and reconstituted potato, together with peas out of a tin, Sim made his way through the shop, relocked the door behind him and walked the few paces to Sprawson's. It was broad daylight but on the right-hand side of the building there was nevertheless a light in Stanhope's window. The town was quiet and only a jukebox in the Keg of Ale disturbed the blue summer evening. Sim thought to himself that the alleged silence of the stables was not really necessary. They might well hold their small meeting—but meeting was hardly the word for three people—might well hold it in the street; but as he thought this, a helicopter, red light sparking away, flew the length of the old canal, and as if to rub in the point a train rumbled over the viaduct. After both machines had passed, his ears, newly sharpened perhaps, detected the faint chatter of a typewriter from the lighted window where Stanhope was still working at his book or a broadcast or his column. Sim ascended the two steps to the glass door and pushed it open. This was familiar ground— solicitors and the Bells to the left, the Stanhope door to the right—at the other end of the short hall the door which gave on to the steps down to the garden. It was all an absurdly romantic area to Sim. He felt, and was aware of, the romance and the absurdity. He had no connection whatsoever with the two little girls, had never had and could expect none. It was all pure fantasy. A few, a very few visits to the shop—

There was a clatter from the stairs on the left. Edwin appeared tumultuously, a man this time of gusto, who threw his long arm round Sim's shoulder and squeezed it tremendously.

"Sim, my dear fellow, here you are!"

It seemed so silly a greeting that Sim detached himself as quickly as he could.

"Where is he?"

"I'm expecting him. He knows where. Or I think so. Shall we go?"

Edwin strode, larger than life, to the end of the hall and opened the door above the garden steps.

"After you, my dear fellow."

Plants and shrubs and smallish trees in flower trespassed on the path that led straight down to the rosy-tiled stables with their ancient dormer windows. Sim had a moment of his usual incredulity at the reality of something that had been so near him and unknown, for so many years. He opened his mouth to speak of this but shut it again.

Each step you took down the steps—there were six of them—had a quite distinct quality. It was a kind of numbing, a muffling. Sim who had swum and snorkeled on the Costa Brava found himself likening the whole process at once to the effect of going under water; but not, as with water, an instant transition from up here to down there, a breaking of a perfect surface, a boundary. Here the boundary was just as indubitable but less distinct. You came down, out of the evening noise of Greenfield, and step by step, you were—numbed was not the right word, nor was muffled. There was not a right word. This oblong of garden, unkempt, abandoned and deserted, was nevertheless like a pool of something, a pool, one could only say, of quiet. Balm. Sim stopped and looked about him as if this effect would reveal itself to the eye as well as the ear but there was nothing—only the overgrown fruit trees, the rioting rose stocks, camomile, nettles, rosemary, lupins, willowherb and foxgloves. He looked up into the clear air; and there, astonishingly at a great height, a jet was coming down, the noise of its descent wiped away so that it was graceful and innocent as a glider. He looked round him again, buddleia, old man's beard, veronica—and the scents of the garden invaded his nostrils like a new thing.

Edwin's hand was on his shoulder.

"Let's get on."

"I was thinking how preferable all this is to our small patch. I'd forgotten about flowers."

"Greenfield is a country town!"

"It's a question of where one looks. And the silence!"

At the end of the path down the garden they came to the courtyard, shadowed away from the sun. At some time the entrance had been closed by double doors but these had been taken away. Now the only door was the small one, opposite, that led out to the

227

towpath. Stairs went up on their left hand.

"Up here."

Sim followed Edwin up, then stood and looked round him. To call the place a flat would be an exaggeration. There was room for a narrow divan, an ancient sofa, a small table, chairs. There were two cupboards and on either side open entries led to minute bedrooms. There were dormer windows that looked out over the canal, and back up to the house.

Sim said nothing, but simply stood. It was not the mean size of the room, nor the floor, of one-plank thickness, the interior walls of some sort of cheap boarding. It was not the battered, second-hand furniture, the armchair from which stuffing hung or the stained table. It was the atmosphere, the smell. Someone, Sophy presumably, had been there recently, and the odour of cheap and penetrating scent hung in the air as a kind of cover to an ancient staleness, of food, more scent, of—no, neither a glow nor perspiration—but sweat. There was a mirror surrounded by elaborate gilding on one wall, with a shelf below it on which were bottles, half-used lipsticks, tins, and sprays and powder. Under the dormer, on top of a low cupboard, was a huge doll that leaned and grinned. The central table had a pile of oddments on it—tights, a glove puppet, a pair of pants that needed washing, a woman's magazine and the earplug from a transistor radio. But the velvet cloth on the table was fringed with bobbles, between the patches on the wall where pictures and photographs had once been stuck and left traces of sticking, were ornaments such as china flowers and some bits of coloured material—some of them made into rosettes. There was dust.

Inside Sim, the illusions of twenty years vanished like bubbles. He said to himself yes of course, yes, they weren't looked after and they had to grow up, yes, what was I thinking of? And they had no mother—poor things, poor things! No wonder—

Edwin was delicately removing the objects from the table. He laid them on the cupboard top under the dormer. There was a standard lamp by the cupboard. The shade was pink and had bobbles like the tablecloth.

"Could we get the window open, do you think?"

Sim hardly heard him. He was examining what could only be called his grief. At last he turned to the dormer and examined it. No one had opened it for years but someone had begun to paint the surround, then given up. It was like the cupboard door under the dormer at the other end of the room. Someone had begun to paint that pink and also given up. Sim peered through the dormer that seemed to stare, blearily, back at the house.

Edwin spoke at his side.

"*Feel* the silence!"

Sim looked at him in astonishment.

"Can't you feel the, the—"

"The what, Sim?"

The grief. That's what it must be. Grief. Neglect.

"Nothing."

Then he saw the glass door open at the top of the steps at the other end of the garden. Men came through. He swung round to Edwin.

"Oh no!"

"Did you know about this?"

"Of course I knew the place was here. This is where we had our dolls' tea party."

"You might have told me. I assure you, Edwin, if I'd known I wouldn't have come. Damn it man—we caught him shoplifting! And don't you know where he's been? He's been to jail and you know why. Damn it man!"

"Wildwave."

On the stairs the voice was suddenly near.

"That's what nobody really believes. I don't know where you're taking me and I don't like it. Is this some kind of trap?"

"Look, Edwin—"

The black hat and blasted face rose above the level of the landing. The shock of grey-white hair and the pinched face of the old man in the park followed behind him. The old man stopped on the stairs with a kind of writhing twist.

"Oh no! No you don't Matty! What is this, Pederasts Anonymous? Three cured and one to go?"

The man called Matty had him by the lapel.

"Mr Pedigree—"

"You're as big a fool as ever, Matty! Let me go, d'you hear?"

It was ridiculous. The two strange and unattractive men seemed to be wrestling on the stairs. Edwin was dancing round the top.

"Gentlemen! Gentlemen!"

Sim had a profound wish to be out of it and away from the

ravished building that was so brutally robbed of its silence. But the stairs were blocked. Exhausted for the moment by his efforts to escape, the old man was gasping and trying to speak at the same time.

"You—talk about my condition—it's a beautiful condition—nobody knows. Are you a psychiatrist? I don't *want* to be cured, they know that—so good day to you—" and with an absurd effort at the socially correct thing, he was bowing to Sim and to Edwin above him and at the same time trying to wrench himself away "—a very good day to you—"

"Edwin, let's get out of here for God's sake! It's all a mistake, ridiculous and humiliating!"

"You have nothing on me—any of you—let me go, Matty, I'll, I'll have the law—" And then the man in the black hat had let him go, had dropped his hands. They stood on the stairs, partly visible like bathers on an underwater slope. Pedigree had his face at the level of Windgrove's shoulder. He caught sight of the ear a foot above him. He convulsed with loathing.

"You hideous, hideous creature!"

Slowly and inexorably the blood consumed the right side of Matty's face. He stood, doing nothing, saying nothing. The old man turned away hastily. They heard his feet on the cobbles of the courtyard, saw him appear on the garden path between the overgrown flower beds. He was hurrying away. Half-way up the path he turned, still moving, and glanced under his shoulder at the dormer windows with all the venom of a villain in a melodrama. Sim saw his lips move; but the curious muffling—for after this desecration of the place, that magical quality had declined from a mystery to an impediment—smothered his words. Then he climbed the stairs and went through the hall and out into the street.

Edwin spoke.

"He must have thought we were police."

Windrove's face was white and brown again. His black hat had been pushed a little on one side and the ear was only too visible. As if he knew what Sim was looking at, he took off his hat to settle his hair. Now the reason for the hat was more evident. He smoothed his hair down carefully, then adjusted the black hat to hold it down.

This revelation of a fact seemed to go some way towards making it tolerable for the viewer. Windgraff—Matty, had the old man said?—Matty when he revealed his disability, his deformity, his, one must so call it, handicap, was no longer a forbidding monstrosity but only another man. Sim found himself, before he was aware of making up his mind, sharing round the social small change. He held out his hand.

"I am Sim Goodchild. How do you do."

Windgrove looked down at the hand as if it were an object to be examined and not shaken. Then he took the hand, turned it over and peered into the palm. Sim was slightly disconcerted by this and looked down himself to see if the palm was dirtied in any way, or interesting, or decorated—and by the time the words had fallen through his awareness he understood that his palm was being read, so he stood there, relaxed, and now not a little amused. He looked into his own palm, pale, crinkled, the volume, as it were, most delicately bound in this rarest or at least most expensive of all binding material—and then he fell through into an awareness of his own hand that stopped time in its revolution. The palm was exquisitely beautiful, it was made of light. It was precious and preciously inscribed with a sureness and delicacy beyond art and grounded somewhere else in absolute health.

In a convulsion unlike anything he had ever known, Sim stared into the gigantic world of his own palm and saw that it was holy.

The little room came back, the strange, but no longer forbidding creature still stared down, Edwin was moving chairs to the table.

It was true. The place of silence was magical. And dirty.

Windrave let go his hand and he took it back in all its beauty, its revelation. Edwin spoke. It was possible to detect a little dust on the words, a little touch of jealousy.

"Did you promise him a long life?"

"Don't, Edwin. Nothing like that—"

Windrove went to the other side of the table and that became at once the head of it. Edwin sat down on his right. Sim slid into a chair on his left, three sides of the table and an empty side where Pedigree was not.

Windgrove shut his eyes.

Sim stared round the room, free of it. Here and there were drawing pins that had held up decorations. A rather poor mirror. The divan by the dormer with its rows of, of *bobbles*—the doll with her frills that sat, propped on the far corner of the cupboard and

231

held there by a cushion—those pony pictures and that photograph of a young man, a pop star probably but now anonymous—

The man laid his hands on the table, palms upward. Sim saw Edwin glance down and take the right-hand one in his own left hand and reach across with the right. He had a moment of embarrassment at the idea, but reached out and took Edwin's hand in his, and laid his right hand on Windrow's left. It was a tough and elastic substance he touched, no universe, but warm, astonishingly warm, hot.

He was shaken by a gust of interior laughter. The Philosophical Society, with its minutes, chairman, committee, its taking of halls and assembly rooms, its distinguished guests, to have come down to this—two old men holding hands with a—what?

It was a time after that—a minute, ten minutes, half an hour, that Sim discovered he wanted to scratch his nose. He wondered whether to be brutal and lift his hands away, thus breaking the small circle, but determined not. It was a small sacrifice after all; and now, if one did detach oneself from the desire to scratch one immediately found how far away those others were, miles, it seemed, so that the circle, instead of being a small one was gigantic, more than a stone circle, county-wide, country-wide—vast.

Sim found he wanted to scratch his nose again. It was provoking to have two such disparate scales, the one of inches, the other, universal more or less—the nose must be *wrestled* with! It was an itch just a fraction to the left of the tip, a tickle fiendishly adjusted to set every nerve of the skin throughout the body tickling in sympathy. He fought resolutely, feeling how hard his right hand was held—and now the left as well, squeezed, who was squeezing who—so that his breath came in great gasps with the effort. His face contorted with the anguish of it and he struggled to get his hands away but they were held firm. All he could do was screw up his face again and again round his nose, trying to reach the tip absurdly with his cheeks, with his lips, his tongue, with anything—and then, inspired, he bent down and rubbed his nose on the wooden surface between his hands. The relief was almost as exquisite as the palm of his hand. He lay, his nose against the wood and let his breathing become even again.

Edwin spoke above his head. Or not Edwin and not speech. Music. Song. It was a single note, golden, radiant, like no singer that ever was. There was, surely, no mere human breath that could sustain the note that spread as Sim's palm had spread before him, widened, became, or was, precious range after range beyond experience, turning itself into pain and beyond pain, taking pain and pleasure and destroying them, being, becoming. It stopped for a while with promise of what was to come. It began, continued, ceased. It had been a word. That beginning, that change of state explosive and vital had been a consonant, and the realm of gold that grew from it a vowel lasting for an aeon; and the semi-vowel of the close was not an end since there was, there could be no end but only a readjustment so that the world of spirit could hide itself again, slowly, slowly fading from sight, reluctant as a lover to go and with the ineffable promise that it would love always and if asked would always come again.

When the man in black let go of Sim's hand, all the hands had become nothing more than just hands again. Sim saw that, because as he lifted his face off the wood, he brought his hands together in front of it; and there was the right palm, a tiny bit sweaty, but not in any sense dirty, and just a palm like any other. He sat up and saw Edwin mopping his face with a paper tissue. With one accord they turned to look at Windrove. He sat, his hands open on the table, his face bowed, his chin on his chest. The brim of the black hat hid his face.

A drop of clear water fell from under the brim and lay on the table. Matty lifted his head; but Sim could read no expression in this blasted side of the face.

Edwin spoke.

"Thank you—thank you a thousand times! God bless you."

Matty looked at Edwin closely, then at Sim who saw that now there was indeed an expression to be read on the brown side of the face. Exhaustion. Windrove stood up, and without speaking moved to the stairs, then began to descend them. Edwin jumped to his feet.

"Windgrove! When? And look—"

He went quickly to the stairs and down them. Sim heard his rapid speech indistinctly from the courtyard.

"When may we meet next?"

"Are you sure? Here?"

"Shall you bring Pedigree?"

"Look here, are you, er, OK for money?"

233

Presently there came the click of the latch from the door leading out to the towpath. Edwin came up the stairs.

Reluctantly Sim stood up, looking round him at the pictures and the places where pictures had been, the doll, the cupboard with the gollywog hanging on it. Side by side they left, courteously insisted on each other going first down the stairs and then side by side again up the garden path, up the stairs, through the hall—the typewriter still clattering in Stanhope's study—and out into the street. Edwin stopped and they faced each other.

Edwin spoke with profound emotion.

"You are such a wonderful team!"

"Who?"

"You and he—in the occult sense."

"I and—he?"

"A wonderful team! I was *so* right you know!"

"What are you talking about?"

"When you went into that trance—I could see the spiritual combat mirrored in your face. Then you passed over, right there, in front of me!"

"It wasn't like that!"

"Sim! Sim! The two of you played on me like an instrument!"

"Look Edwin—"

"You *know* something happened, Sim, don't be modest, it's false humility—"

"Of course something happened but—"

"We broke a barrier, broke down a partition. Didn't we now?"

Sim was about to deny it hotly, when he began to remember. There was no question but that something had happened and likely enough it needed the three of them.

"Perhaps we did."

CHAPTER FOURTEEN

12/6/78

My dear friend Mr Pedigree came as far as the stairs in the stables of Sprawson's but would not stay he is afraid we mean him harm and I do not know what to do. He went off and I was left with Mr Bell who still teaches at Foundlings and Mr Goodchild from the bookshop. They expected something words perhaps. We made a circle with ourselves for protection against evil spirits for there were many in the stables green and purple and black. I held them off as best I could. They stood behind the two gentlemen and clawed at them. How do the two gentlemen live when I am not there I ask myself. Mr Bell offered me money it was funny. But I cried like a child for poor Mr Pedigree who is bound every way by his person it is hideous to see hideous. I can only spare him the time I can spare from being a guardian to the boy. If it were not for worrying about Mr Pedigree I would have a happy life guarding the boy. I will be his servant all the days of my life and look forward to many years of happiness if only I can heal Mr Pedigree and my spiritual face.

13/6/78

Great and terrible things are afoot. I thought that only me and Ezekiel had been given the way of showing things to those people who can see (as with matchboxes, thorns, shards, and marrying a wicked woman etc.) because it. I cannot say what I mean.

She had lost her engagement ring she is engaged to Mr Masterman the PT master who is quite famous I am told. We were all looking for it wherever she had been. I told the boys to look under the elms and looked near them myself. Then she came after

they had gone and asked had I looked under the elms I said no
meaning to go on and say the boys had looked for to say I had
looked myself would be a lie but she said before I could speak well
I will look and walked off. She is very beautiful and smiling and I
gave my foolish person a hard pinch as hard as I could for punish-
ment for what it did and I went on looking for the ring. But looking up (I must remember to give it another hard pinch for that but
at the time I did not think) I saw her drop the ring which she said
she had lost and then pretend to find it, she threw her arms on
both sides and cried bingo. She came to me laughing with the ring
held out on the finger of her left hand. I could not say anything but
was quite at a stand. She said I must tell everyone where I told her
it might be—in fact I ought to tell Mr M I found it. This evening I
do not know what to do. Since I vowed to do whatever a person
asked me if it is not wicked I do not know whether what she asks
is wicked. I am lost like it might be the ring. Now I ask myself what
this sign means. Can to lie be a sign I ask myself. She smiled and
lied. She lied by doing not by saying. Her saying was true but not
true. She did not find it but she found it. I do not know.

14/6/78

All day I was in a daze thinking about the ring and what it meant.
She is the terrible woman but why did she give the sign to me? It is
a challenge. It means she does not care if her jewel is lost or not. I
went to bed after my portion and offering myself to be a sacrifice if
it was right. I do not know if what I then had was a vision or a
dream. If it was a dream it was not like an ordinary dream they say
people have because who could stand such a thing every night I
ask myself it may have been like a dream in the Bible. Pharaoh
must have been troubled or he would not have sent to find out. It
was no ordinary dream. Or perhaps it was a vision and I was
really there. It was the woman in the Apocalypse. She came in
terrible glory all in colours that hurt she was allowed to torment
me because of my bad thoughts about Miss Stanhope. Yet it was
not just my fault my thinking about her, she acting so queer with
the jewel it took me all day to see she knew about signs and how to
show them. But the thing is the woman in the Apocalypse put on
Miss Stanhope's face and laughing and caused me to defile myself
with much pain which when I woke up I discovered and was

236

frightened and astonished because since Harry Bummer in Northern Territory I thought I could not defile myself and then i could not either be *frightened or ashamed*.

Then on this day (but no dream) 15/6/78 all day as I worked I tried to be ashamed but could not. The finding I can sin like other men. I cannot say what I mean. I listened to the birds to hear if they were laughing and jeering like kookaburras but they were not. Is she then disguised as an angel of light or is she a good spirit. I can see the sky now. I mean I can look into it and it is very slightly coloured all the way up. The boys came but briefly. I tried to tell them these things about everything rejoicing as it might be with Hallelujahs and that. But I could not. It is like going over from black-and-white to colour. There was a bit of sun on a tree over by long meadow and I. The boys went off to music apprecia-tion. I could hear but only a bit. So I *left my work* and went after them and stood by the garage near the music-room window. They played music on the gramophone it came out loud and I heard it like I see the trees and the sky now and the boys like angels it was a big orchestra playing Beethoven a symphony and I for the first time I began to dance there on the gravel outside the music dept window. Mrs Appleby saw me and came so I stood. She looked like an archangel laughing so I stood. She shouted to me marvellous isn't it the Seventh I didn't know you cared for music and I shouted back laughing neither did I. She looked like an archangel laughing so my mouth shouted no matter what I could do. I am a man I could have a son. She said what an extraordinary thing to say are you alright. I remembered then my vow of silence and it seemed very small but I thought I have gone near enough by talking to the boys so I blessed her with my right hand like a priest. She looked surprised and went away quickly. This is all what Mr Pierce used to call a turn up for the book.

Since writing that down, I mean between the word book and the word since I have been shown a great thing. It was not the spirits and it was not a vision or a dream it was an opening. I saw a portion of providence. I hope that one day the boy will read these words. I understand that his reading of them in the years to come is what made me write them down though at the time I had some foolish thought of evidence to show I am not mad (17/5/65). The truth is that between book and Since the eyes of my understand-ing have been opened. What good is not directly breathed into the

237

world by the holy spirit must come down by and through the
nature of men. I saw them, small, wizened, some of them with
faces like mine, some crippled, some broken. Behind each was a
spirit like the rising of the sun. It was a sight beyond joy and
beyond dancing. Then a voice said to me it is the music that frays
and breaks the string.

17/6/78

I must take what time I have to tell of the wonderful thing that
happened last night after I had repeated my portion. I will write as
quick as I can for in a little while I must ride my bike into Greenfield and see Mr Bell and Mr Goodchild and Mr Pedigree for this
time I think he will agree to go with me. Last night I thought there
was work to do; and I in a way held out the warmth of my person
to the spirits and they drew me gently into their presence. The
elder in the red robe with a crown and the elder with the blue robe
and a coronet was waiting and greeted me kindly. I thanked them
for their care of me and hoped for their continued friendship. I
thanked them in particular for the years in which they did away in
me with the root of a temptation which now of course I am able to
see for the small thing it is. When I told them this they brightened
wonderfully so that it dazzled my eyes. They showed: We saw
how you gazed on the daughters of men and found them fair. I
asked them about Miss Stanhope and the sign of her dropping her
ring and confessed that I could not see what it meant. Then they
showed: All this is hidden from us. Many years ago we called her
before us but she did not come.

I had been standing outside the harness room looking up at the
sky, but now I went into my bedroom and sat on the edge of the
bed. It is difficult my dear, dear boy, to write of what happened
after that because of the strangeness and greatness. At once the
elders drew me to them. They showed: Now we have answered
your questions we will add to your information so that it over-
flows. The cry that went up to heaven brought you down. Now
there is a great spirit that shall stand behind the being of the child
you are guarding. That is what you are for. You are to be a burnt
offering. Now we shall introduce you to a friend of ours and we
shall eat and drink with you.

Although I am now accustomed to them and know my spiritual

238

name and indeed do not go cold when they call me, yet this news was like being in a lower part of heaven as I may say and it made me cold all over again like that time (17/5/65) and all the hair on my person stood up, each on a separate lump. But when every bit of warmth had gone out from me I saw their friend standing between them. He was dressed all in white and with the circle of the sun round his head. The red and blue elders took off their crowns and threw them down and I took off mine and threw it down. I was in great awe of the spirit in white but the red elder showed: This is the spiritual being who shall stand behind the child you are guarding. That child shall bring the spiritual language into the world and nation shall speak it unto nation. When I heard this, my head lowered before them I had such joy for men that the tears fell out of my eyes on the table. Then, still with my eyes lowered I made them welcome at my small table where there seemed to be room. Then the blue elder showed: There is joy in all the heavens today because the like of this meeting has not been seen since the days of Abraham. Then I offered them spiritual food and drink which they accepted. When this was done I had a great desire to sacrifice and asked what I should do and what they now wanted. The red spirit showed: We want nothing but to visit with you and to rejoice with you since you are one of us. And since you are an elder we will share that wisdom with you which though still in the body you ought to have. They did not do this by showing the great book but by a most wonderful opening which even if it was a thing I was able to do it would not be lawful to describe.

All this while the white spirit with the circle of the sun round his head sat across the table from me and after my first being able to see him I had not dared to raise my eyes to his face. Now, because of the glory of the opening and because they had called him their friend and mine I did raise my eyes to his face and the sword proceeded out of his mouth and struck me through the heart with a terrible pain so that as I found out later, I fainted and fell forward across the table. When I woke up again they had put me from them, and

The village clock struck from the church tower. Matty started up from his small table. He shut the exercise book and put it away in the chest of drawers. He hurried down to the harness room and seized his bike from where it leaned against the wall. He drew in his breath with a hiss. The back tyre was flat. He heaved the machine over and stood it on the saddle and handlebars. He hurried to the tap, filled a bucket with water and began to pull out the inner tyre, plunging it under water to find where the puncture was.

CHAPTER FIFTEEN

Ruth shook her head, smiling. Sim spread his hands in the gesture unconsciously imitated from his grandfather.

"But I want you to come! I *wish* you'd come! You've never objected to making a fool of yourself with me before!"

She said nothing but went on smiling. Sim passed a hand over his baldness.

"You always admired Stanhope—"

"Nonsense!"

"Well—women did—"

"I'm not 'women'."

"But I do wish you'd come. Is it too late in the evening?"

Silence again.

"Is it Pedigree?"

"Go along, dear. Have a good time."

"That's hardly—"

"Well. A successful meeting."

"Edwina's coming."

"Has she said so?"

"Edwin's asking her."

"Give her my love if she's there."

It was a week after the first meeting, and the curious man's free afternoon again. What canvassing Sim had been able to do had produced no result—three refusals and one 'might come' which clearly covered the intention not to. Sim thought ruefully that perhaps it might be worth sending a notice of the demise of the Philosophical Society to be inserted in the *Greenfield Advertiser* among the births and deaths. He was still working out the wording of the notice when he reached the hall of Sprawson's. Edwin was standing on the bottom step of his stairs.

"Where's Ruth?"

"Where's Edwina?"

Then there was another silence. Sim broke it.

"Pedigree."

"I know."

"It's Pedigree. He's why they won't come. Not even Ruth."

"Oh yes. Yes. Edwina would have come in any other circumstances you know."

"So would Ruth."

"She's really a deeply liberal person you know. Only Pedigree—"

"Ruth's the most truly charitable person I know. Charity in its true sense, Greek sense."

"Of course. It was the business over the babies in prams you know. The cruelty to the young mothers. The deliberate psychological torture. She felt so deeply. She said once she'd have castrated him with her own hands if she'd caught him in flagrante delicto."

"She didn't say flagrante delicto!"

"She said assaulting a child. Pushing a pram away with a baby in it can be construed as an assault."

"I thought she meant—"

"Oh no. She wouldn't talk about that would she? I mean she's widely and deeply experienced but there are some things—"

"I remember when she talked about castrating, Ruth agreed with her. Warmly."

Edwin glanced at his watch.

"They're a little late. Shall we go on?"

"After you."

Softly they descended the steps and trod, almost on tiptoe, down the garden path and into the courtyard under the stables. Edwin switched on the light at the bottom of the stairs; and there was a sudden, startled movement in the room at their heads. Sim expected to see Pedigree after all, when he got to the upper level, but it was Sophy, standing by the divan on which she had been sitting and looking, he thought at once, white and strained. But Edwin went straight into action.

"My dear Sophy what a pleasure! How are you? Sitting in the dark? But I'm so sorry—oh dear! Your father you see, he told us we could—"

The girl put her hand up to the curls at the back of her head then took it away again. She was wearing the white sweatshirt with BUY ME stencilled on the front and really, thought Sim, nothing else under it, nothing else whatever, so that—

"We'll go away Sophy dear. Your father must have made a mistake. He told us we could have the room for a meeting of—but how silly! I mean it sounds silly and of course you wouldn't want—"

Then they were all three silent and standing. The single, naked bulb made a black shadow under each nose. Even Sophy looked monstrous, huge, black eye-hollows and the Hitlerian moustache of shadow caught by the light under her nostrils. Sweatshirt, jeans, flip-flops; and surely, some sort of cap? A knitted cap back there, hidden by the curls.

She glanced away from them at shopping bags, plastic ones, leaning against each other on the end of the divan. She touched her hair again, licked her lips and then looked back at Edwin.

"Meeting? You said something about a meeting—"

"Just a silly mistake. Your father, my dear. Sim, d'you think he was pulling our legs? 'Putting us on' I think you'd say, Sophy, according to my latest information. But you've come home to stay, of course. We'll go to the hall and intercept the others."

"Oh no! No! Daddy didn't make a mistake. I'm just going, you see. I'd turned out the light. You can have the place and welcome. Look—just a moment—"

Quickly she moved about the room, switched on a table lamp under the dormer, a table lamp with a pink and bobbled shade. She flicked off the single, naked bulb and the hideous shadows were wiped from her face to be replaced by a rosy and upward glow; and she glowed at them both.

"There! My goodness me! That dreadful top light! Toni used to call it—But I'm glad to see you! It'll be one of your meetings won't it? Make yourselves at home."

"Aren't you taking your, your shopping bags?"

"Those? Oh no! I'm leaving everything! Oh yes indeed! You've no idea. I shan't want any of the stores tonight. Too boring. Just let me put the things out of the way for you—"

Astonished, Sim stared at her face in its rosy glow and could not believe that the smile owed everything to the lamp. She was highly excited—and there, flash from an eye as if it were phosphorescent—and she seemed full of, full of purpose. At once

243

his mind jumped to the usual, dreary conclusion. Sex, of course. An assignation. Interrupted. The really courteous thing, the understanding thing would be to—

But Edwin was talking.

"Au revoir then Sophy dear. Let us see something of you won't you? Or let us hear of you."

"Oh yes. My goodness me."

She had got her shoulder bag and slung it; was sidling round them.

"Remember me to Mrs Bell won't you? And Mrs Goodchild?"

Glow of a smile and then the girl gone away down the stairs, rosy glow left behind, suggestive and empty. They heard the door out to the towpath open, then close. Sim cleared his throat, sank into one of the chairs by the table and looked round him.

"I suppose they call this Brothel Pink."

"I hadn't heard. No."

Edwin sat down too. They were silent for a while. Sim inspected the cardboard box that lay beneath the other dormer. It was full of tinned food, as far as he could see. There was a coil of rope on it.

Edwin had seen it too.

"She must have been going camping. I hope we haven't—"

"Of course not. She has a young man you know. In fact—"

"Edwina's seen her with two young men. At different times, I mean."

"I saw one. Oldish, I thought, for her."

"Edwina said she thought he had a married look about him. The other one she said was younger, much more suitable she said. I mean Edwina's the last person in the world to spread scandal but she said she couldn't help noticing it going on under her nose."

"Dreary. It makes me feel dreary."

"You are such a moral old thing, Sim! Moralistic."

"It makes me feel dreary because I'm not young and with two young men. Well. Two young women."

Then there was silence again. Glancing at Edwin, Sim saw how the feminine lamp was providing him with a delicacy and smiling mouth that he had not got. Perhaps for me too. Here we are, dreary, and with smiles painted on our faces, waiting for— waiting, waiting, waiting. Like the man said.

"They're very late."

Edwin spoke absently.

244

" 'Having if off' they call it nowadays."

He looked quickly back at Sim and perhaps there was a little more intensity under the glow.

"I mean one hears these things. The boys, you see, and then, one reads—"

" 'Getting laid'. Is that American?"

"Incredible isn't it, what you hear? Even on the box!"

Silence again. Then—

"Edwin—we'll need another chair. Four of us."

"There were four chairs last time. Where is it?"

Edwin got up and wandered round the room, peering into corners as if the fourth chair had become not absent but merely less visible and could be seen if you looked closely.

"This used to be their toy-cupboard. I remember when Edwina and I came to tea they showed us every doll—extraordinary the names they had and the stories about them—you know, Sim, there's genius in those girls. Creativity. I don't just mean intelligence. Real, precious creativity. I wonder if their dolls—"

He reached out and opened the cupboard door.

"How very odd!"

"What's odd about keeping dolls in a cupboard?"

"Nothing. But—"

The fourth chair was placed in the centre of the cupboard, facing outward. There were lengths of rope attached to it, to the back and to the legs. Each rope had had the end carefully fused to stop it unravelling.

"Well!"

Edwin shut the door again, came back, laid hold of the table.

"Help me, Sim, please. We'll have to use the divan for the fourth man. Though I must say it won't seem quite, quite seancelike, will it? Takes me right back to the dolls' tea party. I told you about it didn't I?"

"Yes."

"But heaven only knows what she was doing with a chair like that and ropes and things."

"Edwin."

"Yes?"

"Listen carefully. Before the others come. We've stumbled on something, you see. We've no business to have seen that chair."

"What harm—"

"Listen. It's sex. Don't you understand? Bondage. Sexual games, private and, and shaming."

"Good God!"

"Before the others come. It's the least I—we—can do. We, you and I must never never never let on, never by the faintest breath—Remember how startled she was when we switched the light on and then when she saw who we were—she was there in the dark, waiting for someone or perhaps getting things ready for someone—and now she's gone away thinking, *Oh God I hope to God they don't ever think to open that cupboard—*"

"Good God!"

"So we must never—"

"Oh but I wouldn't—except to Edwina of course!"

"I mean after all—there but for the grace of God—I mean. After all, we all, I mean."

"What d'you mean?"

"I mean."

Then there was silence in the rosy room for a long, long time. Sim was not thinking about the meeting at all, or the seance, which was what it would be better called. He was thinking about the way in which circumstances could seem to imitate the intuitive understanding that so many people claimed to have and so many others denied was possible. Here, in the rosy light, with the shut cupboard, a few sticks and twists of artificial fibre had betrayed the secret as clearly as if they had spelt it out in print; so that two men, not by a mystic perception but by the warmth of imagination had come simply to a knowledge they were not intended to have and ought not to have. The man who looked too old for Sophy, and the brothel light—His mind dived into the explanation of it all, glamorous and acrid, so fierce an imagination he caught his breath at the scent and stink of it—

"God help us all."

"Yes. All."

More silence. At last Edwin spoke, diffidently, almost.

"They're a long, long time."

"Pedigree won't come without him."

"He won't come without Pedigree."

"What shall we do? Ring the school?"

"We couldn't get hold of him. And I have a feeling he'll be here any minute."

"It's too bad. They might have told us, if—"

"We gave our word."

"Wait for an hour, say. Then go."

Edwin reached down and slipped off his shoes. He climbed onto the divan and crossed his legs. He held his arms close to his sides, then extended the forearms, palms upward. He closed his eyes and did a great deal of breathing.

Sim sat and thought to himself. It was all the place, just that and nothing else, the place so often imagined, then found, with its silence but also with its dust and dirt and stink; and now seen to have the brothel image added, the pink lights and bobbled femininity—and at the end, like something out of the furtive book in his desk, the perverted chair.

I know it all, he thought, right to the bitter end.

Yet there was, after all, a certain sad satisfaction, and even a quivering of salt lust by association in this death of an old imagination. They had to grow up, lose the light of their exquisite childhood. They had to go under the harrow like everyone else; and doubtless at the moment it was subsumed under *having a good time* or *being with it* or *being into sex, into bondage*. Heaven lies round us in our infancy.

Edwin honked suddenly. Glancing across at him, Sim saw him jerk his head back up. Edwin had meditated himself asleep then woken himself with his own snore. That reduced everything, too. He felt, in the wake of Edwin's snore, an overwhelming sense of futility. He tried to imagine some deep, significant spiritual drama, some contrivance, some plot that would include them both and be designed solely for the purpose of rescuing Pedigree from his hell; and then had to admit to himself that the whole affair was about Sim the ageing bookseller or no one.

Everything was all right after all, just ordinary. Nothing would happen. It was as usual a matter of living among a whole heap of beliefs, first-class, second-class, third-class, and so on, right through to the blank wall of his daily indifference and ignorance.

Nine o'clock.

"He won't come now, Edwin. Let's go."

Matthew Septimus Windrove had the best of all reasons for not coming. He had mended the tyre slowly and methodically. Then with what for him was an unusual saving of time and energy he

247

had carried the bike over his shoulder to the garages so that he could blow the tyre up in a few seconds with the air pump. But he could not find Mr French to explain to him. He found the garage doors open, which was strange; and he went through to the back of the garages, wondering why Mr French had not turned the lights on. As he moved to the door of the office that opened out of the garage at the back, a man stole round a car and hit him hard on the back of the head with a heavy spanner. He did not even feel himself fall. The man dragged him like a sack into the office and pushed him under the table. Then he returned to his work, which was the placement of a heavy box against the wall of the garage where it backed on to the bookstore. Not long after, the bomb went off. It destroyed the wall, brought down the watertank over the bookstore and broke open the upper face of the nearer petrol tank. The water ran into the burning tank, and instead of putting out the flames, sank down and pushed the petrol up. The burning petrol flooded out in a blazing tide as the fire alarms went off.

There were figures, not known to the school, running towards it. Sophy's idea worked perfectly. Fire drill was not intended for coping with bombs. There was chaos. No one could believe in the extraordinary sounds that were just like shots. In the chaos a strange man dressed as a soldier was able to carry a burden out of the school. It was wrapped in a blanket from the end of which small feet protruded and kicked. This man stumbled on the gravel but ran as fast as he could towards the darkness of the trees. But the flaming tide made him take a curving run and as he did so, a strange thing happened in the fire. It seemed to organize itself into a shape of flame that rushed out of the garage doors and whirled round and round. It made as if on purpose for the man and his burden. It whirled round still and the only noise from it was that of burning. It came so close to the man and it was so monstrous he dropped the bundle and a boy leapt out of it and ran away, ran screaming to where the others were being marshalled. The man dressed as a soldier struck out wildly at the fire-monster, then ran, ran shouting away into the cover of the trees. The fire-monster jigged and whirled. After a time it fell down; and after some more time it lay still.

Sophy, when she left the stables, hurried along the towpath to the Old Bridge and then up into the High Street. She ran to a phone box and dialled a number but the phone rang on and on. She came out. She ran back to the Old Bridge and down to the towpath but there was still a rosy light in the dormers of the stable buildings. She stamped her foot like a child. For a time she seemed lost, taking a few steps towards the green door then coming away, going towards the water then backing off. She ran again towards the Old Bridge then turned round and stood, her fists clenched and up by her shoulders. All the time, in the glare from the street lighting over the bridge, her face was white and ugly. Then she began to run along the towpath, away from the town and the light. She left the stabling, she passed the broken roofline of what had been Frankley's, then the long wall of the almshouses. She passed on, light of step, but panting now, and once, slipping in the mud of the towpath.

A voice talked inside her head.

They must be at the crisis if it's on. I hope it isn't on. Lights out for little boys. Little men. There flashed into her mind the image of a poster the day after tomorrow. BILLION FOR BOY. But no, no. It is impossible that I that we are now at this very moment it may be.

Be your age. Well. Be more than your age.

There was a loud thumping noise in the hedge and it stopped her dead. Something was bouncing and flailing about and then it squeaked and she could make out that it was a rabbit in a snare, down there by the ditch that lay between the towpath and the woods. It was flailing about, not knowing what had caught it and not caring to know but killing itself in an effort just to be free, or it may be, just to be dead. Its passion defiled the night with grotesque and obscene caricature of process, of logical advance through time from one moment to the next where the trap was waiting. She hurried past it, hurried on, a chill on her skin that competed successfully for at least a minute with the warmth from her thrusting speed.

All of a glow.

That was where the children were playing. The rubber boat is still tethered there. That means they will be back, tomorrow, perhaps. I must remember that. What's a girl like etc. And the woman. Family life. Where's Dad? In his column room. Where's Mum? Gone to God or in New Zealand. Well it's much the same thing dearie, innit? That's the lock and that's the bridge and that's the old barge. Those are the downs up there all a-glimmer under.

That's the sunken road to the top with trees over. No one would come down that way, not with a car, he wouldn't. Not with a parcel in his arms. Would the water in the canal cover a car? We ought to have found that out. If I walked up the sunken road or along beside it I could see the valley and the slope over the school. That would not be sensible. It is more sensible to stay here where I am placed to warn anyone off. To stay here is sensible.

She turned left and moved into the sunken road. The walking in the groove under the trees was a slower business than walking on the towpath; and some of the things in the air seemed to catch up with her and hang at her shoulder so she hurried as much as she could. The cloudy moon made a dapple everywhere and between the stems and trunks of the trees that had invaded the old road the sides of the downs floated and glimmered, made mostly of two-tone cloud and sliding moonlight.

Then she stopped and stood.

It was a question of direction. You could try to persuade yourself that a straight line to the sky directly over the school was not just *there* and that coincidence could stretch—a real coincidence as the lanky blonde might think it—could stretch to there being two entirely disconnected fires on that line, one, a small, controllable fire, the other—

It was a rose-coloured patch, half-seen over the shoulder of the downs. There was nothing nasty, nothing direct, just a rose petal or two; and now opening and spreading, taking in another cloud corner, the rose lighter and brighter in hue. They said it took the fire engine fifteen minutes to reach the valley by the school when called for. Phone wires cut. But this light in the sky must be beckoning; and in that school of all others there would be some form of communication they could not get at, could not cut—

And he will bring the boy here, down by the canal, to carry him along the towpath to the stables—we could use the old barge, the cupboard up in the front of it, that old loo—

The light brightened over the downs. Suddenly she knew it was her own fire, a thing she had done, a proclamation, a deed in the eye of the world—an outrage, a triumph! The feeling stormed through her, laughter, fierceness, a wild joy at the violation. It was as if the light, shuddering on the other side of the downs, was a loosening thing so that the whole world became weak and melting

250

like the top of a candle. It was then she saw what the last outrage was and knew herself capable of it. She shut her eyes as the image swept round her. She saw how she crawled along the long passage that led from one end of the old barge to the other. She ceased to feel the rough bark of a tree-trunk between her hands and against her body, where she clung with eyes shut. She felt instead the uneven planks of the flooring under her knees, heard the wash of the water under it, felt the wetness well over her hands. Somehow Gerry's commando knife was in her hand. There was a sound like a rabbit thumping that came from that cupboard, that loo right up in front. Then the thumping stopped as if the rabbit was too terrified even to move. Perhaps it was listening to this slow, watery approach.

"All right! All right! I'm coming!"

The thumping would start again, a girl's voice, well, natch.

She addressed the door conversationally.

"Just wait a moment, I'll get you open."

It came easily enough, swung wide. The first thing she could see inside was the ellipse of the little round window, the porthole. But there was also a small white rectangle on the midline of the boat and directly above the seat of the loo, the elsan or whatever. This rectangle was moving violently from side to side and she could smell wee-wee. The boy was there, arms bound behind his back, feet and knees bound. He was seated, bound, on the loo like he might have been in the cupboard and ropes held him on either side to the walls of the boat and there was a huge pad of sticky stuff stuck across his mouth and cheeks. He was jerking as violently as he could and there was a whining noise coming out of his nose. She felt an utter disgust at the creature itself sitting there on the stinking loo, so disgusting, eek and ooh, oh so much part of all weirdness from which you could see that the whole thing was a ruin and

I chose.

Should have brought a gun only I don't know, it is better with the knife—oh much better!

The boy was motionless now, waiting for her on the flat stone. She began to fumble at his jersey with her left hand and he made no move; but when she pulled out the front of his shirt he began to struggle again. But the bonds were beautifully done, Gerry had done a super job, just amazing, the way in which the boy had only

251

a limited kick with his stockinged feet was lovely, should he not have been in his pyjams, the nasty little creature must have been up to something, and she swept her hand over his naked tum and belly button, the navel my dear if you must refer to it at all and she felt paper-thin ribs and a beat, beat, thump, thump at left centre. So she got his trousers undone and held his tiny wet cock in her hand as he struggled and hummed through his nose. She laid the point of the knife on his skin and finding it to be the right place, pushed it a bit so that it pricked. The boy convulsed and flailed in the confinement and she was or someone was, frightened a bit, far off and anxious. So she thrust more still and felt it touch the leaping thing or be touched by it again and again while the body exploded with convulsions and a high humming came out of the nose. She thrust with all the power there was, deliriously; and the leaping thing inside seized the knife so that the haft beat in her hand, and there was a black sun. There was liquid everywhere and strong convulsions and she pulled the knife away to give them free play but they stopped. The boy just sat there in his bonds, the white patch of elastoplast divided down the middle by the dark liquid from his nose.

She came to herself with a terrible start that banged her head against the tree-trunk. There was a roaring and a great clittering of insect stuff and a red, mad light that swirled along the side of the downs. It passed overhead then swung up over the skyline to drop down towards where the fire was. She was trembling with the passion of the mock murder and she began to let herself down the tree-tunnel, back towards the old barge and her knees sagged. She came to the field bridge over the canal—and there was the car coming, no lights, heaving over the uneven track. She could not run, but waited for it. The car stopped, backed, turned and was ready to get away. Then she went to it, giggling and staggering to explain to Gerry about the old men in the stables and how they must use the boat but it was Bill there in the driving seat.

"Bill? Where is he? Where's the boy?"

"There's no bleeding boy. I had him and some burning bugger come out at me and—Sophy it's all gone wrong. We got to get away!"

She stood, staring into his face that was pallid on one side and glowing on the other where a cloud burned in the sky.

"Miss! Sophy—come on for fuck's sake! We got minutes—"

"Gerry!"

"He's all right—they got your boyfriend as a hostage—now come on—"

"They?"

Ever since he saw her without the wig, I knew. Something told me only I refused to believe it. Treachery. They think they've done a swop.

The rage that burst in her overwhelmed triumph and fierceness, bore her up so that she screamed at him, at them, and cursed and spat; and then she was down on hands and knees and screaming and screaming into the grass where there was no boy but a Sophy who had been used and fooled by everyone.

"Sophy!"

"Get lost you dumb beast! Oh shit!"

"For the last time—"

"Sod off!"

And when at last she stopped screaming and began to understand how she had torn her cheeks and how there was hair in her hands and how there was now nothing else, not him nor them nor her but a black night with a dying fire over the crest of the downs the tears rained down her cheeks and washed the blood from them.

Presently she knelt up and spoke, as if he were there.

"It's *no good* you see! All those years, no one—You think she's wonderful, don't you? Men always do at first. But there's nothing there, Gerry, nothing at all. Just the minimum flesh and bones, nothing else, no one to meet, no one to go with, be with, share with. Just ideas. Ghosts. Ideas and emptiness, the perfect terrorist."

She got up, heavily, and glanced across at the old barge where there was no boy, no body. She slung her shoulder bag and wondered how much damage she had done her face. She turned away from the boat and the fire and began to pick her way back along the towpath, where there was now nothing visible but darkness.

"I shall tell. I was used. They'll have nothing on me. Take the ropes off that chair. He said we were going camping, my lord. I've

253

been very foolish my lord I'm sorry I can't help crying. I think my fiancé must have been part of it my lord he was friendly with, with—I'm sure my Daddy had nothing to do with it, my lord. He wanted us out of the stables my lord, said he wanted to use them for something else. No my lord that was after he had been to a chess meeting in Russia. No my lord he never said."

CHAPTER SIXTEEN

As they let him out of the back of the building Sim adjusted his coloured spectacles with movements so habitual they seemed to have become a part of his automatic life. They were one of three pairs he had acquired during the weeks of the inquiry. His walk was automatic, too, a stately progress. He had learnt that it was fatal—almost literally fatal—to hurry. That way he would attract notice and raise the shout of, *there's one of them*, or, *that's the fellow who gave evidence today*, or even, *that's Goodchild!* It seemed his name was peculiarly attractive to them.

Stately, he walked down the side road to join Fleet Street and thus avoid the queue of those who still were unable to get in. He was inspected by a passing policeman, and even in the twilight of his coloured glasses, he thought the man looked at him with amusement and contempt.

I could do with a cup of tea.

The further you got away from the inquiry, you would have thought, the less there was a chance of being recognized? Not a bit of it! Television made everywhere the same. *There's the fellow who was giving evidence*—No escape. The real ruin, the real public condemnation, was not to be good or bad; either of those had a kind of dignity about them; but to be a fool and to be seen to have been one—

At the end, when we can go away, they will have exonerated us. Until then, we are pilloried. And after?

The woman on the bus—*there's one of them! Aren't you one of the fellows who was in those stables?* And then the spit, incompetent spitting, badly aimed, hanging on the sleeve of his heather-mixture greatcoat—We did nothing! It was a kind of praying!

There was a crowd round a shop. Drawn as he always was, despite himself, to this extension of a place and time, he stopped and stood at the back. By dodging this way and that, he could contrive to see brokenly into the window where at least fifteen television screens were showing their identical pictures; and then he saw a smaller one, high up and at an angle, so he ceased to dodge.

It was the afternoon round-up, he saw. There was a split screen, Mr Justice Mallory and his two coadjutors occupying the bottom third of it, and the smoking school above it, now a very famous film indeed. Athough he had never seen the school itself in the days when it had stood untouched and dignified, he could nevertheless identify the various windows from which various children of this royalty or that princedom or that multinational had jumped or been thrown. The top picture changed. Now it was harking back to London airport—there was Toni, her hair dazzling, there was the young ex-officer (that hurt) who had been her accomplice; there, close to him and at the wrong end of his pistol, the weight-lifter who had been engaged to the other sister—was he part of it? It was unbelievable—what was which and who? There was the plane taking off—the picture changed again and with a dull pain at his heart he saw what was to come. The bug was looking down into a small room where three men were sitting round a table. One of them was writhing and then suddenly laid his head down on the table. Their hands were joined. The man opposite lifted his head and opened his mouth.

The film cut to the inquiry again, everybody laughing, the judge, legal persons, press and those odd bodies whose function he had never quite understood, and who were perhaps special agents as a back-up to the armed soldiers who stood here and there against the walls. There was another cut, back, this time, the film of the three men in slow motion, his own head bowing jerkily, then Edwin's mouth open—and this time the people who stood round the shop window were laughing like the men in the inquiry.

"It wasn't like that!"

Fortunately no one noticed. He hurried away, not able to bear the thought that he might see once more (it was such a popular item) his own evidence that Mr Justice Mallory had described as a moment of low comedy in this terrible affair—

"You say, Mr Goodchild, you were not in a trance?"

"No my lord. My hands were held and I was trying to scratch my nose."

And then the roars of laughter, on and on—oh, it must have been for whole seconds.

I wouldn't believe it myself. I wouldn't believe we were—are—innocent.

I heard her in the street, the other woman nodding and talking at the same time the way they do, *there's no smoke without fire that's what I said*. Then they both shut up because they saw me.

The tube was roaring and crowded with rush-hour traffic. He hung on a strap, keeping his head down, looking where he would have seen his feet if a man's stomach hadn't got in the way. It was almost restful to hang there with no one to recognize the fool.

He walked from the station, coming up out of the earth to the street with a sense that once more he was vulnerable. Of course we all had something to do with it! We were there, weren't we?

The man who looked like an accountant but was from the secret service or whatever they call it, the one who did the bugging, said they'd been on to her sister for nearly a year. Who used who?

I had nothing to do with it. Nevertheless I am guilty. My fruitless lust clotted the air and muffled the sounds of the real world.

I am mad.

In the High Street he walked straight and painful, tense. He knew that even the brown women, cloth drawn across the lower part of the face—but in his case as he passed, drawing it higher still, to avoid contamination—even the brown women looked, glinting sideways.

There he goes.

Even Sandra looked. She came fatly, clumsily, but all gleaming and alive with excitement—"My mum wants me not to come but I said as long as Mr Goodchild wants me—"

Sandra wanting to be connected with terror, no matter how far off.

There was a sound of rapid footsteps beside him that slowed to his pace. He glanced sideways and it was Edwin, chin up, fists driven together in the pockets of his greatcoat. He wove a bit and brushed Sim's shoulder. Then they walked on, side by side. People made room for them. Sim turned into the lay-by where he kept his van. Instead of walking the few steps to Sprawson's, Edwin came with him. Sim opened the side door and Edwin followed without saying anything.

In the little sitting-room behind the shop there was dim light. Sim wondered whether to pull the curtains aside but decided against.

Edwin spoke in little more than a whisper.

"Is Ruth all right?"

"What is 'All right'?"

"Edwina's with her sister. Have you heard where Stanhope is?"

"Staying at his club, they say. I don't know."

"Some newspaper's got Sophy."

" 'He stole my heart away, says terrorist's twin.' "

"You're moving I suppose."

"Selling to the shopping-centre people."

"A good price?"

"Oh no. They'll pull the place down and use the ground for access. Big firm."

"Books?"

"Auction. Might make a bit. We're famous for the time being. Roll up!"

"We're innocent. He said so. 'I must state here and now that I think these two gentlemen are the victims of an unfortunate coincidence.' "

"We're not innocent. We're worse than guilty. We're funny. We made the mistake of thinking you could see through a brick wall."

"I'm being encouraged to resign. It's not fair."

Sim laughed.

"I should like to go to my daughter, get the hell out of it."

"Canada?"

"Exile."

"I think, Sim, I shall write a book about the whole affair."

"You'll have the leisure."

"I shall track down and cross-examine everybody who had anything to do with the whole ghastly business and I shall find out the truth."

"He was right, you know. History *is* bunk. History is the nothing people write about a nothing."

"The Akashic records—"

"At least I'm not going to make the mistake of fooling with that kind of idiocy again. No one will *ever* know what happened. There's too much of it, too many people, a sprawling series of events that break apart under their own weight. Those lovely

258

creatures—they have everything—everything in the world, youth, beauty, intelligence—or is there nothing to live for? Crying out about freedom and justice! What freedom? What justice? Oh my God!"

"I don't see what their beauty has to do with it."

"A treasure was poured out for them and they turned their back on it. A treasure not just for them but for all of us."

"Listen!"

"What is it?"

Edwin held up one finger. There was a noise, someone was fiddling with the door of the shop. Sim jumped up and hurried forward. Mr Pedigree was just closing the door behind him.

"We're not open. Good day to you."

Pedigree did not seem so defensive.

"Why was the door open then?"

"It shouldn't have been."

"Well it was."

"Please leave."

"You're in no position, Goodchild, to come the heavy. Oh I know it's only an inquiry, not a trial. But we know, don't we? You're in possession of my small property."

Edwin pushed past Sim.

"You're an informer, aren't you? You did it, didn't you?"

"I don't know what you're talking about."

"That's why you wouldn't stay—"

"I went because I didn't like my company."

"You went to switch the bug on!"

"Edwin, does it matter? That secret service man—"

"I said I'd get the truth!"

"Well. I want my ball. There it is, on your desk. I paid for it. Matty was really honest, you know."

"Just a moment, Sim. We know why you want it don't we? Do you want to go to jail again?"

"We might all go to jail, mightn't we? How do I know I'm not speaking to a very clever pair of terrorists who put those girls up to it? Yes of course she was—as bad as the other! The judge said you were innocent, but we, the great British Public, we—how odd to find myself one of them!—we know, don't we?"

"No, Sim—let me. Pedigree, you're a filthy old thing and you ought to be done away with. Take it and go!"

Mr Pedigree gave a kind of high whinny.

"You think I *like* wandering round lavatories and public parks, desperate for, for—I don't want to, I have to! Have to! Just for, no not even that, just for affection; and more than that, just a touch—It's taken me sixty years to find out what makes me different from other people. I have a rhythm. Perhaps you remember, or are you too young to remember, when it was said that all God's children had rhythm? Mine's a wave motion. You don't know what it's like to live like that, do you? You think I *want* to go to jail? But every so often I can feel the time coming, creeping up on me. You don't know what it's like to want desperately not to and yet know you will, oh yes you will! To feel the denouement, the awful climax, the catastrophe moving and moving and moving—to know that—to say to yourself on Friday it may be, 'I won't, I won't, I won't—' and all the time to *know* with a kind of ghastly astonishment that on Saturday you will, oh yes you will, you'll be fumbling at their flies—"

"For God's sake!"

"And worse; because many years ago a doctor told me what I might become in the end, what with obsession and fear and senility—to keep some child quiet—do I sound verging on senility?"

"Give yourself up. Go to hospital."

"Only they did it while they were young. Willing to kidnap a child—not worrying who got killed—imagine it, those young men, that beautiful girl with all her life before her! No, I'm nowhere near the worst, gentlemen, among the bombings and kidnappings and hijackings all for the highest of motives—what did she say? We know what we are but not what we may be. A favourite character of mine, gentlemen. Well, I won't thank you for your kindness and hospitality. I'm sorry we shan't meet inside—unless of course they turn up more evidence."

They watched him in silence as he wrapped his coat round him, held the big, coloured ball to his chest, and went with his curious springy, tottery step and let himself out of the side door. A moment or two later he shadowed the chinks of boarded-up shop window and was gone.

Sim sat down at the desk, wearily.

"It can't be happening to me."

"It is."

"The real hardship is that there's no end. I sit here. Will they ever stop showing that film of us round the table?"

"Have to, sooner or later."

"Can you stop watching it when it's on?"

"No. Actually not. I have to, like you. Like, like—no, I won't say like Pedigree. But every newstime, every special report, every radio programme—"

Sim stood up and went into the sitting-room. The sound of a man's voice swelled and the screen flickered into brightness. Edwin stood in the doorway. They were going through it all again on the other channel. The shot of the school appeared, was panned slowly, to take in the shattered and smoke-blackened wing. Then, endlessly after that, were Toni and Gerry and Mansfield and Kurtz herding their hostages towards the plane; and again, as a preliminary, before the day's advance, the new News, there was Toni in Africa, broadcasting, beautiful and remote, the long aria in that silvery voice about freedom and justice—

Sim cursed at her.

"She's mad! Why don't people say so? She's mad and bad!"

"She's not human, Sim. We have to face it at last. We're not all human."

"We're all mad, the whole damned race. We're wrapped in illusions, delusions, confusions about the penetrability of partitions, we're all mad and in solitary confinement."

"We think we *know*."

"Know? That's worse than an atom bomb, and always was."

In silence then, they looked and listened; then exclaimed together.

"Journal? Matty's journal? What journal?"

"—has been handed to Mr Justice Mallory. It may throw some light—"

Presently Sim switched the set off. The two men looked at each other and smiled. There would be news of Matty—almost a meeting with him. Somehow and for no reason that he could find, Sim felt heartened by the idea of Matty's journal—happy almost, for the moment. Before he knew what he was about he found himself staring intently into his own palm.

Mr Pedigree, wearing his ancient pepper-and-salt suit, had the overcoat slung over one arm and carried the ball held between his two hands on his way to the park. He was a little breathless and indignant at his breathlessness because he traced it to the talk he had had a few days before with Mr Goodchild and Mr Bell—a talk at which he had voluntarily spoken about his age. Age, then, had leapt out of its ambush somewhere and now went with him, so that he felt in himself even less able than usual to cope with the graph of his obsession. The graph was still there, it was so, no one could deny it, how else do you find yourself at that time of autumn when the day is still warm but these evenings suddenly cold—how else do you still find yourself going towards, despite the desperate words spoken only an hour before, and not just then but here and now as feet took themselves along despite you—no, no, no, not again, Oh God! And still the feet (as you knew they would) took you along and up the long hill to the paradisal, dangerous, damned park where the sons of the morning ran and played—and now, with the still open iron gates ahead, his own breathlessness seemed to matter less; and the *fact*, the undoubted *fact* already standing there, that he would spend tonight in a cell at the police station and overwhelmed with that special contempt they did not feel for murderers—that undoubted *fact* which he tried to rely on to support the 'no, no, no, Oh God!' that versicle without any response, the *fact* was diminishing in importance and was now overlaid quiveringly with an anticipation that really, one could not disguise it, tended to promote the breathlessness of age, not old age, but age, none the less, or its threshold as he said Τηλίκου ὥς περ ἐγών—

Still breathing deeply, astonished and sad, he saw his feet move him forward now again up the steep lip of his obsession, up to the gate on to the gravel, the feet themselves looking, peering at that far side where the boys shouted and played—only half an hour and they will be home with mum. Only another half hour and I would have held out for another whole day!

A wind took a scurry of autumn leaves across his feet but they ignored them and went on fast, too fast—

"Wait! I said wait!"

But it was all reasonable. Only the body has its reasons and feet are selfish, so that as they tried to pass the seat he was able for a while to arrest them and he pulled the coat round him, then slumped on the iron slats.

"Overdone it, you two."

The two did nothing inside their shining boots and he came to himself a little, feeling sheepish and wrapped in a cloud of illusion. Heart was more important than feet and protested. He hung over it, hoping that something nasty was not going to happen with its thump, thump, thump; and as he detected the first slowing of the beat he said inside, not daring even to risk giving the words air, since air was what heart wanted and must have to the exclusion of any other activity—

That was a narrow escape!

Presently he opened his eyes and made the brilliant colours of the ball take firm shape. The boys would not stay at the farther end of the park. Some of them would come this way, they must, to get to the main gate, they would come down the road and they would see the brilliant ball, bring it back to him when he threw it—the ploy was infallible, at worst would lead to a moment's banter, at best—

A cloud moved away from the sun and the sun itself seized him with many golden hands and warmed him. He was surprised to find how grateful he was to the sun for his mercy and that there was a little while to wait until the children came. If thought and decision was an exciting affair it was also a tiring one, hysterical sometimes and dangerous. He thought his heart would be the better for a little rest until he had to go into action, so he nestled into the huge coat and leaned his head down on his chest. The golden hands of the sun stroked him warmly and he was conscious of sunlight like waves as if someone were stirring it with a paddle. This was impossible of course but he was happy to find that light was a positive thing, an element on its own and what was more, one lying very close to the skin. This led him to open his eyes and look about. Then he discovered it was a function of this sunlight not merely to soak things in gold but also to hide them for he seemed to be sitting up to his very eyes in a sea of light. He looked to the left and saw nothing; and then to the right and saw without any surprise at all that Matty was coming. He knew this ought to surprise him because Matty was dead. But here Matty was, entering the park through the main gate and as usual dressed in black. He came slowly to Mr Pedigree who found his approach not only natural but even agreeable for the boy was not really as awful to look at as one might think, there where he

waded along waist deep in gold. He came and stood before
Pedigree and looked down at him. Pedigree understood that they
were in a park of mutuality and closeness where the sunlight lay
right on the skin.

"You know it was all your fault Matty."

Matty seemed to agree; and really the boy was quite pleasant to
look at!

"So I'm not going to be preached at Matty. We'll say no more
about it. Eh?"

Windrove continued to weave and hold on to his hat. Mr
Pedigree saw that it was the extraordinarily lively nature of this
gold, this wind, this wonderful light and warmth that kept
Windrove moving rhythmically in order to stay in one place. There
was a long period then, when he felt that the situation was so
enjoyable as to make it unnecessary to think of anything else. But
after a time, random thoughts began to perform themselves in the
volume that Mr Pedigree was accustomed to regard as himself.

He spoke out of this thinking.

"I don't want to wake up and find I'm inside, you know. That's
happened so often. What they used to call chokey in my young
day."

Windrove appeared to agree; and then, without words, Mr
Pedigree knew that Windrove *did* agree—and this was such a joy
of certainty that Mr Pedigree felt the tears streaming down his
face. Presently, when he was more himself, he spoke out of the
certainty.

"You're an odd chap, Matty, you always were. You have this
habit of popping up. There've been times when I wondered if you
actually existed when no one else was looking and listening if you
see what I mean. Times when I thought—is he all connected with
everything else or does he kind of drift through; I wonder!"

Then there was another long silence. Mr Pedigree was the one
to break it at last.

"They call it so many things, don't they, sex, money, power,
knowledge—and all the time it lies right on their skin! The thing
they all want without knowing it—yet that it should be you, ugly
little Matty, who really loved me! I tried to throw it away you
know, but it wouldn't go. Who are you, Matty? There've been
such people in this neighbourhood, such monsters, that girl and
her men, Stanhope, Goodchild, Bell even, and his ghastly

264

wife—I'm not like them, bad but not as bad, I never hurt anybody—*they* thought I hurt children but I didn't, I hurt myself. And you know about the last thing the thing I shall be scared into doing if I live long enough—just to keep a child quiet, keep it from telling—that's hell Matty, that'll be hell—help me!"

It was at this point that Sebastian Pedigree found he was not dreaming. For the golden immediacy of the wind altered at its heart and began first to drift upwards, then swirl upwards then rush upwards round Matty. The gold grew fierce and burned. Sebastian watched in terror as the man before him was consumed, melted, vanished like a guy in a bonfire; and the face was no longer two-tone but gold as the fire and stern and everywhere there was a sense of the peacock eyes of great feathers and the smile round the lips was loving and terrible. This being drew Sebastian towards him so that the terror of the golden lips jerked a cry out of him—

"Why? Why?"

The face looming over him seemed to speak or sing but not in human speech.

Freedom.

Then Sebastian, feeling the many-coloured ball that he held against his chest, and knowing what was to happen, cried out in agony.

"No! No! No!"

He clutched the ball closer, drew it in to avoid the great hands that were reaching towards him. He drew the ball closer than the gold on the skin, he could feel how it beat between his hands with terror and he clutched it and screamed again and again. But the hands came in through his. They took the ball as it beat and drew it away so that the strings that bound it to him tore as he screamed. Then it was gone.

The park keeper coming from the other gate saw him where he sat with his head on his chest. The park keeper was tired and irritated for he could see the brilliant ball lying a few yards from the old man's feet where it had rolled when he dropped it. He knew the filthy old thing would never be cured and he was more than twenty yards away when he began talking at him bitterly.